Acclaim for

MAGGIE SHAYNE

"Shayne's talents know no bounds!"
—*Rendezvous*

"...the magnificent Ms. Shayne demonstrates why
she is ranked among the top writers of any genre!"
—*Affaire de Coeur*

Praise for

CAROLINE CROSS

"A superb craftsman, Ms. Cross delivers masterful
characterization and a stunning passionate intensity."
—*Romantic Times*

"Ms. Cross looks deep into the human heart
with a blazing intensity every reader will cherish."
—*Romantic Times*

MAGGIE SHAYNE

Maggie Shayne is the author of more than thirty novels, including women's fiction, romance, suspense and paranormal fiction. Maggie has made a name for herself on the *USA TODAY* and *New York Times* extended bestseller lists, and is the winner of numerous awards, including two *Romantic Times* Career Achievement Awards, a National Readers' Choice Award and the coveted Daphne du Maurier Award. She has been nominated seven times by the Romance Writers of America for the RITA® Award. Maggie resides in the town of Otselic in central New York State with her family and faithful bulldog, Wrinkles. Visit Maggie on the Web at www.maggieshayne.com.

CAROLINE CROSS

Caroline Cross writes romance because life can be challenging and she believes we all need an occasional reminder that good people and true love do exist— if one just looks hard enough and has faith in happy endings.

Winner of numerous awards, including the prestigious RITA® Award bestowed by her peers in Romance Writers of America, she lives in the Pacific Northwest with her husband of over two decades, has two delightful daughters and depends on her family and a handful of wonderful writers and friends to keep her grounded. And even so, she has regular conversations with Maddy and Quinn, whom she suspects are angels in dog and cat disguises.

MAGGIE SHAYNE

CAROLINE CROSS

AN UNEXPECTED FAMILY

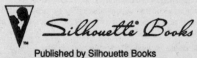

Silhouette Books

Published by Silhouette Books

America's Publisher of Contemporary Romance

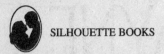

SILHOUETTE BOOKS

ISBN 0-373-23030-3

by Request

AN UNEXPECTED FAMILY

Copyright © 2004 by Harlequin Books S.A.

The publisher acknowledges the copyright holders of the individual works as follows:

FOREVER, DAD
Copyright © 1996 by Margaret Benson

THE BABY BLIZZARD
Copyright © 1997 by Jen M. Heaton

Visit Silhouette Books at www.eHarlequin.com

Printed in U.S.A.

CONTENTS

Dear Reader,

I am so pleased that Silhouette is reissuing this novel. It's a very special one to me, among my earliest forays into the realm of romantic suspense. It was one of those rare stories that sucked me right in. It was written during the summer months, but there's one scene that takes place in a blizzard. As I finished writing that scene, I lifted my head from the computer screen to look past it at the window and the sky outside, and for this one brief, surreal moment, I was shocked to see green grass and sunshine instead of snowdrifts and dark skies.

I love suspense, I love thrillers and I love stories with children in them—probably because I have five of my own. And I've noticed the kids in my stories tend to get older as my own do! Go figure. If you like this story, know that it, and a handful of other Intimate Moments novels, were where I got my training in suspense fiction. Then take a look at *Colder Than Ice,* my latest romantic suspense title from MIRA Books (on sale in November) to see where that training has led me.

Don't forget to visit me on the Web, at www.maggieshayne.com.

And happy reading!

Maggie Shayne

FOREVER, DAD

Maggie Shayne

Chapter 1

"Everyone is looking for it, Palamaro. I'm telling you, *someone* is going to find it. Soon." D.C. Wayne shook his head, pulled off his Ben Franklin specs and massaged the bridge of his nose with two fingers, looking every last one of his sixty-plus years.

"And you're not embellishing just to get me out of retirement? Not even a little?"

D.C. shot him a glare that would've nuked a small city. "You know better."

"I'm not so sure I do." Torch Palamaro dug a cigarette out of the crumpled pack in his shirt pocket and stuck it, unlit, between his lips while he thought it over. D.C. had argued long and loud when Torch had announced his retirement almost a year ago. The man had done everything but handsprings trying to convince Torch to stay on.

The I-CAT's bureau chief hadn't, though. Doug Stern had been glad to see Torch go. Hell, he'd have fired him personally if he'd had a single solid cause. All Stern had ever had, though, were suspicions.

And a healthy lust for Torch's dead wife.

"This job used to be your lifeline, Torch."

"Used to be my life, period. To the exclusion of everything else." He took the cigarette from his lips, rolled it between two fingers. "And even then, I screwed up."

D.C. shook his head. "Don't start with that crap. You were a good husband, a good father to your kids."

"So good I got them blown to bits."

D.C. fell silent.

"So good Doug Stern suspected I'd set the bomb myself."

Torch took a breath, swallowing the old rage. Stern's suspicions had infuriated him. And Torch hadn't exactly been cleared. But Stern had never been able to gather any real evidence against him. Still, Palamaro had found it impossible to continue working under the man.

Glancing down at his clenched hand, Torch opened his fingers one by one. The cigarette was reduced to bits of white paper and brown tobacco flecks. Kind of like his life. Refuse and litter. No meaning. Not anymore.

"What happened to Marcy and the twins wasn't your fault," D.C. said softly, his gruff voice gentling in a way it rarely did. "And just so you know, Stern isn't involved in this."

"How the hell can he not be involved? He's in charge of everything I-CAT does."

"Not this. Look, I can't say more. Just trust me. Someone a lot higher up than Stern wants you in on this. We need this thing found and brought in, Torch. I think you might be the only man who can do it."

Torch sighed, shook his head. "I swore I'd never take

on another mission. Not after I dropped the ball last time.''

''Torch, you saved hundreds of lives. All those people would have died—God knows, no one else had a clue what the target was. Do you remember how desperate we were? Do you remember the chaos around here when that bomb threat was phoned in?''

Torch remembered. He remembered everything. Too well. Especially at night, in his dreams. Oh, he remembered it all then.

D.C. rocked back in his chair. ''It was a mess. We had agency men and feds and every bomb squad in the city on standby. But no one knew the target. We only knew the damn caller meant business.''

Yeah. Because he'd given his name. Or the name he went by, at least. Scorpion. The most successful terrorist in the world. Harder to catch than smoke. With the morals of his namesake. The bastard had no particular cause. He hired out to the highest bidder, doing their dirty work for a price. He was responsible for more deaths than Torch could count, but there were only three that mattered to him. Three that he even bothered counting. Marcy, Josh and Jason. His wife. His sons.

The twins had only been four years old.

Word had it, the man who called himself Scorpion had never been thwarted. At least, not until this last time.

''We played that tape over and over,'' D.C. said. ''Everyone and his brother analyzed it, Torch. But no one figured it out. 'What once stood tallest will be brought to ruin.' Wasn't that how he put it? Tucked that one-liner in among all his anti-American rhetoric so everyone else thought he was talking about the U.S.A. itself. You were the one who picked up on it. You made the connection. The Empire State Building was evacuated and the bomb squads found enough C-4 to bring down a city block.''

Torch listened. He could have tuned D.C. out, could have got up and left. But it wasn't as if he didn't go over this in his mind, day and night. Refusing to listen to D.C. wouldn't kill the memory. Nothing would.

He'd been so damned pleased with himself. The only man ever to throw a wrench into one of Scorpion's attempts. He should have known there would be a price. He should have known.

''You couldn't have guessed the bastard would retaliate, Torch. No one could. It was totally against his MO to carry out an attack based on a personal vendetta. He'd never done anything unless he was being paid.''

Somehow, the bastard had learned the name of the man responsible for stopping his little fireworks display from going off. Somehow, he'd tracked him down, when doing so should have been impossible. Scorpion had learned where Torch lived and planted another bomb.

The malicious son of a bitch had detonated it by remote control. From somewhere close by, where he could watch. Torch hadn't know that then, of course. He'd only known that he was home, after one hell of a day's work. He'd only known that Marcy stood in the doorway, smiling at him when he pulled in the driveway, and that he couldn't wait to get to her. He'd carry that image of her with him for the rest of his life. Loving him, trusting him. Depending on him.

He'd gotten out of his car and taken a single step toward the house when it exploded. The white flash had blinded him, the impact had sent him flying, the heat had seared the skin of his face, singed his hair, scorched the suit he'd been wearing. Melted the wiper blades and the rubber bumper guard on his car and bubbled the paint. Intense heat. Killing heat. There hadn't been a spot of snow left within fifty yards of the house, though there had been a fresh three inches the night before. And he'd struggled to his feet in the middle of the street where he'd landed hard on his back. He'd tried to go to them. Even knowing they couldn't be alive. Even knowing there was no chance, he'd tried to go in. Maybe he'd just wanted to die with them. Maybe that had been it.

His nearest neighbor had stopped him. Actually his nearest neighbor's respectable right hook to the jaw had stopped him. Nothing else could have.

"…you couldn't have known, Torch," D.C. was saying. "And a year is too long to let this thing eat your guts away. Damn, you keep it up there'll be nothing left."

It hadn't been a year. Not yet. There were still a couple of months to go.

Torch stopped staring at the shapeless wad of paper and tobacco in his hand and brushed it all into the unobtrusive gray wastebasket beside D.C.'s cluttered desk. "When I want to discuss my mental state, I'll go to a shrink, D.C." He'd had enough. He couldn't think about it anymore. Not now, not in front of his old friend. "Just stick to the subject, okay? This case you want me to take on, this mad scientist's missing formula—you say 'everyone' is after it. Be more specific."

Rising from his chair, which resembled a Barca-Lounger on casters, D.C. paced in a small circle. Torch didn't want to upset the man any more than was necessary. No sense taxing the pacemaker that had given D.C. his nickname. He was pretty riled already. Hell, he had reason to be. He'd been passed over for that promotion again last week. And now, word had it, he was being "urged" toward early retirement. Hell, the man might be slacking off lately, but he didn't deserve this. He'd been good, in his prime. And he'd given everything he had to give. The International Crises Aversion Team—I-CAT—had been his life. D.C. had supported the team from the spark of an idea to a full-blown operation that the UN would be hard-pressed to do without. When negotiations, sanctions and overt UN intervention failed, the men of I-CAT entered the picture, individually or in force. And the problem was quietly solved.

Torch sat still, observing D.C.: the pallor of his face and the two high spots of color on his cheeks. The light in his eyes. Hell, his gnarled hands were shaking. This must be something major.

"So, who's after this formula, D.C.?"

D.C. stopped pacing and fixed Torch with a steady gaze. "You know I can't be specific until and unless I know you're taking the case."

Torch watched D.C.'s eyes but saw no hints. "Shall I tick off terrorist groups on my fingers then? Just nod if I get warm, okay?"

"Pick one. I told you everyone. I meant everyone. And, dammit, Torch, the only safe place for something this powerful is in the hands of the UN. No, I take that back. Even that isn't safe. I want it destroyed. I want every trace of it eliminated. I want the damn thing never to have been discovered."

Torch nodded, absently flicking stray bits of brown tobacco from his palm, not particularly curious. "Okay, so it's important. Vital, even. I don't think you'd be this stressed out if it wasn't. On to the next question. Why me?"

D.C. walked around the desk to stand right in front of his chair. "Because you can do it. There aren't many men around who have the skills, the ability, let alone the guts."

"Not many, but a few. So again, why me? And don't tell me it's because you're worried about me, D.C. I know you too well to think you'd let personal concerns influence a decision this sensitive. I'm an explosives expert, not a chemist."

D.C. shook his head. "Of the few who might pull this off, Torch, you're the only one I trust." He averted his eyes. "And there's another reason."

Torch lifted his brows and waited.

D.C. chewed the inside of his cheek, as if trying to decide on the right words. Finally he sighed. "There are powers out there who'd pay anything they had to get this formula. Do you understand that? The man who finds it could name his price."

Torch lifted his brows. "Think I could get a yacht outta this deal?"

D.C. scowled. "It's no joking matter, Palamaro."

"Who's joking? The houseboat's nice, but it's getting cramped." *Yeah, real cramped, just me and the accusing eyes of my wife and kids, and the nightmares. Taj Mahal would be too cramped for all of us.*

The old fists clenched. Palamaro saw them and cut to the chase. "All right. Okay, I'll get serious. How much does the job pay?"

"One million dollars on delivery of the formula. Once we verify it's genuine, that is."

"And if I can't deliver it?"

"We'll reimburse your expenses."

"Thoughtful of you."

D.C. closed his eyes. "You'll be offered ten times that if you find it, Palamaro. You'll have to prepare yourself for that."

Palamaro nodded and thought it over.

"I hope your powers of deduction aren't as rusty as they seem to be right now, Torch. Did you hear what I just said? A man could name his price."

"I heard." Torch closed his eyes. He didn't want to take the job, even though the knowledge that he wouldn't have to work with Doug Stern made it more enticing. He didn't want to do much of anything, except kill time until he could get off the damned planet. He didn't have the heart for it anymore. Not for living. Certainly not for working.

"A man could name his price," he repeated mechanically. "Terrorist groups, and a few Third World despots, too, I imagine, will be willing to pay…to pay…" Torch's eyes opened. His head came up slowly, and he met D.C.'s troubled gaze. And what he saw there lit a fire in Torch's soul. One he hadn't felt in the past year. He put the question into a single word. "Scorpion?"

"CIA has a tip that he's in the U.S., after something big. I'd lay odds this is it."

Torch swore long and low.

"You're the only one ever to outwit that bastard, Torch. That's why I want you on this case. And I'm not going to beg," D.C. told him.

Torch held D.C.'s stare, but he wasn't seeing it. He was seeing the two faces that haunted him, day and night. Twin angels, with twin sets of dimples and twin sets of blue eyes and twin heads of dark satin curls. His heart. His soul. All gone in a blinding white flash.

Torch's guilt was compounded by the fact that he hadn't loved their mother. At least, not in the passionate, can't-live-without-you definition of the word. They'd been best friends. And they'd both been lonely. One night a little too much liquor and a little too much mutual comforting had led to something more. And a couple of months later Torch had found himself married. A father, before he knew it. He hadn't minded. Marcy had been his best friend. They'd been making it work.

He cleared his throat. He wanted the bastard who'd killed her. And if Scorpion and Torch were both after the same thing, Torch would be bound to run into him, sooner or later. He'd beat him at his own bloody game. And this time, he'd kill him.

He lifted his gaze to D.C.'s and nodded just once. "What have you got so far?"

D.C. sighed and for the first time, sank into his chair looking a little more relaxed. Torch watched him for a long moment, waiting. D.C. lifted the black briefcase he'd been carrying all morning. He set it on the desk, right in the middle of a mishmash of papers and file folders and notepads. D.C.'s office always looked as if one of Torch's bombs had recently detonated there. He punched a code into the panel on one side and snapped the case open. His eyes seemed tired now, or maybe that was just the relief of having shifted the burden. The old coot ought to take them up on the early retirement they were offering. But he was too stubborn.

Torch took the four-inch-thick stack of papers and folders that emerged from that briefcase, and he prepared himself for a crash course. He hoped to God he still had the stuff for this. He'd be calling on skills he hadn't used in almost a year.

On top was an eight-by-ten color photo of an elderly man with snowy hair and coal chips for eyes.

"Alexander Holt," D.C. intoned. He was all business now. "Until six months ago he was a research scientist in the employ of Uncle Sam. Was working on Gulf War Syndrome, trying to find out what our boys were ex-

posed to over there that's making so many of them
sick.'' D.C. cleared his throat. ''That's classified, by the
way. According to the government, they were exposed
to *nada* and their symptoms have nothing to do with
their tours of duty.''

''Hurray for the red, white and blue,'' Torch muttered.
He flipped the photo over, then sucked in a breath. The
next photo looked as if it ought to be autographed and
sent to some drooling fan. Except for the white lab coat,
the woman looked like a starlet or a model. Tall, slender.
Perfectly straight jet hair that gleamed all the way to her
hips, pulled back and held with a barrette. Huge brown
eyes and full lips. But she looked at the camera as if
half-afraid of it. As if she resented its invasion of her
privacy, her life. She seemed almost to be drawing herself back from it, and her eyes were wary.

''Who is she?'' His voice was a whisper, and even as
he asked the question, he was thinking that eyes like
those belonged on a wild thing, something untouched by
the poison of society. A doe, hidden away in a virgin
forest, never seen by man.

He blinked and gave his head a shake. Where the hell
was all the fairy-tale crap coming from?

''Holt's daughter, Alexandra,'' D.C. supplied. ''She's
an M.D. She works at a clinic for low-income types, sees
lots of AIDS patients. Her father raked in decent money
working for the government. She works for peanuts,
sometimes for nothing. At least, she did until six months
ago.''

Torch nodded, listening, absorbing the information.

''It's ironic, really. Here she is trying to help people
survive the plague of the twentieth century, while dear
ol' Dad's busy developing a new and improved ver-
sion.''

"They don't get along?"

"That's the kicker. Sources say she worships the ground he walks on."

Torch felt his eyes narrow as he studied the photo. He searched the bottomless, velvet brown eyes for answers and found none. The only things he could detect in those eyes were wariness and hurt. A dull pain that had been there so long she didn't remember being without it. He recognized that look. He saw it every morning in the mirror.

For just a second he wondered what had put the pain in such a beautiful pair of eyes. It didn't belong there.

"Six months ago, out of the blue, Alexander Holt turned in his resignation. His daughter gave notice at the clinic, and the two of them vanished without a trace. Since his work was sensitive, his disappearance set off plenty of alarm bells. When the research lab discovered every one of Alexander Holt's files missing, and all his work erased from the computer he used, every diskette gone, they got suspicious and started going over his work for a clue. The man is known for being brilliant, a freaking genius. But he wasn't so smart he didn't leave a clue behind. Seems the modern-day answer to Einstein was a little bit absentminded."

"A walking stereotype?"

"Nah," D.C. said. "He isn't your likable, nutty professor, the way Jerry Lewis was in the movie. The guy's cold as ice, from what we've learned. They say he refused to attend his daughter's graduation from medical school. One of his former colleagues told us he called her degree worthless because she hadn't attended an Ivy League university."

Torch flinched, glancing again at the brown eyes,

thinking maybe he had an inkling now about where all that pain was coming from.

"Anyway, his few flaws paid off, because a page from one of his notebooks was found under his desk." D.C. nodded toward the stack Torch held.

Torch set the photo of Alexandra Holt aside, though he didn't want to. For some reason, studying those brown eyes had become addictive. He tore his gaze away and stared instead at a photocopy of a sheet of ordinary notebook paper, and a few lines of the worst handwriting he'd ever seen in his life. He squinted, trying to make it out.

"...highly contagious during the incubation period, but noncommunicable after that, and so far, always fatal. Released, this synthetic virus could very well annihilate the population of a small country in a matter of weeks. And with the formula I've developed, anyone with access to a laboratory could produce the virus in quantity."

Torch felt a little sick to his stomach as he laid the paper on the desk.

"See that notation on the bottom?"

Torch glanced down at the row of letters, numbers and symbols, then up at D.C. again. "Looks like it's written in some kind of code."

"We thought so, too. Ran it by the boys in Cryptography."

"And?"

"And they say it might be a coincidence...but apply the right key, and it reads 'Sting of death, from desert sands.'"

Torch nodded. "Scorpion."

"Right. And the chances of that being coincidental are slim to none. So we have to assume Scorpion knows about Alexander Holt's little discovery."

"And we both know he's either on someone's payroll already, or planning to auction it off to the highest bidder," Torch added.

"Scares the crap outta me, too," D.C. said. "That's why you have to get it first."

Torch swallowed hard, then he nodded. Alexander Holt might have run, but there would be no place he could hide. That modern-day Dr. Frankenstein better hope to God Torch found him before Scorpion did. The bastard would make Mary Shelley's mob scene look like a walk in the park.

But it would be the last thing Scorpion ever did. Because even though finding the formula for this virus was probably the most important mission Torch had ever undertaken, he was making it priority number two. His foremost objective here was vengeance. He was going to find that bastard, and when he did, Scorpion was going to pay for murdering the three most important people in Torch's life. He was going to pay with everything in him.

Chapter 2

The wind outside moaned a little louder than before. It wasn't like Alexandra to be afraid of the wind. Then again, it wasn't like her to be this desperately lonely. Father had been gone for five months now. And she should be used to the loneliness. She told herself that she hadn't really been any less alone when he was alive than she was right now. He'd barely spoken to her, and never *talked*.

But she'd loved him. Adored him, really. He'd been all she'd had.

Except, of course, for Max. His furry body pressed against her shin as she stood staring out the window into the night. The darkness was different here. Star-spangled and natural. Alive and real. Nothing like night had been in the city. The night here spoke in whispers, but at least it spoke. That was more than her beloved father had done.

The fact that her father had never shown any signs of

loving her back didn't bother her, though, she reminded herself. She was good at reminding herself of it. She'd had a lot of practice. Father had been a genius, a special, one-of-a-kind man. Brilliant. It wasn't his fault his mind was too busy seeking solutions to the world's problems to allow time for emotional nonsense like love.

At least, that's what he'd been too busy with for most of her life. Those last few weeks…she'd begun to wonder whether he'd had any mind left at all. It was as if he'd gone completely insane all in the space of twenty-four hours.

She'd never forget her shock when he'd walked into her shoebox apartment—he hadn't bothered visiting since she'd moved in—and announced that he was leaving his job and going into isolation. She'd almost choked.

"You can come along with me, Alexandra, if you want to. And if you don't, that's fine, too. Just know that once I leave this city, you'll never see me or hear from me again. No one will."

She'd blinked in utter shock. "Dad, what are you talking about? Why are you—"

"Don't ask foolish questions," he'd snapped. And she remembered searching his eyes, wondering if he was in the middle of a stroke or something. "I can't answer them anyway. You know my work is sensitive."

Sensitive. As in classified. But as far as she knew, he'd been doing nothing more than researching Gulf War Syndrome. And yes, that was supposed to be classified, but he hadn't seemed concerned about that when he'd told her…months ago, over dinner, when she'd been all but begging him to make some effort at dialogue. He'd talked about his work, of course. For Alexander Holt, there was nothing else.

"Are you coming, or not?"

She'd been worried about him, thinking maybe he
needed to check into a hospital for some tests. And half-
convinced she'd be able to talk some sense into him
before they spent more than a night or two away. One
thing was for sure, she wasn't going to let him go off
on his own.

It had seemed to Alexandra that for the first time in
her entire life, her father needed her. She'd waited so
long to feel that she was more than just an inconvenience
and a constant source of disappointment in this great
man's life. She wouldn't have wished it to happen like
this, of course, but the fact remained, he needed her. She
wouldn't let him down. Not this time.

"Well, of course I'm coming with you," she'd told
him.

"Then pack."

"What? Now?"

"Right now," he'd barked. "Call those do-gooders
you work with and tell them you need a leave. But don't
say why or where you're going."

"Where *am* I going?" She'd been getting more and
more afraid for her father, more and more certain he was
in the grips of some sudden onset of senility or a blood
clot in the brain. "Dad, maybe you ought to see a doctor."

"You *are* a doctor. You've got your two-bit degree
from your two-bit school to prove it, don't you?"

She remembered those harsh words, the pain they'd
caused. It truly had devastated him when she'd been
turned down by every Ivy League school on his list. But
her grades just hadn't been good enough. She'd swallowed the sting his words inflicted and cleared her throat.

"Maybe you'd better tell me why you feel you have to go into hiding?"

"Someone might come after me, Alexandra. And that's all I can say."

He'd refused to tell her more. Caught up in her concern for her father, Alexandra had accompanied him to this massive tumor on the face of the Adirondacks. Aunt Sophie's Gothic mansion fit into the wilderness of this place like a square peg in a round hole. But here they'd come and here they'd remained. Father had made some veiled comment that no one was likely to trace them there, since it had been left to Mother before she'd married him, and the deed was still filed under Mother's maiden name.

Alexandra hadn't severed all ties, though. She hadn't cleaned out her bank accounts the way her father had ordered her to do. And she hadn't canceled her credit cards, though she had tucked them away in the back of her wallet, promising herself she wouldn't use them until he was himself again. She imagined he would have badgered her into canceling them eventually, but the fact was...

He'd died. He'd died in his sleep one night, just three weeks after they'd arrived here. And Alexandra had been surprised to find that he'd made a will and left it with an attorney in the one-horse town of Pine Lake, at the base of this mountain. He'd had the will drawn up the day after they'd arrived here. Almost as if he'd known...

But he couldn't have known. Other than his odd behavior, he'd exhibited no symptoms whatsoever. Alexandra had suggested an autopsy...but both her father's lawyer and the county coroner had objected to the idea so vehemently that she'd backed down. The letter with her father's will stated that he detested the idea of his body being autopsied, and with the lack of any real symptoms, Alexandra had been hesitant to go against his wishes. The coroner's report stated "natural causes" had killed her father. And despite her nagging misgivings, she'd concurred. It was, she'd decided, what her father would have wanted. He'd made that clear.

Again…almost as if he'd known. But he would have told her if he'd known, wouldn't he?

No. Probably not. Her father never told her much of anything. Except for his constant reminders of what a huge disappointment she was to him. One disappointment after another. All beginning the day her mother had died giving birth to her.

She'd thought, in the end, that maybe by coming out here with him, caring for him through whatever crisis, real or imagined, he was having, she would finally earn his respect. But there hadn't been time.

After he'd died, after she'd carried out the instructions in his will to the letter, having his body cremated and the ashes sealed in a vault at the cemetery, she'd stayed here in these mountains.

Despite his attitude toward her, her father had left her a wealthy woman. Mainly, Alexandra assumed, because he had no one else to name as his heir. So there'd been no need to go back. To face daily failures, to feel inadequate, to wish she could be more than she was. There was simply no need. She'd been feeling the effects of burnout even before she'd left the city. So much death…so much hopelessness facing her every day. She'd been handling it all well enough, until her recent physical exam. The results had been one more blow to her self-esteem. A staggering one.

She liked it here. Isolated and alone. No expectations

to fulfill, no demands to be met—or to fall short of meeting.

The house tended to creak in response to the wind outside. It was as if the wind moaned a question and then the house creaked an answer. What were they saying to each other? she wondered. What secrets were they sharing?

But that was just her imagination working overtime again. Too much time out here alone, she supposed. Gave her mind too much time to think. Gave her heart too much time to regret that she'd never been able to live up to the greatness of her father. And to mourn the fact that she'd never known a mother's love…and she'd never know a child's.

She paced away from the window, letting the sheer silvery curtain fall back into place, bending to stroke Max's head. There was nothing out there. Nothing. Just tree-covered mountains and lakes and a speck-on-the-map town a few miles away where old men still sat around a checkerboard in the general store, chewing and spitting.

She ought to try to go back to sleep, she supposed. She turned toward the curving staircase and started up it.

Then she stopped dead in her tracks and listened to what sounded absurdly like an upstairs window scraping open.

A heartbeat later, the doorbell chimed, and her stomach turned queasy.

Licking her lips, she tried to decide which to investigate first. She turned toward the door, wondering who could be way up here in the middle of nowhere, so late at night. She never had visitors.

A hunter who'd gotten lost, she told herself. Or maybe

one of the locals needed something. Still, the hairs on her nape stood erect, and her sweat-dampened hand on the doorknob trembled a little as she turned it and pulled the door open.

The door opened slowly, without so much as a "who is it?" first. And Torch found himself face-to-face with the woman whose photo he'd studied, memorized.

She was tall, slender. Her long, jet hair hung loosely, all the way to the waist of the sensible white flannel nightgown she wore. Her feet were long and narrow, and bare right now, beneath the hem.

He'd saved her eyes for last deliberately, knowing they would be a letdown. There was no way they could be as arresting in their mystery as they'd been in that photo. He looked up…and saw that they were. No. More arresting. Stunning. Wide and dark brown, filled with questions and a nameless fear. The wariness he'd seen in the photo still haunted her big eyes. She reminded him of a wild deer backed into a corner. And beyond the skittish fear, he saw the pain. More intense, more real, more clearly branded in the brown velvet than he could have imagined.

Her skin looked softer, smoother, up close than it had in the photo. And when her scent reached him, he flinched at its subtle allure.

He forcefully tore his gaze from her, reminding himself of his mission, and looked past her, scanning the dim interior of the house and seeing no one else. Still, he hadn't liked the looks of that black van parked at the end of the dirt path that passed for a road. He'd only managed to track the Holts down today. Today, Alexandra Holt had made a mistake. She'd used her credit card…first time since she and her father had disappeared over six months ago, according to the company. She'd bought some supplies at a general store in the nearby town. According to the clerk, she usually paid in cash but had apparently left her billfold at home. She'd reluctantly used the plastic rather than make another trip.

Torch had been to that general store, but when he'd asked the old proprietor where he could find Alexandra Holt, the man had replied, "Looks like Ms. Holt is in for some company tonight, then. You're the second one to stop and ask for directions up there."

Scorpion's resources would be the same as Torch's. He'd know enough to keep tabs on those credit cards. And he had enough people on his payroll to help him pull it off.

"Is there something I can do for you?" she asked.

Torch blinked again. Her voice was like smoke, dark and deep and soft. She didn't look like a doctor. She looked like an angel. A frightened angel.

She stared up at him, waiting, and he had to jerk his gaze forcefully away from those eyes. Damn, they ought to be certified as lethal weapons.

"I'm looking for Professor Alexander Holt."

There was a quick widening of her doe eyes. A jolt in the tall, flannel-ensconced body. But she recovered fast and tilted her head to one side. "Never heard of him. Sorry."

He narrowed his gaze at the reaction he'd seen in her when he'd said the name. Fear. No doubt about that. A new fear...of him. He had to remind himself that the angelic look of the woman, the innocent brown eyes, were only the surface. A diversion, though an effective one. She knew all about her father's formula. She must, or she wouldn't be up here in the middle of nowhere with him.

"You'll find," he said slowly, "that it's not a real good idea to lie to me...Alexandra."

She blinked rapidly, drew in a shallow breath. "Who are you? How do you know...?" She glanced over her shoulder again. Third time she'd done that. Was the professor standing behind her, coaching her? Or someone else? She cleared her throat. "My father isn't here," she said at last, as one hand gripped the door, pushing it shut.

"Sorry, hon. I'm not buying it." He moved her aside without much effort and shouldered his way into the house. Then he blinked again, and did a double take. The place was dark, lit only by candlelight, and the candles were scented. The aroma and the flickering shadows made him think of slow, soul-stirring sex. There was a fire crackling from the huge marble fireplace on one wall. A big plush rug in front of it added to the pictures swirling in his mind. Her legs, under that nightgown, were long. Endless, he imagined. Slender, in keeping with the doe image.

He blinked, erasing the erotic thoughts from his mind. What was she, some kind of witch or something? Were those candles laced with a mind-altering drug? Or maybe an aphrodisiac?

Or maybe, he admitted silently, his libido was just picking a lousy time to come back to life after its long slumber. He didn't think that was very likely, but he supposed it was as likely as drugged candles.

He focused once more on the task at hand and continued scanning the house, from a more objective point of view. The one thing he didn't see was the professor.

"So, where is he?" As he said it, he took a deliberate step toward her.

She shook her head rapidly, backing away from him,

brown eyes wider than ever. "I'm—I'm calling the police. And then I'm going to turn my dogs loose, and—"

"You're not calling anyone, because there's no phone up here. And I can tell you that I'll be a lot easier to deal with than whoever comes through that door next." When he said it, her eyes jerked toward the darkened archway and the base of a broad, curving staircase beyond it, but came right back to him.

"Someone's upstairs, hmm? Who, Alexandra? Your father?"

She shook her head but averted her eyes. She was breathing too fast. Not from agitation. Something else. Her chest rose and fell harder, faster than it should have, and each time it did, her small, unbound breasts pressed themselves to the fabric that covered them, making perfect outlines in the cloth.

A sound came from upstairs then and her eyes told him it shouldn't have. When had he seen a face express every thought the way this one did? Something wasn't right in this house.

He yanked the gun from his waistband automatically. When she saw it, her gasping got worse. She pressed her hands to her chest, whirling and running right out of the front room through the huge, dark archway before he could stop her. He hadn't expected it, and something, instinct maybe, made him hesitate before going after her.

He saw where the broad staircase began, saw her stop at the base of it, snatching a bottle of some sort from a stand there, bringing it to her lips as she fought to breathe, and then sucking loud bursts of medicine from the thing.

She bowed her head, apparently exhausted, apparently waiting for relief to come. Asthma? he wondered. She stepped around the staircase, just out of his line of vision. And the second she was out of his sight, he heard her scream.

It was a pathetic, frightened wail, punctuated by harsh gasps. Torch ducked to one side of the doorway, peering around it, straining his eyes.

She stepped into sight again, a white angel appearing in the darkened room, whimpering in fear, but it had little effect on the brute who held a gun barrel so tight against her temple that it was likely biting into her skin. His arm crushed her breasts and held her back tight to his chest.

A low growl came from Torch's right, and he jerked his gaze around, only to see a black cat the size of a mountain lion arching its back and hissing. Then it scrambled away, disappearing under the sofa.

Torch cussed mentally, bringing his attention back where it belonged. Alexandra Holt's eyes were rounder than ever. The guy who held her so cruelly was dressed all in black, almost invisible in the darkened room, and he apparently wasn't aware of Torch's presence. Experience and caution had caused Torch to park his heap a little farther down the dirt track than that van so they wouldn't have seen that, either.

And he had no doubt it was "they" and not just "he." Because this wasn't Scorpion. This man was too short, his build too slight. This was one of Scorpion's henchmen, and while their boss worked alone, his thugs worked in bunches.

Torch sidled his way to the front door and slipped through it, unseen, into the night.

Alexandra clung to her inhaler. Her attack was easing now, thanks to the spurt of medicine she'd inhaled before he'd grabbed her, but she had no doubt this kind of fear would instigate a relapse before long.

Damn her asthma! She might have managed to get away if she hadn't been weak and dizzy from the attack. Father had always called it a weakness, always told her it would keep her from amounting to anything. And it had. The frequent illnesses and hospitalizations had made her miss too much school. Her grades had fallen, and kept her from getting into what Father considered a good university. Now the damned condition might just help get her killed by madmen in her own home.

She was afraid, so afraid she felt sick and dizzy. She had no idea what was going on, why these people were treating her this way. The man's grip was too tight on her, crushing her chest. The gun barrel pressed painfully against her skin. Her eyes scanned the room for Max. Her poor cat would be terrified by all this disruption. He was probably hiding, likely scared half to death.

"Where is your father?" the madman rasped into her ear. His voice carried a cadence she couldn't place. When she didn't answer instantly, the gun barrel drove harder into the side of her head, breaking the skin, and she cried out.

"Where is he!"

"I don't—"

"Is he here, in this house?"

"I don't know what you're—"

The barrel embedded deeper. She felt white-hot pain, and warm blood trickling down the side of her face. "No!" She screamed the word. "Not here!"

The pressure eased a little. Maybe now he'd leave, go search for her father somewhere else. What did he want with him? Why was this happening?

Someone might be after me, Alexandra.

No. Her father had been delusional, sick, when he'd said—

The man shoved her through the archway, into the front room, to the door. She tripped over Max, and he let out a howl before streaking out of the room to hide. She stumbled on the rug, but couldn't fall down. The madman's grip on her was too tight for that.

"You will take us to him, then," he said.

She'd never been so afraid in her life. And she wondered for an instant if these men meant to kill her. And where was the other one? Was he with this brute, or did he have his own reasons for bursting into her house in the middle of the night?

"I know who you are, Alexandra Holt," the man with the gun whispered into her ear, and his strange, exotic accent made his words seem even more frightening. "You will take us to your father or we will kill you. A very simple choice, really. When we have him, we will let you go."

"But my father isn't—"

The gun pressed harder. "No talk. You will take us to him."

She bit her lips to stop them from shaking. She had a feeling that no matter what she said, this animal would kill her anyway. And she couldn't have spoken a coherent phrase even if she'd wanted to. Could Father have been sane all along? Was this what he'd been running away from, hiding from? Had he been telling the truth when he'd told her that someone might try to follow him?

He pulled her backward, through the front door. "You'll come with me, pretty one. And you will take us to him. If not, we have men waiting in line for the chance to interrogate you. Each believes his methods will be the most effective in making you talk. There have been wagers laid on who will succeed.'' He stopped just outside the door, turning again, staring down the gravel driveway into the darkness beyond. ''It won't be pleasant for you, I'm afraid. But great fun for the men.''

Alexandra stared into the darkness, but there was no help for her there. Pine boughs sighed in time with the wind that whispered through their needles. Early winter's chill laced the air, and it tasted like snow. It seemed like such an ordinary night. How could any of this be happening to her?

He backed down the steps and turned to wave, and she saw the van parked at the roadside, black, sharp-nosed menace, like a shark waiting there to devour her. Even the windows were tinted.

The van crept into the driveway. The man shoved Alexandra forward, and the van stopped. A second later, its side door slid opened.

She caught her breath as she saw another man, crumpled on the van's floor, dressed entirely in black just like the one who held her. Then a foot nudged the body, and it rolled out onto the gravel.

The man holding her pushed her to the ground, shouting a curse and lifting his gun toward the van's dark interior. He got one shot off before the other man—the first one she'd encountered tonight—leapt on him, knocked him to the ground and with a single punch, put him out for the count.

Panting, he turned to Alexandra. She pulled herself up off the ground, gasping, pressing the inhaler to her mouth and sucking in blasts of medicine. Her eyes never leaving his, she backed away a step, then two. The bastard who'd rung the doorbell and shouldered his way inside. Damn him. He'd saved her from the two men in black, but for what purpose?

He bent down to take the gun from the other man, and when he straightened, she saw the blood on his shirt.

It didn't matter that he'd been hurt, she told herself. He was no better than the other two and she was getting the hell out of here.

She turned to run.

"Don't make me hurt you, Alexandra."

The words were low, and she could hear the pain that laced each one. It was enough to make her pause and look back. Only to see him pointing the gun at her. "You're either going to have to deal with me, or more like these two. Believe me, they won't be long in arriving."

She shook her head, shock seeping like ice water through her veins. She lifted her hands to press them to either side of her head, biting her lips to keep them from trembling. She was dizzy with fear.

"Dammit, get a grip. Tell me where your father is or he'll end up dead…or worse."

He was bleeding. The gleaming scarlet stain on the front of his shirt grew and spread. His left arm hung useless at his side while his right one gestured with the gun as he spoke.

She took another step backward. "I don't know what any of this is about. Just get out of here and leave me alone!" Hysteria grabbed her, but she fought it. Her car was in the garage. If she could only get to her car…

One of the men on the ground moaned, and she went rigid and still.

"Snap out of it, Alexandra! Your life is in danger, or haven't you figured that out yet? You don't really want me to drive off and leave you to these two, do you?"

His long, dark hair was wild, and his eyes seemed as untamed. His arm must be hurting. His unshaven jaw was rigid, suggesting grated teeth behind those thinned lips, and she could see the corded muscles in his neck standing out. Oh, yes, he was in pain. A lot of it. He came closer, lifted the wounded arm, gripped her shoulder in a hand that dripped blood. "Dammit, where is your father?"

She blinked, tearing her eyes from his to look down at one of the forms on the ground—the one that groaned again and moved a little. Then she focused on those intense eyes. In the moonlight she saw them, pain-glazed but piercing all the same.

"My father is dead," she whispered, because she couldn't seem to speak louder. Fear made her throat swell nearly shut.

"Dead?" He almost shouted the word. She only nodded.

The man swore fluently. "All right. Okay, we'll have to search the house." His hand finally fell away from her, but she felt the sticky warmth it left behind. "Get me some rope, so I can keep these two from kicking the hell out of me. And make it fast. We have a few hours at most."

Alexandra blinked, not moving. This wasn't happening. This couldn't be happening. My God, what did this man want? What did it have to do with her father? Why did he want to search her house?

Of all the questions swirling in her mind, she only voiced one. "A few hours until what?"

"Until some friends of these guys show up, or maybe some other guys who'll be just as nasty. The rope, Alexandra."

"My God...my God, what is this all about?"

He scowled at her until his dark brows touched. She shook herself and turned toward the little shed beside the house. The one that held all Father's gardening tools. He used to love to putter in a flower bed during the tiny fragments of time when he wasn't working. Spent more time digging in the tiny patch of brown dirt than he did talking to her.

Alexandra hated gardens.

She went into the shed and found some rope.

Chapter 3

The two thugs were bound, gagged and struggling in the living room of Alexandra Holt's Gothic monstrosity of a house. Torch had blown out most of the candles. Didn't want their thrashing to start a fire. He'd turned on lights, instead, half-surprised they even had lights this far up in the middle of nowhere.

She didn't like the lights. Her face told him so without her lips speaking a word. She squinted and shielded her eyes from them. It was as if she'd rather scamper off into the woods, into the dark, away from him and every ugly human being ever to draw a breath. To live out there, with her own kind. The wary woodland creatures.

Stupid to keep thinking of her that way, but it was just such a fitting image. She seemed like something rarely seen by mortal eyes. Something that only came out of hiding when she was certain no one was near. Always afraid of being hurt. Or something.

She was definitely afraid of something.

The thugs most of all, at the moment, anyway. She wouldn't walk by them even though they were tied up. She followed Torch through the house, questioning him once or twice in a voice soft with fear, but still deep and smoky. But when he passed the terrorists, she hung back.

He stopped at the bottom of the staircase, staring up at the seemingly endless hall above, the countless doors lining it. "Damn. You couldn't have lived in a quaint little cottage, could you?"

His shoulder raged and nagged for attention. It was only a matter of time before more guys-in-black showed up. And here he was with a search grid the size of Arkansas.

"You won't get away with this," she was telling him, like some heroine in a murder mystery. Only she had the balance wrong. There ought to be more defiance, less fear in her voice. "Someone will be coming along any minute now, and you—"

"Someone will be coming along all right, but they won't be much help."

She stood just inside the archway, and though she'd been speaking to him, her eyes were glued to the two wriggling black bundles hog-tied on the floor. Her skin looked like chalk, and her lower lip trembled. Her fear was palpable, and something softened inside Torch's granite heart. The feeling shook him right to the core, so he looked away from her. But not fast enough.

Her wide brown eyes stayed right there in his mind's eye. He couldn't make them leave. Damn. There was something about her that made him want to touch her. Stroke her hair and her face, run his palms real slow down her back and up again and over her shoulders, and tell her it was going to be okay.

He cleared his throat, the friction of it scattering the

images forming in his mind. "Look, I don't have time to search the whole place," he told her, and it was an effort to sound as cold and hard as he wanted to. "So I'm gonna have to trust you. Where are your father's notes?"

She blinked, and her gaze finally tore free of the thugs and met his. "Notes?"

"The project he was working on just before he resigned, Alexandra. The formula he developed. Where is it?"

Her eyes narrowed. She was either completely unaware of the mess her father had created, or a very good actress. Torch hadn't decided which.

"I don't know."

Torch pushed a hand through his hair, rolled his eyes, swore—none of which helped the situation. When he looked at her again, she was staring at the floor near his feet. He glanced down, saw the bloodstain on the carpet, saw fresh drops raining down from his arm to add to the mess.

"You're going to bleed to death." She said it matter-of-factly, as if she could care less.

She had a point. Torch stuffed the thug's gun into his waistband and used his good arm to tear his shirt open. Then he shrugged out of it, balled it up and dropped it.

She emitted a soft gasp that drew his eyes back to her face. And then she amazed him. Because she straightened her back and she lifted her chin. Sending one last, fear-filled glance toward the men on the floor, she bit her lip, fixed her gaze on the pulsing wound in his shoulder, and she came to him. She walked right past those two, though she was shaking visibly as she did. She took his good arm in her hand.

Firm grip, but cool. Fear tended to lower one's body

temperature. She drew him up the curving staircase and through one of those countless doors, flicking a light switch as they entered. Her hand never relaxed on his forearm as she drew him into the plush, gleaming bath-room and gently nudged him onto a dainty chair he wasn't sure would hold him. He found himself sitting at a vanity, with an oval mirror at its back. And when he glanced at his own reflection, he figured it was little wonder she was afraid of him. Shirtless, bloody, his eyes as dark blue and merciless as the depths of the ocean, betraying no hint of feeling. His hair was too long, no longer the regulation above-the-ears cut he used to wear. He'd let it grow out during his brief attempt at retire-ment, and hadn't bothered cutting it again for this job. It was a dark tangle that hung to his shoulders.

He heard water running and turned to see her coming toward him with a clean, wet cloth. She reached out and he leaned backward, away from her.

She frowned, meeting his gaze. "You'll have to hold still."

He couldn't believe it. He'd had a moment of inex-plicable fear when she'd reached for him. *Him*, Torch Palamaro, afraid of a fragile-looking, not to mention beautiful, woman. Why?

He could have analyzed it, but he didn't. Fact was, he simply didn't want her touching him.

Rather than admit that, though, he held still. Alexan-dra, with a surprisingly gentle, if trembling, touch, cleaned the gunshot wound on the front his shoulder. Then she leaned closer, bending over him to clean the exit wound on his back.

And he inhaled the good, clean, woman scent of her. Her breasts were too close to his face. So close he could see their outline right through the white flannel, and he could tell she wore nothing beneath it.

Not a moment too soon she turned away, rummaging in a medicine cabinet and coming back to him with gauze and tape, and some ointment in a tube.

"Why are you doing this?"

She stopped two feet from him, her hands full, and she blinked twice, as if asking herself the same question. Then she shook her head, shrugged. "I'm a doctor. It's...what I do." She smeared ointment on a gauze pad, used another to dab the new blood away. "Or maybe I just don't want you dropping dead before you tell me what this is all about."

He didn't like her caring for his wound. And he knew why. He tried not to think of Marcy, but he thought of her anyway, and those thoughts brought searing pain with them. Marcy, small and soft and fair. She used to touch him this way, her hands gentle. They might not have been in love, but they'd been lovers. He couldn't remember it, not the way he should. But he knew it had happened. Often. She'd squeeze scented oil onto her fingers and rub it all over his back at the end of a stressful day.

Marcy. Gone now. Barely enough left of her to bury. Nothing at all left of his sons. Their markers stood over empty graves. All because he'd failed.

And him, here, studying the shape of some other woman's breasts. He closed his eyes as the pain intensified.

Alexandra pulled her hand away. "Did I hurt you?"

"No." His voice came out like tree bark.

"Are you going to tell me? What this is about, I mean?"

She was nearly finished. She'd get away from him in a minute, and he'd snap out of this morbid guilt-fest.

When she did, he looked up. "You mean to say you really don't know?"

She shook her head, her gaze pinned to his, too brown and too innocent.

"Then why did you quit your job in the city and move out here with him?"

She shrugged. "Father was determined, and I...I couldn't very well let him come out here by himself. He was old, and..." She sighed. "His mind wasn't just right. He thought people were out to get him...." She glanced through the open door, toward the stairs, and shuddered a little.

"Yeah, well, your old man wasn't as crazy as you thought he was."

She blinked at him, as if reaching the same conclusion. Then she turned to the basin, on the pretense of washing her hands. But he was too astute not to notice that she only turned on the cold tap, or that she held her wrists turned up to the flow to counteract the shock. "What was it my father was working on? What are all you people after?"

He didn't like her lumping him in with all the others, and almost said so. But he stopped himself. He didn't give a damn what she thought of him.

"I'm not at liberty to give you details. Suffice it to say that he created a formula that could be used as a weapon, and as a weapon it would be more devastating than the A-bomb."

She shut the water off, dabbed her hands with a towel and lifted her face to the mirror in front of her, meeting his gaze there. "My father wouldn't be involved in anything like that."

"Your father *was* involved in something *just* like that. When he realized what he had, he must have finally understood what the repercussions could be. He took all his notes, erased his files from the computer and vanished from the face of the earth, for all intents and purposes. Problem was, he was sloppy. He left a page from a notebook. The formula wasn't on it, but there were enough hints to make it clear what he had. The information obviously leaked. Now every two-bit despot and terrorist leader in the world is itching to get his hands on him and his formula."

Clutching the towel in her hands, she turned to face him. "And which two-bit despot or terrorist leader sent you?"

He blinked. Her voice was a little stronger now, and her eyes had gone cold. "That's classified."

"Then so is anything I might know."

He rose slowly from the chair, recognizing a standoff when he saw one. He hadn't expected it. Not from a woman as easily frightened as this one was. Seemed there was a little toughness in there after all. Buried…deeply buried. But there. The path to her steel lay in her old man. Say something bad about the sainted Alexander Holt, and find his daughter's anger.

But he couldn't tell her what she wanted to know. Hell, the very fact that I-CAT existed was top secret. And it had to stay that way.

"I can't tell you."

"Then you might as well leave."

He smiled just a little, knowing he had her beat. "And what do you plan to do with those two downstairs, Alexandra, or the backup crew who are probably on their way right now?"

"Nothing. I'm leaving, too. If I didn't learn another thing from my father, I learned how to hide."

Now that was more in keeping with his image of her. To scurry away into the woods. To burrow into a den somewhere in the forest with the other timid, wild things.

"But I found you," he told her. "They found you. They'll find you again."

"And I'll run again."

"That's no way to live."

"That's my problem, isn't it?"

She was tougher than she looked. Still shaking, shocked right to the core by what he'd accused her father of having done, scared half out of her mind, but tough. She wouldn't tell him. The determination was right there in her frightened eyes.

He battled a grudging admiration for her.

"All right," he said slowly. "I'll tell you this much. The people I work for want that formula, but not to use as a weapon. They want it so they can make sure every trace of it, and the research that led up to it, is destroyed."

She stepped closer, her eyes narrowing, staring so deeply into his eyes that he felt their touch on his soul. She was trying to see inside him, he realized, trying to see if he was lying to her. She licked her lips, a quick, nervous dart of her pink tongue.

"How do I know I can believe you?"

"You don't."

She stood there a moment, deep in thought. Finally she shook her head. "It's all a mistake. My father was a genius and a great man. He wouldn't have done this."

"He did it."

"No." She blinked, and he saw tears threatening to

spill over. "I don't believe it. He'd have told me...."
She let her voice trail off, uncertainty clouding her eyes.

"Would he?"

Her chin came up, and her gaze met his. "He couldn't
have done what you say he did."

"Okay. I say he did it, and you say he didn't. There's
only one way to prove which of us is right."

She closed her eyes, clenched her teeth. "I...I have
to think—"

"There's no time to think, Alexandra. I'm not lying
when I tell you more men like those two downstairs will
be showing up soon. And they'll do everything they said
they'd do to you...and then some."

Her eyes opened and she faced him. He thought
maybe she'd come to a decision.

"If I tell you...where to find the papers...will you
leave me alone?"

He was not going to leave her alone. She'd end up
dead if he did. "Sure," he lied.

She swallowed hard, nodding slightly. "After...after
my father died, I was going through his things and...and
there was a receipt. He'd paid for a safe-deposit box in
a New York bank. If there is anything to be found, that's
where it will be."

"I want the name of the bank, hon. And then I want
the key."

She frowned, as if searching her mind again. Then she
turned and left the room. Torch was on her heels. He
followed her down the hall, into a bedroom that had to
be hers. The rumpled bed attested to a sleepless night.
That beast of a cat peered out from underneath it. When
she yanked open a dresser drawer, he half expected her
to pull out a file containing all her father's secrets, and
he allowed himself a sigh of relief. It was cut off when

she only took out a pair of jeans and bent to step into
them, tugging them on under the nightgown, snapping
them around her narrow waist. Giving him a brief
glimpse of supple skin and the dark well of her navel.
Making him feel something he had no business feeling.

"What the hell are you doing?"

"Getting dressed. I'm going to give you the key and
then I'm leaving. All right?" She didn't wait for an answer. She dug through the dresser again, emerging this
time with a sweatshirt. Turning her back, she tugged the
nightgown over her head.

Torch stood motionless, staring at the length of her
bare arms, the curve of her spine, the soft, smooth round-
ness of her shoulders. And for just an instant, he battled
an overwhelming urge to run his hands over her silken
skin. To turn her around and look at her breasts and her
waist and…

He averted his eyes, gave his head a shake, tried to
focus on something else besides her. The fireplace on
one wall, not burning. The neat stack of kindling and
wood on the grate, ready for the touch of a match. The
brass log holder, filled with fragrant, seasoned cherry
wood.

"You'll leave me alone? You promise? If there's anything to be found, it will be in that box. And whatever
you do find, it's only going to prove you're wrong about
him."

He looked at her again. The sweatshirt was in place,
concealing her lovely flesh from his gaze. Thank God
for small favors.

"Give me the name of the bank, and give me the key,
Alexandra. You're not in a position to—" He went silent
at the sound of tires crunching gravel. "Damn, they're
here. We're out of time." He saw her fear return, chas-

ing all that false bravado right back into whatever closet she kept it in when she wasn't using it. "I lied about leaving you alone. You're coming with me, you understand? If you want to survive this, don't argue about it. Now get the damned key and let's get out of here."

She looked so crestfallen it would have been laughable if the situation hadn't been so deadly. Turning, she dumped a jewelry box onto her dresser, pawing through a small mountain of trinkets. He saw the key as she snatched it up, and before he'd even extended his hand for it, she'd tucked it into her jeans pocket.

The car stopped. "Oh, God," she whispered. But she never stopped moving. She swooped down on a pair of sneakers that had been hiding under the bed, stuffed her feet into them. She was shaking again. Breathing hard. She snatched the inhaler from the dresser where she'd dropped it, clutched it in a white-knuckled grip.

"Is there a back door?" Torch whispered harshly.

"We'd have to go back downstairs."

He lunged for the window, shoving it open as she watched, baffled.

"What are you doing?"

Torch stuck his head out the window. "No fire escape? Nothing?"

She only shook her head, her face draining of color when the front door opened audibly below. Then she blinked. "Just rope ladders in the bedrooms. Father insisted on it." She turned to the closet and hauled a flimsy-looking rope ladder from an upper shelf.

Torch took the bundle from her, anchoring the two end hooks on the window ledge and letting the rest fall free.

"Come on," he whispered harshly. "Hurry. Get out there."

"I don't want to leave my cat!"

"You'll leave him on angel wings with a harp in your hands if you don't get your butt in gear!"

She sent a desperate glance toward the bed, where the cat had been only seconds ago, but the beast had gone into hiding. She shook her head, staring at the open window, then at him. "I...I can't—"

"You damned well better. Move it!"

Torch heard heavy footfalls on the stairs. Alexandra bit her lip and, her entire body shaking, she stared at the flimsy rope. Torch took her shoulders in his hands, gave her a shake. "You don't have a choice, Alexandra."

Her eyes cleared a little and she nodded. Then, awkwardly, she climbed through the window, slowly making her way down the ladder.

It wasn't Alexandra Holt climbing down that rope ladder in the middle of the night while brutal killers invaded her home. It just simply wasn't. Alexandra knew that *her* reaction would have been very different. She'd have been hiding under the bed, with Max, shivering in fear.

But something had happened to her up there, something she hadn't been aware *could* happen. She'd suddenly stepped out of herself, standing aside, quiet and trembling with fear, just watching events unfold like watching a scary movie. And something else had taken over. Something stronger and braver than timid Alexandra could ever be. She didn't recognize that thing. It was like an alien presence, summoned to life by a strong pair of hands gripping her shoulders, and by intense blue eyes boring into hers. He'd roused some new, unfamiliar part of her to life. She didn't know how, but she was grateful. Enough so that she almost felt guilty for lying to him about the safe-deposit box.

For just a few seconds, Alexandra had found courage she'd never known she possessed, and she managed to hang on to it until her feet were on the solid ground once more.

She stood, trembling on the ground below her bedroom window, watching the man descend. She heard the others, inside, and she felt no further hint of that brave alien. Only stark terror.

He jumped when he was still ten feet from the ground, rolled to his feet and gripped her arm. But she couldn't move when he tugged her. Fear had rooted her feet to the ground.

"Come on, Alex! Don't freeze up on me now!" He made a harsh whisper seem like a barked order, and it shook her enough to make her move. He'd called her Alex. No one had ever called her that before. It seemed different than Alexandra. Better. He pulled her into the pine forest beyond her back lawn and never slowed his pace.

He seemed to know where he was going. That gave her a little confidence. Becoming lost in the Adirondacks was not an appealing prospect. Usually she knew this section of forest like the back of her hand, but in this state of mind, God only knows where she'd end up. Still, getting lost in the forest was a far more appealing prospect than falling into the hands of those men back at the house.

He veered westward, cutting a diagonal path through the forest that would bring them to the only road that led up here. She had to struggle to keep the pace he set. Briskly cold, pine-scented night air rushed in and out of her burning lungs. She kept looking back over her shoulder as they ran, expecting to see an army of men in black giving chase. None in sight. Not yet, anyway. They'd have to know where to look for them, though. The rope ladder was still hanging in the window.

Maybe Max would find it and use it to escape. Or maybe he'd stay hidden until those men left. The poor thing. She hadn't intended to leave him behind. She'd intended to send this man off on a wild-goose chase and then gather up her cat and disappear herself.

Right after she went through her father's papers and found proof of his innocence. Now she'd have to wait until she could get away from this crazy man who clung to her hand with his strong, warm one and pulled her through the pitch-dark forest at a dead run.

Finally he stopped at the edge of the woods near the winding dirt road. He wasn't even winded, though Alexandra panted more loudly than she would have liked. She sank to the ground and its cushion of pine needles, watching him stare out at the road. And she automatically pulled her inhaler from her pocket and took a dose.

He tilted his head, listening. He seemed even to sniff the air.

Then he turned to her and jerked his head. She rose, though she wanted to stay right were she was. Taking her arm, he led her out onto the road. A car sat a few yards away, and that was where he drew her. Alertness marked his every movement, and his feet on the road made barely a sound. He stopped beside the car, slipping a penlight from a pocket. Then he was on his belly, shining the light underneath. What in the name of...?

He got up, checked the car's interior and opened the driver's door. "Get in."

She hesitated. "But—"

"Get in, Alex. The keys are in the switch. Don't start the engine. Not yet. Count to one hundred, slowly, beginning when I leave. Then start it. I'll be back before you can count to a hundred a second time. If I'm not, get the hell out of here.''

"You're leaving? For what? Where are you—"

"No time. Just do as I say, okay?"

"I don't think I can—"

"You'll be fine. Just do what I tell you."

She clamped her lower lip between her teeth and nodded, sliding into the car. He opened the back door, snatching out a small satchel. Then he closed both doors without making a sound. He turned and ran into the woods.

Her sweaty hands slid back and forth over the steering wheel as she counted. "One, two, three…how in the name of God did I end up in the middle of this insanity? Six, seven, eight, nine…I can't possibly sit still all the way to a hundred! Where *is* he? Twelve, thirteen…I've never been so scared in my life…fifteen…"

She did it. Somehow, she sat there, imagining she saw dark shapes moving just beyond the tree line, only to discover they were branches swaying in the wind, hearing sounds that turned out to be her own body brushing against the plush seat of his car. His car. A sports car with what appeared to be fangs where the grill should be. Jet black, inside and out. Expensive. It smelled new. "Ninety-nine, one hundred. There. Made it that far."

She closed her eyes, prayed her pursuers were all hard-of-hearing, checked to be sure it was in neutral and turned the key.

The beast of a car came to life and sat purring like a contented lion. She started counting again and adjusted the mirror so she could see behind her. She checked the emergency brake. It was on. When she got to fifty, she depressed the clutch and slid the stick shift into first.

But when the passenger door was yanked open and

he dove in, she was so startled her foot slipped off the clutch and the car stalled.

He swore. "Come on, Alex! Go!"

She twisted the key again, released the brake and managed to take off this time. "Are they following us?"

She looked up at the mirror.

"Shift! We're in a hurry here, the object is to go fast!"

She shifted, negotiated a curve, picked up speed and shifted again. Behind her she could only see a cloud of brown dust. Ahead, only darkness. She reached for the headlight switch. He covered her hand.

"Not yet. No lights."

"I can't drive in the dark!" She shifted again, but fourth gear was all she dared on this road. She'd get them both killed if she tried to go any faster. "Are they—"

"Yeah, they're coming."

Her foot pressed harder on the accelerator. "This is insane. I'm running for my life in the middle of the night with a total stranger. I can't drive this car! I've never driven a car like this in my life!"

"You're doing fine."

"God, I don't even know your name!"

"Palamaro," he said.

She glanced at him briefly, not daring to take her eyes from the barely visibly road ahead for more than an instant. He was turned in his seat, staring behind them, and he held something in his hand that she couldn't identify. Not a gun.

"Palamaro?" she repeated stupidly.

"Torch Palamaro," he said.

"Torch?" She swung the wheel and the car veered

wildly. She'd almost missed that corner. ''That's not your real name, is it?''

''Nickname.'' He was a man of few words, it seemed.

She frowned, again glancing his way. ''Why Torch?''

His answer was a slow grin, and he lifted the thing he held, pointing it behind them.

An explosion rocked the very ground beneath them. The car vibrated with it. The night glowed for a moment, and Alexandra jammed the brake and the clutch at the same time, skidding the vehicle to a stop in a cloud of dust.

She looked behind them, saw what had been the van, minus several important parts, the hood being the most obvious. It burned like a motorized torch, pouring black smoke skyward as several men emerged like rats from a burning ship.

They scurried, then regrouped and ran forward, and she heard a rat-a-tat sound she couldn't place at first.

Then the back window exploded, and she screamed.

The man who called himself Torch—for obvious reasons—gripped her waist in his large hands and pulled her onto his lap. Before she could yell again, he was sliding out from beneath her, into the driver's seat. In what seemed like a heartbeat they were flying, and one of his hands rose to the back of her head to push it toward her lap.

''Stay down, Alex.''

Alex stayed down.

Chapter 4

Torch didn't know where that brief flash of courage she'd displayed back at the house had come from, but it was long gone now. She sat huddled in the passenger seat with her knees drawn to her chest and that long hair of hers hiding her face. And he was pretty sure she was crying. Shaking like a leaf, too.

When they finally hit a road with what passed for blacktop, he slowed down a little. Not much, just enough to avoid drawing undue attention. He turned the heat on full blast, but it still didn't make up for the wintry air coming through the shattered back window. She must be cold, as well as terrified. Not to mention sick. He didn't know much about her gasping fits, but he didn't imagine being scared out of one's wits and then exposed to frigid air was exactly good for them. He wished she'd say something, but he didn't expect her to. He found himself wanting to draw her out of the shell she'd crawled into, but he wasn't sure why.

"Are you sick?"

She shook her head, said nothing.

"Is it asthma?" He didn't know why the hell he'd asked that. He didn't want to know anything about Alexandra Holt, except where her father had hidden his formula. He didn't care about her.

"I've had it since I was three."

"Is it bad?"

"Chronic. Not as bad now as it used to be though." She lifted her head a little, so her hair fell back and revealed her face. She closed her eyes. "Used to drive my father crazy, having to take time off from work running me to doctors and hospitals."

Torch looked down at the way her long, elegant hands clasped each other more tightly as she spoke. Her father sounded like a real prince. "What brings it on?"

She shrugged, opening her eyes again, even looking at him for a second. "I haven't had an attack since I found my father, in his bed...." She gave her head a nearly imperceptible shake.

And Torch found himself envisioning her, alone in that mausoleum of a house, slipping into her father's bedroom to check on him, worried maybe, about the man she adored, according to the background check on her. He could see it all so clearly, those wide, expectant brown eyes, growing even wider when she called to her father and got no answer. Wider still when she shook his shoulders and still heard no response. And finally filling with tears when she realized that her father was dead.

Damn, why did his brain insist on conjuring so much baloney?

"When I was younger, it would act up at the first sign

of pollen or cat hair or smoke. Now I guess it's mostly stress induced. Even Max's long hair doesn't bother it.''

That was better. She was talking. When she talked he could focus on the words, the inflections in her tone. He could try to hear more than she was saying, maybe pick up on a clue. When she went silent, it was far too easy to start searching her eyes and imagine he could read every emotion in them. Way too easy.

Stress induced, she'd said. Well, then, it was no wonder she'd had an attack. She'd certainly had some stress in the past few hours. But it couldn't be helped, could it? He had to get the formula, and he had to kill Scorpion. Alexandra and her asthma be damned.

''So where is this safe-deposit box located, Alexandra?''

''New York.''

He nodded. ''You told me that.''

She took a few steadying breaths. He thought she might be searching for some more of the tiny reserve of strength she kept hidden so well, way down at the end of some twisting cavern inside her. He kind of thought she'd stumbled onto it by accident when he'd caught a glimpse of it before. Maybe she didn't even know the way back to that place.

She bit her lip, seemingly forcing words now. ''This is over as far as I'm concerned. You can just let me go now. Okay?'' She lifted her head, staring at him from huge brown eyes that were still frightened and now red rimmed to boot.

''I don't think so.'' The words slipped out before he'd given them any thought at all. Why not let her go?

''You don't need me. I'll tell you the name of the bank and give you the key, but only if you swear to let me go.''

He stared at her, searched her face, probed those expressive eyes until he was in danger of being sucked into them as if they were made of quicksand. She was up to something. Damned if she wasn't. He could read her like a book. "Seems to me you'd *want* to go with me, Alex. Seems like you'd want to see what I find in that box for yourself, especially since you're so sure it'll prove your old man innocent."

"I know it will."

"So how do you know I can be trusted to report what's really in there? How do you know I won't lie and ruin his impeccable name no matter what I find?"

Her eyes widened and she bit her lip. "I'm…not cut out for this."

"No, I don't suppose you are." He sighed hard, knowing it was an understatement. She was fragile and frightened and he was about to drag her with him into the hubs of hell. But he had no choice.

"Look, Alex, the truth is that if I let you go those guys are gonna track you down. It won't matter where you go or how well you think you can hide. Sooner or later, they'll find you, and they'll try to force you to tell them what they want to know. They won't believe you don't know anything. And even if you did manage to convince them of that, they'd be obliged to kill you anyway. And by the time they decided to do it, you'd be grateful for death."

She shook her head. "No one is that brutal."

"Don't tell me that, Alex. I know *exactly* how brutal they are. Believe me."

"You've dealt with them before?"

Her eyes took on a new look, a curious, probing one, and they picked his brain. He clamped his jaw, averting his face. He didn't want her digging into his soul, because with eyes like those, she'd have to be capable of seeing right into its blackest, bottomless pit. Right to the heart of his grief. She'd look into the empty place where his soul was supposed to be. But his soul was gone. It had died with his little boys.

"You're not gonna be safe until I get that formula to my boss. Then I'll let you go. Until then, you're stuck with me." He glanced her way. "Now, how about handing over that key?"

She shook her head.

He sent her his meanest glare, but it was ineffective since she refused to look him in the eye. "How about the name of the bank?"

"I'll tell you when we get to New York."

"You care to explain your reasons?"

She shook her head from side to side. "It's not as if it matters anyway. There's not going to be anything there."

"Huh?"

Her white teeth worried her lower lip for a moment. "I've already told you, my father couldn't have done this." She drew a shaky breath. "And...and if he did stumble onto some potentially deadly weapon, then he did it by accident. He wouldn't have done something like that deliberately."

"I don't really care if it was deliberate or not, Alex. Your father created a monster. When he had it, he took it and ran."

"Maybe he wished he hadn't found whatever it was. You said he deleted his files, took all his notes."

"So?"

"So, if this thing ever existed, he probably destroyed it himself."

"That's where you're wrong, Alexandra."

She tilted her head, staring at him, and her eyes pierced his skin again, tears slowly drying on her lashes. "I know my father."

"And I know his type."

She was silent for a long moment while Torch waited. "You don't know anything about him at all," she said softly.

"Alex, this formula of your father's—good or bad— was probably the most significant discovery of his career in science. Do you really think he'd have had the heart to destroy it?" She blinked at him, apparently unable to look away. "I don't. I think he'd squirrel it away somewhere, and maybe he had the best of intentions. Maybe he never intended for another soul to see it or even know about it. But I really doubt he destroyed it. His vanity, his oversize ego, wouldn't let him destroy it."

Her knees lowered until her feet rested on the floor. She tipped her head back, resting it on the seat behind her. "You're wrong about him." But her voice lacked conviction.

"Sure I am. And you're so loyal to him because... what, he was the world's greatest dad?"

She flinched in real pain. Intense pain that brought tears to her eyes. Torch wished he hadn't spoken. He'd obviously touched a raw spot. He rolled his eyes, wishing he couldn't so easily tell when his words hurt her, wishing he could be callous to her pain.

"Look, you could be wrong, and we can't take a chance like that. I have to be sure. This is too important, Alex. Those guys back there would do anything, pay anything to get their hands on this."

She turned toward him, eyes narrow. "And I'm supposed to trust that you won't get it yourself—on the off

chance there is actually anything to get—and sell to the
highest bidder?''

''What?''

She closed her eyes, sighed long and hard. ''If I'm
stuck with a man I barely know, I'm going to hold on
to the key. For all I know, *you* might murder me once I
give it to you and tell you what you want to know.''

''You're kidding, right?''

''I'm going to prove you wrong. I'm not going to let
my father's memory be tarnished like this. For once in
my life, I'm going to do something right, something he
would have expected of me.''

Torch had the feeling she was speaking more to herself than to him. He frowned at her, wondering where
that last remark was coming from. *No way, Palamaro,
you don't want to go there. Leave it alone. You don't
give a damn about her, remember?*

''You're liable to regret it,'' he told her, wisely heeding the advice his practical side was feeding him. Damn,
he didn't want her with him. He didn't want her anywhere near him. She was dangerous. But he didn't see
that he had a choice in the matter.

''I'd regret it more if I let him down again. I'd regret
that for the rest of my life.''

Something close to admiration welled up in his throat.
He'd never seen anyone as scared as she'd been back
there. Scared as she was, though, she was still able to
stand up to him on behalf of this idiot father of hers.
Her loyalty might be misplaced, but it was sure as hell
solid.

''You might need a refill on that medicine of yours
before this is over.'' He gunned the gas and the car shot
forward.

* * *

He came out of the motel office with one key dangling from his good hand, and Alexandra couldn't take her eyes off him as he crossed the parking lot toward the car. He'd donned a leather jacket that had been lying in the back seat, so he wouldn't attract notice by walking in shirtless with a bandage job on his shoulder. But she imagined he'd attracted just as many eyes this way. Striding purposefully toward her with the black jacket hanging open and his unclothed chest beneath it, she figured he looked like some women's fondest fantasy.

Not hers, though. To her, he looked scary. Too big and too hard. A little bit too virile. She'd prefer a less muscular man, one who was all brain and little brawn. She'd prefer a man with short, tame hair. Not the long, wild waves that suggested rebellion and seemed untamable. A man who was shy and sensitive, and who didn't keep his feelings to himself. The way this one did.

When she looked into his eyes, she could plainly see them roiling with…something.

He looked tough, she mused. Like someone you wouldn't want to cross…or even look at wrong. She could never be attracted to a man as ominous and unapproachable as he was. One who seemed to exude subliminal, erotic messages along with his masculine scent.

He got into the car and drove it around behind the motel, parking it between a camper and a pickup truck to conceal its presence. He seemed to think of everything, this guy. He might be muscular, but he was smart, too. Who was he? Who did he work for? What kind of man did this stuff for a living?

It didn't matter, she told herself, wishing she could believe it and stop wondering. She wouldn't be with him long enough to find out.

She didn't trust him. And she didn't want him getting

a close look at that key until she was ready to run. Because if he did, he might realize that it wasn't a safe-deposit box key at all. And she wasn't going to tell him the name of the bank, either, because then all he'd have to do would be to place a phone call, and he'd know her father no longer had a safe-deposit box there. Hadn't had one since right after he'd died.

Rather than trust Torch Palamaro with the truth, she was going to slip away from him at the first opportunity. She had to see for herself what her father's notes had to say. That way she could be sure the truth came out. This was the last chance she was ever going to have to make her father proud of her, to repay him for all the disappointments in the past.

Double-crossing Torch Palamaro, though, was going to be the most frightening thing she'd ever done. She could just imagine what his wrath would be like. She shivered a little.

"Our room awaits," he announced as he got out.

She stopped shivering and stared, wide-eyed. "What do you mean, *our* room?" Opening her door, she jumped out after him.

He didn't stop walking. Just paused in front of a door, inserted the key and opened it with a flourish. "Let's just say I don't trust you any more than you trust me, Alex. And I wouldn't be a bit surprised if you were planning to take that key and go to that bank by yourself. In which case you'd get killed, the bad guys would get the formula, and I'd lose my chance to do my job and collect my money…and it's too much money to risk losing like that."

So he was only in this for the money. She might have guessed as much. Well, he had one thing right, she *was* leaving. But she didn't care if it was with or without the key, and she wouldn't be going anywhere near New York. Doing so would be easier, though, if they had separate rooms.

"I'm not sleeping with you." She blurted the sentence before fully composing it in her mind. "I mean, I'm not—"

"Twin beds, Alex. I think I can manage to stay in mine if you can manage to stay in yours. Okay?"

"No, it's not okay."

"Well, if you're afraid you won't be *able* to stay in yours, that's okay, too. I mean, I'm as red-blooded as the next guy—"

He broke off when her hand came flying up. She froze just before her palm connected with his face, and she stared at her hand, blinking in shock. My God, she'd almost slapped him. That wasn't like her. It wasn't *anything* like her. What was happening to her?

And what in the world was the matter with *him?* He hadn't flinched, hadn't drawn back, hadn't tried to stop her. And now, he just shook his head, clucking his tongue. "Chicken."

"What?"

"Nothing. Listen, I'm the guy with the money, and I rented one room. I'm not renting another one. Should have grabbed your purse while you were making that daring escape, lady."

He held the door open, waved her inside, and she went, too shocked by what she'd nearly done to argue with him anymore. He came in behind her, closed the door and locked it. Then he tossed the key onto the bed, followed by his jacket, and then his body, back first. "I could use a nap."

"Something to eat would be nice."

"Nag, nag, nag."

She stared at him, then quickly looked away. It was oddly disturbing looking at his naked chest when he was stretching sinuously, rumpling the covers with his body.

"Well? Come on, I said nag. What are you waiting for?"

She closed her eyes, shook her head. She didn't understand the man at all. "I do not nag."

"No? Shame. It's a great stress reliever. For now, though, I'll do it for you. You're hungry. You'd like a shower and a change of clothes and then and only then will you feel able to sleep. Am I close?"

Tilting her head, she nodded.

"All right, then." He lunged to his feet and headed out of the room without another word. She watched his broad back and the tight curve of his denim-encased backside when he left, and then she swallowed hard, trying to relieve the dryness in her throat. But it didn't help.

When he came back he slung a duffel bag onto the unoccupied bed she'd decided must be hers.

"There you go. Knock yourself out."

"You have food in there?"

"A veritable banquet. K rations. And help yourself to the clothes." He was on the bed again, but he lifted his head to look her up and down. "They'll be big, but I imagine you'd look good in a feed bag."

She blinked, stunned. Had he just complimented her? Too late to tell, his eyes had closed again. And even as she stared at him, he seemed to fall asleep. The muscled wall of chest rose and fell slowly, expanding incredibly and then collapsing. The room was utterly silent except for the deep soughs of the air filling him again and again, escaping over and over. It hypnotized her.

She shook herself, muttering under her breath that she

was a thousand kinds of idiot, and carefully loosened the drawstring on the duffel. She tried not to hear the mesmerizing music he was making as she dug through the bag. It wasn't easy.

The thing was crammed full. Seemed he had everything but the kitchen sink in here. And it occurred to her that she might learn a little something about the mysterious man who called himself Torch, if she looked through what must be his worldly possessions.

"K rations are in that zippered pouch on the front. And there ought to be a T-shirt right on top."

She nearly jumped out of her skin at the sound of his voice. He'd scared her half to death. She fished out a T-shirt as he'd instructed and left the bag where it was, to head into the little bathroom. And she locked the door before she showered.

But locked away from him in the bathroom, her curiosity about him grew to unreasonable proportions. Did he, perhaps, not want her looking through the duffel bag too thoroughly? And if not, why not? What did he have to hide?

Again she told herself it didn't matter. She had an agenda of her own to keep. Probably the most important one of her life. She didn't dress in the big black T-shirt she'd taken with her. Instead, she put her clothes back on. And then she cracked the door.

He was snoring now, very softly. All right then. This would probably be the best opportunity she'd ever get. She tiptoed out of the bathroom, pausing only long enough to snatch her sneakers off the floor. Torch never moved, just kept snoring, sleeping. His eyelashes seemed thicker and darker now than when he was awake. Or was it just the way they contrasted against his cheeks?

Didn't matter.

She stopped at the door, grabbed the knob.

"Going out for a little stroll, Alex?"

She froze, closing her eyes. "I was...just checking the lock."

"You need your shoes for that?"

She tossed the shoes to the floor, shook her head in self-disgust.

Palamaro sat up in bed, smiling smugly at her. "Don't try that again, Alex. I'm the lightest sleeper you'll ever meet."

She only stared at him. His blue eyes were amused, not angry. And they had a disturbing habit of dipping as he looked at her. So he didn't just look at her face but at her entire body, head to toe, over and over again. Almost as if he couldn't resist doing so. Or maybe he was just trying to shake her, keep her off balance.

"Get some sleep," he told her. "You're gonna need it."

"I couldn't sleep if I wanted to."

"Suit yourself." He swung out of the bed. "Meanwhile you can help me with a little problem I just recently discovered."

He dug into the duffel, tugging out a fresh pair of jeans and tossing them onto her bed. She watched his every move, though she told herself repeatedly to look away. Her eyes refused to obey. They seemed terribly interested in the way the muscles in his back and shoulders flexed and relaxed and rippled beneath his taut skin. And the way his dark hair fell over his neck, just touching his shoulders. It looked...incredibly...soft.

There was strength in this man. And she sensed it went deeper than just the physical aspects.

"What problem?" She wished he'd locate a shirt and put it on.

He turned toward her, the duffel dangling from his right arm. Its weight made his biceps stand out, and for a second her gaze was riveted to that arm, tracing the corded bulge beneath the taut skin. She jerked her gaze elsewhere and ended up staring at his belly. Hard. Tight. She felt hers tighten in response. What was wrong with her? Hadn't she ever seen a well-developed male before?

Not really, she admitted silently. Not up close. Not alone in a room with no one but him and his damned unclothed, hair-sprinkled chest and his scent.

"The problem of how the hell I'm supposed to leave you alone long enough to take a shower."

A lump rose in her throat. She couldn't seem to swallow it.

"The minute I turn on the water, you'll be out of here like a scared rabbit, won't you, Alex?"

She shook her head, speaking past the lump, since it wouldn't dislodge. The result was a squeaky, raspy-sounding voice. "I'll stay," she told him.

"I don't believe you. But listen up, Alex. If you try to leave, I'll come after you, and if I have to chase you down in that parking lot buck naked and dripping wet, I'll do it. Don't think I won't."

His words evoked images she'd rather not see. She only nodded and croaked, "I'll stay."

"You'd better." He was back to digging through the duffel again. He bent over it, drew out another black T-shirt. As he did, a photograph fluttered to the floor and he went utterly still. It landed faceup, and as he stared down at it, his face altered. The tough-guy glaze vanished, evaporated like dew under a blazing sun. And what remained was a pain so stark and so intense that she almost gasped in surprise.

Since he didn't move, she did, stepping forward and

dropping to her haunches. The photo's corners curled slightly inward, and it looked old. He must have carried it for a long time. It was of a beautiful, petite blond woman and two little boys. Twins, apparently. And their dark hair and blue eyes looked enough like Palamaro's to make her wonder if they might be his children. Or maybe his nephews or something.

She frowned and turned her gaze to the man who seemed to have turned to stone as his blue eyes remained riveted to the photo on the floor. She tried to picture him with a family, a wife and two little boys. But it wasn't easy. He just didn't seem the type.

She reached for the photo, then jerked backward when he swooped down and snatched it up with the speed of a striking rattler.

She caught his gaze only briefly, and it amazed her. He was hurting. A vulnerable, aching mortal man battling unseen demons. Intense pain blazed from his eyes. Sorrow, remorse and more. It was in the way his shoulders bowed just slightly, the lowering of his chin, the softening of his jaw.

Then he turned away, tucking the photo into one of the duffel's side pockets.

"Who are they?" She asked the question before she could think better of it.

He said nothing. Only straightened, lowering the bag to the bed, keeping his back to her. Something compelled her then. And she should have known it would. She was the consummate nurturer, after all. It was why she'd gone into medicine. She liked caring for people, had this insane urge to feel needed. Because she wasn't, she supposed. No one had ever needed her. Not really. Well, except for Max. She missed that lazy cat. He was another reason she couldn't stay away for very long.

She'd tried to care for her father, but he'd never allowed it. She'd gone so far as to follow him, leaving her job and her life and her home, just to care for him in what she'd thought was severe senility or worse. When she saw someone in pain or in trouble, the urge to heal them overcame her. She'd been that way as long as she could remember. It was stupid, she supposed, for someone to long to be needed as desperately as she did, but it was there, nonetheless. Someday someone would need her, and she'd be theirs for life. Until then, she'd just have to live with her compulsion to heal and sympathize and comfort.

When she was younger, she used to dream of growing up and having children. Sweet, beautiful children who'd love her unconditionally. Who would need her as no one ever had. But that dream had shattered just recently...with her recent physical. A few unexplained cramps. An ultrasound. And the discovery that her ovaries were withered and not functioning. A birth defect, more than likely, the gynecologist had told her.

She'd never have children.

Sweet, beautiful children like those two in the photo.

Her hand rose, slowly, softly, and she watched it, almost surprised at the movement. Then she settled it on his hard, broad shoulder, and she felt him stiffen at her touch.

He drew a deep breath that shuddered its way into his chest. But he didn't speak to her. He didn't even turn to face her. He simply walked into the bathroom, his steps fast and sure. Alexandra's hand lingered in the air for a moment. She shouldn't have asked about the photo. He'd made that clear, hadn't he?

She stared at him in the bathroom. He hadn't bothered to close the door. But he turned toward her, and every trace of emotion was hidden behind the hard features that became handsome only when he slept. Because then the granite went out of his face. The facade of hardness fell away.

His hands went to the button of his jeans.

"You might want to turn around, Alex. I'm gonna leave the door open, just in case you decide to try and leave."

His fingers freed the button, lowered the zipper. He hooked his thumbs in the waistband. "Or you can watch. It's all the same to me."

He shoved the jeans down. She managed to convince herself to spin around as he did it, and she heard his deep chuckle, heard the material rasping over his thighs. Then she heard the water running. The sound of it changed when he stepped into the spray.

Alex chanced a quick glance over her shoulder and was rewarded with an unobstructed view of his wide back, dimpled buttocks and rock-solid, hair-smattered thighs. He stood in the tub, shower curtain wide open. Water pummeled him. Steam rose from his tanned skin, and again she couldn't look away.

Until he turned, sending her a wink. "You're not as bashful as I thought, are you, Alex?"

She was gaping, she realized. She clamped her jaw and hurried to the bed, deciding it might be time to get some sleep after all. But she didn't sleep. Because when she closed her eyes, it was only to see a naked, wet man grinning at her. And it was only to realize, with a sickening sensation in the pit of her stomach and a foreign ache in her loins, that she was attracted to Torch Palamaro. Powerfully attracted. To the man who seemed determined to ruin her father's good name.

God help her.

Chapter 5

The bandages came loose in the shower and the wound hurt like hell. Those were the least of his worries, but he supposed he'd have to take care of them.

Alexandra Holt was too insightful and too damned softhearted for her own good, or for his peace of mind. She'd seen the photo, and she'd seen the pain he never revealed to anyone. His most private hell. She had no damned right to see it! It belonged to him and him alone. He had no desire to share his grief or his guilt. Especially not with her. She'd invaded his most private place when she'd put her hand on his shoulder.

She'd only been trying to comfort him. He knew that. But he didn't want her damned comfort. When she'd almost touched the photo of Marcy and the boys...

It was wrong to let her touch it. Touch them. She had nothing to do with them. They were a separate part of his life, safe from invasion by outsiders.

Especially her. The first woman to stir a healthy lust

in him since their death. It was wrong. He had to keep
her away from that sacred memory, that sacred pain. He
and Marcy had had something. Not love. But friendship.
And trust. They'd created something precious together.
Josh and Jason.

He bit his lip against the swelling in his throat and
the burning in his eyes. They'd been his world. And
Marcy had been a big part of that world.

He remembered the phone call, the last time he'd ever
heard the voice of the woman who'd given him twin
sons.

"Try to get home early," she'd said, happiness in her
voice. "Before it gets too dark. Josh finally figured out
how to ride his two-wheeler and he's dying to show off
for you."

"I'll be there. Just one last report to file. I'd have been
home before now, if D.C. hadn't called in sick."

She'd laughed. "Sick, huh? I think he was playing
hooky. The boys and I ran into him at the mall today.
He was talking to some man with—oh, hey, I'd better
go. Someone's at the door. I'll tell you about it later."

"Give the boys a kiss for me," he'd told her.

"If I can get them to come inside long enough," she'd
replied, and hung up. And that was it. That was all. And
apparently she *had* gotten Josh and Jason to come inside,
because they'd died with her in that damned explosion.

And the pain was his. It was his alone. This job, this
mission he was on was for them. He'd avenge their
deaths. He'd get it right, this time. And he wasn't sure
why, but he felt certain Alexandra Holt posed a threat
to that. Somehow, she'd try to keep him from exacting
vengeance. It made no sense, but the knowledge was
there, stamped indelibly on his mind. He couldn't let her

do that. Could not allow this woman to come between him and his goal.

He stepped out of the bathroom, wearing his shorts and nothing else. Let her be shocked. Let her throw a prissy little fit and he could despise her for being pretentious and phony.

But she didn't. She lay on the bed, curled on her side with her back to him. All that glossy hair covering her shoulder, a few curling tendrils reaching out over the pillow as if in search of something to twist around.

It damned well wouldn't be him.

She didn't turn, didn't even move. He figured she must be sleeping. He dug the first-aid kit out of the duffel and taped up his shoulder, though doing so one-handed was awkward and nearly impossible. But he managed. When she didn't stir to offer help, he was *sure* she was sleeping. She was too softhearted to let him struggle without jumping in like Mary Sunlight to help him. Even if she'd decided to hate his guts, which he dearly hoped she had.

He ate. But the whole time, the image of her, lying there in the bed wearing his T-shirt now, with her hair spread around her like black satin, haunted his mind. She hadn't eaten. Not a bite. And she should have, because she was going to need her energy at its peak for the trip ahead. Either she was too fussy to settle for the rations, or she didn't have any appetite. Probably the latter.

He ought to wake her and make her eat.

He didn't.

And when he'd cleaned his guns and loaded them and run out of things to do, he sat there on his own bed and stared at her.

Why did he have to end up with a woman who could make a saint have impure thoughts? Why couldn't this job have provided only the usual risks, bullets flying over his head, that kind of thing? Why her?

Palamaro hadn't been with a woman since Marcy had died. And, frankly, he hadn't wanted to. That part of his soul had died with his family. He hadn't been aroused since the night when his life had gone up in smoke, and that was fine with him. He'd planned to just throw himself body and soul into the job, and hope to God the bad guys would win one of these times. Let them blow him away and put an end to this joke that passed for a life.

But work hadn't made him forget. And with Doug Stern always watching his every move, never quite believing Torch innocent in the bombing that had killed his family but unable to back up his suspicions, work had become impossible.

Hell, he couldn't even blame Stern. The bastard had been half in love with Marcy when she and Torch had had to get married. If he hadn't gotten her pregnant, she probably would have ended up married to Stern.

And maybe she'd still be alive.

Though he never said it out loud, Stern was a constant reminder of that fact. So Torch had chosen retirement. A life of killing time, waiting to waste away. But that hadn't worked out, either.

He'd entered stage three now, he supposed. He was living for vengeance. That was all he cared about. There was no room for sympathy or even lust for Alexandra Holt. No room at all.

So what was it about her that had him feeling...desire? The longer he looked at her, the more he felt it. All he'd done was sit on his bed and look at her, and he was hard. Just like that, after almost a year without a sign of life down there. And it seemed to him that all these months of abstinence were screaming to end. Right now, right here. With her.

Made no sense whatsoever. And he had no intention of heeding their cries. If he could dodge bullets and battle terrorists, he could certainly resist a little uprising of his libido. He wasn't going to be unfaithful to Marcy's memory. Beyond that, he most certainly wasn't going to let himself care about Alexandra Holt. Not in the least. Because it would interfere with the job he'd come here to do. It would distract him, and it would mess up his objectivity, dull his instincts. He knew the drill. She was one of the targets of this investigation, and an operative didn't screw around with a target.

Besides, he'd pretty much given up on caring about people at all. It hurt too much to lose them. Torch knew damned well he wasn't up for dealing with any more pain.

So he sat there arguing with his body's demands, until an hour before dawn. That was when she muttered something in her sleep and rolled over, bending one long leg slightly, causing the T-shirt to bunch up around her waist. And he saw the little white cotton panties she wore, and he wanted to go over there and slide them off her.

He was undeniably aroused, and disgusted with himself for it. Fresh air might help. He pulled on his jeans and T-shirt and headed out the door, paced in the parking lot, stared up at the fading night sky. But it gave him no answers and did little to erase this sudden hunger for a woman he barely knew.

It was only when he heard the soft purr of a vehicle and turned to see the sleek black minivan moving slowly through the lot that he forgot all about his aching need.

Torch ducked into the shadows, pressing his back to

the motel's brick wall and moving sideways until he
could see the van again. There had been two vans at
Alexandra's house. He'd blown one to hell, but not the
other. And to believe this was just some family looking
for a good parking spot was a fool's errand. It was Scorpion, or more of his henchmen. It had to be, and they
were cruising the lot looking for Torch and Alexandra
Holt.

How the hell had they followed him here? Had they
seen his car? Did they know what to look for?

Didn't matter. He'd left two alive back there, two who
could describe him and Alex to a fault. All they'd have
to do would be to question the desk clerk.

But how the hell had they found them here?

The van came to a stop out front, and one of them
headed toward the office.

Torch ducked back into the room, closed the door
quietly and flicked off the lights. He ran to the bed where
Alexandra lay sleeping, her face illuminated only by the
flickering orange glow of the damaged neon vacancy
sign outside. He leaned over her, gripped her shoulders.
"Alex, wake up!"

Her eyes flew open. Sleepy and wide and brown. She
stared up at him, and he knew what she was thinking.
He knew, read it on her face as easily as boldface type.
She thought his reasons for coming to her bed were anything but what they were.

She shook her head slowly, side to side. "I…I don't
even know your real name," she blurted.

Not "get your filthy hands off me, you beast." Not
"make another move and I'll scream this place down
around your ears." Just that she didn't know his name.
Was he supposed to take that to mean that not knowing

his name was her *only* objection to a little game of one-on-one?

He swallowed hard, told himself this wasn't the time or place for those kinds of questions. "We have to leave. They're here."

He saw the fear, the panic in her eyes. She lunged out of the bed and was yanking on her jeans, stuffing her feet into her sneakers even before he added, "Hurry. They're in the office now, they won't hear us leave."

"How did they find us?"

"Damned if I know." Torch tore his gaze away from her, scanning the room to be sure they left nothing behind. As he checked the bathroom, he tried to figure it out, talking it through as he did. "You said you found out about the safe-deposit box when you were going through your father's papers, after he died. Are those papers still in the house?"

She groaned, closed her eyes. "Right in his bedroom. God, why didn't I think of it before?"

"I didn't think of it, either." But he should have. Dammit, hadn't he learned anything? Not anticipating crap like this had gotten his family murdered in their own home. So what did it take to get through to him?

"What is it? What's wrong?"

He shook himself, met her gaze. She was staring at him, and she was scared half out of her mind. "Nothing. Just that they knew where we were going, knew we were in a hurry, took the only sensible route, and started checking motels. Child's play for these guys. My mistake. I'm supposed to know better."

Her brown eyes probed his, narrowing, searching. It was as if she knew his words had some double meaning, as if she were trying, even now, to see the source of his consuming pain. The way she looked at him made him shiver, and he was damned if he knew why. He averted his eyes, slung the duffel over his shoulder and took her arm. He held his gun at the ready in his right hand and opened the door.

"I can't do this. I can't go out there." She whispered the words, but Palamaro either didn't hear or didn't want to. He tugged her through the door and outside into the night. She moved on legs as stiff as boards, which she figured was just as well. If her knees bent at all, they'd probably dissolve.

She tried to look around, tried to search the area for threats, men in black, men with guns. It seemed at first that they were everywhere, but it was only that the parking lot was alive with moving shadows. It took one panicked moment for her to realize the cause—headlights passing on the highway out front, casting their glow slowly as they moved, making the shadows come to life. There could be twenty men in black lurking out here, and they'd be invisible.

Torch Palamaro stood still just beyond the door, and she thought he was testing the air. The motel room behind them was dark. He'd flicked off the lights before dragging her out here. He'd left the door wide. In case they had to retreat? But if they went back in there, they'd be trapped, wouldn't they?

From somewhere on the highway, rock music came faintly, then louder, then faded again. Motors purred and sputtered and roared. She could hear the tinny voices and canned laughter of a TV sitcom coming from one of the rooms nearby. And there was a throaty gurgle of rushing water from beneath the grate just under her feet. Nothing else. Utter silence. But that didn't mean they were alone.

Palamaro leaned close to her. "Give me the key. But don't make it obvious."

She stared at him, but he didn't meet her eyes. His were wide, alert, moving back and forth as he scanned the parking lot's dancing shadows. "I...I don't understand what you want me to—"

"Now, dammit."

His whisper was all but silent, and still managed to be harsh, demanding. He'd given an order. Alexandra prayed she was doing the right thing and reached toward the back pocket of her jeans.

He faced her, moving so suddenly she jumped in surprise. One arm snagged her waist, jerking her against him hard and fast. And tight. So tight she could barely breathe. His mouth covered hers, and he stole what little remained of her breath, taking it into his own body, sucking the very life from her, it seemed. He pressed her back to the wall, nudging her mouth open, thrusting his tongue inside, dipping and tasting and taking without permission or hesitation. His hand slid down over her back, and her eyes fell closed even as she realized his remained open. And he still clasped that black gun in his other hand.

Her wooden legs dissolved, and she had no choice but to put her arms around his neck. She'd sink to the ground if she didn't. His mouth on hers was warm, wet, hungry as it invaded and devoured. When his hand clasped her buttocks, squeezed her there, held her hips to his as they ground against her, she felt her insides turn to molten lava. She tilted her head to accept his tongue's thrusts as her mind spun into madness. Conscious thought receded. Feeling took over. Sensation. The blood in her veins became fire, and every limb trembled. She opened her mouth to his with a soft groan of surrender. She slid her fingers into his long dark hair and kissed him back and even moved her hips against him. He was commanding responses from her very soul as he kissed her. The way his hand moved, kneaded, slid…

Into her back pocket, and then out again, with the key.

He could have slapped her and shocked her less.

He straightened away from her, the key now in his fist. His eyes just as alert and sharp as before. His breathing perfectly normal. While she clung to the wall behind her to keep from falling to her knees, and fought to catch her breath, he went about his business, seemingly unaffected. Her heart hammered. She was cold and she shook with it. He turned, scanning the lot again, unmoved by the chaos he'd just brought crashing down on her.

"Now walk very casually to the car, Alex. Open the passenger door and get in."

She swallowed hard, lifting her chin. He was a bastard. He deserved to be horsewhipped for what he'd just done. But she'd be damned if she'd let him see how much he'd shaken her. She took a step toward the car, then two. He kept pace on the driver's side.

She reached the door. Bent to it, put her hand on it.

"Not leaving so soon, are you, Palamaro? The party is only beginning."

The voice sent cold chills up Alexandra's spine. It was too high-pitched, too shrill. She froze, moving only her eyes to find the source of that fingernails-on-a-chalkboard tone. The shockingly pale man stood right behind Palamaro, a gun pressed tight to the base of Torch's neck. Torch's gaze met hers over the top of the car. There was rage in his eyes. But she sensed it wasn't directed at her. He said a single word, and it dripped with hatred.

"Scorpion."

The man behind him yanked the duffel from Torch's back and slammed it down onto the pavement. "Your gun, my friend. Drop it."

Torch did. Alexandra heard the clatter of metal against pavement. She tried not to sink into a well of panic, tried telling herself it was all right. There were other guns in that duffel Torch had slung over his shoulder. Lots of other guns.

The man behind Torch lifted his gaze, and when it met Alexandra's she shuddered in revulsion. Cold eyes. Colorless in the darkness, only igniting with neon fire when the sign flicked and buzzed. But evil, unspeakably evil. She felt its touch when he looked at her. The neon illuminated the scar across his cheek, making it seem fresh. Goose bumps rose on her arms, and she felt a crackle of static race over her nape. His perfectly white hair and glowing red eyes…

"Put those lovely arms up high, Ms. Holt, and walk around the car to stand beside your paramour, will you?"

She opened her mouth to tell him she couldn't. She couldn't move. Her feet were frozen to the ground where she stood. But no words came out. Seemed she was scared speechless as well as motionless. Her gaze jerked back to Torch's, and he sent her a nearly imperceptible nod. And somehow, she managed to raise her hands above her head and put one foot in front of the other until she stood beside Torch, facing the car, with that monster behind them.

"Turn around," the monster squeaked. His voice made her teeth hurt. Torch turned to face him. Alexandra stood still, trembling. Until Torch's hands touched her shoulders, urging her to turn as well.

The monster smiled. His eyes were pale, pink flashing red when the sign flickered its light on them. His skin was ashen. Shorter than Palamaro, though not by much, he was skinny. His long, narrow face ended in a pointed chin. He seemed to Alexandra to be evil personified.

"Good to see you again, Palamaro. I barely trusted my instincts when my men described the agent who'd run off with Ms. Holt and left them bound like calves at one of your American rodeos on her living room floor. I almost convinced myself it was only wishful thinking. But it *is* you."

"You shouldn't be so glad about that," Torch said softly.

"Oh, but anyone else wouldn't even have been a challenge," the monster went on. "I enjoy a worthy opponent, Palamaro. Makes the game so much more interesting."

"This is no game, Scorpion."

"Of course it is. Shall I tell you the rules?" He laughed softly, toying with the action of the gun as he pressed its barrel to Torch's forehead. Alexandra gasped aloud.

"You have something I want," he said. "The key to Alexander Holt's safe-deposit box. Give it to me, and I'll consider killing you quickly. Otherwise…" He smiled again, a slow, meaningful smile that froze Alexandra's heart. "It will be slow and extremely painful."

"What makes you think we have the key?" Torch said, and his voice was low, level, dangerous.

The man shook his head. "Lies will only earn your lady friend more pain, Palamaro."

Torch stared, never once blinking. "You think I'd

keep the key with me? You forget, Scorpion, I've dealt with you before.''

"And you underestimated me then, too, as I recall. I did think it would take longer for you to take a lover, though. Is your dead wife a faded memory already?''

She felt Palamaro stiffen beside her, and instantly thought of the woman in the photo. His wife? Dead? What about the boys? Had they been his sons, then? And where were they now?

"No matter,'' the monster went on. "I'm going to kill this one, too. Will you forget her as quickly?'' His gun moved down over Torch's face, his chin, his neck, finally stopping when it pressed to the center of his chest. The man called Scorpion reached out with his free hand, ran it slowly over Alexandra's hair. She cringed backward, pressed tight to the car, averted her face, but he still reached her. "I won't kill her fast like I did your wife, though. I believe I'll take my time with this one. Shall I make you watch, Palamaro, when I take her? Would you enjoy that?''

Her stomach heaved and her lungs began to spasm. Alexandra whirled, dropping to her knees and retching on the asphalt.

"A weak stomach, Ms. Holt? Such a pity.''

She knelt there until she was spent, and when she finally stopped heaving, she knew she couldn't stand up again if her life depended on it. She collapsed against the duffel, sobs wrenching her body.

Scorpion shook his head disdainfully at her, before returning his attention to Torch. "You might at least have chosen one who might be of help, Palamaro. I never thought weak women were your type.'' He sent her a last glance, then dismissed her with a shrug. "Ah well, no matter. Where is the key?''

"Not here," Torch said calmly, levelly.

Alexandra felt her bronchial tubes clenching tighter, and she gasped for air. Not now, she prayed. Not now! Her damned asthma might get them both killed. She pawed the spilled contents of the duffel in search of her inhaler, sucking in breaths that couldn't sustain her. She felt dizzy already.

"Where, Palamaro? My patience is running thin."

Torch only shook his head. "I can't believe you're here alone," he said. "I thought you never ventured out from under your rock without a half-dozen henchmen at your beck and call."

"For you I don't need help. This is personal now, isn't it, Palamaro? Just you and I."

Alexandra didn't find the inhaler on the ground, so she put her hand into the bag itself, still searching, still panting, growing more desperate for air with every insufficient gasp. She closed her fist around something cold and metallic. Not the inhaler. A gun.

She blinked in stark disbelief. She couldn't do this. She couldn't possibly do this. She gasped and choked, fighting for air, doubling over. And as she did, and her long hair concealed what her hands were doing, she slowly pulled the weapon out of the bag, turned it so the grip was in her palm, closed her fingers around it.

"This is getting tedious," Scorpion whined in his high-pitched, irritating voice. "I'm going to have to insist your lady join me back in the room here. I have methods for extracting information, you know. It won't be pleasant."

Alexandra didn't know if the gun was loaded. She didn't know anything about guns, except that one was supposed to pull the hammer back before firing. Only this one didn't seem to have a hammer. And if she waited much longer, she'd pass out from lack of oxygen. Her breaths were shallow, noisy, wheezing, rapid.

"It's a shame. A waste of a good man, but I'm afraid I'll have to kill you right away, Palamaro. You understand. I don't need you to lead me to the formula when I have Ms. Holt. And she'll be much more pleasant compan—"

She lifted the barrel and squeezed the trigger.

Palamaro's first thought when the shot exploded in his ears, was that Scorpion had shot him. It took only an instant to realize that wasn't the case. Scorpion swore aloud and swung his gun down toward Alexandra. But Torch brought his clasped fists down on Scorpion's gun hand, and the weapon dropped to the ground. The man never missed a beat. He lunged away, running for all he was worth, heading for the black van at the other end of the parking lot. And Torch itched with everything in him to go after him. To kill him. To make him pay. The haunting images of Marcy and Josh and Jason, smiling at him from that photograph he carried everywhere he went, drove Torch to do it. He reached down to Alexandra, yanking the Ruger from her cold, trembling hands.

He made the mistake of glancing at her as he did it, though, and then he paused. The red haze of hatred faded a little, enough so he could see her hunched on the cold pavement, choking for air. Her eyes were wide and glazed in the neon glow, swimming with tears that had left red streaks on her face.

He heard the van door slide open. Damn. No doubt Scorpion had other weapons in there. He bent down, caught sight of the inhaler and grabbed it, lifting it to her lips, fitting it between them. She didn't move.

"Take it." Still no response. "I said take it, Alex!"

Finally her hands closed over his. Damn, she was cold. He stuck the gun into his jeans, bent to grip her under the arms and hauled her to her feet. He wanted to take the supplies, too, but they were scattered and there was no time to gather them all. He settled for grabbing the half-filled duffel as he opened the car door. "Get in, Alex. Quick!"

She blinked twice, staring at the ground, still gasping for breath, though she'd finally shot a blast of medicine into her lungs. All at once she crouched and snatched something up, before finally scrambling across the seat and huddling in the passenger side.

Torch dove behind the wheel. The van had started toward them. He jammed the car into gear, spun the tires as he took off. He sped into traffic, cutting just ahead of an eighteen-wheeler and getting a blast of air horns for his trouble. All the while, one hand was elbow deep in the duffel bag. And he finally found what he wanted, a little cocktail for his pal, Scorpion. He anchored the bottle between his thighs, worked a lighter from his jeans pocket, flicked the flame to life and touched it to the cloth. He didn't even open his window. Just chucked the Molotov right out the back, through the missing windshield.

The explosion caused cars to skid sideways behind him, effectively blocking Scorpion's pursuit. Changing lanes, passing everything ahead of him, he managed to leave the minivan and the small fire in the distance. But even when the chaos was far behind him, he didn't let up on his speed. He was taking no more chances with Scorpion. He couldn't afford to make another mistake.

Some miles later, only beginning to allow himself to feel confident of their escape, he glanced over at Alexandra. She sat utterly still, her pupils dilated. Her breathing had eased. He saw the inhaler on her lap. And then he blinked. The photo lay there beside it. Marcy and Josh and Jason, smiling from the curling picture. All he had left of them, really.

A horn blew, and Torch jerked his attention back to the highway and swerved into his own lane. She'd grabbed the picture off the ground before they'd left. He gave his head a slight shake. Why?

He looked at her again, keeping one eye on his driving this time. She was shaken, maybe in shock. White as a sheet.

"Alex? You okay?"

Her answer was a vague nod. She licked her lips. "Did...did I hurt him?"

"Scorpion?" The question surprised him. He supposed it shouldn't have, though. She was a doctor. In the business of healing people, not putting bullets into them. "You missed by a mile, Alex. But you got our butts out of one tight spot, anyway. That was quick thinking."

She tilted her head, frowned a little, finally looking at him. Her expression seemed a little confused.

"You did good back there," he clarified.

She closed her eyes, lowered her head. "I got sick on the ground and almost passed out."

"Yeah, but you kept your head and used your wits. Not too many women I know could have done that."

She shook her head. "It was an accident. I was looking for my inhaler, and I found the gun by mistake."

Torch frowned, wondering why she was so determined not to take any credit. "Did you fire it by mistake, too?"

"No."

"I rest my case."

She said nothing for a long time. When she did, her voice was almost normal. "What happens now?"

Torch shook his head slowly. "They know where the box is."

"But they don't have the key."

"Neither do we...not anymore."

He saw her frown. She sat a little straighter, her eyes beginning to clear. Good. If thinking about the task at hand would erase the fear from her eyes, all the better. He'd never seen anyone so afraid. But she hadn't frozen. The woman had steel she wasn't even aware of.

"I dropped the key through that grate in the parking lot," he told her.

She frowned harder, giving her head a slight shake. "Why? Why throw it away after you...went to so much trouble to take it from me?"

His head jerked around. He couldn't tell if that was pain or anger in her eyes. She was still showing mostly fear, and it camouflaged everything else. "I suppose I ought to apologize for, uh, for that. I...knew Scorpion was watching. I could feel him, and I didn't want him to see me take the key from you. It...was the first thing that popped into my head."

Yeah, right. Actually, kissing Alexandra like that had been teasing his brain since he'd first laid eyes on her. But he'd never imagined her response would be pure, mind-blowing desire. Hell, he hadn't imagined what her response would be. But not that. When she'd turned to liquid fire in his arms, he'd almost forgotten all about Scorpion. When she'd moaned in a deep, throaty voice, and opened her mouth for him, and raked his hair with her fingers...

Damn. He'd known she'd be a distraction.

"Don't ever do that to me again," she said softly, her voice shaking.

"Yeah, I could tell you really hated it."

Her eyes widened and she stared at him, wounded right to the quick, he thought.

"All right, I won't lay a hand on you. Feel better?"

She looked away, eyes straight ahead. "Why did you throw the key away?"

"As a precaution. Not that it matters now. Scorpion knows where that box is. I don't imagine not having a key will stop him from getting his hands on the contents. And even if it did, we couldn't just show up at the bank. He'd be there, waiting. He'd take us the second we stepped out of the building."

"Then...then it's over? We've lost?"

He glanced sideways at her, sent her a wink. "Not by a long shot. I'm good at what I do. One of the best, and even though it's risky, I still think I can reach that box without getting my head blown off."

She flinched when he said that.

"It's just gonna require some creativity. Now, I think it's about time you gave me the specifics on that bank. I don't like that bastard Scorpion knowing more about this than I do."

He looked at her, and he knew the second he saw her face that there was more. Something she hadn't told him. Guilt clouded her brown eyes, and she gnawed her lower lip.

"Well?"

She cleared her throat. "I can't let you risk getting shot when..."

"When...?"

"There is no safe-deposit box in New York."

He blinked, swinging his head around, gaping. "What the hell do you mean?"

"I lied."

Chapter 6

Torch swore until he ran out of breath. Then he inhaled and started over, jerking the wheel without signaling and pulling the car off onto the first exit ramp they came to.

"How can there not be a safe-deposit box, Alex? Scorpion saw the papers saying there is one. That's what led him to us."

She chewed her lip, keeping her eyes lowered. "There was one once. Just like I said, in New York. And I really did find out about it after Father died, and Scorpion probably saw the same papers I did. But..." She let her words trail off.

"If you stop now I'll wring your pretty neck, Alex. But what?"

She lifted her chin, her wide brown eyes meeting his head-on. "I could see no sense in keeping a safe-deposit box in New York when I wasn't even sure I'd ever be going back there again."

The question that sprang to the tip of his tongue was

why. But he bit it back. It didn't matter to him what her
reasons were. He didn't give a damn why a talented
young doctor would want to hide herself away in the
mountains alone, and never emerge into the daylight
again. It didn't matter. All that mattered was finding this
damned formula before Scorpion did. And then killing
the bastard.

So why was it so hard to keep from asking the question?

"Lovely," he said instead, braking for a light at the
end of the ramp, then turning right, having no idea where
the hell he was going, just driving. "Go on. And tell me
the truth this time."

She looked at him with wary eyes. Half afraid of him.
Half something else, something he hadn't quite put his
finger on yet. He would, though. She was too easy to
read for it to take very long.

"We're on the same side, Alex."

"No, we're not. Our goals are completely different.
This is important to me, Palamaro. My father is dead.
In my whole life I never did anything but let him down,
and I'm not going to do it again this time. I have to clear
his name. I owe him."

The questions were burning in Torch's mind again.
Questions that had nothing to do with this case. Questions about her. Just what had convinced her she'd been
such a big disappointment to her old man? What horrible
letdowns had he suffered at her tender hands? The
woman's perceptions were definitely skewed.

Again he clenched his fists, forcibly resisting the urge
to ask, to delve into her psyche, to search for the source
of all that pain and wariness in her eyes. He took the
next left. "So what did you do with the box?"

"I sent the key and the number to Father's lawyer in

Pine Lake. I asked him to have the contents of the box sent to him there. I just wasn't up to going through any more of Father's things at the time. Jim stored them for me, said they'd be there whenever I was ready. As far as I know, they still are.''

Torch pulled the car to a stop on the shoulder. ''You're telling me that this safe-deposit box in New York City isn't even your father's anymore? That none of his stuff is in it? That it was up there in Pine Lake all along?''

She nodded.

Torch rolled his eyes and blew a sigh through clenched teeth, resisting the urge to throttle her. ''And the key you gave me?''

''Just an old PO box key.''

He swore some more. ''So I was supposed to trot all the way to New York on this wild-goose chase you set up, and then what? While I sat around trying to figure it out, you were going to try to give me the slip, right? You were going to head back up to your precious mountain retreat and grab your father's notes on your way.''

She swallowed hard, audibly, and nodded again.

''And then what, Alex?''

''Then I'd know…I'd have proof that my father didn't develop this weapon you keep talking about.''

''Oh, yeah?''

''And I'd have sent everything to you, to clear my father's name.''

Torch drummed his fingers on the steering wheel. ''And what if you'd found just the opposite? Hmm? Would you have let me know about that, too? Or would you have tried to cover it up, the way he did?''

''My father is innocent!''

''Yeah, and I'm Santa Claus.''

"I don't understand why you're so angry!"

He turned toward her, gripped her shoulders in his hands, and stared right into her eyes. "Dammit, Alex, you just aren't getting it, are you? This plan of yours could have worked! You could have pulled this off, and if you had, I'd have been completely stumped. Pine Lake would be the last place I'd look for you. And dammit, you'd have probably ended up dead!"

She shook her head slowly, her eyes probing his, confusion clouding their liquid brown depths.

"Dead, Alex. Cold and stiff in the ground. No more talking or laughing or flashing those big brown eyes. Nothing. One minute you're going about your business and the next…it's just all over. It's all freaking over…."

His hands had tightened on her shoulders. A little too much maybe. "Over," he said, his voice lowering, growing harsher and rougher than it should. "All over… for you anyway. Not for me. There would be one more innocent life on my shoulders, and let me tell you something, Alex, one more is more than I can take."

Her eyes slowly came into focus through the haze of grief that had been clouding his vision. Her eyes, so damned intense they could see things no normal eyes could see. He knew it. He had the feeling she was reading his scarred soul just then as easily as reading a book. He gave his head a shake and he released her. But he knew it wasn't soon enough. She'd managed to shake him right out of his coldness, right out of his mannequin state, and she'd copped yet another peek at the hell that lived inside him. She'd seen way too much.

He looked away, relaxing his hands, knowing his fingers had been digging into her flesh. He steadied his breathing, but he could feel her eyes on him. And when he glanced back at her he saw the way they darted rapidly over his face, the way she lifted her hand, as if to press it to his cheek, only to stop in midair, maybe because of the look in his eyes.

"You're in agony, aren't you." It wasn't a question, the way she said it. More like an observation. One that made his heart bleed. Torch didn't want her sympathy. He could handle just about anything but that.

He shook his head from side to side. "You're changing the subject. We were talking about you—"

"No. I don't think we were."

When traffic cleared, he pulled a U-turn and headed back the way they'd come.

"She was beautiful, your wife."

He only nodded, trying to focus on driving, trying to work out his next step in his mind. Revenge. Justice. The blood and pain and death that he'd inflict on Scorpion. Those ought to be foremost in his mind right now. Ugliness, blackness, violence.

"Tell me about her," Alex said softly, and her voice was hypnotic…a whisper of music, a soothing melody that pierced the darkness and somehow penetrated the stone of his heart. "What was her name?"

"Marcy." He said it automatically, without stopping to think about it first. Then he bit his lip, knowing he shouldn't have answered. He didn't talk about Marcy and the boys. Not to anyone.

She was silent for a moment, and Torch thought maybe she'd decided to grant him a reprieve.

"And what about the boys?"

You don't talk about the boys to anyone. You don't talk about the boys to anyone. You don't talk—

His thoughts were interrupted by his own raspy words. "Josh and—" his voice broke, and he cleared his throat "—and Jason." Why was he talking to her? What was

compelling him to answer her gentle questions? Why
didn't he just tell her to shut up and mind her own
damned business?

"They look like twins in the picture."

"They...were."

"No...." Her hand rose to her lips, and moisture filled
her eyes. Then she touched him. There was no stopping
her this time. Her hands covered his white-knuckled
ones on the steering wheel, warming them through.

Torch's foot hit the brake without his permission. The
car jerked to a stop in the middle of a narrow road, and
the pickup behind him blasted its horn before going
around. Torch barely noticed. Grief blinded him, and the
lump in his throat had swelled to encompass his entire
chest. It was suffocating him, choking him. His hands
on the wheel clenched tighter and he closed his eyes,
shook his head. "I can't do this."

"Yes, you can," she whispered, just as if she knew
exactly what he was talking about. "It's all right. Come
here."

And he did. Damn him, but he did. He turned toward
her and let the fragile and frightened little thing pull him
into her arms. She cradled his head on her shoulder,
massaging his scalp with one hand, rubbing his back
with the other. And it felt good, dammit. It felt good. So
good that he put his arms around her waist and he
squeezed her closer. So good that he didn't pull away
when she turned her head and pressed her soft lips to
his cheek. He felt the moisture, the warmth between his
face and hers, and he wasn't sure whose tears dampened
his skin. It didn't matter. He was sinking in a stagnant
sea of guilt and remorse and pain. And she was suddenly
here, just when he'd been about to drown. Buoyant and
light. The sensation washed over him like a cleansing,

fragrant wave of revelation. Somewhere inside, a voice whispered, "Cling to her and save yourself, Palamaro. She's your only hope."

And for one, insane moment, he did. He turned his face to her and slid his mouth over the satiny skin of her cheek and her jaw, and finally covered her lips. He felt them tremble and then part in timid invitation. And it was an invitation he couldn't turn down. He took and tasted and drank from her mouth, plunging his tongue inside again and again, stroking and petting her, holding her. She was sweetness and light, innocence and fire, and he'd been without those things for so damned long they were drugging to him. Addictive. All he wanted was more of her, more of her, more of her, more of her. Because to let her go would be to return to the blackness of reality.

It was her whispery sigh that snapped him back to sanity. And as he returned to himself, he knew what he'd done. He'd encouraged her fantasy that there might be a hint of feeling between them. He'd set a deadly fire in an innocent, one he had every intention of putting out. He couldn't go on with this. It wouldn't be fair to use her that way, to let her think things that were utterly impossible. He shouldn't do anything that might make her believe she cared for him. Because he had nothing inside to give her in return.

Grating his teeth, he straightened away from her. He was ashamed of using her this way, and embarrassed by the emotions that had swamped him like a tidal wave just now. His cheeks were still wet.

So were hers. And her eyes, round and glistening as if coated in liquid diamonds. Her swollen lips remained parted, and he wanted them again when he looked at them. He wanted them in ways she wouldn't even dream of. So he looked away.

He was supposed to be tough here, strong. He was supposed to be in charge, protecting her from Scorpion and his thugs. Not turning to her for comfort like one of her bleeding young patients. Not punishing her by letting his pain become passion and by spending all of it on her. She didn't deserve that. What the hell was wrong with him? How did she manage to dig so deeply into his soul with those eyes of hers, extracting his most painful secrets with no more than a word, a look?

"Sorry," he muttered, blinking his eyes clear and driving again.

"There's nothing to—"

"It won't happen again."

"Maybe it should," she whispered. "Maybe you need someone right now, to—"

"I don't discuss my family with strangers, Alex, and I certainly don't have sex with a stranger for comfort." With anyone, for that matter. But she needn't know that. "I am human, though, so I'd appreciate it if you'd keep your distance."

He didn't have to look at her to know his barb had stuck. He knew she winced, could see the pain in her eyes without even turning his head. Too bad. She was one of those females who thought she could heal the world with her soft touch and her smile and a little TLC with her incredible body. And her eyes, don't forget those. Well, she was wrong. And he damned well didn't want her poking around an old wound just to prove it.

He was stuck with her for a few days, at most. Long enough to find the missing formula and send Scorpion to hell. That was it. The sooner she got that through her head, the better.

"I didn't offer you sex for comfort," she told him in a wounded voice.

"You could have fooled me."

She was silent for a long time while he drove. He was, too, though his mind was working overtime. It took some effort to put his grief and the faces of his dead children back into the deep well of pain that used to be his heart. Something about being with Alex seemed to drive those ghosts to the surface more often than ever before. But he had to keep them locked away. He couldn't think of them now.

And he couldn't think about how remembering them didn't hurt so much when Alex held him in her soft arms.

It took still more effort to bring his thoughts back on track. A plan was what he needed.

"Where are we going?" she asked him at last.

"Where do you think?"

She gave him a look that made him feel like a demon for trying to hurt her. Deliberately trying to hurt her. Shooting thorns right into her skin, his automatic defense mechanism, apparently designed specifically for her, would keep her from getting too close to his private hell ever again. He couldn't help it. It was necessary.

"We're going back to Pine Lake," he told her. "But we have a few stops to make first."

His sons. Those two adorable little boys in the photo, who looked so much like him. Taken from him without warning or reason. God, it was no wonder he was so nasty. The man was in more pain than any human being ought to bear in a lifetime. And his came all at once.

But he'd let her hold him, even if it had been only for an instant. He'd turned to her with that grief, turned to her as if for salvation. In his eyes she'd seen something she'd never seen before. A desperation, a plea he couldn't or wouldn't or didn't know how to voice. *Help me, Alexandra.*

Maybe he wasn't even aware of it, but Torch Palamaro was going to bleed to death from the arrows in his heart if he didn't pull them out and start to heal.

He'd released a tiny bit of his grief in her arms. It wasn't a great leap of the imagination to guess he hadn't done so often. Perhaps not at all. The rage and turmoil bottled up inside him were visible in his eyes. That swirling, riotous emotion she hadn't been able to place before. The man was going to explode like one of his bombs if he didn't do something.

And it was none of her business, was it? She barely knew him, and what she did know of him made him her enemy. Why, then, was she so compelled, so drawn to him? Why this urge to hold him until his grief was spent? Oh, she knew she was always drawn to the wounded. The more serious the wounds, the more she wanted to help. Came of that need to be needed, she supposed. And the knowledge she'd never have children to nurture. So she naturally longed to nurture others. But it shouldn't extend to this man. Common sense ought to have some say in the matter, and common sense certainly decreed she keep a safe distance from a man with cactus skin. A man who lashed out just to keep her away. A man who'd told her in no uncertain terms that he didn't want her help.

His wounds were too deep, too dangerous. The darkness inside him was devouring him, maybe already had. And if she got too close it would snare her, pull her in, destroy her the way it had destroyed him. She knew it would. She felt the warnings prickling up and down her nerve endings and dancing over her skin. Stay away, they whispered. Stay away.

If she had any sense at all, she'd heed those warnings. But she never had been as smart as her father, had she? And maybe she just wasn't bright enough to listen to the voice of common sense.

She'd try, she vowed in silence. She'd try to keep a cool distance. She'd stop asking about things, she'd stop caring about his pain. He was nothing to her, why should she care? She'd force herself not to reach out to him again. She could do that. It wasn't such an impossible task.

Was it?

They rode in silence through the small town they'd discovered nearby, pulling in at a used car dealership where Torch went inside…alone. His jaw had been like granite as he'd left the car, never so much as looking at her.

The man was as cold as a stone and twice as hard.

The man was in pain.

But that was nothing to her, right?

His hardness, the hunk of rock that passed for a heart in that broad chest of his, was a little easier to understand now, though. He must have been a different man, before they'd died. She tried to picture him happy, content, affectionate. But it was a terrible stretch of the imagination.

"Mrs. Jones?"

There was a tap on her window and Alexandra jumped, then turned to see the smiling face of the salesman staring in at her. She cranked the window down.

"Mrs. Jones, come take a look. Can't have your husband making a purchase this important without your input now, can we?"

Mrs. Jones? Her husband?

Frowning, she opened the door and got out, allowing the man to lead her around the lot to where Torch was just stepping out of a motor home the size of a tank. He met her confused gaze and smiled...*actually smiled* at her. The perfect image of the devoted husband. He crossed to where she stood, draped an arm around her shoulders.

"Well, honey, what do you think?" He waved his free hand toward the house on wheels.

His arm felt warm and comfortingly heavy on her shoulders. She had to forcibly resist the urge to lean into his embrace, to tilt her head sideways until it rested on his shoulder, to slide her own arm around his waist and give it a squeeze and tell him that he was going to be all right.

The man does not want to be comforted, she reminded herself.

"I...uh...I'm not sure *what* to think."

"It has everything. Perfect for our trip to Yellowstone. Go on inside, take a look."

She blinked at him. He'd converted himself into the image of the American sightseer, evincing images of campgrounds and hot dogs and cold sodas. It was incredible.

Without a word she stepped into the camper, but she wasn't really looking at it. She just sank into a padded seat and tried again to figure him out.

Had he gone camping with his wife and sons? Was this what he'd been like then, before tragedy had turned his heart to stone?

He'd kissed her desperately, hungrily, in the car. Even though he was insisting she keep her distance now, he'd turned to her then.

So maybe the solid stone heart of Torch Palamaro had a small chink in it. And maybe he wasn't quite as un-interested in her as he pretended to be. Maybe he needed her. Maybe he sensed, too, that she was the only one who could help him. And maybe that feeling frightened him and that was why he was being so cold toward her.

And maybe she was allowing her fondest dream—that of someone truly needing her—to interfere with rational thought.

The very idea of being Torch Palamaro's savior was so appealing that it was difficult to dismiss. It was also ridiculous. Imagine someone as strong and sure of him-self as Torch needing a little nobody like Alexandra Holt. It was absurd.

She had no idea how long she'd sat there, staring into space, when he poked his head in. But he was back to cold distance now. "Drive the car. Follow me." His eyes were sapphire chips. His words fell like icy rain, chilling her right to the bone.

She only nodded. He started to pull back, but she stopped him. "Come in for a second. Close the door."

Frowning, he did. She glanced out the window, saw the salesman heading into the office with a wad of bills in his hands. Turning to face Torch, she tilted her head. "Why...?" Lord, this was hard. But she had to know. She'd drive herself crazy wondering if she didn't get a definitive answer soon. She cleared her throat. "Why did you kiss me the way you did?"

He closed his eyes as if completely out of patience with her. "I told you why. I'm human, Alex."

She shook her head and remained silent, waiting.

"And I haven't had any in a while, if you get my drift."

She looked at his mouth, and as she did, she remembered the kiss. The thrust of his tongue against hers, the press of his hands against the small of her back, and the curve of her buttocks. "And that's all?" she asked, her voice very soft. Very unlike her own. "Because it really seemed as if there were…aspects of that kiss that went beyond just…that."

"That's all, Alexandra. Don't even think there was anything more. I don't *have* anything more."

He turned and stepped out of the camper before she could respond. He'd slapped her, without lifting a hand.

Alexandra sat very still, blinking in shock, because the slap hadn't connected. He'd been lying through his teeth. It showed in his eyes. Was written all over his face. When she'd asked her question, he'd actually been afraid—of *her!*—just for an instant. And now, she figured she was doomed. She didn't want to think that Torch Palamaro was a man in such intense pain that it was eating him alive from the inside out. And she certainly didn't want to think that she could help him. Could reach the heart he'd buried beneath a layer of solid stone. Could heal wounds too horrible even to look at.

She didn't want to think this man might need her, as no one in her life had ever needed her.

But she was thinking it anyway.

He wasn't sure exactly what he was looking for, but he'd know it when he saw it. Torch drove the oversize camper, keeping one eye in the extended side mirrors on the car that followed. Alexandra. She was nothing but one giant thorn in his side. First lying to him about the safe-deposit box, then digging around in things that were none of her business.

And then holding him in her arms and making herself

seem to him like the very essence of heaven and salvation and peace.

Dammit.

He didn't want to think about Alexandra right now, because every time he did, his mind went back to what had happened between them in the car. The way the emotional floodgates had parted, just for a second, and the way they'd kissed. The way she'd felt in his arms. The way she'd tasted.

It had been the same the first time, back at the motel. At the time, it had seemed like a simple, quick method of getting that phony key out of her pocket, all without letting Scorpion see what he was doing. He'd known the bastard was there, watching. He'd felt him.

That sixth sense had paled to transparency, though, the second he'd pulled Alexandra's trembling body up against his. And he knew he'd taken it way further than he'd needed to just to get the key. And dammit to hell, she apparently knew it, too.

It hadn't been necessary to kiss her so deeply or for so long, or to hold her so tight to him that he could feel every curve of her body. It wasn't necessary to dip his tongue into the sweet warmth of her mouth, to taste her. He could even now taste her when he thought about it.

He still wasn't sure why the hell he'd done all that. And he was equally confused about his actions in the car. He was way too susceptible to Alexandra Holt. And maybe that was because it had been a long time, and he was only human, as he'd told her. His libido responding to her musk. Hell, she was a beautiful woman. He wasn't exactly made of stone. So maybe he'd given in to a natural, long-denied desire, for a few crazy moments.

He told himself that was it. The one and only reason for his weakness against the allure of her. But deep inside there was a little voice whispering that he was wrong. A voice his wary mind refused to let him hear.

Torch swore and glanced into the rearview mirror again. She was still there, still following. He didn't want to want her. But he did. And even though it meant nothing, even though he knew it was no more than chemistry, a physical attraction, a bodily need he'd denied too long crying out for attention, it still hurt.

He didn't want to want her. He didn't want to ever want another woman again. And he didn't deserve to have one. Not after the way his negligence had cost him the first.

Marcy, Josh and Jason. He tugged the photo from his shirt pocket and studied their faces. And he tried to remember them as more than just this one-dimensional image on paper. He tried to remember them animated, moving, laughing. The sounds of their voices, their facial expressions. But as always happened when he tried to bring up the memories, a solid wall slammed down inside his mind, blocking them.

He didn't deserve the happy memories, he supposed. It was his fault they were dead, and he'd lost even the past they'd shared. His image of his family seemed to be sealed in one tiny moment. The way they looked at him from this one-dimensional photograph.

They were the reason he was involved with Alexandra Holt right now. They were all that mattered. Their murders would be avenged, and soon. And Torch knew that even killing Scorpion wasn't going to end his pain or in any way lessen his culpability. But it had to be done. He owed his family that much. Maybe then he'd be able to remember them the way he wanted to. Happy, laughing, talking. Maybe then his conscience would allow the good times back into his mind, his heart.

He blinked the rage away, shoved the photo back into his pocket. He was glad Alex had retrieved it for him. He needed it. Needed to look at it, just to remind him what he was doing here. What was important. A glance at the photo would be enough to dampen any desire that tried to flare in him for Alexandra Holt. He wouldn't let himself get distracted. Not now. Not when he was so close.

With his focus back, he rededicated himself to the task at hand. That being finding a place to hide his car. And as if his decision had been approved by whatever gods lived in this hellish world, a farm came into view, with an old, decrepit barn, standing gray and hunched like an old man, beside a shiny new building.

Torch pulled into the barnyard, killed the engine and stepped out of the RV. Alex pulled right in behind him and shut the car off. But she didn't get out. She stared at him, her hands clutching the steering wheel a little too tightly. And her eyes held his captive for a long moment before he managed to look away.

"Something I can do for you folks?"

Torch swung his head around, plastering the old, practiced expression on his face. The one that said, "I'm just a normal, well-adjusted, happy family man on vacation." The one that didn't look as if it belonged on the face of a soulless mannequin. "Sure can," he told the farmer, a fiftyish man in faded jeans and aromatic, green rubber boots. "I'm looking for a place to store my car for a couple of weeks. Had a little accident, and I don't want to interrupt our vacation to wait for repairs. God knows if I leave it at a garage it'll cost me a fortune."

"They'll rob you blind, all right." The man stuck his hands into the pockets of his Carhart coat, rocking back on his heels.

Torch nodded. "I was hoping you might be willing to let me store it in your barn. Like I said, just for a couple of weeks. I could pay you. Say, a hundred dollars? In advance."

The farmer nodded, considering. "Suppose you take off and don't show up for six months, friend? I'm gonna be tearing that old barn down, soon as winter's over."

"If for any reason I'm not back in time, you can sell it. Or junk it. It's up to you. Paperwork's in the glove compartment."

The man's eyes widened. "You trust me not to sell it the second you're outta sight?"

"You have an honest face." Torch took a hundred dollars in twenties from his wallet. "So what do you say?"

The man nodded and took the money. But he didn't pocket it. Only looked at it, narrow eyed. "The car's not stolen, is it?"

"No. I promise, this is legit. I can show you the registration in my name and—"

The man held up his hands. "All right, I'll take your word. You don't look much like a car thief, and I s'pose I've yet to see one off on a camping trip with his wife. I'll open the barn door for you. Drive it right in."

"Thanks." Torch went back to the car where Alex still sat behind the wheel. He didn't look into her eyes, aside from one quick glance. He didn't like looking into her eyes. There were things going on in her mind that he'd rather not try to figure out just yet, and her emotions were too plainly visible in her face. Especially in her eyes. She was still stinging over his anger with her, and over his harsh words to keep her at bay. She was still wary of him. Not quite trusting him, not quite sure of him. She still didn't believe the truth about her saintly father.

And she was still thinking about that kiss. Analyzing it. Trying to read more into it than there had been. Knowing there was more to it than what he'd admitted to her. He liked that least of all.

He opened the door. She stared up at him, those huge brown eyes of hers compelling him, almost daring him to meet their steady gaze. He looked everywhere but at her. "We're gonna leave the car here for a while. In the barn, out of sight. We'll take the camper from here."

"Why?"

She hadn't moved. Just sat there, staring, pulling his eyes to hers with some kind of invisible magnet.

"Because Scorpion's seen the car."

"But why a camper? Why not a pickup truck or a station wagon or a compact? Why that huge RV?"

"Why all the questions?" he countered. "Look, I do this kind of thing for a living. I know my job, okay?"

He made the cardinal mistake of looking into her eyes as he snapped at her, and there was no mistaking the way she flinched at his tone. She looked away too quickly.

Torch cleared his throat. "The last thing Scorpion would find suspicious is a vehicle like this. And having a place to sleep might come in handy. No more ambushes at motel parking lots. We can't exactly take up residence at your house in the woods again, Alex. Hell, Scorpion probably left men posted there in case we come back."

"I don't think Scorpion would have any reason to do that." She thinned her lips, tilted her head, still not looking at him. "But what do I know? You're the expert on all this stuff. I suppose I should have been able to figure all of that out for myself. Sometimes I'm not very smart. Slow on the uptake, Father used to say. But I didn't mean to question your judgment.''

Torch blinked. He didn't know what he'd expected to hear from her but not that. ''You're a doctor, for crying out loud.''

She got out of the car, snatching her inhaler off the dash as she did. ''Yeah, well, you don't have to be a genius to be a doctor.'' She headed toward the RV, got in without ever looking back at him.

Chapter 7

Alexandra waited in the RV. In the passenger seat. Torch drove the car into the barn, helped close the door, and after another brief word with the farmer, he came to join her. He slid behind the wheel and started the engine. And without even looking at her, he said, "You know, Alex, I'm one of the best there is at what I do."

It didn't sound like idle bragging. Sounded more like he had a point to make, and this was the opening argument. She looked at his profile. Strong. And attractive, if not exactly handsome. It drew on something inside her. Some instinct that made her fingers itch to trace his cheekbones and the square line of his jaw. It made her palms ache to run over the dark shadow of stubble growing there. She resisted the urge and instead remembered his actions back at her house with those two armed thugs. "I believe that," she said softly.

"You outwitted me, though," he said. "I'm not happy about it, but you did. And I already told you, your plan wasn't half-bad. Pine Lake is probably the last place I'd have gone looking for you. If you'd managed to ditch me, you just might have pulled this off."

She frowned, sending him a sideways glance. "You think?"

He nodded. "Yeah. And I'll tell you something else, I don't get outwitted very often."

"No?"

"Almost never."

"Hmm."

He glanced sideways at her as he drove. "What?"

She shrugged. "I just wondered why you suddenly felt compelled to tell me how tough it is to outwit you."

"Because you seem, somewhere along to line, to have picked up the notion that you're...slow on the uptake, isn't that how Daddy Dearest put it?" He made a disgusted sound deep in his throat. "But you're not."

"I didn't say I was stupid, Palamaro. Just that I'm no genius."

"So who the hell is?"

"My father was."

He nodded slowly, as if he were beginning to understand something he probably never truly would. Ever. "Must have been tough, trying to live up to the standards of a genius."

She shrugged. "My father only wanted me to succeed."

"And did you?"

She said nothing, only bit her lip.

"You graduated with honors and a degree in medicine. Most people would call that success."

She closed her eyes, tried to tune him out.

"But I guess it just wasn't up to your father's lofty standards, was it, Alex?"

"You don't know anything about this."

"Sure I do. I did my research."

She shook her head again, doing her best to ignore him. For some reason, she didn't like the idea of Torch Palamaro studying her background, reading about the many failures in her life.

"Your father isn't here anymore, Alex. But I am. And you've already proven that you can match wits with me, and that's saying something."

"So?"

"So I can't have you working with me if you keep questioning your judgment. We're liable to end up in situations where a second's hesitation could be the difference between life and death. Don't stop to second-guess yourself. If you're in a pinch and you see an out, take it."

She stared at him, listening, hearing, not really sure she believed him. "I don't know if I could do that. I've spent my whole life second-guessing myself."

"You can do it. You did, back at the motel when you pulled that gun out of the duffel and took a potshot at Scorpion."

She tilted her head. "I...I guess I *did*, didn't I?"

"Damn straight, you did."

Her lips curved at the corners, almost on their own. For a second she smiled, and felt her back straighten just a little more than usual and her chin come up a fraction. She *had* used her wits back there. And she'd probably saved Torch's life, as well as her own.

Father wouldn't have been proud if he'd seen her actions. No, he'd have called her foolish for risking her life by pulling a gun on an armed criminal. He'd have called her weak for the asthma attack that had overwhelmed her in the middle of all of it. He'd have called her simpleminded for having wound up in this situation in the first place.

But he *wasn't* here, and he *wasn't* saying any of those things. Torch Palamaro *was* here. And he was some kind of expert in these matters. And according to *him,* she'd been darn near brilliant.

Deep inside, part of Alexandra cringed at the imagined condemnation from her father. But another part, a very small part, swelled a bit in pride at what she'd done.

Maybe she was a little stronger, a little smarter, than she'd realized. Maybe her father just hadn't seen it in her.

"You seem surprised."

"Hmm?" She jerked her attention back to the man beside her, frowning.

"You seem surprised," Torch repeated. "Did your old man do such a number on your self-esteem that you're actually surprised you did something right?"

Alex felt her smile die, felt her jaw go rigid. "If you don't want me talking to you about your family, Torch, how about returning the favor? Your opinions about my father are way off base, so please keep them to yourself."

"Sure. I can do that."

Only, he didn't really want to keep his opinions to himself. And he knew that was a mistake, because none of it mattered to him. He could care less whether her father had messed up her head.

But he knew. That was the problem. He'd done the research, he'd read all the reports, and according to everyone who knew him, Alexander Holt had treated his daughter like a poor relation. No matter what she'd ever accomplished, the man had never seemed to find it sufficient. He'd criticized her often enough in public that it was on the record. And if he'd done it that often publicly, he must have really ripped her down in private.

The bastard should have been horsewhipped.

If Torch had harbored any doubts about Holt's parenting skills, they'd been erased just now. There'd been a decided glow about Alexandra when Torch had told her she'd outsmarted him. He couldn't help but notice it, though he'd been deliberately trying not to look at her too much or too closely. She'd seemed pleased, delighted. For crying out loud, she'd apparently had so little praise in her life that a few words of it could change her entire mood. Her father must have been one hell of a sweetheart. *Genius.* Right. If he was so smart, why didn't he know what he was doing to his kid?

And why had Torch ruined it all by saying what he thought of the old idiot? He'd taken away her pleasure with a single sentence. He ought to remind himself often not to say anything against the father she still worshiped.

He couldn't help but wonder what it was going to do to her to learn the truth about the man. She was too damned sensitive, too vulnerable. It was going to tear her world apart.

The thought of that made his throat go a little dry, even as he told himself it was nothing to him. At least then she'd have something on her mind besides trying to offer comfort to a man who was far beyond its reach. And maybe she'd stop trying to analyze that kiss, too.

Torch drove north until noon, and when he stopped to get them a bite to eat, he didn't use one of the restaurants right off the exit ramp, but instead, drove into the nearest town and meandered around until he found a diner that probably catered more to locals than passers-through.

For some reason, he'd stopped being furious with the woman beside him for her lies. He couldn't really blame her, could he? Hell, he'd probably have done the same thing in her situation. So his anger had died... somewhere around the same time he'd seen the glow come into her eyes. How could he be mad at her for outsmarting him when she was apparently so damned proud of it?

He didn't like not being angry with her, though. Because anger was a good buffer. And he needed one between her and him. He needed one badly.

"Hungry?" he asked as he found a parking space big enough for the beast he was driving.

"Starving."

"Come on, then. But let's get something to go."

She nodded and slid out the door. The clouds overhead were ominous. She looked around as she headed for the diner, then stopped, pointing. "There's a department store across the street. Maybe we ought to pick up some things before we leave."

"Good idea."

In the diner, Torch was uneasy. Too many eyes on them, eyes that could describe them later, should Scorpion stop by asking questions. But he figured the chances of the bastard checking every diner in every town were slim. And since he'd expect them to continue south, they were even slimmer.

No one in the place seemed to be paying undue attention to them. He breathed a little easier and headed up to the counter. Alexandra was already there, ordering a club sandwich and a soda to-go in a soft, deep voice that made a person really listen when she spoke. Torch stepped up beside her.

"You two together?"

He blinked at the waitress's question. It seemed to take Alexandra by surprise, as well. She looked up at him, and he met eyes filled with uncertainty. He had to tear his gaze away before he got lost in hers. He gave the waitress a curt nod. "Yeah. I'll have the same."

She was still looking at him. He felt the satin touch of her eyes as the waitress punched keys on an old-fashioned cash register that chucked and clicked and pinged. Still touching his face, those brown eyes, as he took the wallet from his pocket and handed over a ten-spot and waited for the change. Why did she find it necessary to *look* at him like that?

There was a country song wafting from a radio behind the counter. And another waitress was busy tacking strands of green garland to the edges of the counter, reminding him of the approaching holiday season. Someone had sprayed the place with a pine-scented air freshener. A memory slipped into his mind. He heard young boys' high-pitched laughter, and the crinkling and tearing of gift wrap. The memory was brief but vivid, real. And it took him by surprise, because he'd been denied any real memories for almost a year.

The bell over the entrance jangled, and he glanced behind him, watching his back as he always did. And then he felt a hot blade slip right into his chest and twist slowly, tearing his insides to shreds.

The little boy was no more than five. All dark curls, baby blue eyes and dimples as he grinned up at his father. And as the pair moved inside, talking and laughing, finding a table, Torch felt the black emptiness in his soul reaching up to claim him. To draw him into the depths of loneliness, despair, endless grief. He closed his eyes to blot out the image of the child who looked so much like one of his own.

They should have been outside playing. Dammit, why the hell hadn't Josh and Jason been outside? They never came in until Marcy called them for dinner. Never. Why this one night, had they come in earlier?

He felt a warm, firm hand on his shoulder. He swung his head around. Alexandra's eyes were wider and browner than ever, and they were damp as they probed and questioned him.

He gave his head a slight shake and simply walked out. The door swung closed on the child's laughter, and Torch blinked in the crisp November air, wishing it were colder, wishing it could slap his face and snap him out of this grief. But it wasn't and it didn't. Nothing ever had. Maybe nothing ever would.

Alexandra stared after him. Part of her wanted to go to him, try to help him through the haze of pain he was obviously battling. But another part knew he wanted to be left alone. She stopped herself from intruding, with an effort.

"Miss?"

She turned back to the counter, to see the woman on the other side holding out a handful of change. Alex took it. "Is there a rest room I can use while I'm waiting for the sandwiches?"

The woman nodded, pointing toward the back of the building. Alex tried to put Torch's heartache out of her mind and walked into the ladies' room. She took her time, washed her face and finger-combed her hair, and stared at her reflection in the mirror, telling herself she'd never hold a candle to the blond woman in Torch's picture. Some twenty minutes later, when she pushed the door open to head back out, she glanced up to see a man dressed all in black, leaning on the counter where she'd been standing. And for just a second, she stiffened. It was that color that did it. Everything black, right to the ski cap on his head. He had everything the thugs at her house had, except the mask.

She shook her head, chiding herself for an overactive imagination. And then she saw the waitress hand a photo back to him, and saw her lips form the words "rest room" and her head tilt toward where Alex now stood. And, as if in slow motion, she saw the man's head turning toward her. She ducked back inside and closed the door, turning the lock, panting. She gasped as she felt her bronchial tubes spasm, automatically pressing a hand to her chest.

"Not now," she whispered. "Not now, the inhaler is in the RV." She leaned over the sink, cranking the tap and splashing handfuls of cold water on her face. What should she do?

Was she imagining things? She didn't think so. And Torch had told her to trust her instincts. She certainly wasn't going to march back out there and pick up their food when the man might very well be one of those working for Scorpion.

She scanned the rest room. There was one squat window, on the back wall, too high to reach from the floor. Alex looked around for something to stand on, and settled on the trash can. It only took a second to remove the rounded top and flip the can upside down. She silently apologized for the mess she'd made as she climbed up. The window locked from the inside, and she turned the clasp to the unlocked position, mentally crossed her fingers and shoved at it. It opened easily, and Alex thanked her lucky stars. She climbed up on the ledge, peering outside first. She saw no one, but there was no way to be sure. Well, she couldn't just sit there waiting for the jerk to get sick of being patient and come in after her.

She slipped over the edge, turned and lowered herself until she dangled a few feet above the ground. Then she let go and landed with an ungraceful tumble. She looked around, hoping she hadn't been seen as she got to her feet and brushed the dust from her jeans. Carefully she made her way back to where the RV was parked out front, keeping the vehicle between her and the diner.

Torch was there, and Alex thought she'd never been so glad to see anyone in her entire life. He stood in the tiny kitchen area, unloading a bag of groceries into the cupboards. Or pretending to. Actually, he was waiting. For her, she realized. He was fully expecting her to try to comfort him again, the way she'd done before. And he was dreading it. The expression he wore stated clearly that she was to ask no questions, offer no solace and keep her hands thoroughly to herself.

Well, he'd get his wish this time. She drew a couple of steadying breaths to calm her quivering lungs, and went right to the front, sat down in the driver's seat and started the motor. Then she put the thing in gear and pulled slowly out of the parking lot.

A second later, Torch was standing behind her, one hand on her shoulder, but only to steady himself, she was sure. "What's going on?"

"One of them…back there, in the diner. I saw…" She bit her lip. Her words were coming out in bits and pieces, and she was starting to breathe too fast again. She hadn't realized she was this shaken up.

"Easy," he said, and his hand squeezed her shoulder. She closed her eyes because it felt so good to have that strong grip there. "Drive nice and slow, Alex. Take your time. No one's gonna look twice at a camper, unless it's careening through town, taking curves on two wheels.''

She eased up on the accelerator, nodding, fighting to steady her breathing. Safe now, she kept telling herself. She was safe now.

"You need this?" Torch held her inhaler in one hand. She hadn't even seen him reach for it.

"I don't think so."

He returned it to the glove compartment. "Now tell me what happened."

"I went to the rest room. When I started to come out there was a man at the counter, dressed all in black. He was showing a photo to the waitress, and the waitress pointed toward the rest room. I was the only one in there."

"And?"

"I ducked back inside and locked the door and climbed out the window." She looked up at him to gauge his reaction to that, and was surprised to see him smile a little.

"Good girl. The guy's probably still sitting there waiting for you to come out."

"Do you think it was—"

"No, Alex. To be honest, I doubt it was one of Scorpion's henchmen. They'd have to be bloodhounds to track us to that diner."

She breathed a relieved sigh, felt her muscles relax a little. "I overreacted, didn't I?"

He shook his head. "Hell, no, you didn't overreact. You did exactly what I told you to do—followed your instincts. We can't be too careful, Alex."

"I didn't get our sandwiches."

"We'll get some more sandwiches, Alex."

She bit her lower lip, turned to look at him again. "I'm scared."

"I shouldn't have left you alone in there."

"It's all right," she said quickly. "I—"

"It's not all right." He drew a breath, let it out slowly and finally moved up to sit opposite her in the passenger seat. "It's been ten months," he said softly. "I ought to be handling things better by now."

Alexandra blinked in surprise. *He'd* brought the subject up. Not her. "It...can't be easy."

Torch was staring straight ahead, deep in thought. Alex had to make an effort to keep her eyes on the road. "After...after it happened, and Scorpion got away clean, I resigned. I couldn't focus on the job anymore."

"But you came back to it," she prompted when his words faded to silence.

"Yeah. The minute I found out Scorpion was involved. I thought I could handle it, after so much time. But I'm not doing too great so far, am I?" He looked toward her, met her eyes, gave her a sad smile. "Turn left at this light, we need to get back on the highway up ahead."

She did as he said, waiting for him to continue, but her own mind was filling with new thoughts, new fears. One, in particular, that wrapped an icy hand around her heart and chilled it through and through. "Torch?"

"Yeah?"

"You said you only came out of retirement to take this case when you realized Scorpion was involved. Will you tell me why?"

He laughed, but it wasn't really a laugh. More like a short burst of air being forced from his lungs. "He murdered my family, Alex. I want him to pay."

The icy hand clenched tighter. She battled a shiver.

"You're going to catch him and turn him over to the proper authorities," she said softly. "You're going to see him go to trial and be convicted, and spend the rest of his life in prison. Right?"

She had a feeling she knew the answer already, but she had to hear it. Torch didn't oblige, though. He didn't give her any answer at all. Not with his voice, at least. But in his eyes…in his eyes there was something blacker than the pain that filled his heart.

"Right here," he said. "That's the on ramp. See it?"

She nodded and flicked on the signal light.

Chapter 8

They arrived in the town of Pine Lake just after dark. If she hadn't known this place so well, she might have let Torch drive right through. Because "town" was really a misnomer. In truth, Pine Lake was just a bend in the rutted gravel road that had a few more houses in closer proximity than other places along the same route. The general store was the focal point. The thing was the size of a barn and carried everything from food for humans to grain for livestock. In the front, an ancient red gas pump leaned tiredly to one side.

Torch pulled the RV off the narrow road but left it running.

"So now what?" She was uneasy, and she knew it came through in her voice, but she'd never been very good at disguising her feelings. She just wasn't sure *why* she felt as much dread as she did.

"We go talk to your lawyer friend and get our hands on those papers of your father's."

She nodded. He hadn't said another word about the family he'd lost, and she hadn't asked. She wanted to. She wanted to know how it was that he felt responsible for their deaths, and she wanted to know what he planned to do to Scorpion. Or maybe she just wanted something to focus on besides what might lie ahead.

But he'd made it clear he didn't want to discuss his family. So she forced herself not to bring them up again. She bit her lip, cleared her throat, left with no choice but to look at the present and the very near future.

"There's not going to be anything there," she whispered, but it was like a wish. Like a prayer, and she was pretty sure Torch knew it. She didn't want to look at him. Didn't want him to see the doubt that must show in her eyes right now. So she stared up at the ghostly gray clouds skittering over the moon, their color just a shade paler than the dark sky, their shapes as ominous as specters. "It's going to snow."

"Probably."

"We ought to go up to the house."

"No."

"If it snows, we might not be able to."

"Snow melts, Alexandra."

She bit her lip to keep from arguing. Max hadn't been fed today. He'd be climbing the walls by now...if he was able. Those men they'd left behind at her house might have done something to him.

The thought made her have to blink away tears. The one that followed was worse. That she was worrying about her pet because she didn't want to think about what had been in that safe-deposit box, or why her father had kept it even after breaking every other tie he'd had in the city. What secrets were about to be revealed?

"Where does the lawyer live?"

He has a one-track mind, doesn't he?

"Just drive through town. It's a big house at the north edge, on the right. I'll tell you when we get there." Why was she having all these doubts now? Her father was innocent. She'd known that all along. There would be nothing but proof of that at Jim's office, which was no more than a converted spare room in his house's huge basement.

Torch put the rig back in gear and pulled onto the road again. In a few minutes, they were turning into the driveway of James McManus, attorney-at-law. And a light snow had begun falling into the twin beams of their headlights.

Torch walked beside her to the door. She didn't think he could tell how terrified she was of this moment. How frightened she was of what they would find. If her father had been working on something...something he shouldn't have, that would explain his actions at the end. So would senility or stroke, she assured herself. So would a lot of things. He couldn't possibly have done what Torch had accused him of doing.

She didn't realize she'd frozen on the top step until Torch's arm slid around her shoulders, squeezed just a little. "It isn't gonna matter what's there, Alex. It can't hurt your father now."

She lifted her chin, turning to look Torch in the eye. "It can hurt me, though."

"You can handle it." His hand cupped her chin, and his eyes plumbed hers as if he truly cared what she was feeling right now. "You're tougher than you think, Alexandra Holt."

She thought that if she were so tough, she wouldn't be trembling. She wouldn't be staring at his eyes, and noticing that *they* were staring at her lips, and wondering and wishing and...

Her thoughts ground to a halt when a dog started barking from the next place over. The noise drew her gaze, and she saw curtains part, a face peering out at them. The neighbor's dog kept up his barking, which in turn made her wonder where the McManus's dog was, and why *he* wasn't barking right now. She turned, staring first at the door, and then at the rest of the house, noticing for the first time the darkened windows, and the way the cold wind riffled the pages of three newspapers lying on the porch.

"Torch, I don't think anyone's here."

He followed her gaze, then left her standing there, while he ran down the steps and over to the garage, to peer through the glass. "No car inside. Dammit."

Alex poked the doorbell with her forefinger, let up and poked again. But even when she gave up and started knocking instead, there was no response.

She didn't feel relieved. She'd worked up enough strength, she thought, to get her through this. The anticlimactic ending of this day only left her tense and jittery, and with the beginnings of a headache throbbing to life behind her eyes.

"Three newspapers," Torch muttered, coming back to the porch. "Looks like they might be gone for a while."

"They never go away for very long."

"It's almost Thanksgiving."

Alex bit her lip. "That's right, it is. I forgot about that." Torch frowned at her, and she shrugged. "It's been a while since I've celebrated any holidays," she said by way of explanation.

His lips thinned. He was going to say something nasty

about her father, she thought, but he bit it back. Instead, he just said, "Me, too."

That admission made Alex's eyes sting. "We can check down at the store. Someone will know when they're expected back."

"Or we can break in and get what we need tonight."

"No!" She was so shocked at his suggestion that her jaw fell and her eyes widened. "We can't go around breaking into people's homes."

He shrugged. "Maybe *you* can't—"

"Torch, please. Let's wait." She glanced again at the house next door, pointed at the face still peeking through the window. "Besides, we'll be seen. Let's at least wait until later, when the neighbors are in bed."

He sighed—in disgust at her reluctance, she was sure—but finally nodded. "Okay, all right, but it has to be tonight. We don't have time for finesse, Alex."

"I know."

He turned and headed back to the RV. And then they were driving again, through snow that fell thicker with every passing second. Torch was looking for a hidden spot to park for the night, and Alexandra was worrying about her cat. So she directed him to an old fire road cut into the forest. And he followed her instructions but looked less happy about it the farther they drove. The snowfall had already coated the narrow dirt road, but not enough to make driving hazardous. Not yet, anyway.

"This seems like it sits awfully close to where your house is, Alex. Are you playing games with me?"

"No games," she told him as he chose a spot off the fire road, in a little copse of pines, and drove carefully onto it. "The house *is* nearby. If you follow the fire road for a half mile, and then veer off to the right, and cut through the pines, you'll end up in my father's *precious* flower bed.''

Torch frowned and shut the motor off, then the lights. ''You say that as if you're not overly fond of flowers.''

''He spent more time digging in that dirt than he did with me,'' she blurted before thinking better of it.

''But he was a saint, all the same, right?''

She lowered her head. ''I loved him.''

''But he didn't love you back, did he, Alex?''

A single tear fell. It dropped from her cheek to splash onto the back of Torch's hand, just as he reached out to cup her face. His thumb ran over her cheekbone, and he lifted her head to stare into her eyes.

''You should have been disappointed in him, Alexandra, not the other way around. You need to open your eyes and see that one of these days. He didn't deserve a daughter like you.''

No, Alex thought. He'd deserved a much better one. Aloud, she said, ''I thought I asked you not to talk about my father.''

''I was talking about you.''

She shook her head slowly, taking her gaze from his. ''I want to go home,'' she whispered. ''I want to go up to the house.'' And for the first time, she realized why. It wasn't Max. It was…that the place had become a haven in her mind. She'd run away from her entire life. She'd been hiding there. And she wanted to hide again.

''We can't. Not yet. Do me a favor and be patient, okay?''

She'd try. But, God, she craved space. Room, lots of it, between Torch and her. It was killing her to be this close to him and pretend nothing had happened between them. Which was exactly what he expected, even silently demanded, that she do. She needed space…time alone, to come to grips with the very real possibility that her loyalty to her father had been sorely misplaced. She'd always known he wasn't a very nice person. Not a very honorable person.

Maybe she'd only loved him so much because she'd had no one else to love.

"Okay?" Torch repeated.

"Yeah. Okay." She turned in the seat, looking back into the living quarters of the RV, squinting in the darkness. "So what do we do for light and heat?"

"Propane," Torch said. "The dealer threw in a full tank. I just have to go outside and hook it up." He tilted his head. "Loan me my jacket and I'll do it right now."

She'd been wearing his black leather for lack of anything else. Chivalrous of him, and unexpected, but nice. She liked wearing his coat. It smelled of leather and of him, and it was almost as nice as being held in his arms.

She shrugged out of the coat and handed it to him. Torch put it on and went into the back, bending to one of the cupboards and emerging with a flashlight and an oversize pipe wrench.

"Where did you get that?"

"Pipe wrench came with the camper. I picked the flashlight up at that department store while you were playing hide-and-seek with the goon in the diner. I grabbed some extra clothes, too. In the drawer under the bunk. Some sweatshirts and heavy socks and an extra pair of jeans for each of us."

"That's good. Tell me there's a three-pound flannel nightgown in there, too."

"What do I look like, an idiot?" He tugged up the zipper of his jacket, flipped up the collar and opened the door while Alex was still feeling the rush of heat in her cheeks, and the surge of warmth his last comment had instigated.

He paused in the doorway, swearing softly.

"What is it?" she asked him.

He turned to send her a narrow-eyed stare. "It's really coming down out there. The road must be damned near impassable by now."

"Oh."

"No way in hell we'll get back to the lawyer's house tonight."

"It's just as well," she said. "Maybe by the time the roads are cleared, the McManuses will be back."

"And maybe you planned it that way."

She only shrugged. "Maybe I did."

He sighed, shook his head. "Tomorrow, Alex. The second the roads are cleared. And I don't care if I have to break in with the whole damn town watching." With that he walked out the door, closing it behind him.

So this was it, at least for tonight. And they were together in even closer quarters than they'd been in the motel. How was she ever going to sleep? Even in bunk beds, she'd be far too close to him. Far, far too close.

Torch came back inside and stood in the doorway brushing snow from his shoulders. She went to him automatically, her hands dusting the white stuff from his chest and his upper arms. She reached for his dark hair, ruffling it with her fingers to shake the snow away. And then she stopped. His hair was soft and damp, and her fingers were buried in it. She stood very close to him, too close, maybe, and when she looked up, he was staring right down into her eyes.

He laid his hands gently over hers, still buried in his hair, and he lifted them away. Alex blinked, turning abruptly. "Do we have matches?"

"Top drawer," he said, and she thought his voice was the slightest bit hoarse.

Of course it was, he'd just been out in the cold.

She found the matches. "Better get the pilots lit. Shine the light, will you?"

He did, and Alex lit the pilots of the little gas lamps on the walls, and then turned the knobs. In seconds the lamps glowed, washing the camper in liquid gold. It did erotic things to a man's skin, that amber light. It did even more disturbing things to his eyes. She lit the pilot on the small two-burner range next, then handed the matches to Torch. "You can do the heat. I haven't got a clue."

He nodded, took them from her and fiddled around in the little closet next to the cubby-size bathroom. The place was toasty a few minutes after he emerged.

Torch shrugged off his coat and sat down at the table. So now what? Alex wondered. She poked around in the cupboards to see what he'd bought by way of food, finally settling on a can of beef stew and some instant hot cocoa. She located a can opener, some bottled water and a pair of small pots. Seemed Torch had thought of everything.

"You, um, you don't have to go back there with me tomorrow," she said at last, unsure whether she'd be treading on forbidden ground to broach the subject that had been on her mind since they'd left Jim's house. "I'll go alone, get the papers and bring them back here."

"Sure you will. Or maybe you'll decide to take off for parts unknown with them."

She met his eyes, shaking her head slowly as she sank into the seat across from him. "I won't do that."

"You'd do just about anything to protect your father's good name, Alex. Don't kid yourself."

"If I tell you I won't, then I won't."

"Even if those papers prove your old man did exactly what I told you he did?"

She held his gaze with hers and nodded. "Yes, even then." She wanted to add that she knew that wasn't going to be the case, but her doubts were too strong. And growing all the time. "I'll swear on his memory, if it'll make you feel better."

He held her gaze for a long moment, searching it, finally nodding. "I almost believe you would. But I'll go with you, anyway, Alex."

"You…you might not want to."

He sighed long and low, letting his chin fall to his chest. "I saw the bicycles in the garage, Alex. I know they have kids."

She got to her feet, turning to stir the stew but watching his face, wondering if speaking about this would hurt him more or help him. "Their grandchildren stay with them quite often. Especially during the holidays. I hadn't thought of it before, but chances are if they do get back tomorrow, they'll have the boys with them." She licked her lips, cleared her throat. "You don't have to put yourself through that, Torch."

"Don't."

"I saw your face at that diner. I saw what looking at that little boy did to you. I'd have to be blind not to see it."

"Don't," he repeated.

"Going there tomorrow will only hurt you more," she whispered. And she was thinking of more than just the children. She was thinking of the little things scattered all over the place that would remind Torch of his lost sons. Toys and books and games and small clothes. There would be evidence of the children everywhere.

He lifted his chin, met her eyes without blinking. "Nothing could hurt me more, Alex. Pain is something I've learned to live with."

"But—"

"And it's my pain, not yours. It has nothing to do with you, do you understand that?"

She blinked, searching his eyes, wanting with everything in her to reach out and touch him, take him in her arms and make it all right for him.

"I want you to leave it alone." He got up, reaching past her to snap the burner off. "You're burning the stew."

"Torch…"

He froze her with a single glance. "Just leave it alone, Alex. Please."

She swallowed hard, bit her tongue against the flood of words that wanted to escape. Words of comfort that would do little good anyway. She grated her teeth, closed her eyes. "I don't suppose you thought to buy plastic flatware, did you?"

When Alex opened her eyes again she saw his shoulders sag in relief, heard the breath escape him in a long sigh. "Yeah. As a matter of fact, I did." He reached past her again, scraping open another drawer to reveal the white spoons, forks and knives. "Paper plates, too. No bowls though. Guess we make do."

"I guess so."

She left it alone. And Torch was grateful, because it was harder with her. He still hadn't figured out why that was, but when Alexandra started poking at his wounds, he couldn't stop himself from cooperating, answering her questions, telling her about his secret pain. And he didn't like that power she seemed to have over him. To make him talk about it, to invade his privacy.

He didn't discuss his family with anyone. They were sacred, and that was that.

He looked at Alex when she wasn't looking at him—which wasn't often—and he tried to figure out what it was about her that made him forget his own rules. But there were no answers in her soft brown eyes, or in the way she managed to shovel beef stew into her mouth as if she were half-starved, still looking delicate and graceful and feminine. Didn't make a damn bit of sense.

And then her eyes caught him in the act of staring. Only they were wide, startled. She swallowed hard and said, "Did you hear that?"

"Hear what?"

"Shh!" She held up a hand, tilted her head to one side.

Torch listened, and in a second he heard it, too. The distinct sound of footfalls in the wet snow. His muscles tensed, and before he was aware of moving, his gun was in his hand. Alex didn't move any more than he did. Only enough to reach carefully to her left and crank the little window very slightly open. And the sounds came more clearly then. Closer. A few steps, then silence, then a few more steps. Someone was creeping up on them.

Torch looked into her eyes. Big mistake. She was terrified, and it made a lump come into his throat. Made his stomach clench. "Don't be afraid, Alex," he whispered, though his thoughts should have been on other things. Like surviving a sneak attack, not comforting a scared woman. "I'm not gonna let anyone hurt you. Promise."

Stupid fool, making promises he knew damned well he might not be able to keep. And she wasn't much better, because she actually looked as if those words eased her mind. As if she believed him, trusted him to protect her.

Sure, just like Marcy and the boys did once.

He closed his eyes to blot out thoughts like that. This was no place for them. Slowly he got up, reaching to douse the lights so he wouldn't be perfectly silhouetted when he opened the door. "Put on my jacket, Alex, just in case you have to run."

He heard the leather rubbing over her as she complied. Then she was beside him, near the door. "I'll step out first," he told her. "You come out behind me, but as soon as your feet hit the ground, slip around behind the camper. I'm pretty sure there's only one of them. If anything happens to me, run down toward town. Okay?"

"No."

He froze with his hand on the doorknob, turned to study the shape of her face in the shadows.

"I'm not going anywhere if you get hurt. You might…need me."

Those two words, *need me,* came out on a trembling breath. Unsteady. As if they were terribly important, somehow.

Oh, great, something more about Alexandra for his mind to insist on analyzing while he knew he ought to be planning this mission. Just what he needed.

"If I tell you to run, you'd damn well better run," he told her. He thought she nodded, but wasn't sure. The footfalls drew nearer, got louder.

Torch flung the door open and lunged through it, landing in the snow in a deep crouch, gun leveled at where the sounds had come from. And at that moment, the clouds skittered away from the full moon, giving him a clear glimpse of the intruder as it whirled and leapt away. A white-tailed deer with antlers that resembled a coat rack.

He was still trying to unclench his muscles when Alex's laughter tinkled through the crisp air like the clearest bell.

He turned, battling a sheepish grin of his own. "Oh, so you think that's funny, do you?"

She stood in front of the camper, nodding hard, still laughing. "Of course not," she managed to say between chortles. "I'm just overcome with gratitude that you saved me from that killer buck." She laughed some more.

Torch stuffed the gun into the waistband of his jeans, to free his hands. Then he scooped up a snowball and let her have it. Splat! Dead center of her forehead.

Her laughter came to an abrupt stop about the time his began in earnest. "Why you…"

She squatted to arm herself for retaliation, but he ran before she could launch the first volley. He got pegged twice in the back as he ducked behind the camper. Then he leapt out again and got her in the chest.

She fired three at him, rapidly, one after the other, and he took one in the face before he had a chance to weave out of the line of fire.

Time to change tactics. When Josh and Jason used to ambush him with snowballs this little trick had never failed. He let her hit him with one, then fell down onto his back, and lay very still, not moving.

Sure enough, she tiptoed closer.

"Torch?"

And still closer.

"Come on, Torch, I didn't hurt you, did I?"

And closer yet. She crouched down, her hands moving to touch his face, and he sprang the trap. Grabbed her shoulders and flipped her onto her back in the snow while she yelped in surprise. He straddled her to hold her still, and drizzled a little white stuff on her face while she wriggled beneath him.

And then he stopped and sat very still. My God, he'd remembered the boys. He'd remembered the snowball fights. He'd done it without struggling in vain, searching his mind for the memory. And he'd done it…ever so briefly…without a flash of blinding pain. He'd been laughing. Laughing out loud. He hadn't done that since he'd lost them.

He stared down at the woman beneath him. Her cheeks cherry red in the moonlight, her eyes sparkling, her hair spread over the snow, damp with it.

She smiled softly. "All right, I surrender. You win. You're a superior warrior, I admit it."

He got off her, took her hands and helped her to her feet. He didn't know what to say, what to think. Part of him knew he ought to feel badly for remembering his sons without pain. How could he? How could he play and laugh when his little boys were dead because of him?

But there was another part…a long-starved, craving, hungry part that sighed in blessed relief. A sandy, barren place in his soul absorbed what had just happened the way the desert absorbs the blessed rain. And a single blade of new grass struggled to burst forth.

That sensation, though, was one he didn't deserve. So he ignored it.

"I didn't know you had a frivolous, silly bone in your body, Torch Palamaro," she said, brushing snow away from her clothes, then starting on his.

"I…" He couldn't answer her. He was still too overwhelmed.

"I'm glad you do," she said. "I never had anyone to be silly with. I didn't even know I had it in me."

He shook his head, forcing himself to take his eyes off her. She looked like a kid, her hair tousled and snowy, her face aglow, her eyes shining with emotion.

Damn, damn, damn, he didn't like what he was feeling.

"Come on, let's go inside."

Torch followed her, reminding himself over and over why he was here. He had to kill Scorpion. He had to avenge the murders of his wife and children. He didn't deserve happiness, because it was his fault they were dead, and even killing that murderer wasn't going to change that. Nothing would. His family was dead and Torch was alive. That was so wrong, so very wrong that the gods must have gone off duty on that blackest of days. Fate must have taken a vacation, because it just wasn't the natural order of things. It was out of whack. The whole freaking universe was screwed up.

And he wasn't going to forget that it should have been him blown into so many bits there hadn't been enough left to bury. Those markers, standing over empty graves, should have his name cut into their stone faces. It should have been him, not them.

"Are you sure we can't go back to the house?"

It was the fifth time she'd asked him the question as she tossed restlessly on the top bunk. Above him. He answered her mechanically, his mind on other things.

"We can't go to your house, Alex. It wouldn't be safe."

"You can't be sure of that. Why would they leave anyone behind there, when they have every reason to believe we're heading to New York? It doesn't make sense.''

He sighed low. She was right. There was very little chance Scorpion had bothered leaving men at the house, or near it, on surveillance duty. Very little chance. But a chance, all the same. A chance he couldn't take. It would only take them being sighted up here once to bring Scorpion right back to their doorstep. And Torch didn't want the bastard here.

Not yet, anyway. He'd discovered that he'd prefer to have this formula safely on its way to D.C. first. Moreover, he admitted, he'd like it if he could get Alexandra Holt out of the line of fire before it came down to the final confrontation. He didn't want her to see him kill or be killed. She was too damned softhearted to take it.

''Torch?''

''Hmm?''

''I hate calling you that. Torch. What kind of a name is that, anyway? When are you going to tell me your given name?''

''Don't hold your breath.'' She could get it out if him, if she applied herself. He figured there wasn't much he could keep from her if she wanted to know badly enough. Things had a way of just slipping out when she was around. She ought to work for the CIA.

''Do you really think there are men watching my house?'' She leaned over the edge of the bed so she could see him on the bunk below her. Her hair hung straight down toward the floor and her eyes glimmered in the lamplight like virgin silk. ''And tell me the truth, will you?''

''You look like a troll, upside down.''

''A troll?'' Her brows drew together.

''Don't tell me you've never seen one. They're these

little dolls with hair that stands straight up. My kids used to collect…'' He stopped in midsentence, his jaw slack. It had happened again. For just a second, he'd seen the boys in his mind's eye. Sitting in the middle of the living room floor with their troll collection spread out around them, moving the figures around, giving them comical voices.

He'd remembered. Without effort his mind had given him a memory, and no black wall had come slamming down to cut it off before it was even complete. No tidal wave of guilt had come surging in to sweep it away from his grasp.

Twice now in one night. Why? Why now? What did it mean?

She was staring at him. Hanging upside down with her troll hair so long he could have reached out and touched it. She was seeing the emotions cross his face, he knew she was.

''Oh,'' she said softly. Then louder. ''Oh, *those* trolls. The ones with the neon-colored hair, right? A little patient of mine brought one with her to the clinic once. Ugly little bugger. I'm not taking that comment as a compliment, Palamaro.''

Her eyes said more. They touched his soul, those huge brown eyes. They moved over his face and it seemed to Torch as if they smoothed some invisible balm over his deepest wounds. He could see the warmth in them. He could feel the healing power of their touch.

She spoke volumes with her eyes. And he heard her.

''But this troll talk is off the subject,'' she said.

''I suppose it is.'' His voice came out slow, lazy. He had to shake himself before he could remember what they'd been talking about initially. When it came back to him, he blinked, breaking the grip of her gaze, breaking the spell she'd been putting him under. "Alex, why are you so determined to go back to the house, anyway?"

"Why are you so determined not to let me?"

"Because it's risky."

"The risk has to be minimal, Torch. At least admit that much. There's very little chance Scorpion left anyone there, and you know it."

He chewed his lip and nodded. "You're right, there's very little chance. But that's still a chance and it's a chance I'm not willing to take."

"We could at least *look,* couldn't we? I mean, if we head over there at night, sneak a look at the house from the woods, we could see for ourselves if there's anyone around."

He propped himself up on one elbow. "This is about that cat of yours, isn't it?"

Her face was turning red. She nodded upside down.

"Your blood's rushing to your head, Alex. And if you think I'm gonna risk everything for a cat, it must be interfering with your ability to reason."

She pulled her head up, but a second later her legs hung over the side. Bare feet and smooth calves. And then she hopped to the floor, pacing. "He has to be fed, or he'll die."

"He'll catch a mouse."

"I don't have mice."

"A bird, then."

"But he was shut in! He can't get out to hunt, Torch. He needs me." She paced to the little stove and set a kettle of water on the burner, then rummaged in the cupboards.

"Alex, it's just a cat."

She located the box of hot cocoa mix he'd bought,

opened a packet and poured it into a disposable cup. Her back was to him. She wore a T-shirt and, as far as he could tell, nothing else.

She looked toward him, tried for a smile, but it was crooked and endearingly sad. "You want a cup?"

"He'll be okay for another day or so, Alex. A cat the size of that one can certainly last forty-eight hours without food."

She nodded. "Maybe."

"We'll get your father's papers from Jim McManus tomorrow. We'll get that formula into the right hands. After that it won't matter."

Her brows bunched together. "There is no formula," she said, her voice a little stiffer, colder than before. But it sounded to Torch as if she were mainly saying it to convince herself. She tore open a second envelope, dumped it into a second cup, then poured the hot water. "And even if there was, what difference will it make? Scorpion will still come after us if we're seen up here, won't he? How would he know we'd already put this imaginary formula somewhere beyond his reach?"

"He won't know. And yes, he'll still come after us."

She stirred the cocoa, carried a cup in each hand and sat down on the edge of his bed. He sat up, taking his from her hand, touching her fingers as he did so, wishing he hadn't.

"But I'll make sure you—*and* your damn cat—are someplace safe, by then. When Scorpion gets here, there's only going to be one person waiting for him."

She held her cup between her hands, her doe eyes probing him. "You're going to kill him, aren't you?"

He said nothing. Didn't nod, didn't answer. Just averted his gaze and sipped from his cup.

"What if he kills you, instead?"

"He already did that." Damn, there he went again, blurting things that were none of her business. He took another drink, set the cup on the floor.

"He killed your family," she whispered. "But not you. You're still alive."

"My body is, Alex. That's all, though. There's nothing left inside."

"There is." She put her cup on the floor, not having taken a single sip of the liquid it held. He shook his head in denial, but she caught his face between her palms, held it still, staring so deeply he felt her touch his soul. "There is, Torch. I see it, right there in your eyes."

"No...."

"You don't want to be alive anymore, because it hurts. You wish it had been you. But it wasn't, Torch. It wasn't. It was them, and they're gone, and it's horrible and unfair. But they wouldn't want you to stay dead inside. They'd want you to go on. Do your grieving, and miss them and love them always. But go on."

His hands rose, closing over hers on his face. He moved them away slowly, and he shook with emotion. He held both her hands between his. "I can't do that," he whispered roughly.

"You can, if you just—"

"You don't understand, dammit!" His words exploded from his chest, vibrating through the small camper, making Alexandra jerk in surprise. He released her hands, clasped her shoulders hard, his fingers sinking into her flesh. "It's my fault they died! I screwed up. I underestimated that bastard, and he killed them. He killed Marcy and he killed my little boys because of me." He released her suddenly, shoving her away from him as he did. The force of it sent her tumbling off the bed, to the floor. But he'd had no choice, because he'd been damn close to pulling her closer, to clinging to her and embracing the healing light she wielded with her brown eyes.

She scrambled to her feet again, but he didn't want her coming back to him. Not now. If she touched him again, he'd do something utterly stupid. He turned onto his side, facing the wall.

Alex sat down on the bed again, and her hands caressed his shoulders. "It wasn't your fault, Torch."

"It was."

Her fingers wove through his hair. "Why?"

He closed his eyes. He did not talk about this. Not to anyone. He never had. And he wasn't about to begin now.

And even as he assured himself of those things, the entire ugly story was taking shape in his mind, readying itself to be told. To be shared. With her.

He rolled onto his back, looked up into her brown eyes. With one hand, he reached out to tuck a lock of satin hair behind her ear.

"There was a bomb threat phoned in. That's how it started," he began.

Chapter 9

He'd told her the entire story, and Alexandra had tried not to cry at the pain in his voice, but she hadn't been able to help herself. And he hadn't turned away or pushed her away again.

He talked for a long time. It was as if the floodgates had broken, as if once he started he had to tell all of it, right to the end. He told her about his last conversation with his wife, and how D.C., the man Torch called his best friend, had stood by him afterward. D.C. had never doubted him, even when some higher-ranking fellow named Stern had suspected Torch of being involved in the murder of his own family.

She lowered her head onto his pillow, and she put her arms around him, and she held him while he talked. She stroked his hair and his back and his shoulders, and she listened.

"How could he possibly have suspected you?" she whispered, holding him a little tighter.

"The obvious reasons. It was a bomb, Alex. They're my specialty."

"But your own family..."

He stroked her hair. She lay in the crook of his arm, with her head on his chest and her arm anchored around his waist.

"Stern knew Marcy and I only married because of the boys."

Alex frowned. "You didn't love her?"

"I did," he said quickly. "Just not the way..." His words trailed off, and he tried again. "We were friends, good friends. Things got out of hand once, when we were both feeling lonely, and Marcy got pregnant. So we married."

"But it was working out," Alex guessed.

"Yeah. Kids have a way of...of bringing people closer. It's hard to explain it...but you'll know what I mean someday, Alex, when you have children of your own."

That hurt. It hurt beyond belief, but she swallowed the pain, fought it into submission. Talking would do Torch a world of good. She wasn't about to change the subject.

"How did this Stern know about how things were between you and your wife?" she asked, genuinely curious.

"He was half in love with Marcy himself. Hell, I often thought she might have fallen for him, in time, if...if things had been different."

Alex didn't know about that. She couldn't imagine any woman falling for another man if Torch were the competition.

"She never said so, though. Never did a thing to make me think that." His voice was sleepy now. Long pauses came between his words. "She was too kind to risk hurt-

ing me...and she was loyal.'' His hand stilled on her
hair. "A lot like you," he whispered.

The last pause drew out. In a few minutes, she realized
he'd fallen asleep. Exhausted maybe, from the sudden
release of such long pent-up emotions. A soul-deep
sleep, she could tell. His chest expanded, lifting her head
with his deep inhales, and fell smoothly as he exhaled.

She sat up, staring down at his relaxed face. "The
only person to blame for what happened is Scorpion,"
she whispered. "You did your job. You did what you
were supposed to do." She ran her fingers through his
hair. "Torch, they're at peace. They've returned to meld
with whatever force you believe created them. You're
the only one in hell. Can't you see that?"

His eyes were still closed, his breathing deep and
even. He slept as if comatose, and she knew it was his
body's response to the emotional stress of sharing his
past—the past that had almost destroyed him—with her.

Alexandra thought he'd probably never released any
of the rage he'd been feeling over the murders of his
family. Perhaps he'd never talked about it before.

But he had now. And she was glad.

Alexandra slipped silently away from him, pausing to
pull the covers over his still body. She ached for what
he was going through, but she also knew that his past
was coloring his judgment of the present. There was no
danger in going to the house. There were no men hiding
there, waiting for her return. Not when Scorpion believed she and Torch were in New York right now. Even
Torch had admitted the chances of such a thing were
slim. But he was being overly cautious.

And it would be foolish of her to think that was out
of concern for her. It was fear of failure making him so
careful. He was afraid another death would be added to

his list of imaginary sins. He was afraid of what that would do to his soul and maybe even to his mind.

But there was no danger. He wouldn't believe that unless she proved it to him, so she would. She needed to go back there, and her reasons went beyond her desire to be sure Max was all right. Torch wouldn't understand them. She wasn't certain she understood them herself, yet. But she had to go back. There were some things she needed to think through and she couldn't do that here, with Torch and his pain so close, so reachable.

Things about herself…and her relationship with her father. Things she hadn't wanted to delve into before, because they were too painful. But it was time, she realized. It was past time. And for some reason, it would be easier to analyze and dissect these things back there at the house where they'd spent the last days of his life together.

She closed her eyes and turned away from Torch, silently apologizing for what she was about to do. But she wouldn't be gone long enough for him to wake up and perhaps worry. She'd just do what she'd suggested earlier—get close enough to the house to take a look around and assure herself no one was there. And in the morning, she'd tell him what she'd done, and what she'd found, and he'd stop being so stubborn about going there.

Making barely a sound, she picked up her clothes. She pulled on a pair of the heavy socks he'd purchased, and then donned one of the sweatshirts. She finished off with his leather jacket, and she took the flashlight, too. On tiptoe, she slipped into the front of the RV and then out the passenger door, rather than the one in the back, where he might hear.

And then she stepped away from the camper, stretching her arms out to her sides and inhaling deeply of the

clean night air. Snow fell softly but thickly, dusting her
face and hair. And it was colder than it had been earlier.
Quite a lot colder. It wouldn't be a problem, though. She
could find the house blindfolded.

She took a step, then stopped, blinking at the unfamiliar surge of feeling that last thought had evoked. She
felt...capable. She felt sure of herself and...and strong.
She couldn't remember feeling that way before. But she
didn't have to spend much time analyzing it or trying to
figure out where it was coming from. She knew. The
time she'd spent with Torch was changing her.

She looked back at the camper, remembering the way
he'd looked lying there, asleep and drained and even a
little vulnerable. Yes, he was changing her. In more
ways than one.

She only hoped she didn't end up regretting it.

Torch dreamed of his children. Jason and Josh were
playing in a square patch of grass, their faces bathed in
golden sunlight. He heard their laughter, saw the sparkle
in their eyes as they ran and tumbled and rolled in the
lush grass. He saw himself, too, running and rolling right
along with them, and then he remembered. He'd been
teaching them football in the backyard. The summer before...

He stopped thinking and just looked, watched the
scene unfold in his mind's eye and devoured every second of it. It had been so long since he'd been able to
see them like this, alive and happy. So long since he'd
been capable of bringing up a single memory. But now,
it was like being there again. So real. The redness of
their plump cheeks, and the way the wind ruffled their
curls. The comic size of a regulation football when
clutched in the small hands of a four-year-old.

"Josh, Jason, time to come in."

Torch turned at the sound of Marcy's voice. She stood at the back door, smiling as the boys ran toward her. They begged to stay out just a little longer. It was such a familiar scene, one that had played out a thousand times in real life. But it didn't have the feel of a memory anymore.

Smiling, Marcy granted the boys an extra half hour in the backyard. They raced back to their game, and automatically Torch started toward the back door. He had to talk to Marcy. There was something...

"You called them inside," he said.

"They asked for more time."

"Yeah." Torch smiled. "They always ask for more time."

"And I always give it to them."

He started up the back steps. Marcy caught his gaze and shook her head. "No. You need to wake up now."

He frowned, saying nothing, just staring, confused.

"It was my time, not yours," she said softly. "And it's not Alexandra's time yet, either. She needs you. They need you."

He tried to argue, but when he opened his mouth the words that came out had no form, no substance.

"It was my time, not yours," she repeated. "Accept it, and go on."

And then it was as if the lights went out. Utter blackness descended, engulfing everything. He couldn't see Marcy anymore, or the house, or the yard. He couldn't hear the voices of his sons. There was only darkness, and the unearthly howl of the wind.

It took a full minute for Torch to realize that his eyes were opened. He was awake, in a pitch-black camper. It had been a dream, for God's sake. A dream.

He sat up in bed, pushing his hands through his hair, gnawing his lower lip a little, just to be sure he was really awake. Seemed he was. And his first instinct was to call to Alexandra. To hear her voice answering him would be reassuring. It would confirm everything was all right. Just as it should be.

She needs you.

He gave his head a shake, trying to rid himself of the haunting memory of that dream. It had been so real. He cleared his throat and very softly, not wanting to wake her, he said, "Alex? You awake?" He waited, remembering with a flush of embarrassment the way he'd poured his heart out to her earlier. The way she'd held him as he had told her everything. Every single thing he'd vowed not to talk about with another living soul. And how she'd listened, and seemed to understand every word. And how sharing it with her had made him feel like maybe he could survive this hell after all.

There was no answer. Okay, so she was asleep. He shouldn't feel such an intense need to hear her voice, anyway. It was ridiculous.

She needs you!

Torch rolled his eyes at his own apparent mental instability. But he decided there was little use fighting it. He got out of bed, reached for the gas lamp nearest him and turned the knob. The flame came to life, reaching its yellow fingers into the corners, chasing shadows away.

Torch turned toward the bunks, standing now. He'd just look at her, assure himself that she was okay, and maybe he'd be able to get some sleep.

Only, she wasn't there. The bunk was empty. The sight of it was like a blow between the eyes, so much so that he took an involuntary step backward at its impact.

He swore, and checked the bathroom, and swore some more as he poked his head into the cab, finding both as empty as her bed had been. And her shoes and jeans were gone, and so was his jacket and the flashlight.

"Dammit straight to hell, she's gone to that house," he yelled at the walls, the ceiling. Okay, okay, calm down. So, she'd sneaked out while he slept. So she'd deliberately, blatantly done exactly what he'd told her not to do. So what? It didn't mean the world was going to end. He gathered his clothes, picked up his gun. She'd been right from the beginning. There was barely a snowball's chance in hell that Scorpion had left men behind to watch the place. She'd be all right. She'd be just...

He squinted through the windshield, frowning. And then he reached past the steering wheel and down to the side to pull on the headlights.

But even their blazing white glow couldn't penetrate the blizzard blanketing the night. He couldn't see a yard in front of the RV. Not a yard. Sometime while he'd been sleeping, a brutal wind had kicked up, and the result was a blinding snowstorm. And Alexandra was out there somewhere. A chill of foreboding slipped up his spine, and again he heard his dead wife's meaning-laden whisper. *She needs you.*

He swore. It couldn't have been this bad when she'd left. Couldn't have been, or she wouldn't have gone. Alexandra was too smart for that. This was the Adirondack forest, for God's sake. She wouldn't have gone out there alone in a storm like this. He could only pray she'd reached the house safely, before the blizzard had unleashed its fury. He could only hope there had been no one there waiting for her when she had.

He pulled on every sweatshirt that remained, wrapped a pale blue blanket around his shoulders in lieu of a coat and snatched up his duffel bag. Hunching forward, he headed out into slashing white chaos.

She made it halfway, she figured, before the snow began flying horizontally instead of vertically, driven by an ever-strengthening, frigid wind. She lost her bearings. It was ridiculous. Stupid, to get lost in a place she knew so well. All she had to do was follow the fire road, for God's sake. Problem was, she could no longer *see* the fire road, and the flashlight she gripped was a joke against the power of the sudden storm. When she'd left the camper, it had been cold, yes, but not like this. Now there was this bitter, harsh wind that turned wet snowflakes into razors. There was no light, no darkness. Just snow. She couldn't make out the shapes of the trees she moved among, until she was nearly inhaling their bark. There was nothing to guide her. The wind moaning eerily through the boughs overhead seemed to Alexandra like the voice of her father. Condemning. Scornful.

Her nose and cheeks burned, razed by the blizzard's claws. It hurt to inhale the frigid air, and her lungs screamed with every breath. Yet she breathed ever faster as panic crept into her veins. The cold and the fear tried to send her bronchial tubes into spasm, but Alex fought it. She forced herself calm. She ordered her body not to betray her now.

She'd left the inhaler at the camper.

Her hands were wet and slowly going numb, and her feet had long since mutated into solid ice chunks. She couldn't feel them anymore when she stepped on them, so she lurched along, trying to find her way.

But there was no more sign of the path, and she wasn't

sure whether she'd have known it even if she'd somehow stumbled onto it again. She only knew she wasn't on the path now. Somehow she'd veered into the forest. That was obvious by the trees that loomed into her vision with every few steps. Panic crept in again, chilling her even more deeply than the cold wind. But she fought it. There had to be a way to get through this.

She squinted in the snow, trying to see something, anything that would give her a clue, but to no avail. She decided at last to backtrack. She'd either find her way back to the fire trail, or perhaps all the way to the camper if she just followed her own tracks. Turning in place, she bent low, searching for the footprints she'd left in the snow. She had to bend almost double, hold the light only inches above the ground in order to see them. Loose snow swirled and whipped around her lower legs like the ghostly mist in a horror movie. Only more deadly. She finally found a shallow indentation in the snow that marked the place where she'd stepped. Then another. Slowly she started back.

She was shivering now. Shaking so hard her teeth rattled and her muscles burned and the light jerked and danced in crazy patterns. She pulled her hands up into the sleeves of Torch's jacket and wrapped her arms around herself, bowing into the wind that screamed in her ears as she forced herself to keep moving and tried to keep the flashlight's beam focused on the tracks in the snow.

But in only a few yards, the footprints she'd made when she'd come out here vanished. The blizzard had already filled them in. And now just what on earth was she going to do?

Keep moving. Just keep moving, Alexandra, or you'll die out here.

She tried to obey the voice of reason, did for a while. Until it became impossible. Because the asthma came on full force, shutting her bronchial tubes down. She gasped, forcefully sucking minuscule breaths of freezing air into her lungs, but she knew it wasn't enough to sustain her. It was like trying to suck air through plastic. She felt as if she were suffocating. Felt as if, nothing, she *was* suffocating. But she fought, used every ounce of strength in her body to try to inhale. The effort cost her, and the reward was a dismal squeak.

Dizziness came as she'd known it would. She groped for a support, her hand sweeping through the falling snow, finding nothing to grasp. And then the snowy ground reached up to surround her face. Its cold was an icy slap, an injection of awareness. She managed to pull herself up again. But her rally didn't last. She staggered forward a few more steps only to collapse against the skin-scraping bark of a massive pine. Her stinging face pressed to the trunk, and she tasted its fragrance with every desperate, insufficient gasp.

Torch knew which way she would have gone. He left the headlights on, which helped a little. God knows their beam was a good deal more powerful than that of the pathetic flashlight she was depending on.

As soon as he stepped out of the camper, the cold bit right through every layer of clothing he wore. Damn. It was frigid, killing cold, with this wind behind it. She wouldn't last long in cold like this. No one would.

He thought about her lungs, the frequent asthma attacks and the way they were instigated by fear. She'd be afraid right now, if she was out in this storm. If she was lost, she'd be terrified. He felt sick to his stomach thinking about how afraid she'd be. Ducking into the camper, he checked the glove compartment and found her inhaler there. His heart sank. She didn't have it with her. What would she do if she had an attack out there, and no inhaler on hand?

Torch snapped himself out of his panic by mentally insisting she'd made it to the house. She was inside right now, and she was warm and dry and safe. He envisioned her wrapped in a blanket, warming her feet by one of those fireplaces that littered the place. Only the ever-growing knot in the pit of his stomach kept insisting that wasn't the scene he was going to find.

He managed to stay on the fire road. He was soaking wet and shivering before he'd reached what he judged was the halfway point, but the extreme cold only drove him on. Maybe he even picked up his pace, calling her name now as he went. And it seemed to Torch that the storm abated a little. That the wind eased and the snowfall slowed as he moved on. Or maybe he was just going numb and his senses were dulled.

But no. He'd made it.

Torch stopped and stared off into the gloom at his right. There was a glow, very pale, but there. It was like trying to see a streetlight through heavy fog, as he squinted and started toward it. The light led him off the fire trail, into the forest, but it remained visible, even grew clearer as he went. And then the trees he'd been hiking through came to an end. And he was seeing Alexandra's house beyond the veil of the storm, the outdoor light glowing like a beacon, and he ran toward it.

Thank God! If the light was on, she must be...

Halfway across the driveway, he paused, studying that outdoor light now that it was more visible. A huge halogen globe, very much like the streetlights he'd likened it to. The kind of light that came on automatically at dark. All by itself, with no help at all.

He put his observational skills into gear and felt his heart sink into his feet. There wasn't a single light glowing from inside the house. Only this automatic outdoor one.

He wanted to run up the front steps, slam the door open and yell her name. But he didn't. A lifetime of caution wasn't overcome that easily. He drew the gun and moved slowly, his feet making furrows in the snow. Then dents when he walked up the three concrete steps. He stood before the dark wood door with its fan-shaped, snow-encrusted panes of glass, and he listened.

The house was silent. Not a sound or a movement from within. He didn't think Alex was there, and the idea that she wasn't almost put him on his knees. They actually began to buckle. It was a sensation Torch Palamaro had only experienced once in his life.

He steadied himself, trying to focus on positive thoughts, trying to weigh his options. Fortunately, it didn't look as if anyone else was there, either. He tucked the gun under his arm and rubbed his hands together to warm them. It didn't help much. Neither did blowing on them.

He turned to look behind him, just once. Just to be sure. No vehicles. No tire tracks. No footprints. Then again, if there had been any, they'd have been filled in by now.

He tried the brass doorknob and found it unlocked. Then he pulled the gun out again with his right hand, held its barrel steady as he opened the door with his left.

In the bit of light that spilled in from outside, he saw the far wall. The dark, empty fireplace, without so much as a glowing ember to attest to recent use. No one waited in ambush inside. As Torch made his way from room to room, upstairs and down, he found no sign that anyone had been here today. The place had been searched but not trashed. Scorpion's men had been methodical, careful. They hadn't charged through, emptying drawers and turning over chairs the way one saw on television shows. You'd never find anything if you searched a house that way. Scorpion knew that. He'd taught his men well. An untrained eye might not even have known they'd been there.

But other than the signs of a painstaking search, there was not a hint of human presence. And the fact that the place was colder than a tomb was the clincher. If Scorpion's men had stayed, they'd have lit a fire in at least one of the hearths that littered the place. The power wasn't out, so Torch figured a blown fuse must be to blame for the furnace not working. If anyone had been here, they'd have needed heat.

So Alex had been right and he'd been overly cautious. No one was here.

Including her.

He replaced the gun and turned on some of the lights. The more light the better. He didn't care who else might see them right now. These were for Alex, in case he couldn't find her, to guide her in.

But he would find her. He had to.

He strode toward the front door. Something snared his leg with a low growl, and he damned near shot it. The cat released him when he whirled, and it crouched, hissing at him. Accusing green eyes blazed up at him from a furry black face.

"Not now, beast." He turned back to the door and headed out. He kept thinking of Alex, lying in the snow, dying. He kept picturing himself discovering her lifeless body out here, and it was tearing his insides apart. Dammit, she hadn't done a thing to deserve any of this. She'd been dragged into a situation beyond her control, and now she might die because of it.

No. No, she damn well wouldn't die, because Torch wouldn't let her. He was going to do it right this time. He wasn't going to lose another person he cared about. Not again.

Torch swallowed hard, realizing that he'd just admitted he cared for Alexandra Holt. Hell, he hadn't wanted to. But the woman made it impossible to keep a distance. She'd wormed her way under his skin, and yes, he'd let himself care. Combine that with the madness she stirred in his loins, and the woman was more deadly an enemy than Scorpion on his best day.

Didn't matter, though. Alex was out here, somewhere. He wasn't going to quit until he found her.

Alex had found the fire road again by mere chance, for what good it did her. She hadn't realized it at first, but the tree she clung to was right at the road's edge. She could see that now that the storm was easing a little. Or maybe it was just taking a break between rounds.

Finding the road, though, was no help whatsoever. Not now. She panted helplessly, barely clinging to consciousness. The strain of forcing air into her lungs was exhausting her. Her legs were stumps, numb to the knees, and she could barely stand, let alone walk. Her clothes were soaked now, her jeans frozen to her legs, her shoes caked in several layers of snow and ice. She leaned against the tree, wishing it could emit body heat, hugging herself and shaking violently, and she knew she couldn't go on. Once again her foolishness had gotten her into trouble. Maybe it would do her in this time.

Her legs gave out and she sank into the snow at the tree's base. God help her, she didn't think she was going to survive this.

Her father wouldn't have been surprised.

Chapter 10

He thought she was dead when he found her. He'd been meandering into the woods along either side of the road, checking out every snow-covered clump of deadfall that even remotely resembled a body. And then he'd glimpsed a pinprick of faint light on the ground in the distance. He'd raced toward it. The flashlight lay half-covered in snow, right beside Alexandra. And she was utterly still, cold as a stone. A thin layer of snow coated her face and clothes. His heart did things he hadn't thought it was still capable of doing. Like breaking, for instance. He hadn't believed anything could break what had become a hunk of lifeless granite, but the sight of her shattered it to dust.

He fell to his knees beside her, choking on the words he tried to shout at her, brushing the snow and frozen hair away from her face and eyelashes. "Alex! Dammit, Alex, talk to me! Come on!"

Her answer was a low moan, but the sound of it shot

adrenaline directly into his veins. "You're alive!" He pulled her limp body against him. Her arms and head hung like a rag doll's, but he held her all the same. "You're alive, Alex. And dammit, you're going to stay that way." He had to release her just long enough to wrestle the inhaler from his jeans pocket. He held it to her lips, squeezed two sharp bursts of medicine into her mouth, hoping she'd managed to inhale some of it. Then he tucked it back into his pocket again to free his hands.

It was closer to the house than back to the camper. Torch was all too aware that just because Scorpion's men hadn't been there didn't mean they weren't watching the place from somewhere else. Or checking in on occasion. But he had no choice at the moment. Her life was in the balance, and Torch was already responsible for more deaths than he'd ever atone for. He wasn't going to add Alexandra's to the list.

He took the blanket from around his shoulders and wrapped her in it. Then he lifted her into his arms and began trudging back the way he'd come. She didn't move again, didn't make another sound. But he couldn't stop to check her, didn't dare stop to check her, terrified beyond reason that he'd find her heart had stopped.

She wasn't gasping. He told himself her muscles would relax when she was unconscious and that her breathing would ease, but he had no idea if it was true. Seemed to him she ought to be in the midst of an asthma attack at a time like this. Why the hell couldn't he hear her breathing?

He looked down at her as he walked into the light outside the house, at her pale skin, the frozen lashes resting on her cheeks. The stillness of her. She looked like an icy angel, a frozen princess under an evil spell.

Why did it hurt this much?

He shouldered the door open, kicking it shut behind him, and headed straight up the stairs to her bedroom. Damn, it was cold in here. A little warmer than outside, though. At least here there was no wind. He lowered her to the bed, and only then did he dare to lay his head against her breast, to listen. When the soft, slightly wheezy sound of her breathing reached him, he closed his eyes tight. "Thank God. Still alive," he whispered.

He tucked the blanket more tightly around her, knowing she might not stay that way long if he didn't act fast. But damn him for a fool, he didn't know what to do first.

He straightened away from Alex, looking around the room, and the hearth in the corner seemed to whisper an answer to him. A fire laid ready, just as it had when they'd left the house. A stack of wood standing neatly to one side. It only took a second to find the matches on the mantel and to light the fire in the fireplace. Torch closed the bedroom door, to keep the heat inside. Then turned, frowning as he realized the window had been closed. And the rope ladder...? He had no idea what Scorpion's men had done with it. He hoped to God they didn't end up trapped here with no way out.

But that worry had to take a back seat for now. For now, his only concern was Alex. The room would be warm in a while. He returned to the bed, pulling the snow-damp blanket away from her. Her clothes were wet, frozen. They were doing her no good whatsoever. He needed to warm her, and he needed to do it fast. Kneeling on the bed, he gently removed the leather coat, then the sweatshirt she wore beneath it. She didn't move as he worked, didn't make a sound, just lay there limp. Lifeless. His throat tried to close off, and his eyes burned inexplicably.

The zipper of her jeans was caked with snow and ice, but he finally managed to undo them. He knelt beside the bed, wrenching the snow-coated shoes from her feet, peeling the socks and then the jeans away. Her skin was cold, clammy to the touch. He hoped to God he'd found her in time. He tugged back the covers and bent to pick her up, to settle her beneath them, but realized his shirts were soaking wet and icy cold. He tugged them over his head, tossing them to the floor before bending over her again. He picked her up, naked and limp and cold in his arms, against his chest. He wanted to cradle her there, to hold her and rock her and speak to her until he drew some kind of response. But he couldn't, not yet. He tucked her into the bed, under the covers, then quickly searched the room, taking every blanket he found and spreading them over her.

Now what?

He turned in a slow circle. Frostbite, he realized, was a danger. Her hands and her feet...

Still shirtless, he ran into the adjoining bathroom. The room where he'd sat on that tiny vanity stool while she'd tended his bleeding shoulder. He snatched several thick towels from the shelf and returned to the fire. He added more logs and then held two of the towels as close to the flames as he dared, warming them. When they were heated through, he went to the foot of the bed, lifted the covers and wrapped a towel around each of her icy feet. He repeated the process with two more towels, wrapping her hands this time.

At last, he heeled off his now-thawed shoes, shimmied out of his jeans and stood naked before the fireplace to take the chill out of his own body. And then he slipped beneath the covers with Alexandra. She was so cold after the heat of the fire. He flinched and sucked air through his teeth as he pulled her chilled body into his arms and held her tight against his own warm skin.

Gently he cradled her, willing his body's heat to move into hers, to warm her, to bring her back to him.

"Come on, Alex," he whispered, a harsh desperation in his voice making it seem like that of a stranger to his own ears. "Come on, wake up. You're gonna be okay. Do you hear me? You're gonna be okay."

God, if only he could be sure of that.

She could breathe again.

It was the first sensation to filter into her awareness. She wasn't struggling and gasping anymore. She was breathing easily, though her lungs ached as if she'd run a marathon.

And she was warm, deliciously warm and wrapped in a wonderful contrast of hardness and softness. She inhaled nasally, and her eyes opened at the familiar, subtle scent.

Torch.

He was behind her and beneath her and surrounding her. His body enveloped hers in its warmth. And she closed her eyes, wondering if this was a dream, or some fantasy-based afterlife. Oh, but it felt too good to analyze. His arms, holding her, warming her. His chest, pressed to her back. His hair-rough thigh, resting atop her legs. His warm breath heating her nape.

She sighed deeply, hoping to stay just like this for several more hours.

He was naked. And...and so was she.

Alexandra came more thoroughly awake. Had something happened between them? Had her waking fantasy come true and had she somehow managed to forget?

The last thing she remembered was clinging to a pine

tree's rough trunk, gasping for air and shivering with cold and teetering on the brink of unconsciousness.

Torch must have found her. He must have found her and brought her... She blinked at the bank of windows with their somber blue drapes and rope tiebacks. She sniffed the air, scenting wood smoke and man.

He'd brought her home. She was in her own bed. And she was all right. She was warm and dry and safe.

Torch Palamaro had saved her life tonight.

She rolled onto her back, better to see him in the dim light of predawn and poststorm. And he stirred. His eyes flicked open, blinked a couple times, then darted rapidly over her face.

"Alex...?"

"I'm okay."

His eyes continued their search, filled with something like disbelief. One hand came up under the covers, to cup her cheek, run through her hair, trace the curve of her neck, as his head moved very slightly from side to side.

"I'm okay," she repeated, knowing he wasn't as sure of it as she was.

He closed his eyes, his arms snaking around her, pulling her tight to him. "Thank God," he said, and sighed. "I was afraid...."

He stopped then. His hands had been sliding down over her back to pull her close, and they'd paused now, cupping her buttocks. As if Torch suddenly realized what he was doing. His hips were pressed to hers, and she felt the unmistakable swelling, hardening of him against her. She lifted her chin, meeting his eyes, knowing he was going to draw away from her at any second, just by the hint of panic she saw in those sapphire depths.

But she saw desire, too. And she knew she didn't want him to pull away.

She didn't have to move much at all in order to press her mouth to his.

He shuddered. His entire body trembled, but he didn't turn away. His lips parted when she nudged them. He lay very still, allowing her to kiss him. To taste his mouth on her own. He didn't move when her hands kneaded his shoulders, or when her fingers threaded into his hair; he only grew harder.

It was an instinct as old as woman that made her hips arch against him. And it was then he came alive.

As if electrocuted, he jerked. And then he held her. He rolled her onto her back and urged her lips wider, his tongue digging deep. She felt his body grow hotter, heard the rasping of his breaths. And she knew, without being told, that it had been a long time for him. Longer for her, though. Far longer for her.

A shiver of fear raced through her. He moved his hands between them, to cup her breasts, to capture her nipples and roll them and gently pull at them. And then his mouth left hers, to explore elsewhere, and he suckled her as if he were starving. His hips worked all the while. And when his mouth took over tormenting her breasts, his hands moved downward, pressing her thighs apart, and cupping her.

She stiffened, a little afraid of what was happening.

He bit her nipple, and she gasped in surprise and exquisite pain and pleasure, which rolled over her in hot waves that drowned most of her fears.

He lifted his head very slightly, his fevered eyes probing hers. "I'll stop," he rasped. "If you want me to stop, I'll—"

"No."

She saw the fire in his eyes blaze brighter before he lowered his head again. Then his mouth worked downward. He sucked the skin of her belly, licked at her abdomen, dipped his tongue into her navel.

Her heart hammered in her chest, and the sounds coming from her throat were foreign, not natural. Animal, guttural sounds.

His head moved lower and she clamped her thighs together, but Torch's hands slid between them and forced them open. Wide open. And then he was bending to her, and his thumbs were opening her, and his mouth was descending and...

She screamed aloud when he touched her with his mouth. The sensation was too wild for containment. He covered her with his mouth, with his lips, and he sucked at her. And then his tongue was stabbing into her as if he couldn't get enough of her taste. Alexandra writhed against his mouth in helpless anguish, straining toward a fulfillment she'd never known.

His teeth scraped and his tongue ravaged, and then her mind exploded. She melted and he moaned as if she were feeding him something he'd craved his entire life.

Slowly he moved up over her body, his mouth blazing a path over her torso, pausing to torment her breasts, burning over her throat and her chin. His hands held her thighs even wider, and he slid his hardness into her. Deeper, slowly and steadily deeper. He wasn't going to stop, not for anything. She opened her mouth, only to feel it filled with his hot, salty tongue. His hands crept beneath her hips, and he held her tight to him, forcing her utter acceptance of his thrusts, his powerful, merciless forays into the very depths of her. He slammed into her, again and again as his mouth worked hers, and his

hands squeezed and held her, and she liked it. She
wanted it.

And then he exploded inside her. She felt the pulse
of his orgasm, felt the way he shuddered, and the sensation drove her to the brink again, as well. Her hands
clutched his buttocks, drawing him deep inside her as
she climaxed, her body milking his until he trembled the
way she did.

And then he collapsed on top of her. But he didn't
withdraw. He simply rolled onto his back, taking her
with him, and he started all over again.

What the hell have you done, you freaking idiot!

Torch looked at her, lying there with the cold morning
sun bathing her naked shoulders, painting the soft smile
she wore even in her sleep.

He'd had sex with her. He'd been wanting it for days,
and damn it straight to hell, so had she. So he'd done
it.

She wouldn't call it that, though, would she? No. She
was female, and as such she'd claim that he had *made
love* to her, which he hadn't. That's the way she'd see
it though. One look at that soft smile was all it took to
know it. She'd think it had been some kind of fate thing.
She'd think he'd been so worried about her, so relieved
to see her awake and alive and well that he hadn't been
able to fight his hidden feelings any more.

But she'd be wrong. Because he had no hidden feelings for her. He was incapable of those kinds of feelings.
His heart had been blown to microscopic bits ten months
ago, and Humpty-Dumpty stood a better chance of healing than that tattered organ.

She stirred a little, snuggling closer to him, one arm
snaking around his waist. Thick black lashes whispering

open, huge dark eyes gazing up at him. The image of the timid woodland creature was back. Only this time it wasn't wary. It was trusting and content.

He was the animal here. He'd used her like a toy, and now he had to make that clear to her. He had to wipe that damned smile off her face before...

Before what, Palamaro? Before it gets to you? Hmm?

Torch closed his eyes tightly, refusing to hear the voice from within.

Yeah, you're right. You're nowhere near ready for this sort of thing.... What do you mean, "what sort of thing?" That sort of thing, fool! The sort of thing that's just about spilling from her eyes. Get the hell away from her before it gets on you!

His throat went dry, and he heard someone whisper, "I'm not ready for this sort of thing."

"Hmm?"

The way she asked it made "hmm?" sound erotic. And it wasn't *until* she asked it that he realized he'd spoken aloud.

"Nothing."

She bent her head to kiss his chest. Torch slid to the far side of the bed. And finally her dazzled expression cleared a little. A tiny frown appeared between her brows. And she looked at him, waiting, and he knew that she knew what was coming.

"Is something wrong?" she asked him slowly, those probing eyes like pins, pricking him everywhere they landed.

"No. It's just..." He shook his head, looked around the room, for a metaphoric hiding place. "I need to throw some more wood on the fire."

"No, you don't." She sat up, leaning her back against the headboard and tugging the covers up with her. "I

get the feeling you have something to say, and I think
your first three words are going to be 'about last night.'"

Torch sat on the edge of the bed, looking with regret
at the soggy ball of denim on the floor. What the hell
was he supposed to wear? He spotted his shorts, damp
but drier than the jeans. And within reach, to boot.

"I don't know what you mean, Alex. Last night was
just sex. What's there to talk about?" This as he got to
his feet and pulled the chilly shorts on, letting the waistband snap into place. Wincing at the icy material on his
skin, he tried not to walk funny when he went to the
fireplace. He hunkered down, cold material finding new
flesh to chill, and made a huge production out of poking
the coals and arranging more wood atop them.

"Just sex," she repeated softly.

"Yeah." *Coward, keeping your back to her while you
deliver the blow.* "Yeah, Alex, just sex. You wanted it,
I wanted it. We're both adults. It didn't mean anything."

She was silent. He was afraid to look at her. Afraid
he'd see tears in those doelike eyes, and afraid of what
that would feel like. He hadn't meant to hurt her. Better
she understand things now, though, than to let her go on
hoping. Better she suffer and cry for a few hours, than
to—

The impact of an unidentified projectile against the
back of his head cut his thoughts in half. "Ow!"

Torch turned, rubbing his head with one hand, holding
up the other when he saw another book coming at him.
Hardcover, too. She could have thrown a paperback.

The second volley ricocheted off his hand to land on
the floor. He eyed the lead crystal lamp on the bedside
stand and tried to judge the distance to the door. She
didn't reach for it, though. She just sat there, glaring at

him as if she'd like to see him beheaded. She didn't say one word. And he didn't ask.

"I...uh...I guess I'll go check on the furnace."

Nothing. Only furrowed brows and blazing eyes as he backed out of the room, into the freezing hallway in nothing but a pair of damp boxers.

He shivered but figured he deserved to suffer a little. Damn, but her reaction had him confused.

Alexandra blinked at the books lying on the floor with their pages folded beneath them like broken wings. She'd thrown them at him. Her frown deepened and she tilted her head to one side. Why?

A short time ago, she knew she would have reacted quite differently. She'd have been hurt, yes. But she'd probably have accepted his rejection. She might even have considered it inevitable.

Not now, though. Without thinking it through, she'd reacted with an anger unlike anything she'd ever experienced in her life. A moment ago she'd been mad enough to seriously hurt Torch Palamaro. Because he'd taken advantage. He'd used her, and dammit, she wasn't going to put up with that.

Now wasn't that an odd notion? Almost as if she were starting to believe she deserved better. Almost as if she thought she deserved...to be loved.

She blinked down her surprise, and turned the idea over and over in her mind. Her outlook had changed a great deal in the few days she'd spent with Torch, hadn't it?

A pathetic wail from beyond the bedroom door, accompanied by scratching sounds, interrupted her thoughts. Alex got up, snatching a bathrobe from the back of a chair and shrugging into it before opening the door. Max leapt into her arms. He nudged her chin with his big head and emitted a purr like a race car, punctuated intermittently by soft pleas for food.

"I know. You've been neglected, haven't you? All right, come on." Without using her hands, she stepped into slippers and headed downstairs. Max brushed his head over the collar of her robe and against her cheek. She ran her hand over his black fur and he arched to her touch, complaining loudly if she dared to stop stroking him for a second.

She was stepping softly, almost on tiptoe, as she descended the stairs. She realized as she crossed the living room that she was *sneaking* through her own house, just because she didn't want to run into Torch again.

Why?

Damn him for making her feel this way. She was bubbling over with the things she wanted to say to him. The problem was, she wasn't sure what those things were. If she opened her mouth right now, she had no idea what sorts of emotional declarations might come out. She was furious with him for the way he'd treated her. And that was such a foreign kind of feeling, she wasn't comfortable expressing it. Not yet. Not until she'd analyzed it a little more, figured out why she felt that way, and what it meant.

The raw intensity of her emotions frightened her. She'd wait until she was calmer, clearer, before she tried to voice them.

She shivered as she scraped cat food from a can into Max's dish. She turned on the faucet to give him some water, but nothing came out.

"The pipes are frozen."

She stiffened at the gruff sound of Torch's voice, but

didn't turn to face him. Instead she shrugged and opened the refrigerator, pouring a little milk into Max's dish.

"Are you all right?"

She set the bowl of milk into the microwave, closed the door, hit the buttons. "Why wouldn't I be?"

He didn't reply. The microwave hummed as thirty seconds ticked by on the digital panel and the timer beeped. She tested the milk with her forefinger before setting it on the floor. Max dove into it, tail straight in the air.

"You spoil that cat."

"I love him," she said. She finally turned around, out of excuses to keep her back to him. Then she blinked. Torch wore a pair of her father's trousers, olive drab, with grass stains on the knees. A memory jabbed her heart. Father, kneeling in that stupid little flower bed out front. No more than three feet by two feet. A small strip that had obsessed him, toward the end. Always digging.

Torch plucked at the front of the sweater he wore. "My clothes are still wet. I hope it's okay that I borrowed some of your father's."

"They fit you." She blinked again, looking him up and down, almost laughing at the bitter irony. "I guess I shouldn't be surprised, should I? You have so much in common."

She saw his frown, saw his lips part as if to ask her to explain that remark, or to deny it. But he seemed to think better of it. He clamped his jaw shut.

"I probably should have said something before, but the furnace has been broken since October. I've been meaning to get it fixed, but—"

"Listen."

She tilted her head, and in a moment realized the ancient oil burner in the basement was running. She lifted her brows in surprise.

"The gun was clogged," he told her, as if she'd know exactly what he meant. "It just needed cleaning out."

She nodded. "That's good. When the house warms up, the pipes will thaw on their own."

"Not that it matters," Torch said slowly. "We're not staying."

"Maybe you're not," Alexandra replied. "But I am."

"Alex, just because no one is here now doesn't mean they aren't watching the place. They might check in from time to time."

She shrugged. "I'm staying. I…need to be here, right now."

Torch frowned until his brows touched. "Why the hell do you need to be here?"

"I don't know yet." She looked at the way her hands were clasped together, wringing each other, and made them stop, bringing them deliberately down to her sides. "I just feel I have to be here. And nothing you can say is going to make me leave. If you want to go so badly, go by yourself."

"You know damned well I'm not going to leave you here alone!"

"Why not, Torch? Why the hell not?"

"Because you could end up dead."

She lifted her brows, searching his face. "That would be a real strong argument, Torch, if you could only name one person who'd give a damn." She strode past him, heading for the stairway, wanting only to go back up to her warm bedroom and put on her heaviest sweater. She was halfway up the stairs when his voice came from the bottom, stopping her.

"Mason 'Torch' Palamaro," he said, and his voice was very low, very soft, "would give a damn."

A chill ran up her spine, and she closed her eyes as all the air left her lungs. She had to fight to breathe again.

"I wasn't trying to force you to say that," she whispered, knowing that was exactly what she'd been trying to do, consciously or not.

"I know."

She turned slowly, met his eyes, saw the turmoil in them. This wasn't easy for him. He was hurting so much. It was palpable, his pain. He was almost writhing with it, and she wanted to ease it for him. She offered him a smile that felt weak, and lifted her brows. "Mason, huh?"

His lips turned up a little at the corners, and the confusion in his eyes cleared. "Yeah. And that's the last time I want to hear you say it."

"All right...*Mason*." She turned around and continued up the stairs. Torch followed, making angry noises. Ignoring him, she went back into the bedroom, rubbing her arms and hurrying to stand close to the fireplace. He came in behind her, but she noticed his hesitation in the doorway.

God, he really was scared to death of her, wasn't he?

After a moment's apparent indecision he came inside and closed the door.

"You, uh...you can bring the cat, if you want," he said, coming to stand beside her. Not too close beside her. Not even close enough.

She realized with a little surprise that she wanted to be close to him, close enough to feel his body heat and hear the pounding of his heart. She wanted to be wrapped up in his arms.

"Bring the cat where?"

"To the camper." He glanced down at her with a wary frown.

"I told you, I'm not going back to the camper."

He swore a long stream, turning in a slow circle, ruffling his hair with one hand. "I thought we settled this."

"We didn't settle a thing. I said I was staying here and I meant it."

"And what about Scorpion's thugs?"

"What *about* them? Torch, they'll find us just as quickly if we leave. There's no way we can get out of here without leaving clear tracks in that new snow out there, unless you sprouted wings overnight."

He opened his mouth. Then he closed it again. Frowned, shook his head, opened his mouth. Closed it again. Finally he lifted his hands, palms up. "Okay. All right. We'll stay."

Alexandra felt her brows shoot upward in surprise. She tilted her head, questioning him without a word.

"When you're right, Alexandra, you're right. We're staying."

She smiled fully. She'd half expected him to spout some obvious, simple solution to the problem of tracks, one that had eluded her. It was nice to be right once in a while, she decided.

And he smiled, too, as if he knew every thought that went through her mind. So she held his gaze, and she thought about the way it felt when he kissed her, when he touched her. His smile faded, and his gaze dipped lower, skimming over her neck and down the front of her robe.

"It's cold," he said. "Why don't you get dressed while I try to find something for breakfast."

She nodded, but he was gone so quickly she wasn't certain he ever saw it.

Chapter 11

He *wanted.*

It had been a very long time since he'd *wanted* like this. Every time she looked at him with those big brown eyes, he had to battle an urge to pull her into his arms. He wanted to hold her very close, very gently, and rock her and warm her, and whisper soft words into her ears. He wanted to kiss her. At the oddest moments, for no apparent reason, he kept wanting to cover her moist, warm lips with his. He was craving her taste. He'd never experienced feelings this intense. Not ever. And he didn't want to experience them now.

Dammit, I'm not ready!

A voice from within laughed at him, and he cringed. Hell, there was no use dwelling on all of this now, anyway. There was one thing in his future, and only one thing. The capture and murder of Scorpion. Torch had nothing to lose, and he wouldn't be able to pull this thing off if that were no longer the case. Nothing to lose meant

nothing he wouldn't do. Nothing he wouldn't give up.
Nothing he wouldn't risk in order to get the bastard. It
was Torch's mission in life, his one chance to make up
for letting his family down. For getting them killed. He
might end up in prison because of it, but that was a price
he was willing to pay. He might end up dying in the
effort to bring Scorpion down. That, too, was a risk
worth taking.

Already his determination was compromised, and it
ate at his guts to know it. He was not, he admitted,
willing to risk Alexandra's life to get Scorpion. Which
was why he had to get that formula and get her the hell
out of here before Scorpion showed up.

By late afternoon the house was warm and the water
was running again. From the looks of the robin's-egg
sky and blinding sunlight, he figured the main roads
were probably cleared by now. If the lawyer had been
coming home today, he'd have been able to get through.

He sat on a cream-colored settee with scrolled hardwood arms and legs, near the window, sipping coffee.
Alexandra came in and sat beside him, and his arm
moved. He caught himself in the nick of time. He'd
damn near slipped his arm around her shoulders and
drawn her close. His body seemed to function on automatic pilot when she got near him. It had all these im-
pulses that just came without consulting his brain for
permission. Damn, he'd never been so out of control
before.

"I don't think I thanked you for coming after me last
night," she said.

Her eyes. Damn how they got to him. She should have
been just fine out there in the forest last night. She
looked so much as if she belonged there.

"I can't imagine how you managed to carry me all the way back here…with your shoulder, I mean."

His shoulder. Funny, how he hadn't given it a second thought last night. It ached now, and common sense said it must have been hurting then. But he'd been too focused on Alex to notice.

"So…anyway…thanks. You saved my life."

"You can thank me by promising not to leave me like that again." He blinked twice. The words hadn't come out the way he'd intended. "I mean—"

"I promise."

Intense, those eyes. Damn, she was reading more into this whole thing than there was.

"It's about time I head out," he managed to say, thinking it high time they changed the subject. "Maybe McManus is home by now. I'll take you to the camper, get you settled in there, before I go on into town."

"You're going alone?"

He nodded. "After last night—after you almost froze to death in the woods last night, I mean—I don't think hiking down this mountain is exactly what you ought to be doing."

"James won't give you my things if I'm not there." She sipped her own coffee, and a tendril of steam rose in front of her face. "Besides, we don't have to walk."

"I know you have a car in the garage," he told her. "I saw it out there the first night. But even if Scorpion's thugs didn't do something to disable it before they broke in that first time, we couldn't drive through all that snow."

She smiled mysteriously. "We don't have to walk."

"What are we gonna do, Alex? I still haven't sprouted wings, and I don't see any sled dogs nearby."

She laughed and Torch went silent, just listening. He

loved to hear her laugh. Her voice was like smoke when
she spoke, but it became a drugging smoke when she
laughed. Entrancing. Mesmerizing. The fragrant smoke
of enchanted incense. Her eyes added to the magic by
lighting when she smiled. He liked that. And he liked
the way her eyeteeth were slightly crooked, and the way
the dimple in her left cheek seemed to wink at him,
and…

I'm not ready for this sort of thing.

Right.

She lowered her head, and a long lock of black satin
hair fell across her cheek. His hand rose up to push it
away and tuck it behind her ear. The feat was accomplished before he remembered to tell his hand not to do
that. She looked up again, still smiling.

"There's a snowmobile in the shed. And we have gas-
oline stored out there, as well. We won't need to walk
into town."

"Oh." It was all he could think of to say.

"So can I go with you?"

He was nodding before he could stop himself. And
the next thing he knew, Alex was in the hall closet,
pulling out heavy coats and mittens and a couple of plaid
woolen scarfs. "Helmets are in the shed, with the machine," she told him.

Torch nodded. He had a small bag of his own packed
and waiting near the door. Things he'd need if it turned
out the McManuses hadn't returned from their trip yet,
some picked from what was left of the equipment in the
duffel. Other stuff scavenged from around the house. He
ought to be thinking about how he would handle that
eventuality, because there was no question Alexandra
would argue.

She'd changed. Right before his eyes, in a matter of

a couple of days, she'd changed. There was something…that core of strength he'd sensed in her from the start, maybe. It wasn't so deeply buried anymore. She didn't have to fight so hard to find it now.

Seemed brushes with death agreed with the lady.

He had to give his head a shake when he realized he was standing still, staring at her, with what had to be a silly smile on his face.

It was no wonder she'd stayed here. Alexandra looked up at the last traces of red-orange sun blazing from the horizon, under a cloudless, multihued sky, as the machine beneath her sped over the snow. Pines with white puffs painting their boughs. Rolling, pristine white hills. It was beautiful here. Before, she'd seen it as a refuge. A place where she could hide from life and its frequent disappointments. Only tonight was she beginning to see the beauty around her.

Maybe because of the company.

She tightened her arms around Torch's waist, figuring she might as well take advantage of the current excuse to hold him. He was so tense, so tightly strung. More so now than he had been before they'd made love. She hoped that was because he couldn't deal with his feelings, and not because he simply didn't have any for her. But she wasn't at all certain that was the case. And she had no idea how to act toward him now.

He seemed to want to pretend last night had never happened. She couldn't forget it even if she tried. She wasn't sure, but she thought she might be falling in love with Torch Palamaro. Mason, she added silently, with a little smile. But the smile died. It was just like her to give her love to men who couldn't give any of their own in return. First her father. Now Torch. What was the matter with her?

Torch maneuvered the snowmobile through the forest, and then over the fire trail. It was dark when they finally emerged on the side of the main road that led into Pine Lake. As he drove, fine white powder rose in an arch behind them, and ice-cold air chilled her right through the heavy coat she wore. At least her face was protected behind the helmet's visor.

In the distance, a huge white circle stood out amid the snowy trees. The lake itself, almost completely frozen. Then the town loomed into view ahead. The first house they came to was James McManus's. And there wasn't a sign of anyone there.

Alexandra's heart fell when Torch pulled in anyway, driving the snowmobile around to the back before killing the engine. He tugged off his helmet. Alex dismounted the machine and removed her own.

"I don't think they're back yet."

"I think you're right," he told her. He swung a leg over the machine and got to his feet, snatching the little canvas bag from under the seat as he did. "As usual."

Torch started for the house, and Alex hurried to keep up. "What are you going to do?"

"Something you're going to have a fit about." He stopped at the back entrance, opened the storm door and tried the next one. "Locked." Opening the bag he'd brought along, Torch pulled out two long, pointy objects that looked like implements of torture, and inserted them into the keyhole.

"Torch!" Her whisper was loud and insistent. "You *can't* break in."

He glanced over his shoulder at her, eyebrows dancing up and down. "I just did." With a twist of his hand, he opened the door. And he stepped inside without a sign of remorse. His form was swallowed by the darkness. There was a soft click, and then the glow of his flashlight. "Come on, Alex. We don't have all night."

She hesitated in the doorway, gnawing her lower lip. A "snap" broke the silence of the night like a gunshot, and she spun around. Squinting, she scanned the backyard from one side to the other. The rising moon's light made everything clear, right up to the tree line. She couldn't see a thing beyond those first few trees. Standing motionless, she listened, waited. Goose bumps rose on her flesh when she saw something move. Her breath whooshed out of her when she realized it was a pine bough swaying in the wind. But what was that noise?

"Probably just an animal. A deer or something," she assured herself, remembering the deer she and Torch had seen before. And their snowball fight. And she felt warm and safe again.

Squaring her shoulders in resolve, she stepped inside and closed the door.

"Here." Torch pressed the flashlight into her hands. "Lead me to McManus's office."

"It's in the basement." She bit her lip. "There's a separate entrance. I should have told you—"

"I saw it already. This was the easiest lock. Lead on."

Alexandra made her way through the McManuses' kitchen, feeling like a thief in the night, which was exactly what she was at the moment, come to think of it. She searched her memory banks. She'd only been to the office twice, but both times Mrs. McManus had insisted she come into the kitchen for coffee or tea. And the basement door, as she recalled, was right...

"Here," she said, and pushed it open. She took a step

downward, only to gasp in surprise when Torch's arm snagged her waist.

"Easy," he whispered. "I just don't want you to fall."

She closed her eyes, resisting the impulse to lean back against him, or to tip her head sideways so she could press her ear to those lips whispering so close to it. Instead, she drew a deep breath and moved on. More slowly now, though. And instead of worrying about being guilty of breaking and entering, she was wondering why he'd be so concerned about her falling if he didn't care about her. And wondering if he felt the same chills and tingles of awareness that she did whenever he touched her.

She reached the bottom. He let go of her. Her disappointed sigh was involuntary, and he couldn't have missed it. He was still too close. She turned left at the base of the stairs, moving the flashlight's beam around until it landed on the office door.

"That's it, Torch."

Torch went to it, tried the knob. "Shine the light on this lock, Alex."

She did. This time he didn't bother with the tools. A simple credit card maneuver that even she was familiar with, and this door surrendered as the first one had. It swung slowly inward, into darkness even more inky than that filling the rest of the house. And then she remembered why. "There are no windows in here, Torch. You can turn the light on."

He did, filling the square oak-paneled office in light. "That will help." Torch turned slowly, scanning the desk's many coffee stains and uneven stacks of envelopes and scattered notes on scraps of paper. He shook his head and turned to the filing cabinet. "Hey, what do you know?'' He pulled a drawer open. ''Unlocked. Let's see, Hollister, Holstein…ah, there we are. Holt, Alexander.'' The file folder slid from the drawer with an ominous hiss.

Alex stiffened, wondering if its contents would shatter everything she'd ever believed about her father. Or vindicate him, as she'd been insisting all along they would.

Torch set the folder on the desk and, to her surprise, stepped away. She looked up and met his steady gaze. ''Go ahead,'' he told her. ''He was your father. You have every right to look first.''

Nodding, she pulled out the chair and sat down. Then, hands trembling, she flipped open the folder. Her father's will sat on top. Beneath that, the letter he'd left behind describing the funeral arrangements he preferred. The cremation. Odd that he'd never mentioned that to her. She never would have guessed he'd prefer that to burial. She flipped more pages, found more papers and finally came to a copy of the one she'd signed, giving James permission to retrieve the contents of the safe-deposit box for her. There was a note on the bottom. It said simply, ''Safe.''

She read the word aloud, lifting her head slowly, turning it until she met Torch's eager stare.

He frowned. ''Safe?''

She nodded, lifting the paper to him, showing him the notation. Torch turned slowly around the room, scanning the walls, stopping when his gaze fell on a tacky painting of dogs playing poker on the wall to the left. He went to it, lifted it down, revealing the small wall safe the painting had been concealing.

''Oh.'' If the single word conveyed a wealth of disappointment, it was no wonder. Alexandra had been hoping to find the truth once and for all tonight. "I guess we're out of luck."

"Sweetheart," he said, and there was a gleam in his eyes. "You're forgetting how I got my nickname."

Alex felt her eyes widen as she leapt to her feet. "You *can't*—"

"I won't hurt anything but the safe, and we'll reimburse them for that."

She shook her head.

"Come on, Alex. What's more important? An international time bomb, or the chance we might mess up some lawyer's office?"

"It's just not…" She'd been turning in a circle out of sheer frustration as she spoke, and then she stopped. "Look! The light on the answering machine is blinking."

"So?"

"Well, if we listen to the messages, we might find out they're on their way home right now. We might find out they'll be here later tonight or early tomorrow. And if that's the case, we don't really need to do this." She turned to face him, lifting her hands. "Do we?"

He grimaced. His chin fell to his chest. But he came forward, reached past her, and pressed the playback button.

Beep.

"James, this is Scotty Mitchell. Five-five-five-six-eight-nine-oh. Call me when you get in."

Beep.

"Wendy, here. Don't forget the bake sale at church, a week from Sunday. You'll be back in time, right? Talk to you soon."

Beep.

Torch glanced at Alex and shook his head to indicate

his opinion of what this effort would produce. But he froze, and the color drained from his face as the next message began to play.

"Hi, Grandma! Hi, Grandpa!" said the child's voice, bubbling with excitement. "Mommy says we're coming to visit you for Thanksgivin'!"

"Ah, God…" Torch gripped the edge of the desk as if he'd sink to the floor without it.

The little voice went on, but Alex hit the button to stop it. Then she turned to him, her hands on his shoulders, her eyes searching his tormented face. "I'm sorry. Are you all right?"

His face was twisted in a grimace of agony, eyes closed tightly, lips thin and pale. "I will be," he whispered. "Just as soon as I kill that murdering bastard."

She took a step closer, hearing pain beyond the anger in his voice, wanting to hold him, to comfort him. But Torch spun away from her, snatching up the bag he'd brought along and taking it with him to the spot in front of the safe. He yanked a chair over there, dumping the bag's contents onto it, and then he was playing with something that looked like clay.

His entire countenance was meant to warn her away. She couldn't reach him in that place where his pain sent him. So she didn't even try.

Minutes ticked by, and he was pressing his clay stuff to the safe, sticking little probes into it. He unrolled wire from a spool as he stepped backward through the room. He backed right out the door, motioned for her to come with him. Then he closed the door, with the wire running underneath it, and finally cut the wire from his spool. Taking a small, electronic-looking device from his pack, Torch attached the wires to it, then held it in one hand. He used his other hand to push her behind him. Then

he moved a knob or a button on the device, and there
was a firecracker-size pop in the office. It made her
jump, but that was all. For a bomb, it hadn't seemed too
terrible.

"Stay here."

She did. When he opened the door, she smelled the
heat, saw the faint tendrils of smoke. Torch went back
inside the office, and a few minutes later, the light went
off, and he emerged with a thick manilla envelope and
the flashlight. He shone the beam on the handwriting
across the front of the envelope. "Holt."

"This is it," she said, and her mouth went dry.

"Maybe." Torch tucked the envelope inside his coat,
reached to grip her hand and started up the stairs.

He was silent all the way back. Silent and angry. And
she didn't have a clue what she could do to help him.

He didn't just want, anymore. He *needed.* Dammit,
when she touched him, she reached past the pain.
Through it. Her very presence soothed the ache. Just
looking at her eased the torture he'd lived with day and
night for the past year. And he was getting used to that.
He'd almost grabbed her when he'd heard that little
boy's voice on the machine. He'd almost wrapped his
arms around her and buried his face in her hair. Like
she was some kind of refuge. Like she could make it all
right. Like if he only held on to her tightly enough, he'd
find salvation. Redemption. Hope.

It was so damned ridiculous it was almost laughable.
Only Torch wasn't laughing. There was no room in
his life for anything like this. No room for *her.* Only
vengeance. Alexandra Holt would take up too much
space. She'd shove vengeance right out of his soul and

fill it with her own brand of goodness instead, if he let her. He knew she would.

He couldn't let that happen. He had to resist with everything in him, and he had to get away from her.

One more night, he vowed. Because tonight he'd find the truth and tonight he'd make arrangements to get Alexandra to safety. Far away from him. Then he'd deal with Scorpion.

That voice, the precious voice on the tape had reminded him why he was here, what his job was. Thank God for that voice.

The house was warm when they returned. He found he was beginning to like the place. Somehow, she'd taken a cold, Gothic monstrosity of a house and made it cozy. Cheerful. Even comforting. The marble fireplace was trimmed in darkly stained woodwork. But the wallpaper was classic Alex. Soft green swirls of vines and leaves on an ivory background. A forest within a forest. She could scamper into that wallpaper and be right at home.

The sofa was an overstuffed teddy bear of brown velour that hugged you when you sat on it. Eggshell-colored drapes, to match the settee, pale green carpeting, light-colored hardwood end tables and rocking chairs with quilted cushions.

He stood there, looking through the parted drapes at the picturesque view of the moonlit night. And he thought that it was too bad, it was really too bad he had to keep his priorities in line. He might enjoy spending more time here.

And who the hell was he kidding? It had nothing to do with the house or the setting or that damned decor. It had everything to do with Alex.

The envelope was clasped in his hands. He tore it

open and pulled a leather-bound book from within. And
when he looked closer, he saw that it was a diary. There
was nothing else.

Well, maybe the formula was in the diary. He
wouldn't give up hope just yet. He opened the cover,
then paused, feeling her gaze on him as surely as he
would feel her touch. He turned away from the window
to face her. Alex stood across the room, near the fire.
Her wide brown eyes filled with more fear than he'd
ever seen in them.

He licked his lips and closed the cover. "A diary is
pretty personal. Maybe you ought to read it first." He
held it out to her.

She came forward, slowly, her legs none too steady.
She extended a hand that trembled as it closed on the
supple leather. The way she looked at that diary in her
hands, he thought she half expected it to grow teeth and
bite her arm off.

She dragged her eyes upward, away from the dreaded
book, to his face. "I will. Not…just yet though."

"Alex—"

"Please. I need some time. I need to…to have…"

"We don't *have* time," he told her. Her brown eyes
pleaded with him, and he felt his granite heart rapidly
turning to mush.

"I've been through more in the past few days than
I've had to deal with in a lifetime, Torch. I need a little
normalcy to bolster me. I can't just wade into that diary
without something." He shook his head, but she went
right on. "A hot bath," she whispered. "A decent meal.
A glass of wine. That's all I'm asking for. Surely we
have time for that."

Knowing full well they didn't, knowing full well
Scorpion could come bursting through the front door

with a machine gun and blow him in half any second now, Torch fell into those velvety brown eyes and said, ''Sure we do. Go ahead, Alex. Get your normalcy fix. The book will wait.''

Chapter 12

But that wasn't good enough for her, was it? Oh, no. Not for Alexandra Holt, the nurturer. The woman who steadfastly defended a father who'd treated her like dirt, and was now soothing the damned soul of a man beyond redemption.

It wasn't enough for her to have her precious normalcy. She had to inflict it on him, as well. And dammit, it was hard enough being near her when people were shooting at them. *This* bull was almost *impossible*.

He was afraid she had a repeat of last night on her mind. But when she came down from her hour-long soak in the tub wearing sweats and a ponytail, he decided that theory might be off the mark. She'd suggested he take a bath, as well, but he'd settled for a quick shower. And when he'd rejoined her there was a fire snapping in the living room hearth. He knew it before he got to the foot of the stairs. He smelled the burning logs, heard the snapping and hissing of the resin.

And he smelled something else, too. Something spicy and Italian that made him hurry his pace. But he slowed it again when he saw the dancing candlelight in the living room. Half a dozen blue tapers chased lively shadows up and down the walls.

He lifted his chin, swallowed hard. He didn't want to go to bed with her again. Much as he'd denied it all day long, that first time had damn near shattered his sanity. It had been too intense. Too hot. Too frantic. And just too damned good.

He hadn't stopped thinking about the way it had felt to hold her in his arms since. At least, not until he'd heard that voice on the McManuses' answering machine. That voice jerking him back to reality the way a pail of ice water would have done.

How could he have forgotten so easily in Alexandra's arms?

It was wrong. And he wouldn't let it happen again. He had to keep his focus, keep his anger, his hatred, alive and burning. He had to.

She came in from the kitchen with a wineglass full of pale pink liquid in each hand. "Thought you could use a little relaxation, too." She handed him one.

He took it, sipped it.

"Dinner's almost ready. Pasta marinara."

"You waxing domestic on me, Alex?" His words came out sounding sarcastic and cold. She flinched and her lips thinned. But that wasn't enough for the bastard inside him. "Look, I don't know what you're expecting this to lead to, but it's not gonna happen. I told you, last night didn't mean a damned thing."

The stricken look in her eyes faded fast. It was replaced by a look of fury. She snatched the wineglass out of his hand and, with a flick of her wrist, applied its contents to his face.

"It's my house. If I feel like cooking I'll cook. If you don't like it, you can always leave."

Even as the last words left her mouth, she was spinning on her heel, leaving him there with wine dripping from his chin and burning his eyes. Maybe he was being just a little bit vain to think that seduction was what she had on her mind. But what the hell was he supposed to think?

He played with that idea for a while. Twenty minutes later she was back, a steaming plate of food in her hand, her wineglass brimming and the bottle tucked under her arm. There was more wine in her glass than there had been before. So she must be on her second. Or third.

She put the plate on the coffee table and sank onto the sofa, curling her legs under her body, sipping deeply from the glass.

"Don't hit the wine too hard, Alex. We have to stay sharp."

"You stay sharp," she snapped. "And if you want to eat, do it in the kitchen. I know it's a shock, Torch, but I don't want your company right now."

He rose to the bait, though he should have known better. With a meaningful glance at the firelight and candles, he said, "You could have fooled me."

"Contrary to your conceited assumptions, Palamaro, the fire and the candles are for my benefit, not yours. They relax me when it feels like things are falling ap—" She licked her lips, cleared her throat. "If that brain of yours knew how to function, you might recall I had a fire and candles burning that first night you showed up to rain chaos down on my entire life."

She had a point. There had been candles glowing that

night. And she hadn't been seducing anyone then. He drew a breath, thinking maybe he had been wrong.

"I'm sorry if I jumped to the wrong—"

"I don't think there's anything wrong with me. I really don't." She drained the wine, reached for the bottle, refilled her glass.

"Who said there was anything wrong with you?" He frowned, worried. She was going to get plastered if she kept it up. Her gaze seemed fixated on the dancing firelight, so he took the bottle and set it on the floor beside the sofa, out of her sight.

"Is there?"

He swallowed hard. She hadn't touched her food. "No, Alex, there's nothing wrong with you."

She met his eyes. She wasn't drunk. If she was, he wouldn't be able to see the hurt in them.

"You lie," she said. "There are lots of things wrong with me. The asthma, for starters. And then there's the fact that I can never have children. I don't suppose your background checks on me turned up that little tidbit, did they?"

Torch flinched when she said it. "You can't believe that would matter to me."

"Matters to me," she told him, and he could tell by the pain in her eyes that it did. It mattered very much.

"Alex…"

She shook her head, heaved a long sigh. "This isn't working. I can't relax and pretend things are fine. My brain just isn't buying it." She closed her eyes. "Hand me that stupid book, and then please leave me alone while I read it."

He pursed his lips and finally nodded. He was only just beginning to realize how much she dreaded reading her father's diary. Maybe she sensed something.

Maybe…somewhere deep inside her, it was something she'd known for a long time but hadn't acknowledged. Now she'd be forced to see the truth, ready or not.

He should have been a little more understanding about this.

"Okay." He took the book from the mantel, carried it to the sofa, set it down beside her. She didn't even look at it. "Are you sure you'll be okay alone?"

"I've always been okay alone, Torch."

It wasn't what she wanted to say. What she wanted to say was that he was the biggest fool she'd ever seen in her life. That if he'd just let go of his anger, he'd realize there was more to live for than revenge. She'd thought she might be able to get him to do that tonight. She'd foolishly thought with a few comfort items like candlelight and food and wine, he might relax enough to open up his eyes and see her, and maybe…maybe let her into his heart. She only wanted to help him, couldn't the idiot see that?

No. He could only see that she wanted him, which, okay, she did. But he wanted her, too. Physically at least. He was too damn bent on vengeance to let her get close to him emotionally. Or maybe it wasn't the vengeance keeping him at a distance. Maybe he just didn't think she was good enough for that kind of closeness. Maybe he saw her as lacking in some way, just as Father always had.

Father.

She glanced down at the book beside her, swallowed the cold fear in her throat and opened it to the first page. She reached over the arm of the sofa, unerringly closing her hand on the bottle Torch thought he had hidden. Refilling her glass once more, she began reading.

* * *

She'd said to leave her alone. He didn't. Not really. He left for a few minutes, long enough to eat a plateful of food and pour a glass of milk, though he was dying to sample that wine *internally*. And when he finished, he went very quietly into the big foyer, where the stairs landed. He sat down on the bottom step, his milk in his hands, and he watched her.

She read. Her hands trembled a little, then a little more. Blinking as if dazed, she laid the book down, staring straight ahead. What she was seeing, though, wasn't in the living room with her. It was in her mind. And whatever it was, it wasn't pleasant. Not with those tears springing into her eyes. Not with her lower lip quivering that way.

Grating her teeth, squeezing her eyes tight, drawing three deep breaths, she seemed to gird herself. Then she looked at the pages again, and she read some more.

It was killing him not to go in there. At first, his eagerness had been based on his hope there would be references to the formula in the diary. But that concern had faded now to the dimness of a pinprick of light from a distant galaxy. Now all he wanted to know was what that book could hold that would hurt Alexandra like this. Because it *was* hurting her. Pain etched itself more deeply into her face with every page she turned. Torch knew pain. He knew it too well not to see it cutting her heart to ribbons right now. And he wanted to go to her.

It was an hour before she stopped reading. She looked shell-shocked when she closed the cover, laid her father's diary on the table and got to her feet. Her knees wobbled, but he was there before she could fall. He grabbed her shoulders, and the warmth of her skin sank right into his palms. He wanted to hold her. Lord, how he wanted to hold her.

"Let go."

Two words. A harsh whisper wrapped in hurt and anger. He didn't let go. He pulled her to his chest and slid his arms around her. He stroked her hair, wishing he could snap the band that held it captive. "What is it, Alex? What did the bastard write that hurt you this bad?"

With a strength that surprised him, she pulled free. He didn't try to hold her when she did. Her eyes were tear glazed and distant when they met his.

"You don't care. Why are you asking when you know you don't care?"

Torch gave his head a shake. She bent over the coffee table, and when she straightened, she held the diary out to him. "Here. Take it. It's what you came for. It's why you stayed. Take it and read it. Maybe your precious answers are in there. I don't know. I couldn't...didn't finish it."

"Alex—"

She pressed the book into his hands and turned away, the ponytail snapping with the motion. Torch threw the diary onto the floor. "I don't give a damn about the book right now, Alex." He touched her shoulder, and she stopped walking away from him but didn't turn around. "Come on, talk to me. Tell me what's wrong, maybe I can help."

"I don't need your kind of help, Torch. Just..." She drew a breath, tears shuddering on its surface like dew on a windblown leaf. "Just leave me alone."

She ran away, out of the room and up the stairs. He heard the bedroom door slam, and that was all.

"Damn."

His gaze was drawn downward, to the diary on the floor. He could go upstairs after her, but he had a feeling she wouldn't tell him a thing. Or, he could leave her alone as she'd asked and read the book for himself.

He squatted on his haunches and picked it up.

Alexandra lay facedown on the bed, crying, heartbroken. He'd never loved her. Her father had never...

No. Not her father. He hadn't even been her father.

The words he'd printed in his poisonous ink, about her mother, were etched indelibly in Alexandra's mind. "I couldn't stand the woman. Marrying her was the biggest mistake of my life. And I should have known all along the brat she carried wasn't mine. When she died shortly after giving birth, I was hoping the child would die along with her. It didn't. And its mother held on long enough to name her after me. No doubt she hoped the irony would get to me every time I spoke that name."

"All those years," Alex whispered, and she slowly sat up. She brushed the hot tears with the back of one hand and was surprised when no fresh ones fell to singe her face. "All those years, bending over backwards to please him. But it didn't matter what I did, what I *was* or what I became. None of it mattered."

She felt her eyes dry, felt the salt on her skin. "None of it mattered," she said again, and finally it was beginning to sink in. Her eyes were opening. She was understanding. It hadn't been that she wasn't good enough. It had never been that. She could have been crowned queen of the world and he still wouldn't have loved her. She could have won the Nobel prize for medicine, and he still would have despised her.

She shook her head, frowning. "It wasn't me. It wasn't me, it was him." Pushing both hands through her hair, she sat, stunned, on the edge of the bed. It wasn't a revelation, though. Not really. It was merely confirmation of something she'd been feeling for a very long time. But she'd been unable to acknowledge it. Because if it were true, then it would mean her father was no good and selfish and cruel. Truly unworthy of her love, just as Torch had said, and not the other way around. But he was the only one she had to love. So rather than face the truth, she'd seen her entire life through the warped glass of a lie. Like seeing her reflection in a fun house mirror. She'd let herself feel inadequate, unintelligent, not worthy of the great man's love, when deep down, she'd known better. None of those things were his reason for resenting her, even despising her. Those reasons didn't exist.

Alex sniffed and yanked open the drawer in the nightstand. Her photo album lay there, and she took it out now. Opened the cover. There she was five years old, getting on the school bus for the first time. The mother of the little boy next door had taken the picture, certainly not her own father. Alex happened to be in the shot because they got on the bus together. And the woman had sent her son in with a copy for her a week later.

She'd been terrified to get on that big yellow bus. Her father had called her a coward.

"But I wasn't," she whispered, remembering now more vividly than she ever had before. "That boy... Jimmy...he was just as scared as I was. But his mother came to the bus with him. She hugged him hard, and promised she'd be waiting right there in the same spot when he came home that afternoon."

The pain in her heart softened then and began to change form, to alter into something else. She flipped the page.

There was the shy little girl in the second-grade production of *The Wizard of Oz.* Only she'd had no proud parent in the audience. Her father had said he might be willing to take the afternoon off if she'd gotten the lead role, but he certainly wasn't missing work to see her play an extra.

"I thought if I could only be better...just be better, he'd love me."

The pain became an ember, and as she flipped more pages, relived other disappointments, other times when he'd made her feel worthless, the ember glowed hotter and brighter. And she found that she was capable of feeling anger toward a man for whom she'd never allowed herself to feel anything but love. More than love. Sheer adoration. Idolatrous hero worship. She'd *ached* to win his affection. But he'd never once given it.

"Damn you," she whispered, when she flipped a page and found a photo of him, accepting some award. She stood up, tearing the cellophane away, peeling the photo from the book, holding it at arm's length in a white-knuckled grip, and she said it again, louder this time. "Damn you! How could you do that to a child who adored you? How?"

Rage welled higher, flooding her soul and spilling out of her. It had built there all her life, but it had been denied. No more. No more.

"It wasn't me, you selfish bastard! Do you hear me? It was never me. It was you! You're the one who wasn't good enough. You didn't deserve the love I lavished on you. And you were wrong to throw it away! You were stupid to throw it away! And so is that idiot downstairs!"

Crumpling the photograph into a tiny wad, she drew a shuddering breath and she felt strong. She felt free of a terrible burden she'd carried too long.

"I *am* good enough," she told the wad in her hands.
"I always was. You were too filled with hatred to see
it. And Torch…Torch is too filled with guilt, and this
damned quest for vengeance of his. I love him. I love
him a hundred times more than I ever loved you!" She
fell to her knees in front of the hearth, her chin falling
to her chest, her eyes filling again, blurring the crushed
photograph she still held. "But he can't return that feeling any more than you could, can he, Father? No. No,
of course he can't. And I'll tell you something, Father,
I'm through. I'm not going to waste any more of my
heart on men too stupid to know how much they're
throwing away when they decide I'm not worthy of their
love. I *am* worthy, dammit. And one of these days, I'll
find someone who's worthy *of me.*"

She opened her clenched hands and tossed the photograph into the fire. Red flames licked at it, devoured
it, turned it into a charred ball of ash, which she thought
resembled her father's black soul. "I will," she whispered. "I swear to God, I will."

"Alexandra…"

She stiffened, not turning at the sound of Torch's
hoarse voice coming from the bedroom doorway. How
long had he been there? How much had he heard?

It didn't matter, did it? She'd made a decision. She
thought maybe she was beginning to know herself as she
truly was for the very first time.

She got to her feet, choosing to ignore the intrusion.
Crossing the bedroom, she opened the closet and located
a cardboard box in the back. Bending to it, she flipped
it over, emptying its contents onto the floor and tossing
the box onto the bed. Then she crossed the room again,
her steps fast and sure. Her hands closed on the photo
album, and she slung it into the box.

Torch came inside. She felt him coming to her, and then his hands rose, as if to close on her shoulders. But they paused in midair, hovering, uncertain. And finally he lowered them to his sides again as she returned to the nightstand.

It was the framed portrait of her father she snatched up this time. She threw it at the box as if she were trying to pulverize it. The satisfying sound of breaking glass came to her with the impact.

"I know you're angry," he said. "You have every right to be."

She tipped her jewelry box upside down, shaking the contents onto the dresser, shoving the piles around. The class ring. He'd complained about the cost but finally shelled out the money for it in lieu of a birthday present. It felt hard and cold in her palm, and then it sailed through the air like a missile, the box its target.

"Will you stop? Will you just talk to me for a minute? Please?"

The painting. The damned painting on the wall just outside her room. A dull gray abstract thing she'd always detested. She lunged into the hall, yanking it from the wall so hard she cracked the frame.

"Alex!"

"He said I'd like it if I were smarter. He said I simply didn't understand complex geometric design, that it was beyond the scope of my intelligence." She carried it with her into the bedroom and, holding it by its sides, she lifted it, then brought it crashing down on a bedpost. The post tore through the canvas. She ripped it free and threw it into the box.

Torch grabbed her arm. "Stop this. Alex, we have to talk."

She stood still, panting with her rage. She couldn't look at him, she couldn't...

His fingers touched her face, lifted her chin, and she met his eyes. "I'm sorry, Alex. I don't know what else to say."

She wanted to fold herself into his arms, just melt against his strong chest, and let him rock her, hold her. She wanted that so much!

But she stood still, unblinking. "Did you find what you wanted in the diary?"

He shook his head. Searched her face.

She was tired. Drained. Slowly her taut muscles unclenched, and she managed to stop grating her teeth and calm her breathing.

"Tell me what other bombshells you found in that damned book," she said, the words falling from her lips without inflection or emotion.

Torch cleared his throat. "He developed the formula deliberately, Alex. It was all prearranged. He made a deal with a terrorist to develop a chemical weapon capable of wiping out entire nations in short order, and that's exactly what he did. It's all in the diary."

"Chemical weapon?"

"A synthetic virus. He was paid a great deal of money for it."

Alex closed her eyes, nodding slowly. "He always complained he was unappreciated. Worthless bastard wasn't even capable of loyalty to his own country, was he? Or even to mankind."

"No."

Swallowing hard, she opened her eyes again, faced Torch's blue ones, wished she didn't see so much concern for her in their depths. "What else?"

Torch cleared his throat. "He collected half the

money up front, and was supposed to get the rest on delivery of the formula. But it seems he got cold feet.''

"Oh?"

"He accidentally exposed himself, Alex. Once he realized he was dying, he seemed to find a modicum of conscience. Either that, or he wanted time to try to develop a cure. Whatever his reasons, he decided to back out on the deal. He knew the man he was involved with wouldn't take that lying down, so he decided to drop out of sight.'' Torch searched her face. "For what it's worth, he waited until the incubation period had ended to contact you. He knew he was no longer contagious by then.''

"The man was a saint," she whispered.

"The man was a fool."

"So are you." She held his gaze for a long moment. He didn't argue. In fact, he lowered his eyes as if in silent concession.

She swallowed hard, looked away from him. "I'm a doctor. Why didn't I see symptoms of this virus before it killed him?"

"You couldn't have, Alex. The symptoms were subtle, and he only recognized them himself because of the research he'd been doing. Forgetfulness was one, which explains why we found that notebook page in his lab. The rest he could have hidden easily enough. Fatigue. Night sweats. And sudden death.''

True, Alex realized. All true. "Did the diary say what he did with his notes?"

Torch shook his head.

She sighed long and low. "That's it, then."

He looked up, met her eyes, brows raised in question.

"You wasted your time coming up here and dragging me into this whole thing," she said, and she fought to keep her voice level, to sound rational and calm. "And I really think it's time we ended it, don't you?"

"I can't leave, Alex. You know that."

She shrugged. "Then I will. You can have the place to yourself, Torch. Tear up the floorboards looking for the formula. Knock yourself out. I don't want anything more to do with it." She picked up the box she'd been filling, and started for the door.

"Alex, you can't just leave! Alex!"

He followed her, but she did her best to pretend he wasn't there as she descended the stairs. She carried the box through the foyer and to the front door, then balanced one side of it on her hip while she got the door open. She didn't hesitate. She stepped outside into the frigid air, and snow reached past her shoes to chill her ankles.

Torch was right behind her, yelling questions all the way, but she ignored him. This was between her and her father. The icy wind stinging her cheeks felt good. It cleared her head, numbed her heart a little to the hurt he'd inflicted so deeply for so long. She trudged through the snow, across the lawn, to the tiny rectangle that had been his garden. And there she tipped the box upside down, spilling its contents there on the snow.

"There you go, Father. You always preferred the company of this stupid patch of dirt to mine. You should have been buried right here. It would have suited you, wouldn't it? No time for a daughter who loved you. No. But plenty of time for all that puttering. Out here all the time, digging. Always digging. That was all you ever..."

Alexandra let the cardboard box fall from her hands, and she went still and silent, blinking down at the snow around her feet. And just like that, she knew. She simply, clearly *knew*.

Without lifting her head or turning to face Torch, she said, ''Get me a shovel.''

Chapter 13

He ought to be excited, knowing he was so close. But instead, as he aimed the flashlight's beam inside the shed, looking for the shovel, he was thinking about Alex. Trying to understand every emotion that she'd experienced in the past few hours. As if getting inside her head—inside her heart—had suddenly become more important than finding the formula. More important than getting Scorpion. More important than anything.

Ridiculous. He knew that. But still his mind worked the puzzle of Alexandra almost to the exclusion of anything else. She'd gone from devastation to rage, to something else in a matter of minutes. He still hadn't identified the final emotion. The one she'd reached as she'd stormed out into the snow. Acceptance maybe. And a determination to leave all of this behind her. To start fresh somewhere, without the emotional baggage she'd been lugging around all her life.

If only it were that easy.

Hell, when he'd heard her upstairs, ranting at her dead father, he'd had no choice but to go to her. He'd wanted to help her, to comfort her somehow. The way she'd managed to comfort him. He blinked in shock at the thought but slowly realized it was true. She *had* comforted him. She'd found a way, despite his determination not to let her. She'd reached right through his pain and she'd held his frozen heart in her gentle hands, warming it. Thawing it. She'd even begun to heal some of the fractures he'd thought went far too deep to mend.

He'd never known anyone who felt things as deeply as Alexandra did. To cry so easily for a pain that wasn't even her own...the way she'd cried when he'd told her about his family. And he'd never known anyone with a more soothing way about her. Every time she touched him, even if it was only with her eyes—no, *especially* when it was with her eyes—it felt as if she were coating his deepest wounds in a magical balm made of nothing more than her own essence.

She deserved better than what her father had given her. And in spite of himself, Torch knew she deserved better than what *he'd* given her.

Upstairs, when she'd been raging at her dead father, she'd blurted out that she loved him. *Him.* Torch Palamaro, a man so broken and battered that there was nothing left but a shell. Or was there?

He was beginning to think there might be, because he didn't *feel* like a shell of a man anymore. He felt as if maybe there was some spark of life left inside him. Something that had been comatose for the past year. Not quite as dead as he'd thought. He *felt* as if it had taken Alexandra's magic to stir it awake.

He located the tools, picked them up and pocketed the flashlight. Closing the door behind him, he walked back from the shed, a pick and a shovel anchored over his shoulder. *Hell of a time to be thinking this way, Palamaro. Hell of a time. Because if you dig up what you think you're going to, it's all over. Time to get her as far away from you as possible. Time to stash the formula somewhere safe and lay in wait for Scorpion. Time to exact the punishment he so richly deserves.*

No. There aren't going to be any fairy-tale endings. Not here. Not now. Not for you, Palamaro. Never for you.

He dropped the pick and shovel onto the ground, half-hoping she was wrong about this, just to prolong his time with her. And he knew that was a foolish thought. But he also knew it was an honest one. Maybe the first honest one he'd had in quite a while.

"Come inside," she said, and her low, husky voice was nearly lost on the night wind. "We need coats, and gloves. Some more lights…"

"Yeah." He didn't want to stand around knee-deep in snow, digging in the frozen ground. He wanted to wrap her in his arms and carry her up those stairs and make her forget the pain she was feeling right now. The pain her father had caused. The pain he himself had added to.

But he knew that was impossible. He had a job to do. He owed a debt to his sons. He couldn't let them down.

She huddled deeper in her down-filled parka, wondering how on earth Torch could stand to work with no coat at all. He'd started out with one, but had shrugged it off as his body heated with the effort of breaking the frigid ground. He wore a sweater, a wool blend, pale brown like a deer's coat. One of her father's. He bent to his work, in the knee-deep hole he'd chipped from the frozen earth. Lumpy brown chunks of frosty ground lay scattered around him like cobblestones. He'd put an ugly brown scar in the snow's flawless face.

And then he stopped, staring downward, not blinking. "I think I found something."

He turned slowly to face her, and the red-orange glow of the kerosene lamps painted his face, made its sweat sheen glimmer.

Alex swallowed the lump in her throat. It wasn't fear of what she'd learn about her father this time. She'd already been dealt that blow. And it had staggered her and hurt her and taken her breath away. But she'd survived it. Her heart was sinking now for a far different reason.

They both knew that once the formula was found, their time together would end. It hadn't been spoken, but it was there, real and black and devastating. To her, at least.

She lifted her chin deliberately. "Let's see what it is."

He held her gaze for a long moment, and there was something there in the sapphire depths of his eyes, some fire in them that went beyond the lamplight they reflected. Then he dropped to his knees in the frozen dirt. Holding the shovel at the junction of metal and wood, using it like a whisk broom, he scraped the rest of the dirt away. When he tossed the shovel aside, he worked with his bare hands, digging down along the square outline's edges with his fingers. Alex picked up the flashlight they'd discarded in favor of the lamps, and aimed its beam down into the hole. Torch grated his teeth as he worked the box free. Yes, it was a box…made of metal, she saw as he finally pulled it up.

He stared at the box while she stared at him. "This is it," he said, his words so soft they were all but lost in the slight breeze that ruffled his sable hair. "It has to be. What else would he bury out here?"

Her throat burned. "There's a padlock."

Torch nodded. "That's easy to fix."

"You're not going to blow it up, are you?"

It should have been funny. He should have laughed and then she should have joined him. But instead he only looked into her eyes as his lips twisted in a sad little smile. She wanted to cry.

He set the box down on battered brown earth, reaching for the shovel again. Then he jammed the shovel's head down on the padlock...once, twice, again. And when he stopped, the lock had sprung free.

And again, he surprised her by seeming more eager to see what was going on in her eyes than what was inside that box. He paused, searched her face. "You want to go inside for this?"

Inside? Yes, she wanted to go inside. And she wanted to throw herself into his arms and beg him not to open that Pandora's box. Not yet, at least. She wasn't ready to say goodbye.

"No," she heard herself tell him, and oddly enough, her voice gave no indication of her turmoil. "Let's do it right here."

Torch nodded. He worked the misshapen padlock's hasp until it came free. He opened the box, And he pulled out a simple spiral notebook. The kind you could pick up at any drugstore for ninety-nine cents. The kind kids used to take notes in science class. It didn't look as if it were capable of destroying the world.

Torch dropped the box and stepped out of the hole onto the level, snowy ground nearer the lamps. He flipped open the cover. Without conscious volition, Alex moved closer to him. Her flashlight's beam illuminated the white pages, and her eyes scanned line after line of numbers and symbols. Some of which she understood, and others she'd never seen before.

She knew enough, though, to realize that this was a chemical formula. Any scientist worth his salt could create the virus that had killed her father, with no more than this notebook, the proper ingredients and a lab in which to work. A recipe for death, right there, in Torch's callused hands. Somewhere deep inside her, the new-found anger toward her father blazed to life all over again. To think she'd spent her life feeling unworthy of him! To think of the times she'd tried to please him, and of his constant disapproval! Damn him for his oversize ego and his unending criticism. Damn him!

"Well. Seems I've arrived just in time for the festivities."

She gasped, whirling at the familiar, whiny voice. Her surprise at seeing the monster standing there in the snow paralyzed her for an instant. It didn't dampen her anger. It only made her forget about it for the moment.

Scorpion stood not two feet away from them, a gun leveled on Torch. "I'll take that journal, Palamaro."

"The hell you will." Torch's low, level tone did nothing to disguise the fury beneath it.

Scorpion shook his head, smiling, chilling her with the evil that seemed to glow from his pink eyes whenever he looked at her. "You have two choices. I shoot you, and take the journal. Or you give me the journal—" his grin broadened "—and *then* I shoot you."

Alex must have moved, though she wasn't aware of it, because Scorpion's alien eyes jerked toward her all of a sudden. "As for *you,* pretty lady, you just stand perfectly still. You surprised me last time, but I won't make that mistake again. You're obviously not quite as brainless as your father thought.''

She said a word she'd never uttered in her life as a blinding, white-hot rage exploded in her brain. And her foot slammed down hard on the shovel, sending its handle upward, right between Scorpion's legs. The impact was fast and brutal and he fell to the ground howling.

Only it wasn't just an agonized howl. He was howling…a name, a command, even as Torch slammed the notebook into Alex's chest and leapt on Scorpion.

Lights blazed in the distance as some tank-size four-by-four bounced toward them. Its path vaguely followed that of the dirt road, crushing the snow that covered it. Its spotlight swung left and right, finally stopping when its beam illuminated the tangle on the ground where the two men struggled for the gun.

Alex acted without forethought, making a mad dash for the snowmobile they'd left parked near the front steps. And if she had given it any forethought, she might not have done it, because the second she stepped away from their boss, the men in the mutant pickup began shooting at her. Puffs of snow appeared in front of her feet where the bullets hit. She stuffed the journal inside her coat as she raced onward. Tires spun in snow as the approaching vehicle sought traction, then lurched, then spun, then lurched, making its way ever closer.

She swung onto the snowmobile, almost shouting in triumph when it started on the first try. Gunning it, she shot easily over the snow. And when she reached the spot where Torch and Scorpion still wrestled for the gun, she jerked the handlebars and hit the brake, skidding around sideways.

She screamed his name.

And she wasn't even sure he heard her. Then he

landed a blow to Scorpion's chin, and Scorpion's head snapped backward. Instead of proceeding with the main event, Torch shoved himself to his feet, gave one leap and landed squarely behind her on the seat. One of his arms wrapped around her waist, and his body bowed over hers, pushing her forward and down so she couldn't even see through the windshield. Then his other hand closed over hers on the throttle, and they shot off into the forest with bullets zinging after them.

He was frozen half to death by the time they reached the town. Not that it mattered, in the overall scheme of things, that he was shivering and his teeth were chattering. That was nothing compared to what would happen if those idiots in the four-by-four caught up to them.

Fortunately, by the time they got that oversize beast turned around and back down the mountain, he and Alex would be long gone.

He and Alex. He'd thought they'd be going their separate ways. That he'd remain behind to await Scorpion. But the bastard had shown up early and ruined his plans. And Torch found himself ridiculously glad.

He pulled the machine around behind the general store and killed the engine. And only then did it occur to him to ask. "Alex, where's the journal?"

She patted the front of her coat. "Right here. Don't worry."

As she said it, she turned to look at him over her shoulder, and he had to battle the urge to kiss her. And then he asked himself why he had to battle it, and he kissed her anyway.

It was brief. His lips caught hers, drew on them for a moment. He wanted more, but...

He cleared his throat. "There's a car out front."

"And we're going to steal it," she said, sounding less than pleased but sort of resigned.

"Borrow it. Come on." He got off the sled, took her hand and together they ran around the building. Torch glanced in through the driver's side window, and smiled when he saw the keys dangling from the switch. "Palamaro catches a break," he muttered, like some sportscaster calling a game. He nodded to Alex and she went to the other side.

When he jerked his door open, she did the same. They landed simultaneously in the front seat, and when the two doors slammed there was only one bang. By the time the old man who owned the station wagon was on the porch shaking his fist, they were rounding the first bend in the road, out of sight.

And as they got farther away and safety seemed almost within reach, Torch knew he wanted to say something or *do* something to let Alex know…know… *something*.

But what?

That he wanted her to stick around, maybe. Yeah, that he wanted her to stick with him a little longer. Long enough so he could figure out just what this…this *something* was going to turn out to be.

He opened his mouth to try to vocalize that, and he'd already said her name before he realized how utterly stupid it would sound.

He realized something else, too. This wasn't over. And he had no business even thinking about involving Alex in his future—if, indeed, that *was* where this train of thought was leading—until he knew he had one. The formula wasn't delivered yet. Beyond that, Scorpion was still breathing. Until Torch killed the bastard, there was no reason to think about anything else. Because he might very well die trying. And that wouldn't be fair to Alex.

She was looking at him, waiting for him to finish what he'd started to say. Those big dark eyes of hers drawing the heart right out of his body and into her own. She made love to his soul when she looked at him like that. How did she *do* that?

Torch cleared his throat. "You were fantastic back there. Saved our butts once again."

"I was mad. Too mad to be scared, I guess."

"You were smart. And yeah, mad as well. Too mad to take time to question your own judgment. You trusted your instincts. You ever notice how every time you do that, your instincts turn out to be right on target?"

She smiled at him, and his heart stopped. "Yeah. I *have,* actually."

He held her gaze, searching her eyes and seeing something in them he hadn't seen more than a hint of before. Pride. Self-confidence. Awareness of her own strength.

It was with a little regret that he jerked his attention back to the road ahead. He liked seeing those things in her beautiful eyes. It made them even prettier. Nodding slowly, he said, "It's about time."

Chapter 14

A hotel room. Cold, impersonal and sterile. It wasn't where he'd wanted to bring her. Everything in him, every cell in his body, it seemed, joined together in an insistent chorus of whispers, urging him to take her home. Home, to the houseboat bobbing serenely in the bay. To keep her there, safe from everything in the world outside. From Scorpion and his thugs. Even from Torch's own persistent demons. The ones that drove him. Were still driving him.

Hell, that idea had been taking shape in his mind for hours now. He wanted to take her into his home, into his life...and he wanted to ask her to stay. For a while, at least. He wanted to tell her that he wasn't sure he could ever be a whole human being again, but that he'd like it if she'd stick around and help him try to find out.

Maybe it wouldn't be fair of him to ask it of her. He didn't think he'd be able to get past the loss of his sons. Not ever. There was a huge part of him that had died with them. He didn't think he'd ever get that part of him back. But there was another part of him, a vital part, that was beginning to heal, and he knew that it was because of her. Selfishly, perhaps, he wanted that healing to go on. He wanted to keep her close to him, he wanted to try…to try to love her.

For a very brief moment in time, a moment that spanned from somewhere during their flight to Washington, D.C., to the present one, he'd seen the possibility of a future for him. A future that included Alexandra. It had hovered in the distance like a glimmering beacon of light at the end of a black, lifeless tunnel. For that one, fragile moment, he'd even thought he might be able to put aside his burning need to murder Scorpion.

But it had been only that. A brief moment in time. A split second when the possibility of moving past the pain and into a new stage of life—with Alexandra—had seemed logical, natural. Even attainable.

And then the moment had passed. Right here in this hotel room. It was shattered by three short, simple words coming through a telephone line.

"Scorpion is here."

Torch's grip on the receiver tightened painfully. His gaze followed Alexandra as she sat in front of a mirror and ran a brush through her long, satiny hair.

"Did you hear what I said, Torch? He's here, in Washington. He must have followed you."

"I hear you, D.C." Torch's voice was strained, and he tried clearing his throat. His ridiculous ideas about trying to make a future for himself and Alex dissolved like sugar in hot coffee.

"I can only assume his presence means you have the formula," D.C. said. "He wouldn't be following you otherwise. Am I right?"

"I have it."

There was a relieved sigh. "What about the Drs. Holt? We need to take them into custody, and it—"

"No." At the force he put into the single word, Alex turned from the mirror to stare at him. Those probing, innocent eyes, searching his face. He shifted in his chair but couldn't break the hold her eyes had on his. "The father is dead," Torch explained, more calmly. "And the daughter had no knowledge of his crimes."

D.C. was silent for a long moment. When he spoke, it seemed he chose his words carefully. "Torch...we'll take your findings into account, and they'll carry a lot of weight. But she has to be brought in. There has to be an investigation into her involvement, before—"

"No investigation, D.C. I want it clear, right now. No charges against Alexandra Holt. Give me your word, as a friend, or I won't bother bringing in the damned formula at all."

"Don't be ridiculous," D.C. said quickly. "If you don't turn it in, you don't get your money."

"You can take that money and—"

"All right!" He could hear the gulp as D.C. swallowed hard, then the long, slow breath he drew. "All right, Torch. Okay. You say she's innocent, she's innocent."

"She is."

Alexandra laid her brush on the dresser and stood up. She came to him while D.C. was still speaking, and the sight of her slow approach made him lose his hearing for a moment. D.C.'s voice faded to nothingness as she ran one palm over the side of his face and mouthed the words "thank you," her eyes brimming.

Torch closed his eyes at the pain her touch evoked.

And even then, couldn't stop himself from turning until his lips touched her palm, kissing her there, slowly.

Her smile was tremulous, maybe uncertain. She went into the bathroom and closed the door.

"….if she's that important to you, you're not going to want to risk it," D.C. was saying. "So I still want her in custody."

Torch shook himself. "Risk what?"

"Try listening this time, Torch, this is vital."

Torch nodded, grunted and wished D.C. would get to the point.

"Scorpion is here. He obviously knows you still have the formula, obviously knows you haven't given it to us yet. He'll try to get to you before you have the chance to turn it in. And that means tonight, Torch. We need to take some precautions. If we don't, you and the woman might both end up dead, and that formula in the worst possible hands."

It was true. If Scorpion was here, then he must be planning another attempt. And he'd kill them outright this time. He wouldn't risk being bested again.

"I can bring it in right now," Torch suggested.

"No. Scorpion knows enough to watch the building. He might try to take you before you get inside. I have a better idea."

"Shoot," Torch said.

"I'll come to you. He'll be watching for you to arrive, not for me to leave. So it shouldn't be hard to slip out of here unnoticed. You can turn over the formula, and then you and the woman come in with me. We stick you in a safe house with armed guards—"

"Protective custody." Torch grimaced at the thought.

"Just until we manage to let Scorpion know it's too late. That the formula has been destroyed. We'll try to pick him up before he skips the country again, but this way, even if he gets past us, he'll still have no reason to bother you or the woman again. You'll be safe.''

Torch shook his head. ''You know what I'm gonna say.''

D.C. only sighed.

''You of all people, D.C., should know exactly what my answer to your plan will be. You know me better than anyone alive.'' D.C. started to speak, but Torch went on. ''I'm not coming in.''

''Torch—''

''Come to me like you said, and be damn sure you're not followed. I'll give you the formula, and then you take Alexandra to that safe house, and you guard her with your life, D.C. This woman—'' he cleared his throat ''—she means something to me.''

''Yeah, well, she won't if you're dead, Palamaro.''

''We do this my way or no way,'' Torch told him, keeping his voice level.

''All right. Okay. Go on, what else?''

''That's it. Take her somewhere safe. Put that damned formula down the nearest toilet once you verify it's the real thing. But don't let it slip that you have it. I want Scorpion to think he still has a chance.''

''But, Torch, he'll still come after you if…oh. I get it. That's what you want, isn't it? He'll come after you tonight, and you'll—''

''Better than letting him get away again, don't you think?''

D.C. sighed, but didn't argue. ''You'll need to tell me where you are, Torch.''

''Yeah.'' Torch looked toward the bathroom door, where he could hear the shower running, and he thought of how furious Alex was going to be with him for this.

She wouldn't go willingly. He knew she wouldn't. "Give me a couple of hours, okay?"

"Sure, Torch. Whatever you want. I owe you for this one."

Torch gave him the address and hung up the phone. A few minutes ago, he'd been wondering if he could convince Alexandra to stay with him. Now, he was trying to think of a way to make her willingly leave. Only one way came to mind.

He seemed so pensive tonight.

She wanted to know what he was thinking, what he was feeling, but she wouldn't ask. If he had something to say to her, something to tell her, he'd have to do it on his own. She was through offering her heart on a platter only to have it handed back to her, bleeding. She couldn't go through it again.

He'd ordered an extravagant dinner, with candlelight and expensive wine. And for a moment, she thought maybe he *was* trying to tell her something. Maybe he was ready for their relationship to take a new turn, to move onward. A bubble of joy rose up inside her...and then she looked at him. *Really* looked at him, probing deep into his eyes. And he didn't have the look of a man about to declare his feelings. More like...he'd lost another loved one. Or was about to.

His face was expressionless, but in his eyes she could see turmoil. His shoulders weren't square and firm, but slumped a bit. As if he were utterly tired of carrying this burden, fighting this fight. As if he couldn't take much more. She wanted to see Torch smile again, to hear him laugh, the way he had when they'd had the snowball fight outside the camper. She wanted to see his eyes alight with passion the way they had been when he'd made such exquisite love to her in the house.

But he barely spoke, and when he did it was in monosyllables or grunts. Distracted? Deep in thought? Worried about something? What was wrong with him?

It was only when they'd finished eating, and she'd reached the end of her patience, when he reached across the table, his hand covering hers, his eyes lowering— almost guiltily—that she'd known. This was it. He was getting ready to say goodbye.

"Alex—"

"Don't." She pulled her hand away, a flutter of panic taking flight in her breast. Not now. Not yet. Torch's eyes rose to meet hers, and she saw so much feeling in them. So much emotion. How could he pretend not to care when it was so visible in his eyes? "You're going to say it's over, aren't you?"

He closed his eyes, nodded.

"And what if I say I don't want it to be?"

"I don't want it to be either, Alex." He met her gaze again, held it, and she almost thought there were the beginnings of tears in his eyes. "I'd like you to stay right here with me. Live with me. Make love to me every night. I'd like that a lot."

"But?"

His jaw clenched. He averted his eyes, and his next words came as if he were forcing them out. "But I don't love you. I never will. And I think you've come too far to settle for that. Haven't you, Alex?"

She shoved away from the table, shot out of the chair. His straightforward rejection didn't even try to ease the blow. It was almost deliberately cruel. "Damn you, Mason Palamaro!"

He bit his lip but didn't face her.

"I don't deserve this. You know I don't."

"I know."

"Then tell me why, Torch. Why?"

She heard the way her voice had grown softer, squeezing through a smaller space as her throat closed off. She saw the regret in his eyes. Another layer of brutal pain on top of the one that had been there before. And the anger went out of her, leaving her weak and shaken. She sank into the chair again, out of strength. The fight gone. Only heartache and confusion remained. He didn't want to do this to her. So why was he?

Torch came around the table and she felt his hands close on her shoulders. She didn't resist as he pulled her close to him. Her face pressed to his hard belly. His hands tangled in her hair.

"It's me, baby, not you. Don't ever think it was you," he whispered.

She swallowed hard, trying not to cry, as she pushed away from him. She stood again, her legs wobbling, and she meant to turn away, to put some distance between them, but he kissed her. He kissed her and her insides melted down. And her mind whirled. He kissed her with his mouth and with his teeth and with his tongue, and the way he held her to him made her think he never wanted to let go. She knew he'd meant what he'd said. That he'd like her to stay.

His lips were still touching hers when he whispered, "I want to make love to you, Alex."

She shook her head, finally managing to take that single step that took her away from him. The air felt cold without his arms to warm it. "I can't."

"Alex—"

"No, Torch. It's over. As much as I want to give in…I just can't do that to myself again. I've…I've spent

my whole life loving a man who couldn't love me back.
I'm finished with that. I deserve…more.''

The look that flashed in his eyes could have been one
of pride, only that would have made no sense. There
was pain there as well. She saw it very clearly.

"You could love me, Torch. I know you could, if
you'd only let yourself. But you won't, will you?''

"I…" He couldn't look her in the eyes for more than
a second. "I'm sorry,'' he whispered, his voice tortured
and coarse.

She drew a breath, stiffened her spine. "I'm not going
to beg.'' Closing her eyes, searching inside for strength,
she forced herself to end this torment, to say the final
words, to break free. "I'd like to leave tonight.''

He lowered his head in acceptance when what she
wanted the idiot to do was beg her to stay.

"That's probably for the best.''

So this was it. It was over.

*This might be over. But not my life. My life…is just
beginning, really.*

She nodded in agreement with the small voice—the
new voice—that came from deep inside. She was free
of a father who'd done nothing but try to bring her down.
Free of the self-image she'd dragged through life like a
ball and chain. She'd finally found the woman she truly
was, beneath all the self-doubt and insecurity, and she
liked that woman. Dr. Alexandra Holt. Smart, strong and
capable of getting through anything.

"Even this,'' she whispered, and cleared her throat
when Torch only frowned at her. "I'll go to New York,
for now. Back to the clinic where I used to work, before
all this madness…for a while anyway. I need to practice medicine again. I didn't realize how much I've
missed it.''

His head came up. "I'll book a flight out for you. Tomorrow."

She shook her head. "I told you, I want to leave tonight."

He drew a breath, pinned her with his gaze. "You are leaving tonight. But not for New York." While she tried to make sense of his words, Torch went to the telephone stand, scribbled something on a sheet of paper and ripped it from the pad that sat there. "Take this."

She did. A telephone number.

Alex frowned. "I don't—"

"Keep it with you, Alex. If anything goes wrong—" His words were cut off by a knock on the door.

Torch stared at her a moment longer, and she saw the anguish in his eyes. Then he turned away. She was surprised to see him pull the gun from his waistband before he went to the door. Standing to one side, he asked, "Who is it?"

"D.C.," a voice answered.

Torch nodded and opened the door. The man who entered was a head shorter than Torch, and about fifty pounds heavier. His hair stuck up straight in a snowy brush cut, and his eyes were pale, piercing blue. Like small, pale ice chips, peering at her from behind rectangular bifocals. The color of his eyes matched the suit he wore.

His first act, after closing the door behind him, was to clasp Torch's hand in both of his. "You look good, Torch. I knew coming back to work would agree with you."

Torch shook his hand, then glanced toward Alexandra. She'd been trying to surreptitiously knuckle her eyes dry, trying to bounce back from Torch's cruel rejection.

"Alexandra Holt, this is D.C. Wayne," Torch said, lowering his hand to his side. "We work together."

She nodded, muttering some inane greeting, absently stuffing the slip of paper into her jeans pocket, and searching Torch's face. Something was going on here. He wasn't surprised at D.C.'s arrival.

"The formula?"

Torch nodded, and turned to take the spiral notebook from where he'd tucked it under the mattress when they'd first arrived. Alex couldn't help sucking a breath through her teeth when he handed it over.

And Torch must have heard it, or sensed her concerns, because he turned to her, faced her squarely and put both hands on her shoulders. "I trust this man implicitly, Alex."

"Like I trusted my father?" She didn't know what made her blurt the words. They jumped from her tongue before she could think about them. She looked up at D.C. standing behind Torch. "I'm sorry. No offense."

He nodded, smiling gently at her, looking for all the world like someone's kindly grandfather. Comforting. Understanding.

"It's all right, Ms. Holt. I know this is difficult. Believe me, you'll be as safe as if you were in your own mother's arms."

She blinked at the reference to a mother she'd never known, then frowned as the rest of his words sank in. "What do you mean?" Her gaze flicked back to Torch. "What's going on?"

"I want you to go with him, Alex. He'll take you to a secure place for the night. By tomorrow it should be perfectly safe for you to go on to New York or wherever you want, but—"

She pulled from his grasp, shaking her head. "This

doesn't make any sense. It's over, Torch. You gave the notebook to D.C. I don't under—''

"Scorpion has no way of knowing that."

She blinked. "You don't *want* him to know it. You think he's going to come after you tonight, don't you, Torch? And you want me out of the way."

Torch said nothing, but he broke eye contact, looking down at the floor. She blinked back tears and went to stand face-to-face with D.C. "If you're truly his friend, you won't let him do this. He's not going to arrest Scorpion, he's going to kill him. Or die trying. You can't let him—''

"Now, calm down, Ms. Holt," D.C. intoned, and his big voice was confident and deep and soothing. "Torch isn't gonna do anything foolish. I'm not gonna let him lay in wait all by himself. He'll have backup and plenty of it."

She turned to face Torch, a feeling of dread settling in the pit of her stomach. "Don't do this."

D.C. kept right on talking, as if unaware of the emotional undercurrents snapping on the air between Torch and her. "If he has to worry about keeping you safe, though, he might screw up. Let his guard down. Believe me, Ms. Holt, he'll be far better off tonight if he knows you're somewhere safe, out of harm's way."

"Torch…"

Torch lifted his head. "Go with him. Please, Alex, for God's sake, don't make this any harder than it is."

She shook her head. "No. I'm not—''

D.C. Wayne's hand closed on her arm gently but firmly. "I'm sorry, Ms. Holt. Try to understand, Scorpion is an international terrorist. He's responsible for countless murders, bombings, kidnappings…the list goes on and on. We can't risk his escaping again, no matter what we have to do to prevent it.''

She tugged her arm away, annoyed at his interference in what was a private matter between her and Torch. ''I *said* I'm not going.''

''I have the authority to arrest you, Ms. Holt.''

Her gaze flew to Torch's.

''I'm sorry, Alex. It's for your own protection.''

She looked at Torch in stark disbelief, and the pain in his eyes almost brought her to her knees. ''It's a choice, Torch. You know that, don't you? It's a choice between a chance at living again, with me...and your vendetta against Scorpion.''

He lowered his head. ''This is something I have to do, Alex.''

So he knew. He understood. And he was choosing hatred over love. ''Do you know how good it would have been between us?'' she whispered. ''Do you have any idea what you're throwing away?''

''Yeah.'' His voice was so choked it was barely audible. ''Yeah, I do.''

''I was falling in *love* with you.''

He licked his lips. ''Goodbye, Alex.''

His words stung like the lash of a whip. Tears surged into her eyes, and she bit her lip to stop it from trembling. She didn't have any idea how to fight this, or what she could do to change Torch's mind. So she finally nodded, but she held his gaze, and without uttering another word, she begged him not to go through with this madness.

D.C. patted her shoulder in an almost fatherly gesture and gently led her out the door. She held Torch's gaze all the way down the hall, as he stood in the doorway, apparently unable to look away. D.C. stepped into the elevator, and Alex went with him. And when the doors slid closed, she felt as if they'd sliced her heart in half. The most vital part stayed behind. With Torch.

Chapter 15

The elevator doors closed, and that was good, because it stopped him from seeing the pain in her eyes.

He stepped back into the hotel room, and he closed the door. He felt a quake moving up through his body, until he vibrated with the effort of trying to hold it inside. And then he gave up.

His fist hit the table so hard the plates jumped from the surface, and pain flashed through the wound in his shoulder. He tipped his head backward, a grimace pulling at his facial muscles until they hurt, and he battled the inexplicable acidic burn behind his eyes. He swore at the top of his lungs, berating the ceiling and the walls. And the reason he was punching inanimate objects and swearing a blue streak was because the only alternative would have been to sink to the floor and cry like a baby.

It had nearly killed him to lie to her that way! Torn him apart to have to hurt her, to break her heart in order to keep her alive. He'd known it would be hard. He hadn't realized just how hard, though. He hadn't realized that seeing the pain he'd inflicted, shimmering in those doe eyes, would make him hate himself. He hadn't expected her to tell him she had been falling in love with him.

"Had been" being the operative phrase. He'd ruined it. Because she was right. But…it should be different, shouldn't it? Once she realized he was only sending her away for her own safety. Maybe…maybe if he survived this, he could find her again, explain to her that he hadn't meant the things he'd said. That he'd hurt her because it was the only way he could be sure she'd go with D.C. Maybe she'd forgive him and understand….

Do you have any idea what you're throwing away?

Torch closed his eyes and sank slowly into a chair as her words came back to him in that smoky voice, made huskier by pain. Who the hell was he kidding? He knew it wouldn't matter if he explained himself. Alex knew it, too. She'd been so right. He'd made a choice tonight. He'd chosen to hold on to his need for vengeance rather than let it go and embrace the salvation she offered him. He could have handed that formula over to D.C., taken Alex and left. They could have gone someplace together…started over.

But no. He'd chosen to stay here and await his long-time enemy. He'd chosen a man he hated over a woman he…

What?

He didn't know. Maybe now he'd never find out.

He must be a complete fool.

He showered, dressed, rebandaged his throbbing shoulder, and cleaned and loaded his weapons while he waited. He knew the drill. By now Alexandra was installed someplace safe, and D.C. had twenty men stationed in and around the hotel. Torch knew they'd get Scorpion the second the man showed his face. But he'd get a shot at the bastard before this night was over.

He tried to picture Scorpion's cold eyes in his mind, but instead, he saw Alexandra's. Wide and brown and hurt. Those eyes that healed a man just by looking at him. Those beautiful, sexy, mesmerizing eyes.

He had put tears in them.

Torch laid the gun down on the dresser, closed his eyes, tried to erase the longing for her that grew stronger with every breath, every second. Was this what the rest of his life would be like? Was killing Scorpion worth this?

No.

The answer came to him as clearly and precisely as if it had been spoken aloud. No. It was that simple. Scorpion would be apprehended if he showed up here tonight. It wouldn't matter if Torch was here or not. What mattered…what really mattered right now, was Alex.

He'd made a choice tonight. The wrong choice.

God, he'd thrown away his last chance at redemption. He'd thrown away a woman unlike any other he'd ever known. Or ever would. Alexandra Holt had been falling in love with him. And he'd chased her away.

The sheer magnitude of his own foolishness hit him with the force of a tidal wave. What was he, an idiot? Was he insane?

But it wasn't over yet. It couldn't be over. Maybe there was still time to make things right.

Torch tucked his favorite gun into his waistband before pulling on his leather jacket. Then he paused to inhale, and he smelled Alexandra's scent clinging to the leather. The longing stabbed deeper. He quickened his pace as he left the room, almost ran through the hall to the elevator and then rode it down to the lobby. It occurred to him, as he crossed the marbled floor to the front entrance, that the I-CAT team, who must be here, were doing an excellent job of concealing their presence. And then he hailed a cab and left them to do their job without him. They'd see him leaving. They'd get the idea. They were skilled enough to be able to handle a simple ambush on their own.

As the hotel faded in the distance behind him, Torch felt a peculiar lightness. A stupid grin kept tugging at his lips. He'd made the right decision.

Then tension knotted his stomach as he wondered whether Alex would forgive him for not making it sooner.

Ah, well, he'd soon find out. The cab dropped him off outside the downtown office building that housed the secret I-CAT headquarters. He paid the driver and headed inside, only to run smack into Doug Stern, who was hurrying out.

"Damn, why don't you watch where you're—" Stern met Torch's eyes and stopped in midsentence. "Palamaro. What the hell are *you* doing here?"

Torch sighed. "I know, I'm supposed to be at the hotel waiting for Scorpion, but I've got to see Alex."

Stern blinked. "I don't have a clue what you're talking about."

"D.C. didn't tell you?" At Stern's blank stare, Torch went on. "I knew he didn't let you know I was going after the formula, Stern, but I assumed he'd have brought you in on things now that he has it."

Every drop of color left Doug Stern's face. "Tell me you're not talking about the Holt case."

"That's exactly what I'm talking about. Look, Stern,

I know you still hold me responsible for Marcy's death. I don't blame you. Hell, I wouldn't have done this for D.C. at all, if the chance to get Scorpion hadn't been a part of it. But it's over. I got the damned formula. I did my part. Now I've changed my mind about the protective custody for Alexandra. I want her back.''

"Protective custody? For Alexandra…Alexandra *Holt?*"

Torch nodded. "I think I finally understand why you hate my guts so much, Stern. If you felt a tenth for Marcy the way I feel for Alex…it's a wonder you didn't put a bullet between my eyes a long time ago."

Stern gaped, then drew a breath. "I did worse than that to you."

"What?"

He shook his head. "Look, Palamaro, you're telling me you went after Holt's formula at D.C.'s request. You turned it over to him, and then you let him take the Holt woman into custody?"

"Yeah. For her own protection. I was planning…" Torch swallowed hard. "I was planning to murder Scorpion tonight."

Stern took a few staggering steps forward, sinking into one of the half circle of chairs, backed by a like-shaped bank of windows in the building's main lobby. Then he lowered his head into his hands.

A lead ball began forming in the pit of Torch's stomach. "Stern, what the hell is going on?"

Stern lifted his head. "D.C. Wayne doesn't work for us anymore. Torch, for a year now, I've suspected him of selling information. I've been watching him but haven't been able to get anything solid on him. Not yet anyway."

An Important Message from the Editors

Dear Reader,

Because you've chosen to read one of our fine romance novels, we'd like to say "thank you!" And, as a **special** way to thank you, we've selected <u>two more</u> of the books you love so well **plus** an exciting Mystery Gift to send you — absolutely <u>FREE</u>!

Please enjoy them with our compliments...

Pam Powers

Lift here

Peel off seal and place inside...

How to validate your Editor's
"Thank You"
FREE GIFT

1. Peel off gift seal from front cover. Place it in space provided at right. This automatically entitles you to receive 2 FREE BOOKS and a fabulous mystery gift.

2. Send back this card and you'll get 2 brand-new *Romance* novels. These books have a cover price of $5.99 or more each in the U.S. and $6.99 or more each in Canada, but they are yours to keep absolutely free.

3. There's no catch. You're under no obligation to buy anything. We charge nothing—ZERO—for your first shipment. And you don't have to make any minimum number of purchases—not even one!

4. The fact is, thousands of readers enjoy receiving their books by mail from The Reader Service. They enjoy the convenience of home delivery...they like getting the best new novels at discount prices BEFORE they're available in stores... and they love their Heart to Heart subscriber newsletter featuring author news, horoscopes, recipes, book reviews and much more!

5. We hope that after receiving your free books you'll want to remain a subscriber. But the choice is yours— to continue or cancel, any time at all! So why not take us up on our invitation, with no risk of any kind. You'll be glad you did!

GET A *Free* MYSTERY GIFT...

*SURPRISE MYSTERY GIFT COULD BE YOURS **FREE** AS A SPECIAL "THANK YOU" FROM THE EDITORS*

The Reader Service — Here's How It Works:

Accepting your 2 free books and gift places you under no obligation to buy anything. You may keep the books and gift and return the shipping statement marked "cancel." If you do not cancel, about a month later we'll send you 3 additional books and bill you just $4.74 each in the U.S., or $5.24 each in Canada, plus 25¢ shipping & handling per book and applicable taxes if any.* That's the complete price and — compared to cover prices starting from $5.99 each in the U.S. and $6.99 each in Canada — it's quite a bargain! You may cancel at any time, but if you choose to continue, every month we'll send you 3 more books, which you may either purchase at the discount price or return to us and cancel your subscription.

*Terms and prices subject to change without notice. Sales tax applicable in N.Y. Canadian residents will be charged applicable provincial taxes and GST.

If offer card is missing write to: The Reader Service, 3010 Walden Ave., P.O. Box 1867, Buffalo, NY 14240-1867

POSTAGE WILL BE PAID BY ADDRESSEE

BUSINESS REPLY MAIL
FIRST-CLASS MAIL   PERMIT NO. 717-003   BUFFALO, NY

THE READER SERVICE
3010 WALDEN AVE
PO BOX 1341
BUFFALO NY 14240-8571

NO POSTAGE
NECESSARY
IF MAILED
IN THE
UNITED STATES

Torch's throat was rapidly going dry. "Selling information...to whom?"

"Scorpion."

The word hit Torch like a blow to the solar plexus. So much so that he felt himself flinch, felt the air rush out of him.

"I thought..." Stern went on. "I thought you were working with him. Dammit, you two were best friends even before you joined the I-CAT. He's the one who recruited you. So when it looked like he was involved in the bombing that killed Marcy, I assumed you were in on it, too. Especially since the device was so well made...and so much like Scorpion's work. Only you and D.C. knew his methods that well. And only you had the skill to duplicate them." Torch swore, but Stern kept talking. "I figured Marcy knew something, stumbled onto some information she shouldn't have..." Stern trailed off, shaking his head.

But Torch wasn't hearing him anymore. He was replaying that last conversation he'd ever had with his wife. It caught like a scratched LP, skipping back to the same phrase over and over again. *We ran into D.C. today. We ran into D.C. today. We ran into D.C. today.*

"No!"

Torch closed his eyes at the sound of it, gave it a mental kick to make it play out and die away. And then he heard the rest. *At the mall. He was talking to some guy with...oh, hey, I have to go. Someone's at the door. I'll tell you all about it tonight.*

Only she hadn't. Instead, she'd been killed right before his eyes. Killed because Scorpion had planted one of his trademark devices in the house. When he shouldn't even have known where the house was. When he shouldn't have known anything about Torch's family.

So how had he known?

He was talking to some guy with…

With what, Marcy? Torch wondered. With pink eyes and shocking white hair?

Torch grated his teeth. "It was D.C. Good God, it was D.C. all along. Marcy saw him that day, she and the boys ran into him at the mall. They said he was with someone. With Scorpion, probably. Scorpion and D.C., and they both knew Marcy and the boys had seen them. They both knew all it would take was one mention of the odd-looking man, for me to put it together…" His head fell until his chin touched his chest. "They killed my kids. Those bastards killed…"

Torch's head came up fast, and before he knew what he was doing, he had Stern by the front of his shirt, lifting him right up out of the chair. "Those bastards have Alexandra!"

Stern pulled himself free, smoothing his shirt. "They also have a virus capable of wiping out entire nations, Palamaro. We'll get them."

Torch was reeling, his mind spinning out of control. A sheen of moisture coated his face and his neck, and he felt himself beginning to shake.

"I made her go with him, Stern. Dammit, she didn't want to. I…" Torch couldn't go on. All he could see was the hurt in Alexandra's brown eyes. He'd handed her over to a killer.

"We'll have every resource at our disposal on this within ten minutes," Stern said. "We'll get them this time. We'll get that formula, and we'll get the Holt woman." Stern turned toward the revolving doors that led to the street, and the shocked and slightly guilty expression faded from his countenance. He squared his shoulders, once again looking every inch the man in charge. ''Park yourself somewhere. I'll get in touch as soon as we know anything.''

''The hell I will.''

Stern paused in his rush for the door, facing Torch once more.

''I want in on this, Stern. And after what you believed of me, you owe me that much.''

Stern lowered his gaze from Torch's, conceding more easily than Torch had ever seen him do. His back bowed a little, and he shifted his feet. He looked like a man carrying one hell of a burden. A man filled with regret and again, guilt. More guilt than he ought to, if all he'd done was misjudge Torch. More, even, than seemed appropriate for having suspected a man of murdering his own children. What the hell was going on with him?

Stern cleared his throat, nodding hard. ''I owe you a hell of a lot more than that, Palamaro.''

''What's that supposed to mean?''

Stern shook his head. ''I'd like to be alive to close this case,'' he said, and there was no lightness in his tone to indicate he was kidding or being sarcastic. ''So I'll explain it to you later.'' He closed his eyes briefly. ''Dammit, Torch, I'm sorry.''

The remorse was incredible. Practically oozing from Stern's pores.

''I don't have a clue what the hell you're—''

''Come on,'' Stern said, not letting Torch finish. ''I've had a man tailing D.C. for days. I knew he was up to something the second he resigned. We'll call him from my car, see if we can catch up to the bastard.''

Raining. Great. A perfect match for a perfect mood. Snowing up north, no doubt. Raining here. She thought about commuter flights and ice-coated wings, and wondered if it would stop raining by the time she was free to catch a plane to New York. And then she shook her head, knowing it didn't matter. She wasn't going anywhere. Not until she saw Torch again.

She supposed she was a fool for wanting to. Especially after he'd made his feelings—or lack of them—so perfectly clear to her. But she couldn't just walk away without knowing what happened to him tonight. She had to know that he was okay. And beyond that, she needed to know that the formula her father had developed wouldn't be responsible for countless deaths.

And she had to, maybe, look into Torch's eyes just once and see that it was really over. Because she hadn't seen that in those blue eyes tonight. Not at all.

D.C. hadn't said a word since they'd gotten into the car. They'd driven away from the bustling streets and into rural areas, Virginia perhaps. And she was beginning to wonder just how far away this safe house of his was.

The car continued steadily onward, wipers slapping water from the glass, headlights piercing the gloom. And then he pulled to a stop in front of what looked like a warehouse. Only…it seemed abandoned.

"What is this place?" she asked, squinting through the windshield, trying to make sense of what she saw. Broken windows, bowing walls. "Why are you stopping here?"

D.C. didn't turn to face her. Very softly he said, "I'm sorry."

Then the door at her back was yanked open from outside, and she whirled at the unexpected blast of cold, wind-driven raindrops. The interior lights came on when the door opened, and they were enough to illuminate the pink eyes and colorless hair of the albino she'd thought she'd only see again in a nightmare.

Cringing backward, she screamed, lashed out with her feet. His reaction was to simply lean into the car, absorbing her kicks as if he were a sponge. His large claws sank into her shoulders and he drew her toward him. Closer and closer as she struggled and howled. Right out into the frigid, icy rain that pelted her face and soaked her hair. Right up against his chest, with his arms pinioning hers to her sides. She writhed and kicked, but he was oblivious. "Come on, Wayne, I don't have all day. The hypodermic is in my back pocket. Take it and inject her so we can move on with things."

The words terrified her, and she struggled all the more as she heard D.C. hurrying out his side, slamming his door, his footsteps slapping the wet ground as he came around the car.

"No," she cried. "No, you can't—"

And then the fine, sharp tip of a hypodermic pierced the flesh of her buttocks. She stiffened, fighting. But the rain grew louder and louder until it enveloped her. And at last she went limp, unable to do anything more than listen. So groggy.

Scorpion rearranged her, hefting her up and over his shoulder, and she felt the cold rain soaking her back but couldn't move to avoid it.

He opened the car door, tossed her down onto the front seat again. "She won't give you any trouble now," he said, and his shrill voice made her teeth hurt. "You, Asbahd, drive the car around to the back, and right inside, before it's seen. Tie her up. But don't kill her. I might need her later. Mr. Wayne and I have some business to conduct in the office." She felt weight on the seat beside her and then the car was moving again.

* * *

"I'm sorry, Chief Stern," the young I-CAT recruit moaned, lowering his chin and shaking his blond head. "It was as if he knew he was being followed."

"If he knew, then you got too close!"

"He never saw me." The young man's pride was showing now. His eyes flashed and he met Stern's gaze head-on. "There's no way in hell. But he knew, all the same. And he took evasive action to lose me. No one could've done better, not even you, Chief Stern."

Stern waved a dismissive hand in the air, while Torch paced a path up and down the roadside in the pouring rain, wishing the icy wetness could shake the sick feeling from the pit of his stomach. But it didn't. It couldn't. Nothing could.

This was where the kid had lost D.C. Well away from the city, on a country road that branched off in four directions. He could be anywhere.

"He had the woman with him?" Torch asked the kid yet again, stopping his pacing long enough to await an answer. "You're sure of that?"

"Yes. There was a woman with him. She had long dark hair. That's about all I could tell in the dark."

"But she was alive?"

The kid nodded. "I could see her moving her head now and then. Yeah. I'm sure she was alive."

Alive and terrified, he thought in silence. Alive and in the hands of brutal killers, because of him. Dammit, he'd get her out or die trying.

Aloud, he only cleared his throat and nodded toward Stern. "Get on the horn and get us a map of this area. And where the hell is that chopper you asked for?"

Stern answered, but Torch was almost beyond hearing. He had no idea where D.C. had taken Alex. But he knew she'd be turned over to Scorpion along with the formula. Unless he could get to her first.

"Use your brain, Alex," he whispered. "Be smart. Help me, for God's sake."

The thug of Scorpion's choosing didn't obey his orders to the letter. He did drive the car around and then inside the frighteningly dilapidated building. She knew that by the sudden, more complete darkness, and the cessation of the raindrops pelting the roof. Then he simply got out. In the brief flash of the car's lights, she saw the dashboard and the steering wheel. And D.C.'s cellular phone. Hope leapt to life in her breast.

The door slammed and the darkness returned. Even the sounds of the rain died away as the thug closed a large, creaking door. She heard his footsteps approach, then pass and fade in the distance.

He hadn't tied her up or even taken her out of the car. He'd taken the keys, but that didn't matter. She sat up slowly, dizziness whirling in her fogged head. And she found the number Torch had given her, in the pocket of her jeans. And then she fumbled some more, her hands groping for the door handle, missing, groping some more. She found it and shoved it open, and the light came on. Then she snatched up the cellular phone, and with dulled wits and achingly slow movements, she punched in the numbers. Carefully she closed the door again, praying the light hadn't been seen as she listened to the seemingly endless ringing on the other end.

Stern snatched up the car phone and barked at it. Then his face went lax, and his gaze snapped to Torch's. "How the hell...? No. Go ahead, patch it through." He covered the mouthpiece. "Dispatch has a call from Alexandra Holt. Wait, I'll put it on the speaker." He hit a button.

Torch's heart cracked into bits when he heard her slurred voice, so soft, fear filled and obviously impaired.

"Torch? Puh-puh-leease...I nnneed to ssspeak to—"

"Alex, it's me. Are you all right?"

She sighed, long and low.

"Talk to me, Alex!" Torch all but shouted at the speaker.

"Shhh. They'll hear you. T-Torch they...they drugged me."

"I know, baby. Can you tell me anything? Anything about where you are?"

Silence.

"Alex?"

"We...we crossed some tracks."

Torch frowned. "Railroad tracks?"

"Umm-hmm. An' we passed...water." More air than substance, her voice. She wasn't saying the words, but breathing them. Sighing them. "Now I'm in...it's old... and...and *dark*."

He could hear the tears in her voice. "I'm coming for you, baby, I swear to God, I'm coming for you. Hang on, you hear me?"

She didn't answer. Only sniffed, and he could sense her nodding at the phone.

"Now what kind of place are you in? Tell me everything you can."

"Abandoned," she said after a moment. "A fac-fac-factory o-or a warehouse. Something like that." She drew a breath. "It isn't your fault," she said, her words coming faster, more desperately than before. "Torch...'f anything happens...take care of Max." He heard her gasp. "They're coming. I—"

"Alex, don't hang up!"

"But—"

"Listen to me." He prayed she would. "Alex, you're smart and you're strong and you can get through this. You hear me? Use your head, Alex. Stay alive. I'm coming for you. I…" He stopped speaking when the click of the cutoff told him she'd hung up.

Or someone had done it for her.

She hadn't wanted to hang up the phone. It was like cutting off her last connection with Torch. The sound of his voice gave her hope. And there was anguish in his tone…too much anguish for a man who was supposed to be incapable of caring. He did care, dammit. The jerk was just too dense to realize it. She hoped to God she could live long enough to prove it to him.

And there was another reason she hadn't wanted to hang up. Somewhere in her fogged mind she'd thought if she just laid the phone down, without breaking the connection, Torch would have been able to trace the call and find her. She wasn't even sure that was possible with a cellular phone. Probably not, but it was worth a try. But then she'd seen the way the little red light on the phone glowed, illuminating the entire front seat. It only went out when she depressed the cutoff button, which she did just before the driver's door was yanked open again.

She slumped against the seat, lying very still. And then a pair of hands caught her under the arms and dragged her out of the car. "I have just the place for you, pretty one," a deep, heavily accented voice told her.

Her back thudded from the car to the floor, then scraped over rough, cold concrete as the man dragged

her. She heard voices. The man lowered her to the floor
for a moment and turned away to open a door, from the
sounds of the creaking hinges. Only the location was
wrong.

"...pay me now," D.C. was saying. "I kept my end
of the bargain. You have the formula."

"Yes, I do." It was Scorpion's voice. "But not your
loyalty, hmm?"

"What do you mean?"

"Come, Mr. Wayne. Do you really think I don't know
what you've been up to? That you've been negotiating
with certain factions, trying to get yourself a higher bid
on the formula?" Scorpion made a little clucking sound
with his tongue. "You're a fool, Wayne. I know everything you do."

"B-but I didn't go through with it—"

"You might have, though, if I hadn't arrived here and
monitored your every move. You've put me to a lot of
trouble, you know. All the expense and effort of trying
to take the formula from Palamaro before he turned it
over to you, just in case you developed the gall to go
ahead with your plot to betray me."

"None of that matters, now," D.C. all but shouted,
his voice trembling. "I got the formula for you. You
have it in your hands right now."

"Indeed," Scorpion said slowly, calmly. "And as a
bonus, I have a hostage, to ease my passage out of the
country. You've outdone yourself. So your reward will
be that much greater."

"It will?"

"Yes," Scorpion hissed. "I'll kill you quickly."

"Sco—*No!*"

The single gunshot exploded, echoing endlessly
through the hollow building, and Alex jerked in reaction,

then forced herself to be still. She'd be next unless she was very careful.

She heard Scorpion speaking, as if to himself. "You sold out your best friend for a price, Mr. Wayne. You gave me the information I needed to kill his family, for money, and to cover your own hide. I knew all along you would turn on me as well."

Alex cringed, trying not to envision the bulky D.C., lying on the concrete, bleeding, dying, as Scorpion stood over him, watching with those terrible pink eyes.

And then Scorpion's words sank in, and she understood that Torch had been betrayed by his best friend. A man he trusted. But there was no time to think about that now. Her thug was back to tugging at her again. She went limp, then utterly stiff when he shoved her through an opening in the floor. The shock of suddenly falling through space sent every bit of air from her lungs. She couldn't have screamed if she'd wanted to. And by the time she managed to draw in another breath, her back was slamming into the bottom hard enough to force it out again. And then her head snapped backward, hitting the concrete, as well. Pain was a blinding white light before her eyes. And that was all.

Chapter 16

She lifted her head slowly, blinked past the dizziness and focused on the ache. Her fingers gingerly probed at the back of her head, only to find the cut and pull away from it as she winced.

What was she going to do? How could she help end this madness?

She tried to focus on her surroundings, but there wasn't much to see. She was lying on her back, on a cold cement floor, in total darkness. Dankness. She heard an echoing trickle of water from somewhere, a scratching sound from somewhere else.

She drew a breath and swallowed hard. She didn't like this. Forcing herself up into a sitting position, she closed her eyes against the new waves of dizziness washing over the beaches of her mind, carrying things like balance and depth perception away in their brutal undertow.

Okay, just take your time. Get your bearings.

Right. She had to stay calm and stay sharp. She was

thinking clearly now. Before, in the hotel room, she'd been one hundred percent emotional, reeling from Torch's rejection. And after that, when she'd realized what was happening, she'd been overcome with shock and fear. Now she had to use her brain.

She'd gotten to know Torch Palamaro very well in the past few days. Probably better than she'd ever known anyone in her life. And she knew that Torch would not give up until he got her out of here…or died trying. That was what she was afraid of. That he'd get himself killed trying to rescue her. Dammit, she couldn't let that happen. She had to do everything she could to save herself before he did something stupid.

Rising, a little unsteadily at first, she moved forward until she felt a cool, rough wall against her palm. She turned to the right and moved forward, holding her other hand in front of her face. She encountered cobwebs, and then a drip, coming from above. And finally, another wall. She turned the corner, and her shins banged against what felt like a wooden crate, nearly tripping her. She got her balance after a moment and continued in the same way, and when she finished, she knew the shape of her prison. It was a square. No windows. No doors. No stairs or steps or any possible way out, other than the way she'd come in. She'd completed the full circuit three times before she made herself believe that, and then she felt her bronchial tubes spasm with fear. She started to pant and gasp.

No, dammit! She wasn't going to succumb this way!

She sank to the floor, calming herself with mental reassurances, forcing herself to focus on her breathing, willing her heart rate to slow down. If she could control the fear, she could control the attack. She knew she could.

And eventually she did.

And then something furry brushed against her leg, and the attack hit her full force.

He waited until Stern was busy with the new arrivals. All of them gathered together while Stern organized a search grid, charting it on a map. At the same time, Stern manned a walkie-talkie, giving instructions to the pilot of the chopper that hovered above them. Torch knew I-CAT's standard operating procedures too well. The formula for this virus was—to I-CAT's way of thinking—a much higher priority than the life of one woman. They'd figure out the locale—and soon. Stern had heard Alex's call. The railroad tracks, the water, an abandoned warehouse or factory. It wouldn't take I-CAT long to determine exactly where Scorpion was hiding. And when they did, they'd simply storm the place. Alex would be lucky to survive the first volley of bullets they exchanged with Scorpion and his thugs.

Torch was determined to get her out before that could happen. So he waited until they were all too busy to notice, and then he muttered that he had to sit down for a few minutes, to try to pull himself together. He got a guilt-ridden, sympathetic glance from Stern.

"Go ahead, Torch." Torch. Not Palamaro. Torch. "You've been through utter hell this past year."

Torch heard the unspoken completion of Stern's sympathetic words. *And I'm about to put you through more by getting your girlfriend blown away. So go ahead, rest. You'll need your strength.*

But Stern didn't say that. He just looked guilty as hell, and Torch wondered if his plans were the reason, and then decided they couldn't be. He'd been acting guilty before he'd had a chance to devise the plan. Torch sighed, shaking his head. Stern's change in attitude was something he'd worry about later.

He turned and headed through the crowd of I-CAT men, earning several friendly slaps on the shoulder as he went, and emerged behind them all. He picked up his pace as he neared Stern's car. Then he got inside, closed the door, took a quick look to be sure no one was paying any undue attention to him. Most of them were looking at Stern. Like Patton speaking to his troops, Torch thought. He crouched a little lower in the seat as he reached for the cellular phone. And then he dialed the number for D.C.'s car phone, and he let it ring for what seemed like an hour, before someone—probably one of Scorpion's flunkies—snatched it up.

"Tell your boss Torch Palamaro wants to make a deal. Tell him to come to the phone. Now."

The man muttered, but Torch heard footsteps. And a few seconds later the grating voice he recognized came on the line.

"Palamaro?"

"It's me," he confirmed. "Is she still alive?"

"She is. Is this call being monitored by fifty I-CAT troops?"

"No. I slipped away for a moment. It's like you said before, Scorpion. This is personal. Between you and me."

"That it is." Scorpion chuckled. "So you want to make a deal, eh?"

"She's expendable," Torch said softly. "I'm being straight with you, Scorpion. I-CAT doesn't give a damn if you kill her or not. All they care about is the formula. They'll probably just call in an air strike on that warehouse of yours and call it a day."

Torch heard the harsh intake of Scorpion's breath.

Good. He'd bought the bluff. "But if you had me as a hostage," Torch hurried on to say, "a decorated member of the team, one of their own, it would make a difference. You might be able to bargain for safe passage out of the country. That's what you want, isn't it?"

"You're offering to join her as a hostage, Palamaro?"

"No. I'm offering a trade. Me for her."

"Does it matter to you that I will use you to make good my escape, and then kill you anyway?"

"Not in the least," Torch whispered. "Not as long as you let Alexandra live. She's not part of this, Scorpion."

"Touching."

Torch held his breath while Scorpion breathed slowly and evenly into the mouthpiece. Finally the bastard spoke. "Done. Take a car and drive south for five miles, Palamaro. I'll have men waiting there to…provide you an escort."

His relief was palpable. His body bowed with it.

"If I see the slightest sign you're not alone, I will…*hurt* her, Palamaro. You'll hear her screams in your sleep for the rest of your life, I promise you."

"I'll be alone," Torch said quickly. "If you touch her, Scorpion, I'll kill you. I swear I will."

Torch hung up the phone. He'd get Alexandra out of this. No matter what it took. Even if it meant letting Scorpion walk away.

He stopped, his eyes widening as he realized what he'd just vowed. That he'd let Scorpion go—when he'd thought there was nothing more important to him than exacting his vengeance—in order to save Alexandra's life.

And he'd thought he was incapable of loving her?

"Idiot," he whispered.

Then he started working out what he'd say when he

asked the inexplicably guilt ridden Stern if he could borrow a car to go somewhere. Torch would have to look as if he were beside himself, half out of his mind with worry. He'd have to convince Stern that he was going to break if he didn't get away from all this for a few minutes. Maybe get some sleep or grab a stiff drink somewhere. He had to make it believable.

He closed his eyes and realized it wouldn't be hard.

He had four weapons. Two were his own. He liberated the other two, complete with ammo, from the glove compartment of Stern's car. The Ruger was in a shoulder holster. Scorpion's men would find that. There was a snub-nosed .38 revolver—the infamous Saturday night special—in a pancake holster at the small of his back. The belt in his jeans fit right over the gun's bulge. But if they were careful, they'd probably find that, too. He doubted they'd spot the little derringer he anchored just above his ankle, though. Or the bowie knife on the other leg. His boots covered them.

He discovered something interesting in Stern's glove compartment. A small silver-trimmed crystal flask. Opening it, he sniffed. Whiskey. Okay. He'd take that along, as well.

The asthma attack eased, but not for some time. And it had taken a lot of the strength out of her. It had almost come on all over again when she'd heard the thug tell his boss that Palamaro was on the phone. And she'd heard Scorpion take the portable phone from the man, and heard his end of that entire conversation. She knew what was happening. Torch was coming in, alone. He was going to try to trade his life for hers.

She'd wring his neck when she saw him.

Her writhing in the throes of the asthma had landed

her on her back in the middle of the cold floor again, as she'd struggled for air and clawed at her chest. It had been a bad episode. She'd almost passed out with no medicine on hand to ease her breathing. She'd torn her shirt to ribbons as she'd clutched herself in panic.

Now, though, from this position, she could see the tiny pinstripes of light above her.

And then she heard Scorpion again. "Send one of the men to meet him. Be certain he is alone. Search him for weapons and bring him to me. I want the pleasure of killing him myself."

"And the woman?" the other asked.

"I keep her. A trophy of my triumph over my most worthy enemy. How do the Americans say it? To the victor, go the spoils? The woman…I keep the woman."

Alex blinked back her revulsion and stared up at the wooden hatch she'd been dropped through. It was not nearly as distant as it had seemed when she'd been falling through darkness. The light came down between the boards and touched her face. And she knew it was a way out. The only way out. She couldn't just sit down here in the dark and wait for Torch to walk into a death trap. Not as long as there was a breath left in her body to prevent it.

She calmed her breathing through sheer force of will, and sought out the wooden crate she'd found earlier, then dragged it to the center of the room. She stood on it, reaching up to the hatch door and pushing, testing.

To her surprise, it gave. No locks? What was this?

She shoved it harder, and light streamed in, making her blink like a mole. And she heard their voices again, though not as close. She wasn't up high enough to climb out, just enough to see over the edge. Not daring to lift the door more than an inch or two, she peered out. She saw two pairs of booted feet, moving through a square doorway big enough to drive a truck through, and into another part of the building. She shifted her gaze and saw no one else. Only gray cinder block walls, and a dull, cracking cement floor.

She had to lower the hatch and get down, trying again after turning the crate on its end to make it higher. This time, her head and shoulders emerged from the pit when she pushed the door open. The voices were more distant now. Too far away to understand. She could no longer see them. Good. She looked around, saw no one and wriggled out. Then she lowered the door carefully and ran, crouching, to the nearest wall. Pressing her back against it, she listened. The only sounds were the beating of her own heart and the squeaky wheeze each time she exhaled.

Slow it down, she thought in silence. Easy breaths. In and out. Slow. That's it. That's better.

Her heart rate slowed as if in obedience. The wheezing eased. She lifted her head and looked at the huge portion of the building around her. She'd already seen the gray cinder block walls. They reached up high. Over her head, steel gridlike structures supported the roof. Here and there, long fluorescent tube lights gave the place a dull, artificial glow. Some flickered, obviously worn-out. The result was eerie and surreal.

Her gaze came down again, locking in on the normal-size doorway in one wall. Was that the "office" she'd heard Scorpion mention? With a quick glance to her left and right, she tiptoed across the spiderweb of cracks in the cement floor, gripped the doorknob, pressed her ear to the metallic door. No sounds came from inside. She twisted her hand, and the knob turned.

Her heart in her throat, she pulled the door open and

stepped inside, closing it behind her. Pitch-dark in here.
Her foot hit something that gave with the connection.
Startled, she reached behind her for the door again, push-
ing it open.

The dim light spilled in, and she wished it hadn't.
D.C. Wayne lay on the floor, a neat round hole in the
center of his forehead. Dark red streams had painted a
bloody headband across his brow. And the whites of his
opened eyes gleamed in the light. For just an instant
she'd sworn he was staring right at her.

All of that in a fragment of a moment, and she was
turning to lunge back out the door. Then she heard that
squeal of a voice and footsteps. They were coming back.
She jerked her head around and spotted another door on
the opposite side of the office.

Her decision was made. She pulled the door closed
silently and moved forward, forced to feel for D.C.'s
body so she could step over it rather than trip and give
herself away.

The steps came closer. She lifted her hands, palms out,
and found the opposite wall. Moving sideways, she felt
the door, located the knob, turned it.

Nothing. The door was locked.

Her heart sank to her feet when she heard the approaching steps stop just outside the door through which
she'd entered. Scorpion was talking about dumping the
body. Desperately she closed both hands around the little
round doorknob…and then she felt the protrusion from
its center, poking her palm. The lock…on the inside?
Deftly she turned the small locking device and cranked
the knob again. It turned this time. She slipped through,
having no idea where she'd emerge, having no time to
think about it. She could hear the other door opening as

she stepped out. At the last moment, she flicked the lock again and pushed the door closed behind her.

She'd emerged into what must be the other, gargantuan section of the builidng. The same flickering, insufficient light came from above, and she saw men, three of them, standing in a huddle about a yard in front of D.C. Wayne's black car. A big slab of a door hung from rollers just behind the car. None of the men looked her way, but they would. She stood in the open, the door to the small office at her back, and the wide room in front of her. Less than fifty feet of space stood between her and those thugs. She swung her gaze to the left and spotted a stack of boxes. Moving slowly, praying for invisibility, she went to it, ducked down behind it. No one shouted at her. No one seemed to notice.

She ducked there for some time. Behind her, a ladder was mounted to the cement wall, and she wondered briefly why. Then she forgot all about it, when she heard Scorpion's voice. She peered out, saw him rejoining the others.

"Well?"

"He's on his way, Scorpion. And he's been disarmed," said a voice she didn't recognize.

"You're sure?"

"Yes. Positive. Asbahd is with him. He reports no one is following. As you said, Palamaro had no trouble outsmarting his own people."

"It's going to be a shame to kill him," Scorpion mused. "It's been a challenge, dealing with him."

"They will arrive at any moment," the first man said.

"Good. Get into your positions, just in case. But remember, the kill is mine."

Alex almost cried out. She had to bite her lip.

"Now? Scorpion, I thought you would use him as a hostage…to insure our escape."

"You question my judgment?"

The man fell silent, and Alex saw the flash of fear in his black eyes. Scorpion drew a breath and went on. "I will not keep him alive. He's too dangerous. Better to kill him now. The others will have no way of knowing he's already dead. We'll negotiate as if he were alive."

"Very wise, Scorpion," one man said, and the others muttered in agreement.

"Go now," he ordered. "Into position."

Alex crept out of her boxes and peered around a corner. There was a catwalk, lined with crates, and she saw two men scramble up there, one on each side. She looked around her, at the ladder on the wall just to her left. That's where it went. Up there, to the catwalk. Torch was walking into a trap. She'd be damned if she'd sit here and watch as they killed the man she loved.

Moving silently, she gripped the ladder and made her way up.

A car rolled to a stop outside. The engine died. Alex bit her lip and moved faster. She got to the top, pulled herself onto the catwalk. It stretched just above the I beams that held the light fixtures, so it was dark here. She could see the shape of the man who'd taken position farther along the narrow platform. He crouched, staring down toward the doorway, a rifle cradled in his arms. If he turned around, he'd see her. She held her breath and began crawling forward.

Closer. Closer. She lay on her belly, sliding along inch by inch. The man was within reach now. She held her breath. Someone below pushed the noisy door open. The man tensed, lifting his gun. And Alex pushed him.

He emitted a soft, surprised cry as he fell, and when

he hit the floor, she barely heard the sound of his impact. The door continued creaking and groaning for a few more seconds. No one turned to look her way. No one saw the broken body lying below, in the shadows near the right wall.

She looked at the open doorway.

Torch stood there, dripping wet, his hands raised above his head. Alex receded into the shadows, back the way she'd come. And then she turned at a right angle and crept over the narrow section of metal that spanned the room from side to side. There was another assassin stationed on the opposite catwalk, and she had to try to remove him from the equation, as well.

Torch caught a glimpse of the catwalks on either side of him. Dark up there. Probably snipers waiting.

"Hello, Palamaro," Scorpion said.

Two down here, besides Scorpion. The one who'd driven him was outside, probably standing sentry in the pouring rain. He wouldn't hear much out there. The one who'd opened the door stood behind Torch, with a gun pointed at his back. And Scorpion stood in front of him.

How many up above? he wondered.

Aloud, he said, "Where is she?"

"Within reach," Scorpion said, grinning. "But if you shoot me and search the premises, you won't find her."

Torch was bleeding inside, damned distracted by the incredible need to see her, to hear her voice, to know she was still alive. And Scorpion knew it, the bastard. He'd drag this out all night. Unless he'd already...

No. He couldn't think that way. They'd found the three guns when they'd searched him. He was pathetically underarmed. Down to the knife in his boot, and that little whiskey flask, which he'd modified the con-

tents of a bit. Emptied the whiskey. Filled it with gas-
oline syphoned from Stern's car.

"There's not much time, Scorpion," he said, aiming
a pointed glance behind him for good measure. "The
team will be all over this place any minute. You need
to move fast. Let Alexandra walk out of here and make
your escape. Use me as a shield. It will work."

Scorpion's white eyebrows rose. Fortunately for
Torch, the chopper—or *a* chopper—chose that moment
to pass over the warehouse, reinforcing Torch's words.
A good thing. He was half convinced Scorpion had
planned to just shoot him on sight and try to bluff his
way out of the U.S. Now, it seemed, he was thinking
twice.

"No time to kill me and hide my body, is there Scorpion? And if they find it...or my blood...they'll know
I'm dead and your escape plan ends. Come on. Let Alexandra go and let's get on with this."

Scorpion's pale tongue darted out to moisten flesh-
toned lips. "I'll keep you both with me." He lifted an
automatic.

There was a guttural cry from high above and to the
right, then a crash. Scorpion jerked his head in that direction, eyes widening. Torch jumped in surprise, too.
Had one of his snipers fallen?

The man behind Torch moved off in that direction at
a nod from Scorpion, to investigate. Great. Only one gun
on him now. Scorpion's gaze was back on him, too. He
wasn't even looking off to the right. Torch was though,
and what he saw made his blood freeze.

Alex's unmistakable form slipping silently down the
ladder from the catwalk. The thug who'd gone to investigate had his rifle at the ready, but he was looking down,
at the fallen man. All he had to do was tip his head up,

see her, and she'd be dead. One shot. All over. All Scorpion had to do now was shift his gaze, and he'd see her, as well. In plain sight now, as she moved lower, into the full glow of the overhead lights.

And then it happened. The man on the floor looked up. A split second was all she had left. Torch knew damned well the second he moved, Scorpion would shoot him. He knew it, but he moved anyway. In an instant he'd crouched, snatched the knife from his boot and whipped it end over end even as Scorpion's gunshot deafened him.

It felt as if a truck had hit him squarely in the chest. He flew backward at the impact, landing on his back, hard. But he had the pleasure of seeing the blade hit home and the man who'd lifted his rifle drop it with a shuddering cry.

So fast. It had happened so fast. Where was Alex?

Scorpion stepped toward him slowly, holding the gun steady and smiling. But Torch didn't give a damn. He searched the ladder. She wasn't there. Oh. She was on the floor, ripping the rifle from the dead man's grasp, pulling the butt to her shoulder, pointing it at Scorpion. But she sobbed Torch's name, and Scorpion whirled, his handgun trained on her now.

"You bastard!" she shrieked. "You shot him, you son of a—"

"Put the gun down, Alexandra." Scorpion's voice was like butter. Smooth. Coaxing. "I don't want to have to shoot you, too."

He was going to shoot her anyway. Torch could see the blood lust in his eyes. He was furious at her for screwing up his well-laid plans, and he was going to kill her. He was only playing with her now. The way a cat toys with a mouse before killing it. The damned rifle's safety was on. She couldn't kill Scorpion if she wanted to.

She shook her head fast, tears flowing from her eyes now, her breaths coming faster and faster.

Torch was having trouble breathing, himself. He reached into his pocket for the flask, and the little lighter he'd copped. He waited until her wheezing gasps were good and loud, and flicked the lighter, still inside his pocket. His fingers were in the damned flame, but he managed to touch the cloth he'd left sticking out of the top of the flask.

"Calm down now, Alexandra," Scorpion said, moving closer to her. Not too close, though. Not yet.

Torch pulled the flask from the pocket and used all his strength to hurl it. It exploded right at Scorpion's feet, and flames shot up his pant legs. He screamed, a high-pitched, keening wail, as the fire licked at his long coat, leapt to the sleeves, heated the metallic weapon in his hands. He dropped the gun and began running, beating at himself with his hands. His howl was unearthly.

"Torch!"

Alexandra. She was on her knees beside Torch, even before Scorpion fell into a writhing, and then twitching, and then utterly still mound of charred flesh and flames on the floor. She was ripping Torch's shirt open, sobbing her heart out, and her tears were warm and wet on his face.

"Not now, not after all this," she sobbed. "Dammit, Torch, be all right...."

He tore his gaze from what was left of Scorpion and stared into Alex's eyes. "Alex...baby..."

"Help is coming, Torch. Just relax. Don't try to talk." She opened the straps of the vest he'd been wearing. Damn thing had done little good against a large caliber bullet at such close range. She peeled the vest away, sobbing. He was bleeding heavily. He could feel the warm stickiness coating his chest and his sides and his belly. Her hands worked feverishly, but he didn't know what she was doing. It didn't matter what she was doing, really. Not anymore. Scorpion had shot him in the chest at point-blank range. He was dying.

And it wouldn't be so bad, really. Hell, maybe, if what the faithful of the world believed was true, he'd get to see the boys again. Josh. Jason. God, it would be so good to hold those two angels in his arms again. To hear them call him Daddy.

But not yet. Soon, but not yet. He had to tell Alex...he couldn't leave her believing the crap he'd spouted in the hotel.

"Alex," he began again.

"I said not to talk," she snapped, but she was still crying. Had she told him that? He didn't remember. "Save your strength."

"I want to talk," he told her with surprising force. Then he sucked air through his teeth, because the words had caused him pain. When he spoke again, he kept it quieter, softer. "I want to tell you...that I love you, Alex."

Her hands stilled on his chest. She shook herself and began working on him again. "Oh, sure. Now that you're all shot to hell, now you love me."

He tried to smile but wasn't sure of the results. Alex shrugged her coat off and covered him with it. She dragged a metal box over and propped his feet on it. He heard sirens.

"I loved you all along. All that crap...in the hotel...I didn't mean it."

"Just trying to get rid of me, huh?"

"I thought…killing him was more…important," he managed to say, and his words were beginning to sound the way they did when he'd had too much to drink. "But I was wrong. I changed my mind, Alex. I was coming to tell you…"

She went still again, staring down into his eyes. "You were?"

He tried to nod but felt oddly paralyzed. His entire body numb. "Yeah," he whispered.

He liked it when she ran her hands over his face. And he liked it better when she bent to kiss his lips. Hers were parted and wet and salty with her tears.

The sirens got louder. Men came running, guns drawn.

When her lips rose away from his, he made himself go on. "I love you, Alex. But don't…ah…don't be too sad. You deserve more. You deserve…you deserve a whole man."

"You are a whole man, Torch."

"No. You know I'm not." He drew a breath. Shaky, shallow. He didn't think he was going to draw too many more.

"Don't you dare give up on me," she screamed. "Dammit, Torch, don't you *dare!*"

"Maybe," he whispered, "it's better…this way."

"No!"

His eyes dropped closed. He was fading fast. He couldn't even feel the pain now. He could still hear, though. He could hear Alex's smoky voice screaming for the paramedics, shouting orders. And he could hear them scrambling to obey. And then there was someone else crouching beside him, and she said, "Who are you? What are you doing?"

"Name's Stern," he said. And then Torch felt the

back of Stern's hand connect with the side of his face, and he realized he could feel pain again.

"Stop!" Alex yelled.

But Torch managed to open his eyes. "I told you to leave me the hell alone, Stern."

"And I told you there was something you needed to know, Palamaro. Listen and listen good."

There was nothing this man had to say that Torch wanted to hear. Not now. Nothing mattered now. He let his eyes fall closed again. Stern hit him once more, and this time he felt his skin split.

Torch's eyes popped open again, but it was an effort. He saw Alex gripping Stern's hand to keep him from doing it again.

Then he saw Stern staring down at him, moving his lips.

"Your sons are alive, Palamaro."

Torch's eyes opened wider. Alex uttered a soft gasp.

"You hear me?" Stern told him. "They're not dead. They were not killed in that explosion. They weren't even in the house when it happened. So if you're thinking of going off to la-la-land just to be with them, you'd better think again."

"I don't know what you're doing," Alex said, "but—"

"Relax, lady. I know what I'm doing." He loomed over Torch. "I started to tell you before, Palamaro. You were a suspect. So was D.C., but I didn't have enough proof to fire him or charge him. I knew about Marcy's call to you that day. I knew she and the boys had seen something they shouldn't have. I knew that if it leaked the boys were still alive, whoever had tried to kill them would try again, and I was half convinced it was you. So I put them into protective custody."

Torch lifted a hand, and the motion cost him more effort than he'd thought he had left in him. He closed it on the front of Stern's shirt. "If you're lying to me…"

"I'm not."

"You…kept me from my sons…when…"

"I know. Look, it kept them alive, didn't it? If Scorpion or D.C. had found out, they'd have tried again. Look, it was only because I—"

Torch's hand went limp and fell to the floor. His eyes closed again. He fought to cling to consciousness…to life…and he heard Alexandra's voice, tear roughened. "He's unconscious. Get out of the way so I can take care of him. We have to get him to the hospital, dammit. I can't lose him. Not now."

Those were the last words he heard. He felt himself slipping and grated his teeth, vowing to hang on until he learned the truth.

Chapter 17

She paced the waiting room nonstop, questioning everyone who happened by. She wasn't licensed to practice in Maryland and probably was shaking too badly to be of much help anyway. She knew that Torch would get excellent care here.

Torch was in surgery. The bullet had lost momentum because of the vest he'd been wearing, but because it had been fired at such close range, it had passed through the protective shell. It had broken a rib on the way in, and that had deflected its path enough so that it missed the heart.

But he'd lost a lot of blood, and it was touch and go all the way in. She still wasn't sure if he'd make it.

Footsteps made her turn, and then she glared at the man called Stern. He stopped in front of her.

"How's Torch doing?"

"You're a bastard," she said very softly, very calmly.

Stern smiled. "Yeah, but you can call me Doug."

"How could you let a man spend all those months believing his own children to be dead? My God, do you know what kind of hell he went through?"

Doug Stern had enough grace to look guilt ridden. "I know. All I can say is that it was better to let Torch suffer than to put those kids at risk again. At least, that was the way I saw it." He sighed. "I cared...a great deal for their mother. I did what I did for her."

She shook her head, turning away from the man.

"And for the kids, too. It might end up costing my job when it comes out, Ms. Holt. I risked that, because protecting them meant that much to me. And I still feel I did the right thing. I was wrong about Torch, I know that now. But if D.C. and Scorpion had known the boys were alive, they'd have tried again and again."

She closed her eyes. Who was she to judge this man? Maybe he really had been afraid for the boys. Maybe... he'd even had reason to be.

She met his eyes, saw sincere regret there. "I guess—"

The surgeon came in and she forgot all about Stern and his explanations as she saw him approaching, over Stern's shoulder. She held her breath, waiting.

"He's in recovery," the man said, smiling. "He's going to be just fine. I'll tell you, though, I've never seen anyone come in here in as bad a shape as he was, and still pull through. He has one hell of a lot of fight in him."

Alexandra went limp, not fighting when Stern caught her around the waist and eased her into a chair. She smiled through a flood of hot tears. The doctor smiled back.

"You'll be able to see him in a few hours. I'll have a nurse come for you."

She nodded, thanked him and turned back to Stern, wiping at her tears with the back of one hand. "Where are they?"

"Who?" he asked. "Oh. Them." He took her elbow, helped her to her feet, and then led her down the hall to a waiting area set aside for children. Two dark-haired, blue-eyed boys sat in the middle of the floor. One pushed a toy truck and made motor noises. The other sat very quietly, turning the pages of a children's book.

Alexandra felt her eyes burn. They looked so much like their father. Younger, more innocent, but they had his blue eyes and his dark, silken hair. Where his fell in waves, theirs kinked and curled.

"They knew their father was hurt in the explosion," Doug Stern said softly, leaning close so that his words were for her ears alone. "They understand that. They were both hurt, too. They were in the backyard playing when it happened. I was first on the scene. I found them and arranged for the secrecy. As far as they know, Torch has been recovering all this time. My father's been caring for them as if they were his own."

One of the boys—the one with the truck—looked up at her.

She smiled at him, and he smiled back. Dimples dotting his face.

"Hello," she said, feeling nervous for some reason. "Are you Josh or Jason?"

"Jason," he said firmly. "Are you gonna take us to see our daddy now?"

"Pretty soon."

"Is he all better yet?"

"Almost."

"I'm glad."

"Me, too," said the other one. Josh was quieter, more

shy. He'd backed up a few steps while his brother had spoken to Alex. Now he stopped his retreat, staring up at her. "I missed him so much."

"He's missed you, too," she told them. "You wouldn't believe how much. He would have been with you all this time, if he could have. You know that, don't you?"

Josh only nodded.

Jason frowned, searching her face with eyes as piercing as his father's. "Have you been cryin'?" he asked.

She nodded. "Yeah. I've been pretty worried about your daddy myself. But that was before I knew he was all better," she added quickly when she saw a worried frown taking shape between small eyebrows.

The frown eased. Jason puffed his chest up a bit. "You don't have to worry about *our* dad. He's *very* strong, you know."

"She knows that, fellas. This lady's a doctor. If it hadn't been for her, your old dad might not have been better even now." Stern seemed to be trying very hard to earn brownie points.

"Really?" Josh studied her for a long moment, than moved up to his brother, leaned close to whisper something into his ear.

Jason nodded and resumed his role as spokes-twin. "If you want, you can wait here with us. Then you won't be so scared."

She knew, as she looked at the hopeful expressions in their eyes, that they wanted her to stay with them.

Stern was whispering very close to her ear. "It's been a long time since they've had a woman's comfort, you know. I think it's something they could use right now."

She nodded, smiling and battling fresh tears. Two sets

of blue eyes and deep dimples had melted her heart like butter. They were their father's sons, all right.

"That's nice of you," she told them, moving into the room to sit down. "I'll feel a lot better if I can wait with you guys."

Jason was quick to take the seat on her left. Josh crept forward a little slower. Shyly he stopped before reaching her. He bit his lip, bending to pick up the book he'd been looking at when she'd come in. He held it out to her, eyes uncertain, a little wary. When she took it and opened it, he climbed into her lap.

And as Alexandra felt the small body resting in her arms, her heart swelled until she thought it would burst. She began reading and Jason, beside her, leaned his head against her shoulder.

The first thing Torch was aware of, when he opened his eyes, wasn't a physical sensation. It was a sense of elation. And for a second he wasn't even sure why he felt it, or what had happened to the shroud of grief that usually greeted him when he opened his eyes.

Slowly he became aware of the dryness of his throat, and the pain in his chest. He blinked, bringing the hospital room into focus....

And then it came back to him. Everything that had happened. And that odd fantasy-dream he'd had right at the end. His sense of elation vanished.

It had seemed so real. God, how much of what he remembered was sheer fantasy, then? Was Alexandra really all right? He tried to pull himself up, despite the pain. And he put all his strength into it when he shouted her name.

"Alex!"

He sat up too fast and had to clutch the mattress to

keep from going over the side when pain and dizziness hit him. And then the door was flying open, and he saw her shoving her way past an obstinate nurse to get to him.

She stopped near the bed, breathless, her wide brown eyes probing his. And then she came still closer, sighing in relief. Her hands slipped around his head and she drew it forward, pressed it to her belly, ran her fingers through his hair and whispered his name. "Thank God," she whispered. "Thank God, you're all right. You're really all right."

Torch wrapped his arms around her waist, clung to her. "I'm sorry," he told her. "For what I said at the hotel."

"I know."

"I only wanted you out of harm's way, Alex. I only wanted you safe. I swear it."

"I know, Torch."

"I love you." He pulled away from her, just enough so he could look up into her eyes. "I love you, Alex. Give me a chance to prove it to you."

Her hands came to his shoulders, and she eased him back onto his pillows. She leaned over him, pressed her lips to his mouth and whispered, "I love you, too, you idiot. And you don't have to explain. You told me all of this back in that warehouse when you thought you were dying. You got yourself shot trying to protect me. There's nothing to prove."

He sighed his relief. And then he clung to her. He needed to. Because the details of that dream were coming back to him now. A dream in which someone had told him the impossible, and he'd believed it because he'd wanted to so very badly. And he'd fought to stay alive because of it.

It hurt to wake up to reality after such a wonderful dream. Even with Alexandra's healing love, he didn't think this pain would ever leave.

She eased away from him. "There are some people waiting to see you."

He closed his eyes. They burned. "I don't want to see anyone but you, Alex."

She frowned down at him. "Torch…" And then she must have seen the moisture in his eyes, because she paused, staring at him. One hand came up to cup his cheek, and she plumbed his eyes, his soul. "Don't you remember what Doug Stern said to you in that warehouse?"

Torch's heart skidded to an utter halt. "I…I dreamed that he told me…" He grated his teeth, shook his head.

She smiled gently, tears brimming in her eyes. "Oh, my love. It wasn't a dream." She stepped backward, reached behind her for the door, pushed it open. And then she turned her head and waved her hand at someone outside.

And a miracle happened.

Josh and Jason bounded through that door and right up onto the bed. They threw themselves at him, hugged his neck, laughing and talking at the same time, so loudly and excitely he couldn't make out a word either of them was saying. For a moment he just sat there, stunned, looking down at the angels clinging to him, staring from one to the other, gaping.

And then he wrapped his arms around them both, and he thought his sutures were going to rip apart from the force of their hugs, but he didn't care. It was the sweetest pain in the world.

He *felt* them. Their soft, warm skin, and their silken

dark hair. He looked into their blue eyes and saw their twin smiles. Jason had lost a front tooth!

Alive! His sons were alive! It hadn't been a dream....

"My boys...oh, God, my boys..."

"We missed you, Daddy!"

"I'm so glad you're better now so we can be with you again!"

"I love you, Daddy."

"Don't leave us ever again, okay?"

He was crying. Torch Palamaro's stony heart melted into a puddle of sheer joy, and tears burned fiery paths down his cheeks. "I love you, too, both of you. And you better believe I'm never gonna leave you again. Not ever."

The hugs gentled, but neither child seemed willing to step out of his arms. And it was a good thing, because he didn't think he could let go of them if he tried.

Alex moved to the foot of the bed and cranked it up until he could remain sitting and still lean back against the mattress. The boys settled down a bit, curling up on either side of him, and he held them close.

But his gaze was on her. On Alex. On the tears of joy she was shedding for him. For them.

She moved toward the door. "You guys spend some time. Catch up. I'll check back in later."

"Don't go, Alex."

She met his gaze, and he saw so much love in her eyes that he wondered at it.

"You want to be alone—"

"No, we don't," said Josh.

"We want you to stay, Alex," Jason said.

Torch held her gaze, tried to send her messages with his eyes. "You *can't* go," he said softly. "Look at us."

He glanced from one head of dark curls to the other. "We *need* you."

Her smile was tremulous. But she nodded her acceptance and came to join them. She sat on the foot of the bed, curling her legs under her.

"Then I'll stay."

"For always?" Torch asked her, then he paused, suddenly uncertain. "I know it's a lot to ask..."

She smiled at him, looking at the boys as if she were looking at her very own miracle. "How do you two feel about cats?"

* * * * *

Dear Reader,

Take a rancher who's turned his back on the world and an independent woman about to give birth. Throw them together in the middle of nowhere during a record-setting snowstorm, and you have *The Baby Blizzard*.

Before writing Tess and Jack's story, I often joked that my perfect plot would involve a pitch-black cave; just think, no distracting exterior world to worry about! Just two people revealing themselves and falling in love through conversation.

I know the cave thing would be a hard sell, though. But a blizzard cutting off my couple from the outside world? It seemed a great second choice.

And then I found out why "Be careful what you wish for" is an *old* adage.

Because just a few pages into the book, I made a horrifying discovery; Jack wasn't talking. Not to me, not to Tess, not to his dogs or his horses. That's when I knew it was going to take a truly exceptional heroine—brave, strong, clever and wise—to breach his defenses, get past his silences and teach him to love again.

I hope you like the result.

Caroline Cross

THE BABY BLIZZARD

Caroline Cross

One

By the time the pale blue Cadillac began its horrifying slide across the snow-shrouded road, Jack had been trailing behind it for several hours.

It had passed him first on the highway north of Casper. Although it was hard to believe now, when he had to fight the roaring wind and blowing snow to keep his big four-wheel-drive pickup on the road, Jack had been bored at the time. He'd been bored with the unchanging grayness of the sky, the unseasonably mild temperature, the desolate sameness of the surrounding plains.

It had seemed an oppressively dull January day.

It was that very dullness—and its failure to distract him from the black mood he'd been unable to shake since seeing Jared and Elise at the lawyer's office—that had made him take note of the Cadillac.

Plain and simple, he'd been looking for a diversion.

What he'd received instead was a blow to the armor of his indifference.

He scowled, adjusted his grip on the steering wheel as the wind buffeted the truck, and admitted he just didn't get it. So what if the Caddy's driver was a woman? That didn't explain why something as meaningless as the glance they'd exchanged the first time she passed him should affect him like a punch to the belly.

Hell, she wasn't even pretty. Striking, maybe, with that mane of hair the exact same color as his favorite sorrel mare and the sort of lush, full mouth that put a man in mind of all sorts of sinful things.

But not pretty.

Except maybe...when she smiled.

Which she had, he recalled irritably. She'd smiled straight at him, all *Mona Lisa*-knowing, when he drove past the filling station in Kaycee where she'd stopped to gas up. Just the memory set his teeth on edge. Clearly, she'd misunderstood his reason for slowing, assuming it was so he could take a second look at her. In truth, he'd merely been trying to get a bead on the weather, since it had started to snow.

Now, he narrowed his eyes against the river of white beating against the windshield. Grudgingly he conceded that—although his view of his fellow traveler had been partially blocked by an open car door—for once reality had lived up to the initial advertising. A man would have to be blind not to have noticed that her legs were long and slim, her arms and shoulders willowy, her provocative mouth balanced by a stubborn chin and dark, intelligent eyes. Just as he'd have to be obtuse not to conclude from the way the gas jockey had been scurrying around to do her bidding that the parts he couldn't see were as compelling as those he could.

So okay. For a woman who wasn't pretty, she'd been something to see with that soft, amused smile on her face and all that shiny hair blowing in the rising breeze.

Not that he cared, of course—except in the most elemental way.

Jared and Elise had seen to that. Between them, they'd cured him of caring about much of anything. Just as they'd relieved him of all his pretty ideals, his Pollyanna view of the world, his foolish hopes and secret dreams.

Maybe that was why the discovery that his libido wasn't dead after all was such a shock. For three years, since the humiliating day in the judge's chambers when he'd learned just how big a fool he really was, he'd divorced himself from intimacy. He'd banished *want* and *need* from his vocabulary. And he hadn't felt a twinge of desire—for anything or anyone.

Until today.

Jack gave a snort of disgust and wondered what had come over him. There was a whale of difference between viable lust, where you had an actual acquaintance with the person you hankered to touch, and some pointless fantasy about a total stranger. That's why it was so galling to have to admit that ever since the stranger in question had overtaken him again at Crazy Woman Creek— and had the salt to wave as she whipped past—he'd found himself wondering all sorts of things.

Such as whether that russet-colored hair was natural or not. And if her wide, full-lipped mouth would taste tart, like cherries, or as sweet as ripe berries. And how it would feel to have those long, luscious legs wrapped tightly around his waist.

And whether she made a habit of smiling at just anyone.

Foolish. Simply acknowledging such thoughts was

enough to make the tops of his ears feel hot. Particularly when there were far more important matters to be pondered.

For example: Where exactly did she think she was going? He'd assumed she was headed for Gillette until an hour ago, when she'd gone north at Buffalo. Then he'd guessed she must have friends or family in the tiny town of Gweneth, until she drove straight past the turn-off. He'd been hanging back, puzzling over that, when she'd stunned him by slowing down and turning onto Johnson County Road Number 9.

That was when he'd decided she was either lost or crazy or both. Because other than the Double D, which they'd passed some twenty minutes back, the only ranch for the next forty miles was his. And he knew damn well she wasn't coming to see him. Except for business, nobody came to see him anymore.

Not since he'd given away his son.

The familiar anguish splintered through him. Ruthlessly, he forced it away, reminding himself that it was over and done. It was then that the Cadillac began its inexorable slide across the road.

Jack watched in disbelief as the vehicle drifted sideways through the heavily blowing snow, spun slowly around in a heart-stopping three-hundred-and-sixty-degree turn, then disappeared from sight as if sucked into a black hole.

Instantly he eased up on the accelerator. There was no question of driving on. Jared had always claimed he was a Boy Scout at heart and, as Jack had been bitterly reminded in Casper again today, old habits died hard.

But he wasn't going to think about that now. It was over, done, past. He was alone, irrevocably on his own.

Or would be, as soon as he made sure the Cadillac's driver was okay.

The thought brought him up short. Dismay splintered through him. Hell. He was actually going to have to meet this woman. *Leave it to you, Sheridan. You can't even enjoy a little red-blooded, from-a-safe-distance fantasy without reality screwing it up.*

In the very next second, he clamped down on his wayward emotions. This wasn't about him, he reminded himself harshly. This was about someone in trouble, someone in need of help. At the very best, she was going to be bruised and shaken, distraught about what had happened. And at the very worst—

Jack shoved the idea away. It was bad enough he had to get involved at all. No matter what condition this woman was in, he wasn't going to let himself care on a personal level. He'd do what he could to help, one stranger helping another, but that was it.

That was how it had to be.

Keeping an eye on the dim outline of the fence that marched along the road to his left, he let the truck roll to a stop and took a long look around.

Nothing. He could see nothing but swirling sheets of snow reflected in the beams of his headlights. He let loose a single scathing curse. Shifting the transmission into park, he pulled on the emergency brake and doused the lights. He squeezed his eyes shut, allowed them a moment's rest from the eerie onslaught of white, then slowly opened them and surveyed the area.

There. Ahead, and down a long, shallow slope to his right, was a gleam of red. He released a breath as he identified it as a taillight. Now that he knew where to look, he could see the rest of the Cadillac, too. It was barely visible, resting at an angle, with the wheels on

the passenger side sunk into the shallow creekbed that
paralleled the road. Snow, driven by the howling wind,
was already starting to pile against the hood and windshield. The car's pale blue paint blended perfectly with
the monochromatic landscape.

His heart gave a twist. In another few minutes, with
twilight graying swiftly to night, he never would have
seen it.

He switched the headlights back on, then reached
around and grabbed the coil of nylon rope and the
heavy-duty flashlight he kept behind the seat. He
shrugged into his sheepskin-lined coat, flipped up the
collar and jammed his Stetson more securely on his
head.

After a moment's consideration, he elected to leave
the truck running as a hedge against the cold. That decided, he hefted the flashlight, shoved open the door and
plunged into the heart of the storm.

She was not going to panic, Tess Danielson told herself firmly.

Okay, so she'd had a little accident. On a remote, not-
so-well-traveled road. In the middle of nowhere. During
what was distinctly starting to look like a blizzard.

While she was willing to concede that the situation
didn't look good, she was not going to give in to the
dread skating along her spine.

Although…a nice loud scream might make her feel
better.

A smile curled through her. Slowly, she let loose the
breath she hadn't known she was holding and forced
herself to breathe deeply and evenly. Things couldn't be
too bad if she still had a sense of humor. Well, they
could; as a Wyoming native, she'd grown up on tales of

hapless motorists who got caught in this kind of weather and weren't found until the first spring thaw.

But that wasn't going to happen to her.

She refused to let it. She hadn't spent twenty-nine years bending the world to her will to give up now when it really mattered. Not when she'd only recently come to understand what was really important. Not when there were still so many things she wanted to experience. And not when she had someone else—she glanced protectively down at the ripe curve of her belly—depending on her.

She tugged on her seat belt, frowning when the buckle refused to budge. Stymied, she sat there and reconsidered that scream, but only for a second. The first thing she'd done once the car came to rest was turn off the engine. Already the air around her was starting to turn . frosty. While that was better than risking carbon monoxide poisoning from a blocked or bent exhaust pipe, it was still far too cold for useless gestures.

She reached over, snagged her oversize down parka from the passenger seat and draped it around her.

And told herself—again—not to panic.

After all, she wasn't going to freeze to death in the next few minutes. If worse came to worst, she'd simply find her handbag, grab her nail scissors and hack her way through the belt.

If the scissors were there to grab.

Tess resolutely raised her chin and told herself she was not going to worry about that, either. She had an ace in the hole, she reminded herself, recalling the big, fierce-looking cowboy with whom she'd been playing car tag for the past several hours. He hadn't been that far behind her. He must have seen what had happened.

More than likely, he was on his way to help her at this very moment.

Unless his heart turned out to be as black as his expression and he simply drove on.

Tess gave herself a shake. *Knock it off. This is Wyoming, remember? Not L.A. or New York. Around here, people look out for each other. He'll stop. So he looks a tad forbidding. He'll probably turn out to be reserved or shy, a real cupcake of a guy—*

"Ma'am?" came a forceful baritone shout.

A light flashed through the window. Momentarily blinded, Tess brought up her hand as the car door was unceremoniously wrenched open.

"Are you okay?" Her rescuer had to holler to be heard over a sudden roar of wind. Even so, his voice was distinct—dark and demanding. A perfect match for his face, Tess decided, as she stared at him in the faint illumination of the dome light.

Forget shy. Forget reserved. Forget cupcake.

Think intense. Think guarded. Think formidable. From what she could see beneath his hat—shadowed eyes, a straight blade of a nose, a slash of cheekbones, an imperious mouth—he was even more forbidding up close than he'd been from a distance.

"Are you hurt? *Answer me.*"

Intimidating or not, she'd never been so glad to see anyone in her life. Relief slammed into her, making moisture sting her eyes and her voice catch in her throat. She swallowed hard, suspecting as she looked up at that uncompromising face that he'd hate it if she burst into tears. She knew for a fact *she* would. She swallowed again and tried gamely for a lightness she didn't feel. "It's about time you got here."

He froze in the act of hunkering down. His eyes, pale green in the murky light, narrowed. "What?"

Forget a sense of humor, too. Tess raised her voice. "I'm fine."

He continued to stare, as if he didn't believe her. "Are you sure?"

She considered the dull ache in her lower back, concluded the pain scored no more than a two on a scale of one to ten, and opted to ignore it. "Yes."

"All right, then." Relief lightened his face, but did nothing to soften its angular planes. "Give me your hand and let's get you out of there. This storm's getting worse by the minute."

She shook her head. "The seat belt is jammed. I can't get it unfastened."

His eyes flickered over her jacket-covered body. Inexplicably, his jaw bunched for an instant before his expression smoothed out. He hooked the flashlight to his belt, twisted sideways so that he faced her, leaned close and reached around her. His forearm, hard and warm even through the padding of his heavy coat, brushed against the mound of her belly. "What the—?" He went very still. "What is that?"

Tess stiffened. "What's what?"

"That…lump."

She stared at him in disbelief, oddly aware of the weight of his arm against her. "That's not a lump," she informed him. "That's me. I'm pregnant."

He gave her a long, blank look, then snatched away his hand and rocked back on his heels. "Well, hell," he muttered, looking away. "It figures."

The words, clearly not meant for her ears, carried with crystal clarity during a momentary lull in the wind. She raised an eyebrow. "Excuse me?"

For one long second, he remained silent, the hard line of his mouth even harder now. Then he shook his head and gave the slightest shrug. "Forget it," he murmured. He leaned forward and once more reached around her, and an instant later the belt gave way. He ducked back as if he couldn't get away fast enough. "Come on." His voice gruff, he stood.

She stayed where she was. "But the car—"

"Isn't going anywhere. Not now. Probably not for a while. Even if I could see to winch you out, the road's too icy to get any traction. In case you haven't noticed, it's dark—and getting darker."

Tess looked around in surprise. He was right. As incredible as it seemed, with the snow falling and the wind roaring, she'd been so intent on him, so totally taken with their exchange, she'd actually forgotten about the weather.

Which appeared to be getting worse. And still she hesitated. "I don't even know your name."

"Oh, for—" Annoyance flashed in those leaf-green eyes before he quickly got himself under control. "Jack," he said flatly. "My name is Jack Sheridan, okay?"

"And I'm Tess—"

"Terrific. So listen, *Tess*. We need to get to my truck. Now. While we still can."

He was right, of course. Annoyed at herself for behaving so foolishly, Tess swung her feet to the ground, trying to figure out why she felt compelled to challenge him.

The answer came a moment later, as she began the awkward process of extricating the rest of herself from the car. Without warning, Jack leaned in, grasped her firmly above each elbow and lifted her out. Then, in a few brusque, capable movements, he bundled her into her parka, zipped it, reached into the car and retrieved her car keys, pocketbook and overnight bag. "Here." He handed her the first two items. "Put your keys away and sling the shoulder strap of your purse around your neck so your hands are free, okay?"

That's when Tess knew. She'd never done very well with authority figures, and this guy was more than a little bossy. He was autocratic.

Which was a pretty petty concern, she chided herself a second later, when the wind nearly knocked her off her feet and he immediately leaped forward to steady her. Holding her firmly against his broad, hard chest, he turned to block her from the wind. "You okay?"

She lifted her chin and nodded, surprised to find that his face was several inches above hers. She was tall herself, and it wasn't often she had to look up at anyone. For a heartbeat, they stared at each other. His eyes really were the most extraordinary color—

"Shoot." He uttered the sibilant word with such disgust it sounded like an expletive. "What the hell is your husband thinking, letting you run around like this in your condition?"

It wasn't a question, and Tess knew it. For some reason, she wanted to answer him, however. "I'm not married." She had just enough presence of mind not to add that if she was, it wouldn't be to anyone who thought in terms of "letting her" do anything.

"Forget it," he replied, in what she was starting to recognize as his stock answer in awkward moments. "I've got a line running to the truck," he went on, all business again. "All you need to do is stay close to me and we shouldn't have any problems. When I turn around, I want you to put your hands under my coat and grab on to the back of my belt. Whatever you do, don't let go. Understand?''

Tess didn't need to be told twice. The driving snow stung her face and brought tears to her eyes, while the cold was so bitter it hurt to breathe. "Got it."

He searched her face. Satisfied with whatever he saw there, he finally gave a curt nod. "Good."

He turned and picked up her overnight bag as if it weighed nothing, then held his ground as she ran her hands up the backs of his denim-clad thighs and over the hard curve of his small masculine behind. Beneath the heavy coat, his cotton-clad back felt firm and solid. Heat rolled off him like a furnace. She took a half step closer and curled her fingers around his belt.

He set off, adjusting his step to her shorter stride. She held on tight, her universe condensed to the broad back in front of her, and concentrated on putting one foot in front of the other. It was no mean feat, given the sloping, uneven ground and the clumps of frozen bunchgrass that kept trying to trip her up.

Although the entire trip probably didn't last much more than a few minutes, to Tess it seemed to take forever. Accustomed to being fit, she'd found the change in her center of gravity in the past few months exasperating. Now, she gritted her teeth, frustrated by her own helplessness as she repeatedly stumbled and slipped. In several instances it was only her rescuer's iron strength that kept her upright. By the time they reached the truck, her lungs burned, the pain in her back was a solid six, and her face felt frozen.

"You okay?" Jack asked as he tossed her bag into the pickup's bed before he yanked open the door.

"Sure," she lied, leaning wearily against the wheel

well. Out of breath, she mentally apologized to him for her earlier intolerance.

"Good."

He'd lost his hat. He looked younger without it. His windblown hair was dark and thick, as glossy as a child's. For some reason, that bothered her. Before she could decide why, he stepped over and dusted the snow from her head and shoulders with his gloved hands. Then he lifted her up, swung her around and deposited her on the car seat, where he brushed off her pant legs, stripped off her snow-caked boots and tossed them, the rope and the flashlight into the narrow storage area behind the seat. "Scoot over," he instructed. Stamping his own booted feet, he yanked off his gloves, shrugged out of his coat and climbed in beside her.

Tess slid over to give him more room, steeling herself against the pain squeezing her back. The well-insulated cab seemed hushed after the din outside. It was also pleasantly warm. In contrast, Tess felt chilled to the bone. She began to shiver, her teeth chattering like maracas.

Something that might have been compassion flared briefly in Jack's pale eyes. He turned up the heater fan, retrieved his coat from the back of the seat and tucked it around her. "That better?"

She nodded, incapable of speech.

That appeared to suit him just fine. Mouth set once again in a grim line, he pulled her shoulder harness around her and buckled it. Then he secured his own, released the brake and put the truck in gear. It rolled forward, fishtailing a little before the tires caught.

Tess pulled his coat tighter around her, burying her face in the soft shearling collar. The distinctive scent of horses and damp leather, familiar from her childhood, tickled her nose. Oddly comforted, she leaned back and closed her eyes.

She wasn't sure how much time passed, but eventually she began to feel less like a Popsicle and more like a person. She stretched, sighing with pleasure at the stream of hot air from the heater that blew over her stocking toes as she tried to find a position that would alleviate the persistent pain in her back.

She wound up canted sideways, toward her companion. Veiling her gaze with her lashes, she covertly studied him. She had to admit she was a little intimidated by his continuing silence. Her reaction surprised her. She'd grown up around cowboys, and she was no stranger to private, taciturn men.

Jack didn't seem to be thinking so much as brooding, however. And that tight look on his face was hardly benign. In point of fact, he had the air of an individual who kept to himself not because he preferred his own company, but because he didn't trust anyone else's.

And yet…he *had* come to her rescue. And for all his brusque manner, his hard-fingered hands had been carefully gentle every single time he touched her.

More to the point, what did it matter? Soon they would both go their own ways, never to clap eyes on each other again—

"Didn't anyone ever teach you it's rude to stare?" Jack asked abruptly.

Tess started, then forced herself to relax, the willful part of her nature asserting itself. It was one thing to privately confess that she found him intimidating. Letting him know was something else entirely. "You're right," she said calmly. "Sorry."

"You want to explain what you're doing out here?"

Why, she wondered, did he have to be so abrupt? "Visiting my grandmother."

"Ah." He imbued the single syllable with a wealth of disdain. "But instead you got lost."

"I wasn't lost. I missed my turn."

"Right." He didn't sound as if he thought much of that, either. "I don't suppose it occurred to you when the snow started to fall that maybe you were out of your league?"

"I grew up here," she said patiently. "I know about snow."

"Huh. Could have fooled me."

"For your information, the only reason I had a problem was because I slowed down to let you pass, so I could turn around."

He snorted. "Because you were lost."

If he was trying to annoy her, he was doing a good job. "What about you?"

"What about me?"

"I suppose it's all right for you to be out in a blizzard?"

That granite face didn't change. "Damn straight. I've got heavy-duty snow tires, four-wheel drive, and I know what I'm doing. Besides, I've got obligations. If I don't get home, my stock won't get fed."

"Where's home?" She was certain he hadn't lived around here when she was a teenager. She'd remember.

"Cross Creek Ranch. We should be there in another few minutes."

Tess made no effort to hide her surprise. "Oh. But—"

"Look," he said sharply. "I'm not wild about taking you there, either. But we need to get in out of this storm while we still can, and mine's the closest place for miles."

Tess let a moment of silence pass. "Are you finished?" she asked finally.

His jaw bunched. "Yeah."

"Good. For the record, going to your place is fine. It's extremely nice of you to offer, and I appreciate it. I appreciate everything you've done."

"But—?" He kept his gaze glued to the road as he carefully braked to make a wide left turn, the headlights flashing across a sign that bore the ranch's name above a stylized carving of a rocking horse.

"When I lived here, this ranch was owned by some people named Langston."

He shot her a sharp glance as they rumbled across a cattle guard marked at both sides with orange reflectors. Around them, the landscape was hard to make out. The few trees and low-rising hills were nothing more than a series of ebony shadows against a charcoal night shrouded with blowing snow.

He slowed even more as their ride grew bumpier over the graveled drive. "You really used to live around here?"

She sighed at his obvious skepticism. "Yes. At the Double D. Mary Danielson's my grandmother." That earned her a single sharp look. "I can't figure out how I missed the turn for the driveway."

He was silent. He shifted the automatic transmission into low as the truck slid on a shallow grade. "Maybe," he said finally, "you weren't looking in the right place."

She waited for him to say more. When he didn't, she had to swallow another sigh. "Do you think you could explain that?"

He shrugged. "Your grandma cut a new road a few years back, when she had to redrill the well at Shell Butte. That must've been right after I bought out Langston, and that's been—'' he shifted the truck back into regular drive ''—seven years ago.''

''Oh.'' Even though there was no way she could have known, she felt foolish. Perhaps that was why she was less than enthralled with his next comment.

''Too bad you don't bother to come home more often.''

She frowned, taken aback by his obvious disapproval. ''I don't think that's any of your business.''

''Yeah? Well, it is when I'm stuck with you.''

''Trust me. Just as soon as the storm passes, someone from the Double D will be over to get me.''

He gave her another narrow look. ''Your grandma left three days ago for an extended vacation.''

''What?'' She felt momentarily disoriented, the way she had when her car began to slide.

''It's one of those things you'd know about if you kept in touch—or were here because you'd been invited.''

She bit off the instant retort that trembled on her lips. She'd be darned if she'd justify her behavior to him. She wasn't about to explain that she'd both written and called ahead, stating her intention to visit and supplying the date of her arrival. Or that her grandmother's departure was the older woman's oblique reply, an apparent payback for Tess's own decision to leave ten years ago.

For one thing, she didn't go around explaining her behavior to rude, disapproving strangers—no matter how compelling they were.

For another, unless she was mistaken, she had a much more pressing problem.

''Damn,'' Jack said abruptly.

''What's the matter?''

''The power's out.''

Following his gaze, she glanced around as they drove into the ranch yard. Although a pair of dogs had come to attention on the back porch, not a single light glowed in welcome. Not from the pitch-roofed barn with its adjacent corrals, or the covered arena, or the rambling two-story house that looked pretty much the way she remembered it from childhood.

Tess's heart sank as she realized something more. She wasn't in the city anymore. Way out here, when the power went, so did the phones, since the two lines shared the same poles.

The icing on the cake. She took a deep breath. "Jack?"

"What?"

"Do you have a wife?"

He stared straight ahead. "Not anymore. Why? You thinking of applying for the job?"

"No." Tess shook her head, clenching her hands as the pain, previously limited to her lower back, snaked along her sides and wrapped around her middle like an invisible boa constrictor. She gave an involuntary gasp as the painful pressure increased. "I'm in labor."

Two

Jack didn't think. He reacted. *"No."* He swiveled toward Tess and shook his head. "Absolutely *not.*"

Her eyes, big and velvety like winter pansies, widened in astonishment. "What?"

"No way." He shook his head again, adamant. "You're not having a baby. Not here. Not now. *Not with me.*"

For the space of one endless, protracted second, she continued to send him that same incredulous look. Then she abruptly crossed her arms above her rounded middle and shifted her gaze to the darkness beyond the windshield. Her mouth—soft, lush, with an undeniable carnality that was all wrong on an expectant mother—flattened dangerously. "All right."

It was the very last thing he expected. Primed for an argument, he stared blankly at her, struggling to get himself under control. "Good." He knew he was behaving badly. He told himself he didn't care. It was better than having her suspect the anxiety her announcement had brought him.

"Here." She laid his coat down on the section of seat between them. "Thanks for the loan." She shoved open the door and climbed out.

Jack gaped. "Where do you think you're going?"

"To the house. There must be someone there who'll help." She slammed the door.

Stunned, he sat frozen in place, his thoughts churning. Hell! What had he ever done to deserve this? One small good deed, one humanitarian be-a-good-citizen gesture, and suddenly he was stuck with a stubborn, unreasonable, overly independent woman who didn't have the sense to stay out of a snowstorm. A woman who, if she really was in labor, was going to have to rely on *him* to deliver her baby.

Just the idea made his throat tighten. Memories, ruthlessly suppressed for the past three years, flashed through his mind. He recalled how happy he'd been when Elise told him she was pregnant. It had been enough to make him ignore his uneasiness when she asked him to move into a spare room so that he wouldn't disturb her rest. It had sustained him through his loneliness when she insisted on moving into Gweneth her last trimester to be closer to the doctor. It had even made it possible for him to swallow his desperate disappointment when he arrived too late for the birth because someone had forgotten to call him. It had all seemed worth it when he finally held his small, precious, perfect son.

Unbidden, an arrow of longing pierced him. The boy would be almost three and a half now, walking, talking, his big green eyes full of questions—

All of sudden Jack realized what he was doing. This wasn't going to help anyone, he thought savagely, slamming a door on the past. He could rail against fate, he could rehash history, he could sit around feeling sorry for himself indefinitely, but the end result would be the same. The child was gone, forever beyond his reach... and Tess had no one to rely on but him.

He took a calming breath and forced himself to look at the situation dispassionately. Tess's labor had just started. Chances were, her baby wouldn't be born for hours, possibly not even until sometime tomorrow. Hell, by the time she was actually ready to deliver, the weather might well have improved, the phone lines might be restored and he could call for help. Once he did, she would no longer be his problem.

In the meantime, all he had to do was provide shelter and a cursory moral support. As long as they both remained calm, there was no reason why they couldn't get through this like the pair of adults they were. Unless something happened to her, he thought suddenly, as a particularly vicious gust of wind rattled the truck. For example, if she were to slip and fall...

He twisted around to grab his hat, forgetting he'd lost it, and that was when he noticed Tess's damp boots, lying exactly were he'd tossed them earlier.

Damn, damn, *damn.* The little fool was out there without any shoes! His newfound calm evaporated in a flash. He shoved open his door and scrambled out of the truck. Heedless of the fact that he'd forgotten his coat, he stormed across the yard, catching up with her in a few furious strides. Ignoring her cry of surprise, he scooped her into his arms. "You just don't learn, do you?" he shouted over the shriek of the wind.

"Learn what?" she replied, her voice muffled as she

buried her face against the warmth of his thinly covered shoulder.

"To get the lay of the land before you go hightailing off." He marched up the three wide, shallow steps and across the wraparound porch, skirting a trio of wooden rockers that swayed in the breeze as if filled with invisible occupants.

"What do you mean?"

"I mean there's nobody here but me and you!" With a curt command to the dogs to stay down, he thrust open the back door, strode across the mudroom and opened the second door into the big country kitchen.

"What?" For the first time, she sounded uncertain. "What are you talking about? This is a big ranch. You can't possibly..." Her voice trailed off. She cleared her throat. "You can't possibly run it by yourself."

"The hell I can't," he said curtly. "I got rid of my herd a few years ago." His voice, though hardly more than a murmur, sounded harsh and loud in the pitch-dark quiet, but at least he'd managed to state the facts with none of the furious anguish he'd felt at the time. "Now I've just got horses."

Tess, still clutched in his arms, shifted. "Oh," she said in surprise.

Her scent came up at him, delicate, mysterious, feminine. He had a sudden, vivid recollection of how it felt to lie naked with a woman, to touch her in all her soft, silky places—

What was he thinking? She was about to have a baby. Disgusted with himself, he set her on her feet. "Stay here while I get a light. I don't want you banging into something." Despite his terse tone, he took an extra second to steady her, then strode to the big walk-in pantry, grateful for the privacy.

He halted before the shelves where the emergency supplies were kept, wondering what was the matter with him. Three years of living like a monk, and the first time he felt so much as an itch for a woman, she happened to be pregnant by somebody else.

The irony of it sent a bitter smile twisting across his lips—and cooled his treacherous hormones like a plunge into a snowbank. With an impatient jerk, he lifted down two of the half-dozen battery-operated lanterns and thumbed on the switches. There was a dim glow and then a flash as the fluorescent bulbs came on.

He walked back into the kitchen to find Tess standing rigidly, her face pale, her mouth taut with pain. It didn't take a genius to figure out she was having a contraction. He slapped the lanterns on the kitchen table with a clatter, yanked out a chair and strode to her side. "Come on," he said gruffly. "You'd better sit down." He slung an arm around her and tried to usher her toward the chair.

"No." Stubbornly, she held her ground. "Standing...standing is better than sitting and this is...the pain is starting to fade." Another few seconds passed, and then she abruptly relaxed. Her breath sighed out and she leaned against him. After a moment, she straightened. "Thanks. I'm okay now."

Jack was damn glad somebody was. To his disgust, his heart was pounding.

He willed it to slow, watching as she took a quick look around, her eyes widening with surprise when she saw the ultra-modern kitchen with its pale birch cabinets and new appliances. An open counter was all that separated it from the family room, which was dominated by a big flagstone fireplace. The service stairs climbed the far wall, while straight ahead was the hallway that led to the living room, dining room, bathroom and den, and the more formal main staircase.

In the family room, there was a couch and a pair of overstuffed chairs atop a dark area rug, the varying gray, green and cream fabrics bled of color by the room's deep shadows. A built-in entertainment center occupied the wall to the right of the fireplace, notable for the large empty space where the TV should have been.

Jack wondered what his guest would say if he told her he'd smashed it into a thousand pieces the night his wife announced she was leaving him.

Not that it was any of her business. "How far apart are the pains?"

"I'm not sure," she said unsteadily. "Maybe…four minutes?"

"Four minutes?" He loosened his grip and stepped back as if she'd goosed him. "What are you talking about? I thought they just started."

She shrugged. "Actually, my back has hurt off and on since this morning. I just didn't realize what it was."

So much for calling for help tomorrow. He took a hard, critical look at her midsection. Elise, though a full head shorter, had been twice that size when she delivered. "How far along are you?"

"Eight and a half months."

Part of him relaxed; the baby should be all right. But part of him was unexpectedly furious, stunned by her irresponsibility. "What the hell were you thinking, running around the countryside when you're this far along?" he demanded.

A wash of color rose in her chill-pinkened cheeks. "Listen, *Jack*. I didn't do this just to ruin your day. And despite what you seem to think, I'm not some reckless airhead. I saw my doctor yesterday. She didn't see anything to indicate I was about to deliver, and I didn't expect to get caught in a blizzard. Why should I? It wasn't predicted, and until today, this has been the mildest winter on record. However—'' she took a deep breath as she struggled to control her temper ''—it's also not your problem. So if you could just spare me a room, I promise not to bother you.''

''Don't tempt me.'' Despite his words, he felt an unwanted twinge of admiration for her nerve—until he remembered how far her labor had progressed. Four minutes! Hell, she was going to need all the nerve she could scrape together and then some. He picked up the lamp and thrust it at her. ''Here. Hold this.''

''Why?'' she started to ask, only to give a startled yelp as he swept her up in his arms.

''Because I've only got two hands.'' He headed for the service stairs that spanned the interior wall. ''And you're not exactly a fragile flower.''

''Put me down,'' she ordered, clutching his neck for balance.

He gave an involuntary grunt as she jabbed him in the chest with her elbow. ''Forget it. Apparently you haven't noticed, but your socks are covered with snow, which means your feet are probably half-frozen. All I need to round out my day is for you to slip and fall. Now hold still before I lose my balance and break both our necks.''

She gave a little huff, but quit squirming. After a moment's silence, she asked, ''Where are we going?''

Didn't she ever quit talking? ''Upstairs.''

''Why?''

''Because it's cold. Because even with the emergency generator, it's going to take hours to get this place warmed up. Because the only room in the house with a bed, a bathroom and a fireplace—all of which you're going to need—is upstairs. Okay? Satisfied?'' He gave her a quick, impatient glance. ''Or is there something else you have to know? My social security number? My shirt size?''

''Look, I'm sorry—''

''Yeah, right.'' She couldn't be half as sorry as he was, he reflected, angling sideways to avoid knocking her into the walls that enclosed the steep, narrow risers.

But then, he'd cut out his tongue before he admitted that he hadn't set foot on the second floor more than a half dozen times in the past trio of years. Or that when he had, it had been only briefly, to fetch and haul for his mother who showed up periodically to fuss at him about getting on with his life. It was certainly none of Ms. Danielson's business that for him the upper reaches of the house teemed with memories he preferred to ignore.

It was nobody's business but his own.

He rounded the corner at the top of the stairs and made his way down the long hall to the closed double doors that marked the master suite, where he deposited Tess on her feet. Face set, he hesitated for the barest instant, then reached for the polished brass handles.

''Jack—''

Sunk in thought, he jerked his head around in surprise as she laid her hand on his shoulder. *''What?''*

''You don't have to give up your bedroom for me,'' she said softly. ''I'll be fine somewhere else—''

Her sudden concern was worse than her questions. Alarmed at what she might have seen in his face to prompt such an offer, he shrugged off her hand and thrust open the door. ''I sleep downstairs.'' He strode to the fireplace, hunkered down and opened the fire screen. "Hold the lamp steady, will you?"

He wondered what she'd make of the room. It was decorated in what Elise had claimed was pseudo-Victorian, but what he'd privately always termed Neo-Pretentious. A thick white rug, totally impractical for a working ranch, covered the wood floor. Lace swags hid the more practical window shades. The queen-size bed had a fussy floral bedspread and canopy, while the chairs that faced the fireplace were slipcovered in a contrasting geometric pattern. As for the rest...well, anything that didn't have a ruffle or a flounce had a fringe or a bow. The overall effect made his teeth ache.

He checked the damper, then lit the kindling beneath the logs already laid on the grate. To his relief, the fire caught immediately. He closed the screen, glanced pointedly at Tess and jerked his head toward the bed. "Sit down so I can have a look at your feet."

For a moment she didn't move, but then she walked over, set the lantern on the nightstand and sat on the mattress edge.

He knelt and peeled off her socks. Her icy feet were long and slim. "They look all right," he said after a careful inspection, relieved to find none of the telltale white spots that would indicate frostbite. "How do they feel?"

"Cold." He glanced up, surprised to see the corners of her mouth curve up in a tentative smile. "But otherwise okay. Thanks."

He shrugged. "Forget it." Her eyes weren't really blue at all, he saw, but closer to the purple color of the gentian violet he used to treat minor cuts on the livestock.

"Jack?"

"What?"

"Did you and your wife.... Do you have any children?"

He couldn't believe his ears. He stood. "That's none of your business."

"You're right," she said immediately. "I'm sorry. I just thought it might help if one of us knew what they were doing—"

"The bathroom's through there." He indicated the door set into the wall at her right. "I need to move the truck and get the generator started and check on my horses, but I'll bring you your bag, some dry socks and some extra blankets before I go."

"All right."

"Do you have a watch?"

She shook her head. "No, I'm afraid I—"

"Here." Cutting across her explanation, he stripped off his and handed it to her.

She clutched it in her hand. "Thank you."

"I'll see you in a little while." Face set, he strode from the room.

Tess was blessed with an iron constitution. She rarely got sick, but when she did she always bounced back in record time. She was also lucky; despite being both adventurous and athletic, and having tried everything from hang gliding to parasailing, she'd never broken a bone or suffered a serious injury.

That was probably why she was so scared now.

Standing with her hands braced against the mantelpiece, she prayed for the current contraction to ease. As silly as it seemed, she was shocked by how much being in labor hurt—and how quickly that pain was wearing her down. She couldn't seem to rise above it, or outsmart it, or brazen it out, the way she had so many other obstacles in her life. Given that things would likely get worse before they got better, she was starting to suspect that she wasn't going to make it through the next few hours with any dignity whatsoever.

It was a humbling admission. Tess considered her strength, both mental and physical, to be as much a part of her as her utterly straight hair, her too-wide mouth, her tendency to do what she felt was right, regardless of the consequences. But now, when she needed it most, her strength seemed to have deserted her. It had gone missing along with her nerve and her luck—

Stop it. Stop feeling sorry for yourself and think about something else.

Okay. How about that this wasn't even close to what she'd pictured when she envisioned giving birth? She'd wanted her and Gray's child, conceived out of such incredible sadness, to be born in tranquil, joyous circumstances. She'd even had a plan: Beethoven on the CD player in the birthing room at Eastside Hospital; her friend and obstetrician, Joanne Fetzer, in attendance; herself, in control, her life in order, ready to welcome the future after having made peace with her past.

Instead, that past, in the form of her grandmother, had lit out for God knew where. The baby was early. And she didn't have the calm, ultracompetent Dr. Fetzer to depend on. Instead, her designated stork was the ultimate charm school dropout—and an undependable one, at that. True, he'd brought her the things he'd promised. But that had been more than forty minutes ago. While Tess could practically hear her childbirth instructor prattling on about how first births usually took forever, that obviously wasn't the case here. If Jack didn't show up soon, he was going to miss the main event.

Not, she chided herself, that she was counting on him to be much help. He'd made it clear he'd prefer not to be part of the delivery. And as much as she'd have liked to hold it against him, she couldn't—not when her own mind shut down every time she tried to visualize the two of them sharing such intimacy. It would be daunting enough with someone she already knew, or with some- one older or kinder or more approachable. But to even consider it with Jack... Well, the idea was simply im- possible.

Although she supposed that anything would be better than being alone...

The contraction began to ease. She waited until she was sure it was over before she released her stranglehold on the mantel, and even then she didn't lift her head until she heard a faint, unfamiliar rumble. She glanced around, then realized the noise was the sound of the furnace coming on. Her heart started to pound. Moving carefully, she walked to the door and looked down the hall, and was rewarded when a light bloomed on at the base of the stairs. A moment later Jack appeared, a stack of supplies in his arms.

Finally. For the second time that night, tears of relief welled in Tess's eyes. Only this time, she was unable to will them away, and they spilled down her cheeks. Mor- tified, she ducked back inside and shuffled toward the fireplace, praying he hadn't seen her. Her back to the door, she barely managed to strike a casual pose when she heard him stride into the room.

His footsteps ceased. "What are you doing up?" She could hear the surprise in his voice.

Apparently his time at the barn hadn't done a thing to improve his manner. She swallowed. "I was cold," she murmured, her voice raw.

Thankfully, he didn't seem to notice. "So why aren't you in bed, under the covers?"

"My back hurts. I don't want to lie down." She certainly didn't feel compelled to explain that being upright gave her an illusion of control she wasn't ready to surrender.

"Huh."

She could feel him studying her. She pretended absorption in the fire, grateful for the flickering shadows.

"How far apart are the pains?"

"Two minutes."

"Are you sure?"

"Yes." She cleared her throat again. "What took you so long?"

"I had to feed the horses."

"Ah." Out of the corner of her eye, she saw him head toward the dresser.

"I brought some things. Towels. More sheets and blankets. Some scissors and string." Light flooded the room as he switched on a lamp.

"Ah," she said again. She wondered what he planned to do with the string. She'd just decided she didn't want to know when the familiar tightening began to spread across her middle. She bit her lip and pressed a hand to the small of her back, making a wordless little murmur of protest as the contraction rolled through her like a wave. She reached blindly for the back of the chair to one side of her, her fingers digging into the plush-covered frame until the pain began to ebb.

Gradually she grew aware of the awkward quality of the silence, unbroken except for the crackle of the wood in the fireplace and the steady wail of the wind whistling around the house. She swiped at her damp face, feeling foolish when she realized her hand was shaking.

Jack cleared his throat. "You okay?"

"Yes." She straightened and turned slowly in his direction. To her surprise, he was only a few feet away, as if he'd started toward her, then changed his mind. For a moment, their eyes met. The line of his mouth tightened, and she realized how she must look, her cheeks shiny, her nose red, her eyes puffy. She looked away.

"I brought a tarp for the mattress," he said gruffly. He took a step toward the bed, then stopped and gestured toward the thermos sharing space on the dresser with the other things he'd brought. He gestured toward the dresser. "Are you thirsty? I made some coffee."

Just the thought made her stomach roll. She shook her head. "No thanks."

"Okay." He moved to the far side of the bed, peeled back the covers and unfolded a rectangle of canvas. Determined not to dwell on the panic that threatened to overwhelm her, she focused on his hands. They were large, with long, elegant fingers, their every gesture deft, sure and competent. She supposed she ought to feel reassured.

She didn't.

As if he felt her watching him, he looked up. His gaze flickered over her. "Interesting outfit."

She fingered the sheet, folded in half and wrapped around her waist, that she was wearing in lieu of her pants. "My water broke." She couldn't resist the little devil that made her add, "Be glad you weren't here. It wasn't pretty."

He gave her a sharp glance, his hands stilling briefly before he resumed smoothing out the sheet he'd stretched over the tarp. He shook his head. "I bet you were a real pain in the butt as a kid."

She couldn't contain a slight smile. "Still am."

He flashed her another look, and she thought she detected a flicker of surprise in his leaf-green eyes. He pulled the covers back into place. "Yeah, well... I suppose you come by it honestly."

"How do you mean?"

He shrugged. "I've done business with your grandmother. She can be a little...difficult."

Tess made an unladylike sound. "Impossible is more like it. Where Gram's concerned, there's only one way to do anything—hers."

He came around the bed. She tensed as he closed the distance between them, then felt foolish as he reached past her for the poker, squatted down and attended to the fire. "Is that why you left? You couldn't get your own way?"

She looked down at his dark head, taking note of the way the hair feathered over his shirt collar. "I suppose you could say that. I wanted to go to college, see more of the world than northern Wyoming. Gram wouldn't hear of it. As far as she was concerned, the Double D *was* the world."

Jack tossed another log on the fire. "But you went anyway, right?" His voice had an edge she didn't understand.

"That's right." She was darned if she'd explain that she'd written regularly, concerned that her grandmother might worry. Or that every letter had been returned, bearing the single word *Refused* penned in Mary's decisive handwriting. He'd obviously already reached some sort of conclusion about her character—and it wasn't pretty.

He climbed to his feet. He was so close she could see the faint, silvery line of a scar high on his right cheekbone. "So why show up now? Or—" he glanced pointedly down at the taut bulge of her belly "—do I need to ask?"

She wondered again why he seemed so determined to assume the worst. "Look. I'm not indigent, and I didn't come here for a handout or to beg a roof over my head. I came because I thought my grandmother ought to know she was about to have a great-grandchild."

"Yeah? I bet the kid's father is thrilled about that," he muttered.

It was the second time that night he'd brought up the baby's father, and Tess had enough. "Save your sympathy," she said tersely, "at least for Gray. He's dead."

If she meant to surprise him, she'd succeeded. Although his expression didn't change, she could see the shock in his glorious green eyes—and an unmistakable flash of regret for what he'd said.

All of a sudden, she felt exhausted, and more than a little ashamed herself. She turned away, back toward the fire. "Please. Just go away— *Oh!*" She gasped as a bolt of pain lanced through her, doubling her over.

She forgot her anger at Jack as she realized that this contraction already felt far worse than the preceding ones. She gritted her teeth so hard her jaw ached, but it didn't help. Instead, the pain increased, winding tighter and tighter. Tess began to panic. She couldn't do this, she thought frantically, little black dots dancing behind her eyelids as she squeezed her eyes shut. She could handle an accident, a blizzard, Gram's rejection, Gray's loss, a hostile stranger—but not this excruciating, overwhelming, unrelenting pain, too. She swayed, biting her lip to keep from crying out, afraid that if she started, she wouldn't be able to stop.

Suddenly a hard, steely arm came around her.

"Breathe," Jack ordered, his deep, impatient voice close to her ear.

Disoriented, she forced her eyes open. "What?"

He stared down at her, his expression grim. "I said *breathe*. In through your nose and out through your mouth. Like this." He demonstrated.

Gasping fitfully, she shook her head. "I— I—can't."

True to form, he disagreed. "You *can*. Look at me and concentrate."

His certainty—and some last little remnant of bravado—brought her chin up. Clutching his arm, she ignored the tears blurring her vision and attempted to pattern her breathing after his. It wasn't easy. At first she felt so frantic and light-headed that with every breath she was sure she was going to hyperventilate.

Jack wasn't having it, however. Through the sheer force of his will, he kept her focused until she was gradually able to inhale and exhale more and more deeply. At some point, the pain seemed to lessen a fraction.

Even so, an eternity seemed to pass before the contraction finally ended. Dazed, every muscle in her body quivering, Tess sagged against Jack. He felt wonderful, lean, hard, warm and solid, and she was suddenly too grateful for his presence to be concerned with anything else. "Thanks," she said when she finally found her voice.

He tensed, but didn't move away. "Why the hell didn't you take a childbirth class?"

She swallowed a sigh. *Forget cupcake—remember?* "I did. I've just never been very good at following directions."

Silence. And then a grunt. "Huh. I never would've guessed."

"What about you?"

"What about me?"

"Do you practice being rude?" she asked mildly, finally looking up at him. "Or is it a natural talent?"

Their gazes met for a long, measuring moment. Whatever he felt was impossible to decipher, but for once he was the first to look away. "Can you walk?"

"Yes. Can you?"

He shook his head. "What I meant," he said caustically, "was do you think you can make it to the bed?"

She considered. Her lower body felt leaden, the muscles weighted. "I don't know. Why?"

"Because you need to lie down before the baby shows up and drops out on its head."

She sighed, this time loudly and on purpose. "You know, Jack, you really have a way with words."

"Can you walk or not?"

It was only five feet. How hard could it be? "Sure." She let loose of him and took a step.

A second later, a new contraction struck her, and her knees gave out.

Three

"**W**hat is it with you?" Jack demanded as the contraction finally eased and Tess loosened the punishing grip she had on his hand. He sat back, shifting to a more settled position on the edge of the bed. Despite his outer calm and the deliberate way he'd coached her along, his heart was still thundering from how close she'd come to falling flat on her face. "You take an oath against asking for help?"

Tess hitched herself up higher against the pile of pillows he'd placed at her back and sent him a reproachful glance. "Gosh, Jack. Don't start being nice now or I'll really lose it."

The cheeky response tugged at him. All right. So he didn't exactly like her. She was too willful, too smart, too *here*. That didn't mean he couldn't admire her grit. "You just don't quit, do you?"

She shook her head. "No. But if it's any consolation,

this isn't quite how I envisioned having this baby, either."

Their eyes met, and something inside him stilled when he saw the look in hers a second before she glanced away. Hell. If it was anyone else, he'd swear that beneath that glib exterior, she was…scared.

The idea brought him up short. As did his sudden, unsettling realization that ever since he'd yanked open the Cadillac's door all those hours ago, he'd been so provoked by her intrusion into his life and so preoccupied with how he felt about it, he'd taken her seemingly inexhaustible composure at face value. She'd acted as if she could handle anything, and he'd believed it.

Now, as if a blindfold had been ripped away, he could see the quiver at the corners of her mouth, the pulse pounding at the base of her throat, the effort behind her composure.

And he didn't like it. He didn't like it at all. "Hey," he said, more sharply than he intended. "What's the matter?" *Nice. If they were giving prizes for stupid, you'd need a trophy case.*

Thankfully, she was so busy studying the fire, she didn't seem to notice. "Nothing. It just…hurts."

He could see how much the admission cost her. "Oh." Another intelligent response. Frustrated, he searched for something relevant to say. "Yeah, well…I think you're through transition, so it shouldn't take much longer."

The instant the words left his mouth, he knew he'd made a mistake.

Her head came around. Questions suddenly crowded her eyes. How come he knew so much? Where had he come by such knowledge?

It was a measure of her ability to unsettle him that for

an instant Jack was tempted to explain. Except...what the hell would he say? That once upon a time he'd had a pregnant wife? That in an effort to be a good husband, a good father, he'd learned everything he could about pregnancy and childbirth, postpartum care and infant development?

Yeah, right—and then what? *You going to tell her how, in the end, none of it mattered? You going to cry on her shoulder, tell her how Elise left you, explain why you gave up your son?*

No way.

"Jack—"

"What?" He braced, wondering what she'd ask first.

As if she sensed his imminent withdrawal, Tess reached out and entwined her fingers with his, as if to anchor some part of him in place. "Can I get that part about this...not taking much longer...in writing?"

For a moment he was sure he hadn't heard her right. Then he assumed she must be toying with him. Anger flashed through him. He jerked his gaze to her face.

To his surprise, she wasn't even looking at him. As a matter of fact, her eyes were shut, her lips pressed together. She clutched at his hand as the mound of her stomach began to tighten convulsively. "Oh!" she gasped, holding on to him for dear life. "Oh, Jack, it hurts—!"

Her trust, in the face of what he'd been thinking, brought the last line of his defenses crashing down. "Easy. It's okay—"

But it wasn't. The contraction bowed her back, brought her arching up off the bed. She opened her eyes, staring at him in helpless distress.

He felt an edge of panic, and struggled to get a grip on himself. God knew, there wasn't a whole lot he do for her except pretend to be calm. He caught her other hand, as if to lend her some of his strength by the contact. "Stop fighting it," he said forcefully. "I know it hurts, but you're doing fine. Just don't forget to breathe."

She nodded, the flesh across her nose and cheeks taut with strain.

Then there was no more time for conversation, as the contractions began to come one after another, faster and faster. Everything seemed to blur together, the labored sound of her breathing, the muscle-wrenching expenditure of effort, the unrelenting, escalating cycle of pain. Jack didn't know how much time had passed when Tess suddenly gave a tremendous shudder. Her eyes widened. "Oh! I can't— There's something— It's coming—"

Earlier, out in the barn, he'd imagined this moment with dread. Not the mechanics of it; he'd barely given that a second thought. Like every rancher, he'd helped deliver his fair share of calves and foals, and he was more than familiar with the nuts and bolts of birth.

But to share such extreme intimacy with a stranger, especially one he found so disturbing... He'd been sure it would be awkward, uncomfortable, embarrassing for them both.

Yet, sometime in the past hour, he'd ceased to think of Tess as a stranger. As a result, he didn't even stop to think, much less hesitate. "Wait! Don't push, not yet, let me check, make sure it's all right—" Without quite knowing how he'd gotten there, he found himself kneeling in the center of the bed, his hands warm and steady against Tess's cold, bare, shaking knees. As if it were the most natural thing in the world, he looked down, saw the top of the baby's head emerging, and felt a mixture of awe and excitement spiral through him. Moisture, unexpected and mortifying, stung his eyes. He swallowed hard before he looked up at Tess. "So what are you waiting for? Push!"

From somewhere, she found the energy to roll her eyes before she pursed her lips, braced herself against the pillows and began to strain.

Once. Twice. A third time. Jack watched her struggle with a mixture of wonder and growing concern.

"Okay, okay... The head's clear... There's one shoulder...now the other... Come on...you can do it..."

"Ohhh...ohhhh..." She fell back against the pillows, breathing like a bellows. She was white-faced with exhaustion.

"Come on." He was suddenly afraid that if she stopped now, she wouldn't find the strength—or the courage—to resume. "Again."

"I'm so tired—"

"I know." As if his movements were dictated by some power outside himself, he found himself reaching up and gently brushing her hair off her face. "Listen. You can do this. But you have to concentrate."

"Right." Her mouth trembled as she tried to smile. "Wanna trade places...and see...if you still feel...the same way?"

Something alarmingly like tenderness curled through him. "No way. Now, shut up and *push*."

She opened her mouth to protest, then changed her mind, apparently seeing something in his face that convinced her he wasn't going to let up. Gritting her teeth, she dug down deep, and found some last little reserve of strength. Jaw clenched, she pushed.

Jack sat back. "That's right, that's it. Come on. You're almost there—"

She strained again, calling out. For a moment, nothing happened.

And then her cry was answered by a high, wavering baby's wail.

Stunned, Jack stared down at the squalling infant suddenly filling his hands. He felt an instant of unreality, a rush of astonishment. Swift on its heels came an explosion of elation, as bright and intoxicating as champagne. "Tess—" for some reason, his voice was shaking "—it's a girl!"

For an instant she looked blank. "What? I thought— are you sure?"

He nodded. "Yes."

Her lips began to tremble. "Is she okay?"

"She's perfect." Quickly he toweled off the baby, wrapped her in a blanket and handed her to her mother. "Honest. Ten fingers and ten toes."

"Oh. Oh, my." Tess looked down at the little red face and managed a shaky smile. "She's…beautiful."

"Yeah." He swallowed. The damn moisture was filling his eyes again, and he seemed to have something stuck in his throat. Nevertheless, there was something he had to say. "You…you did great."

She glanced up in surprise. For a long moment, their gazes met. Until, with no warning, her face crumpled and she began to cry, great wrenching sobs of exhaustion, relief and joy.

For the second time that night, Jack didn't stop to think.

He simply moved up the bed and gathered her and the baby into his arms.

Jack awoke slowly the next morning.

He was conscious first of the light. It was silvery-white against his eyelids, indicating that it was well past dawn, his usual time for rising. Perplexed, he started to stretch, only to be further disconcerted when he felt the chair at his back. Hell. Why wasn't he in bed? He rolled his head, winced at the crick in his neck—and froze as his cheek brushed against an impossibly silky little head. In nearly the same instant, he registered the soft, slight weight resting against his chest.

The baby. Memory rushed back. The storm, the accident, Tess... And then later, the accelerated labor, the incredible moment of birth...

He raised his head and opened his eyes, forgetting to breathe as he took in Tess's daughter's serene, sleepy little face, so close to his. His gaze traced the fan of spidery black lashes that brushed the rose-petal cheeks, took in the button nose and the Cupid's-bow lips parted to form a perfect O. Beneath his hand, he could feel each delicate bump of her spine, the steady ebb and flow of her breathing, the rhythmic flutter of her heart.

An odd pain squeezed his heart. He hadn't lied last night. She *was* perfect.

For one unguarded instant, he wanted nothing more than to gather her closer, to assure her that he'd never let anyone hurt her, to tell her that he'd steady her if she stumbled and catch her if she fell. He wanted to promise that he'd be there for bee stings and skinned knees, for ponies and tea parties. That he'd see her from teddy bears to proms, from fairy tales to real-life princes, through dreams, disappointments, tears and triumphs.

And then, like a slap in the face, his reason returned. God, he was losing it. Hadn't he learned anything? What was he doing, sitting here spinning pipe dreams about another man's child? A child he knew full well would be gone in a day or two.

Which was exactly what he wanted, he was quick to remind himself. But even if it wasn't, if by some impossible twist of fate she were to stay forever, it still wouldn't matter.

He was done with things he couldn't count on. Like love. And fidelity. And caring. Heck, he was just plain done with other people, regardless of their size.

So why, he wondered, as the baby stirred, her eyelashes fluttering and her dainty mouth puckering before she settled back into sleep, did she have to be such a fetching little thing? Why couldn't she be red and wizened? Or have a pointed head? What was it about her that made him want to hold her close and make ridiculous promises he couldn't keep?

Hell. Who knew the why of anything? All he knew was that he was the same man today that he'd been yesterday. That the only thing that had changed was that yesterday this baby had yet to be born. And he had yet to meet her mother...

Tess. It was *her* fault he was feeling this way. Somehow, with her nerve and her courage and her never-say-die sense of humor, she'd managed to get to him last night, to resurrect the ghost of the man he'd been before. The one who had believed in the Golden Rule. The one who'd been naive enough to think that if you worked hard, played fair and lived right, you'd succeed at life.

Stupid. In the clear light of day, he knew better. After what he'd been through, he ought to—

"Jack?"

The soft sound of his name pinned him in place. His gaze sliced toward the bed, where he found Tess propped up on her side...watching him. His stomach rolled. There was something in her expression, a certain softness about her eyes, a tender twist to her mouth, that told him she expected him to act the way he had last night. And that she'd jumped to some silly, sentimental conclusion—like maybe she thought they were friends or something.

The sooner he set her straight, the better. "You're awake."

It sounded more like an accusation than a statement. Taken aback, Tess sat up, struggling not to show her surprise. "Yes, I am." She met Jack's gaze, trying to square the cool-eyed stranger confronting her with the strong, steady, reassuring man who'd occupied that same big lean body only hours ago.

That man had not only safely delivered her baby and comforted her afterward, but had also taken care of all the things she'd been too exhausted to. He'd matter-of-factly dealt with the umbilical cord and a host of other decidedly unglamorous cleanup chores. He'd weighed, measured, washed and diapered the baby. He'd even helped her wash her face and brush the tangles out of her hair, lent her one of his own flannel shirts to wear and made sure she had fresh sheets to sleep on. As foolish as it seemed now, in light of his guarded expression, Tess had drifted to sleep thinking, *My hero...*

Clearly, it was not a role he intended to accept. Needing a moment to think, she said mildly, "It sounds as if it's still blowing pretty hard outside." As observations went, it was hardly brilliant; the steady howl of the wind was self-evident.

Jack treated it as such and gave a dismissive shrug. "Yeah, I guess."

She scooted a little higher against the pillows, trying to ignore the strident protest of more muscles than she'd known she possessed. She nodded at the baby. "Is she all right?"

"Sure."

He said it too quickly. Puzzled by the trace of defensiveness she could hear in his voice, she glanced briefly at the beautiful pine cradle that had mysteriously materialized last night. "Then why are you holding her?"

"She was fussing earlier."

"Gosh, I'm sorry. I didn't hear her."

"Yeah, well…you were pretty tired. How do you feel, by the way?" His gaze met hers in a silent challenge.

"Me? I'm fine."

His mouth curved sardonically. "Right."

Those guarded green eyes didn't miss much. She shrugged, and sent him a disarming smile. "Okay, I confess. I feel like I was hit by a bus. Happy?" The last thing she wanted to do was argue with him. Not after all he'd done for her. And not when she found him so disturbing, with his disheveled hair, his whisker-shadowed jaw—his quiet but unmistakable withdrawal.

He nodded toward the nightstand to her right. "I thought maybe some aspirin would help."

She looked over, saw the small bottle and the glass of water. He ought to carry a warning label, she thought ruefully. *Caution: Master of the Unexpected.* "Thanks."

There was a considerable silence before diversion arrived in the form of the baby, who had the good grace to choose that particular moment to give a little start and wake up.

Almost imperceptibly Jack's expression softened. He looked down, then lifted the infant higher on his shoulder, gently patting her back in an age-old gesture of comfort. The blanket slid down, revealing the back of the baby's head. Covered in fine dark fuzz, it looked impossibly small compared to his hand. Tess's stomach suddenly felt hollow. There was something so compelling about the picture they made together, the baby so small and helpless, Jack so big, so remote, so watchful.

He climbed to his feet and started toward the bed. "Here. You'd better take her."

"Oh, but—" She opened her mouth to protest, then caught herself. Yesterday, she wouldn't have thought twice about confiding that she'd never held a baby under the age of two. But then, yesterday she hadn't given a whit what he thought of her.

Besides, she *wanted* to hold her daughter. She was simply a little nervous, afraid she'd do something wrong. "All right." Reaching up, she slid her fingers beneath Jack's. Dismissing the inexplicable tingle that danced down her spine as their hands rubbed together, she started to lift the infant away.

"Don't forget to support her head," Jack muttered.

"Oh, of course." She quickly slid one hand beneath the baby's wobbly neck before cuddling her close. "Hey, little one. Aren't you pretty?" She wasn't sure where the words came from; suddenly they were just there, trembling on her tongue. "I'm your mama." Delight curled through her as the baby locked on her voice, her dark blue eyes focusing intently on Tess's face. She touched her finger to one small hand, awed when the baby grabbed hold with an almost painfully firm grip.

"I can't believe how strong she is." She glanced up at Jack to share her amazement—and to ask about the tiny white shirt her daughter was wearing.

For once, she caught him with his normally unreadable face unguarded. His gaze was fixed on the baby; his expression was so bleak it made her heart contract.

"Jack?" She wasn't sure if she said his name out loud or merely thought it.

Whichever it was, the result was the same. He stiffened and gave her a single blank look, then abruptly turned and strode toward the farthest window.

Shaken, she stared after him. She watched as he twitched aside the curtain, yanked up the shade and stared outside. She didn't know what to say. Not that it mattered. The tense set of his shoulders forbade conversation.

And yet she couldn't forget the remarkable sense of kinship she'd felt with him last night. It made that look of anguish all the more unacceptable.

She looked down at her daughter, then back at Jack, trying to think of a way to ease the situation. "So." She cleared her throat. "What's the weather doing out there?" *Oh, good, Tess.*

For a moment, she thought he wouldn't answer. Then she almost wished he hadn't. "Snowing," he said caustically.

"Any sign that it's going to let up?"

"What do I look like? The National Weather Service?"

So much for small talk. She cast around for another subject, but what could she say? That she owed him her baby's life, a debt she could never repay? That even though they'd known each other less than twenty-four hours, he meant a lot to her? That she'd like to be his friend?

She could imagine his reaction.

As if the situation weren't already awkward enough, the baby began to fuss, pursing her rosebud lips and making intermittent little bleats of distress. Not knowing what else to do, Tess shifted the child closer and tried gently rocking her. "Shh... It's all right."

The baby stiffened. The bleats got louder.

"Shh...don't cry. It's all right," she murmured. She stared at the infant's face, which currently resembled a miniature gargoyle's, and told herself she wasn't going to panic. "What's the matter, sweetie?"

It was Jack who answered. "She probably thinks she's hungry," he informed her, a trace of impatience coloring his voice.

She glanced at him in surprise. It wasn't what he'd said that was so startling, but *how* he'd said it—easily, automatically—the way only someone experienced with the subject would respond. It was the same way he'd sounded last night, when he'd coached her breathing and commented on her progress through transition, she realized.

Only then, she'd been in too much pain to dwell on why he knew so much.

Now, she wasn't.

Her gaze sought the cradle, which she suddenly saw with new eyes. Then she glanced at the baby's shirt— and that was when she realized the soft blue blanket her daughter was wrapped in wasn't any old blanket. Not only was it exactly the right weight and size for an infant, but someone had embroidered an elaborate rocking horse on the corner, just like the one she'd seen on the ranch sign when they'd driven in.

She looked over at Jack. He stared stonily back, and something about his expression—its determined blankness, its calculated lack of emotion—turned what until that moment had been mere speculation into certainty.

There'd been a child in his life in the not-too-distant past. A child whose absence still hurt him.

His next words confirmed it. "My son—" his mouth twisted with a hint of self-mockery she didn't understand

"—is three and a half. He lives in Casper with his mother and stepfather."

"Oh." She tried to take it in, to understand the sudden edge to his voice. "Do you see him often?"

"No." His gaze fixed on her. "I don't see him at all." His look defied her to comment further.

Shocked by his callous statement, she tore her gaze from him to her daughter as the baby gave a sudden wail. For a second, her mind was blank, and then she realized there was actually something she could do about *this*. She breathed a sudden sigh of relief. Awkwardly cradling the little girl against her, she began to unbutton her shirt.

Across the room, Jack stiffened. "What are you doing?"

She hoped bravado would pass for confidence. "You said she was hungry. I thought I'd…nurse."

His gaze flickered to the widening gap in her shirt. His jaw suddenly bunched, and he looked back at her face, his green eyes hooded. "Good idea." Despite the words, his tone suggested it was anything but. "While you're doing that, there are some things I should take care of."

"But—"

"But what?"

There was no reason to panic, Tess chided herself. She'd traveled all over the world on her own. Surely she could manage one small baby girl. "Nothing. That's fine."

"All right, then." With a haste strangely at odds with his deliberate manner, he hightailed it out the door as if afraid she'd change her mind if he lingered.

Tess watched him go. A line of Winston Churchill's crept into her mind. The great British statesman had been contemplating Russia and had concluded that it was "a riddle, wrapped in a mystery inside an enigma."

Winston, she reflected, should have known Jack.

It took an hour of hard labor before Jack started to feel better. He pushed himself, cleaning stalls, hauling feed, carrying water, working himself into a muscle-aching sweat, until the tense, edgy feeling that had slammed into him when Tess had begun to undo her shirt receded. By the time he forked a last leaf of fresh hay into the last cleaned stall, he'd regained a semblance of control.

But he wasn't happy about it. Or even particularly relieved. He was too damn tangled up inside to even come close.

He'd thought, when he first woke up this morning, that it was only the baby who had gotten beneath his defenses. He hadn't liked it, hadn't liked the longing that twisted his guts and made him ache with the need to cherish, defend and nurture her, but he'd thought he understood it. Given the hole in his life since Elise had taken the boy, it wasn't strange that the baby, all new and innocent and defenseless, should trigger all those old feelings. He'd told himself it was like phantom pain, a residual ache from a part of him that had been torn away.

But there was nothing ethereal about what he'd felt earlier for Tess. And while he could blow off the anonymous sort of attraction he'd felt for her during the drive from Casper yesterday, he couldn't dismiss this so easily. What kind of man got all lathered up over a nursing mother?

He stalked blindly down the aisle, so familiar with the big barn's layout that he didn't even see the row of stalls to either side or the hayloft above his head. Instead, he concentrated on carefully hanging the pitchfork on the outer wall of the tack room, rather than hurling it at the nearest object, the way he wanted to.

For some reason, the small demonstration of will helped. At least enough that he could finally face the rest of what was bothering him. As much as he wanted to deny it, something had…happened…to him last night. In the instant when he delivered the baby, he'd felt closer to Tess than to anyone ever before in his life.

An aberration, he told himself firmly. An illusion born of the moment. Not all that surprising, really. Birth was a profound experience and, hell—he was only human.

It didn't mean anything. So what if it had felt good to be needed? So what if he'd felt that startling sense of connection? So what if he'd felt a compelling urge to take care of her, to treat her like a queen, the way his dad had treated his mother, the way he himself had once treated Elise?

He'd learned his lesson. Being open and trusting and generous had brought him nothing—unless you counted the loneliness, the anger, the heartache he'd lived with the past three years.

He was never going through that again. He was never going to care about anyone so much that he couldn't walk away unscathed.

The reminder served to steady him. He reached over and picked up a clean bucket, then flipped up the hinged lid of the grain bin and dipped it inside. At the familiar rustling sound, nine equine faces popped over the tops of their stall doors, liquid eyes expectant.

The familiarity of the horses' reaction eased him further. He stripped off his gloves and stowed them in his pocket, then started down the row, taking his time as he fed each of the four mares and five geldings a few handfuls of oats. By the time he got to the end of the line, the gentle tickle of velvety muzzles had lightened his mood even more.

Obsidian, a rangy gray Jack had raised from a foal, stamped his feet as he waited his turn. Jack shook his head but obediently held out a portion of oats, careful to keep his hand flat as the horse greedily scraped at his palm. "Take it easy, you old reprobate." He tugged on the gray's silky forelock. "Bite me, and I'll have a talk with those fine folks who make dog food."

The gray gave a snort that conveyed his opinion of that.

Too bad people weren't so easy to understand, Jack thought with a rueful sigh. Still, it was time to quit belly-aching, to put the past two days in perspective. So there was something about Tess that got to him, so what? He'd had itches he couldn't scratch before. Eventually they went away—and so would she. In the meantime, she'd no doubt divide her time between sleep and taking care of the baby; Elise hadn't gotten out of bed for a week after she gave birth. All he had to do was keep his distance, and in a day or two the weather would improve and they'd part company.

This time next month, she'd be a dim memory.

He fed Sid another handful of oats, gave him one last pat and yanked on his gloves. He switched off the lights and shrugged back into his heavy coat, then did up the buttons, wrapped a scarf around his lower face and neck. Bracing himself, he put his shoulder against the door and slipped outside.

The wind snatched at him, tearing the door from his grasp and nearly knocking him to his knees. He staggered, only to get lucky as he blindly reached out and encountered the guideline he'd strung the previous night.

Holding tight, he pulled the safety loop over his head and around one shoulder.

Normally, the trip to the house took less than a minute. Now, it took five times that, and the visibility was so poor he didn't know he'd reached the porch until his boot hit the first step and sent him sprawling.

He climbed to his feet, cursing a blue streak. He found the stair rail and clambered up the stairs and across the porch. He stopped under the shelter of the overhang. Shivering, he slipped off the safety loop and slapped the snow off his coat and jeans before he tramped into the mudroom.

He unwound the scarf, wondered briefly where the dogs were, his thoughts fuzzy from the intense cold. Deciding he'd wait to shed the rest of his outerwear in the relative warmth of the kitchen, he pushed open the inner door, only to grind to a halt at the discovery that the room was already occupied.

"What are you doing here?" he demanded of Tess, too shocked to temper his voice when he saw her standing by the stove, whisking something in a bowl. The tantalizing scent of frying bacon made his stomach cramp with hunger, while the blast of heat from the fire she'd built in the big fireplace drew him like a magnet. The dogs, the furry traitors, were already there, fast asleep.

"Fixing something to eat. I don't know about you, but I'm starved. I hope you like pancakes."

It wasn't right. She was supposed to be in bed, too wiped out to do more than sleep and concern herself with the baby.

Instead, she'd helped herself to a pair of his thick thermal socks and another of his flannel shirts, this one an oversize blue-and-black plaid, which she was wearing with a pair of stretchy blue pants that must've come from her overnight bag. She'd also showered; her thick chestnut hair had regained its high-gloss sheen and her pale skin had a warm tint of color. She looked a little tired, but it didn't detract at all from the provocative tilt to her mouth.

Goodbye perspective. Hello itch.

She poured batter onto the gas range's built-in griddle. "The coffee's fresh, if you'd like some."

He stripped off his coat and gloves, stalked over and poured himself a cup. He started to take a sip, then stopped. "Where's the baby?"

She pointed to a kitchen drawer sitting in the middle of the table. "Right there. I wasn't quite up to wrestling the cradle down here, but I read somewhere that a drawer would work as a baby bed in a pinch."

He scowled, walked over and critically inspected the makeshift crib, taking in the thick blanket she'd used for padding. The baby, thoroughly if sloppily covered, was wide awake, blinking up at the ceiling. He set his cup down and tucked the blanket more firmly around her, and she promptly switched her focus to him. Even though he told himself not to be foolish, he could have sworn her sweet little face brightened at the sight of him.

He stepped away and sent a hard look at the infant's mother. "You ought to be in bed."

"Probably." She flipped the pancakes. "But I'm not. These won't take very much longer. Why don't you go wash up, and then we'll eat?"

He wanted to refuse. He wanted to order her upstairs and tell her in no uncertain terms to stay there. He wanted to inform her that she had no right to intrude any farther into his life than she already had.

On the other hand, he was hungry, breakfast was almost ready, and pancakes and bacon were his favorites. Why cut off his nose to spite his face? It was one damn meal, not a long-term commitment. He'd eat, he'd ignore her, and that would be the end of it. "All right." He went to wash.

By the time he got back, Tess had moved the baby to one end of the rectangular table, set a pair of places, and was already seated, a fragrant stack of steaming pancakes, a platter of bacon and a ceramic bowl filled with canned peaches in front of her.

Jack sat, as well. His movements deliberate, he filled his plate, dropped his napkin onto his lap, and began to eat, not speaking except to ask Tess to pass the syrup. He felt her scrutiny but ignored it, and after a moment she, too, began to eat. Relieved, he concentrated on taking the edge off his hunger. He polished off a dozen fair-size pancakes and a like amount of bacon slices in a matter of minutes.

Without saying a word, Tess laid down her fork, stood and strolled to the oven. Grabbing a hot pad, she retrieved a second plate of pancakes, walked back, took one for herself—it was her second—and slid the rest onto his plate.

She sat and picked up her coffee cup, waiting patiently as he methodically demolished his second helping. When he was almost done she inquired politely, "Were the horses all right?"

He nodded.

"How many do you have?"

"Nine."

She swallowed a sip of coffee. "That's all?"

He shrugged. "Spring and summer, two or three times that." He resumed eating.

"You take care of that many horses all by yourself?"

He pointed at her plate with his fork. "Your food's getting cold."

"That's all right." She looked at him expectantly.

He sighed. "I have a pair of hands who help out." Her expression didn't change, and his mouth twisted sardonically. "Brothers. They're in Mexico now. Visiting family."

"Ah." She nodded and took another sip of coffee. "So what do you do with the horses?"

"Train them."

"To do what?"

"Cut cattle."

"For whom?"

"Rodeo circuit, mostly." He ate another pancake.

Her eyes narrowed speculatively. "You mean, you train horses for professional cowboys?"

He nodded again.

"But...those horses are expensive." Since it wasn't a question, he didn't respond. "And you're here all alone... Why don't you have a cell phone? As isolated as you are, I'd think you'd want one as a hedge against emergencies."

He set down his fork. "Not everybody wants to reach out and touch someone. Some people like to be alone. Some of us—" he gave her a long, level stare "—prefer it."

She regarded him thoughtfully. "I take it that means you don't want to talk about yourself?"

"You got it."

"All right." At last there was a slight edge to her voice. She put both hands flat on the table, pushed back and stood. She began stacking plates.

"What do you think you're doing?"

"The dishes."

He pushed back his own chair and rose. "I'll take care of them. Why don't you take the baby and go upstairs? Rest or something."

Her eyes glinted dangerously. "Fine." She set down the plates with a clunk. She took a few steps sideways, only to stop. A trace of uncertainty showed briefly on her features.

"What's the matter?" he inquired.

"Nothing. I just—" She pursed her lips, then raised her chin. "Would you mind taking a look at her diaper first? I tried to copy what you did, but it didn't look right."

He shrugged. Whatever it took to get her out of there. He came around the table, irritation prickling through him when she moved over but didn't entirely step away.

He pushed the baby's covers aside and deftly stripped away her too-big plastic pants. Underneath, she was clean and dry, but it was no thanks to the diaper. It was the sorriest mess he'd ever seen, loose and lopsided, sagging clear to her dimpled knees. "What's this supposed to be? Some sort of origami?"

"Very funny."

He unfastened the pins. Told himself to shut up. And promptly heard himself say, "Haven't you ever changed a baby?"

"Yes. Of course. But I used *modern* diapers. You may not know it, but you can actually buy them to size these days. With safe, reusable tapes instead of sharp, outdated pins."

"Those disposable things?" He snorted. "They're bad for the environment. Besides—" he shook out the long rectangular cloth, refolded it and deftly pinned it into place "—all this takes is a little practice."

"Right." A trace of amusement crept into her voice.

"So why don't you go a little faster? That way I could feel even more inadequate." With a slight shake of her head, she leaned forward and gently touched a finger to her daughter's small hand.

He could smell the faint fragrance of soap on her skin. That trapped, edgy feeling crept back, and the silence suddenly felt oppressive. He stared down at the baby. "What's her name, anyway?"

"I don't know yet."

He turned to look at her, then was sorry when his abrupt motion brushed his shoulder against hers. "You're kidding, right?"

"No. I was so sure she was going to be a boy..." A touch of asperity entered her voice. "I didn't pick a girl's name. And before you ask, I've never given a child a bath, or taken a temperature, or done any of the rest of that, either."

"Terrific," he muttered.

"But I'll learn. After all—" she looked down at the blue blanket, then back up at him, a mixture of challenge and something that looked suspiciously like compassion in her eyes "—you did."

His jaw bunched. Damn her. She saw too much.

Without saying a word, he wrapped up the baby and handed her to her mother. "Thanks for the breakfast."

Tess met his gaze over the infant's head. Eyes locked, they stared at each other, neither of them giving an inch. And then she gave an unexpected sigh. "You're welcome." With that, she turned, crossed the room and started up the back stairs.

Jack stayed where he was, watching her ascend until she disappeared from sight. His face felt tired, the muscles stiff from the control it took not to expose his whirling emotions.

His insides felt as tangled as ever.

Four

"Here." Jack tossed the book on the kitchen counter. "I thought maybe you could use this."

Tess let the plate she was washing settle to the bottom of the sink and leaned over to take a closer look at the oversize paperback. The title jumped out at her: *As Easy as ABC: Taking Care of Baby from Birth to Age 3.*

She tried to decide whether to be amused or offended.

Amusement won. After six days, it was clear that not all parents were created equal. Her diapers still sagged, her swaddling shifted, and she had yet to settle on a name for her daughter. As for Jack...well, he might not be big on conversation, but, as the gift of the book indicated, neither was he as aloof or as indifferent as he pretended.

Not that he wasn't doing a great imitation, she thought, twisting around as the door to the mudroom banged shut behind him. That first day, after their breakfast together, he'd braved the bitter cold to return to the barn, where he'd stayed for the rest of the day. When he had come in, it had been well past dinnertime and he'd been in no mood to chat. Moody and monosyllabic, he'd switched on the radio and eaten dinner out of a can. His attitude hadn't improved when he heard the weather forecast, either; he'd seemed to take it as a personal insult that the storm battering Montana and Wyoming was predicted to last through the weekend, still two days away. Minutes later, he'd announced he was going to bed and had withdrawn into his study, firmly shutting the door behind him.

It had been all of seven-thirty.

Since then, Tess had hardly seen him. Either he'd been out in the barn or closeted in the study. He showed up at mealtimes to slap together a sandwich or heat a can of chili, but he didn't linger and he didn't indulge in any idle chitchat.

Clearly, he was avoiding her. And it bothered her; she wasn't sure why. Maybe because he'd shared the most profound moment of her life. Maybe because of her certainty that he'd suffered some sort of major heartbreak. Or maybe because there was a desperate quality to his aloofness; despite his attempts to appear cool and callous, he kept slipping up with small acts of kindness— like finding her the book.

She glanced at the item in question and came to a sudden decision. She wiped her hands on a towel and headed for the utility porch. Hoping to catch Jack before he left the house, she yanked open the door—and crashed right into him.

"What the—!" He dropped the armful of bridles and other tack he was holding, grabbed her as she stumbled back, then caught her close as she swayed forward.

Tess froze, not prepared for the feel of him, big and warm and solid against her open palms. Nor for the way his scent filled her head, a delicious combination of soap, cold air, horses and a faint trace of spicy aftershave.

"You need something?" he demanded, setting her firmly away. His tone implied that whatever it was, it had better be good.

She raised her chin. "Yes, as a matter of fact. The baby's starting to smell a little ripe. I wondered if you'd have time later to help me bathe her?"

He was shaking his head before she finished the sentence. "Look in the book. That's what it's for."

"I'm sure it has good advice," she said patiently. "But it can't tell me where to find the things I'll need, like soap and shampoo and extra towels. And I'm not sure what I'm supposed to do about her umbilical cord—"

He gestured at the tangle of leather littering the floor. "I've got tack to clean."

"I could help."

His green eyes narrowed dangerously in the dim light. "Look," he said abruptly, "it's like I told you. I've got better things to do than take care of you and the kid. Remember?"

"Oh, I remember." She wasn't likely to forget.

Last night, after Jack had made his usual retreat to his study, she'd listened to the radio for a while and straightened the already neat kitchen. Then she'd taken the baby upstairs, fed her and put her down to sleep. She'd changed into her borrowed nightshirt, picked up the paperback mystery she'd found on a shelf in the living room, crawled into bed to read and had promptly fallen asleep.

Hours later, she'd awakened to the deep rumble of

Jack's voice. Although the words had been indistinct, his inflection had been so soft and gentle, so achingly tender, she'd thought she was dreaming. When she'd surfaced enough to open her eyes, however, she'd found he really was just a few feet away, silhouetted by the light from the fireplace. Bemused, she'd realized he was talking to the baby. "Jack?"

He'd jumped as if she'd zapped him with a cattle prod. "You're awake."

"Umm. Sort of." She'd looked around for a clock before remembering there wasn't one. "What time is it, anyway?"

"A little after midnight."

She'd sat up and pushed the hair out of her eyes. A shock had gone through her when he'd turned fully toward her and she'd seen that his jeans were unsnapped and his shirt undone, providing a stunning view of a shallow navel, a washboard stomach, a lightly hairy chest hard with muscle. For some reason, she'd found it hard to swallow. "What…what are you doing here?"

For an instant he'd looked nonplussed. Then, suddenly, he'd gone on the offensive. "What do you think? I came to see what was wrong with the baby."

She'd stared at him, considered the relative silence and wondered what he knew that she didn't. "What do you mean?"

A slight tic had throbbed in his jaw, then miraculously subsided as little—Amber, Jade, Crystal?—let out a plaintive sputter. "That's what I mean. How am I supposed to get any sleep?"

As if sharing his annoyance, the baby had begun to cry in earnest. Galvanized, Tess had tossed the covers back and scrambled out of bed, too intent on comforting her daughter to be self-conscious because all she had on was his shirt. "I'm sorry. I didn't hear her—"

Jack had jerked away, hastily averting his gaze. "Forget it. Just try to be more alert in the future, will you? I've got more to do than look after the two of you." He'd stalked out of the room.

It hadn't been until this morning, when Tess had come along the lengthy upper hallway, descended the main staircase and looked down the hall at the door to the study, that she'd thought to wonder how he possibly could have heard the baby. It wasn't as if the little darling had been howling; while Tess might not be an experienced mother, she *was* a light sleeper, and she knew she couldn't have slept through that. After all, Jack had managed to wake her with a few whispers.

Bottom line, the man had lied. Whatever had brought him upstairs and into the master bedroom, it wasn't that the baby had disrupted his sleep.

"I remember what you said," she said carefully. "But she's so little. And if I give her a bath, she'll be wet, and if she's wet, she'll be slippery." She paused for effect. "What if I drop her?"

That revealing nerve in his jaw jumped to life. His eyes narrowed even more, but when she simply stared inquiringly back at him, he finally gave in. "Aw, hell. All right. Now go inside, would you? You're letting cold air into the kitchen." He stooped and began to gather up the tangle of halters, bridles and other items he'd dropped.

She wasn't about to argue. Returning to the kitchen's comforting warmth, she checked on the baby—Katy? Karen? Katrisha?—who was still fast asleep, then returned to the sink to finish up. Jack came in a minute later. He set the tack down on a chair, got an oilcloth to cover the table, gathered a stack of clean rags, a round tin of saddle soap and a bowl of warm water. In minutes, he was hard at work.

She might have been invisible for all the attention he paid her.

Tess set the last dish in the drainer and went to join him. Intent on the bridle he was dismantling, he appeared not to notice as she selected a piece of toweling, wet it, worked it across the saddle soap and picked up a cinch strap.

But then again, appearances could be deceiving. "Don't get the leather too wet," he said abruptly.

"I won't." She diplomatically didn't point out that she'd grown up cleaning tack. Not just because she had a few questions and a favor to ask, but because she also felt overdue for some adult company and she didn't want to give him an excuse to bolt.

Instead, she worked the soap into the cinch, taking her time, doing it right. Not until she was totally satisfied did she pick up a fresh piece of toweling and begin to dry it, stropping it through the towel in her hand. "Jack?" She inspected the leather.

"Humph."

"I've been wondering…how do you train cow ponies if you don't have any cattle?"

There was a moment of dead silence when she thought for sure he wasn't going to answer. Finally, however, he said coolly, "Your grandma supplies me with a few head as I need them. Right now I don't."

"Oh." It was the last explanation she'd expected. Still, it explained how he'd known Mary would be gone. It also opened up a whole new category of questions. "How is she?"

"Mary?" He shrugged. "I don't know. Why don't you ask her when you see her?"

Then again, maybe not. He was about as chatty as a grizzly bear with a mouthful of porcupine. With an inner sigh, she laid the cinch aside and reached for a headstall. She removed the bit, and pulled the throat latch, head-piece and chin strap free, letting the silence spin out before she spoke again. "Jack? Would you mind if I did some cooking? Maybe started taking care of lunch and dinner?"

His hands stilled and his head came up. "Why?"

"Well, it's not to poison you, so you don't need to sound so suspicious." She rubbed her rag across the soap. "And it's not to pay you back for all you've done, because that's a little more involved than providing a few meals. The truth is—" she glanced up and gave him a quick, wry smile "—if I have to eat another peanut butter sandwich I'm going to start sounding like Jimmy Carter."

He stared stonily at her for a few seconds longer than was polite, shrugged and went back to work. "Suit yourself. There should be some stuff in the freezer."

An understatement. She already knew the appliance in question was packed side to side and rack to rack with enough food to feed a small army for a year. Still, that didn't interest her as much as his stubborn refusal to lighten up. "Thanks."

Again, he shrugged his wide shoulders. "Thank my mother. She does the grocery shopping."

"Oh. That's nice. Does she live around here?"

"No."

"Where does she live, then?"

"Rapid City."

"Is that where you grew up?"

"No."

Be patient, Tess. "Where did you grow up?"

"Cattle ranch east of there. My mom sold out after we lost my dad."

"I'm sorry," she said, meaning it. "Is that when you bought this place?"

"No."

Oh, for heaven's sake! She snuck a peek at him, trying to decide if he was hoarding words for a purpose or just to drive her crazy. It didn't take more than a second to realize the futility of the gesture; not only didn't she have a clue what went on behind those leaf green eyes, but the longer she looked at him, the more aware she became of his intense masculinity. She found herself thinking about last night, about his muscled chest and the modeled flatness of his bare belly. An odd flutter kicked up inside her...

Good grief, where had that come from? she wondered, a little wildly. True, new moms were prone to some weird postpartum hormone imbalances. But still— She drew a shaky breath.

"Look," Jack said sharply, misconstruing the cause of her distress, "my mother sold the family ranch twelve years ago, okay? I've been here six. In between, I spent some time on the rodeo circuit."

"Really?" She latched eagerly on to the subject; anything was better than where her imagination had taken her. "I wanted to do that. When I was fifteen, my consuming ambition was to be the first woman allowed to ride broncs on the men's circuit."

"Yeah?" His gaze flicked over her. "What happened?"

"I turned sixteen and decided what I really wanted was to be a rock star like Madonna."

He couldn't hide a flash of reluctant amusement. "Oh. Well. I guess that's normal."

She widened her eyes. "Wanting to be Madonna?"

One black brow slashed up, giving his face a mocking cast. "No. Kids having idols."

"Who were yours?"

He shrugged. "I don't know. My dad, I guess. And Gaylord Perry. My brother always said—" He stopped. His hand tightened on the rein he was holding. A glob of orange saddle soap oozed up between his fingers.

Without thinking, Tess reached out to wipe it off. "Your brother always said what?"

The curve of his mouth abruptly flattened out. "Nothing. Forget it." He looked down at her hand touching his and jerked away with such force his chair skidded a few inches across the floor. He stood. "I have to go. There's something I forgot to do out in the barn," he said tersely.

She couldn't have heard him right. "You're kidding. Now? Surely it can wait—"

"No. It can't." He gestured at the tack strewn across the table. "Leave this. I'll finish it later." Turning away, he snapped his fingers at the dogs, who were dozing in front of the fire. "Tucker. Kite. Come on. Let's go."

"But, Jack— Hey, wait." She clambered to her feet. "I don't understand—"

The dogs crowding his heels, he kept walking, leaving her to stare blankly at the door as it slammed shut behind him.

All she could think was that he was nothing at all like Gray.

She squeezed her eyes shut, shaken by a sudden wave of loneliness. *Damn you, Gray Maxwell. How could you go off and leave me like this? You were the one who was good at reading people—not.*

She sighed. Lord, but she missed the guy. Not as the lover he'd been for one single, solitary night, but as the anchor, the sounding board, the best friend and confidant that he'd been for nine years.

He'd been funny, smart and kind. And—in stark contrast to Jack—direct, open and easygoing. If he'd been a body of water, he would have been a backyard pool—warm, clear, inviting.

Jack, on the other hand, was white water, turbulent, unpredictable, quicksilver, possessed of hidden depths, stomach-dropping dips, uncharted twists and turns.

Gray had made friends wherever he went.

Jack was so very much alone.

She heard the outer door slam. She walked to one of the windows that overlooked the yard and twitched aside the curtain, narrowing her eyes against the onslaught of white outside. For the moment, the wind had fallen off, but the snow continued to come down, steady and relentless, wrapping the countryside in muffled silence.

From the right, the dogs bounded into her field of vision. They leaped wildly through the ear-high drifts, their plumed tails waving exuberantly despite the chill. Jack appeared a moment later, wading through the snow that been blown onto the path to the barn since he made his last trip.

She had only a brief glimpse of him before he rounded the corner, but it was enough. His head was down, his shoulders were hunched, his mouth was a compressed line. He looked as bleak as the landscape.

Tess sighed. She didn't understand him. She wasn't sure she wanted to. But she was beginning to believe that, more than anyone she'd ever known, Jack could use a little friendliness, a little softness, in his life.

She stared out at the vast sea of white and thought about that for a long, long time.

A promise was a promise.

A man's word was his bond.

There was a sucker born every minute.

Of the three, Jack knew damn well it the last one that best explained why he was standing in front of the kitchen sink with his shirtsleeves rolled up and his hands full of wet, slippery baby.

It didn't matter that the baby in question was a charmer. Or that she looked pretty darn cute as she cooed up at him from the warm, shallow water.

He should never have agreed to this. He should have stuck to his guns when he told Tess she could find all the help she needed in the child care book. Barring that, he should have refused to honor his commitment. God knew, everybody else did.

But not him. It was a rude shock to find that some part of him still believed in the same old outmoded code of honor. And though he had nobody to blame but himself, he knew exactly who was a contributing factor to his foolishness.

He glanced sideways at Tess, who was doing the baby washing while he did the baby holding, and cataloged her most recent sins.

First she'd cleaned the rest of the tack, willfully ignoring his assertion that he'd take care of it later.

Then she'd fixed dinner. Not just any dinner, but fried chicken, with mashed potatoes and gravy and all the fixings, and chocolate cream pie for dessert. She'd brought a tray of it to his study, left it even though he'd told her he wasn't hungry—and hadn't said a word when he showed up in the kitchen for seconds.

By the time he'd finally finished eating, she'd already done the rest of the dishes, scoured and disinfected the sink and had the child care book open to the "Giving Your Baby A Bath" section.

Through it all, she'd been friendly and pleasant, just as if he hadn't bolted from the house earlier without a word of explanation. Short of appearing like the biggest jerk since Attila the Hun, he'd had no choice but to roll up his sleeves and keep his word.

But he didn't have to like it.

Or her.

Broodingly, he gave her another surreptitious look.

Her lush, pink mouth was pursed with concentration. And she'd done something to her hair, piling it on top of her head in such a haphazard fashion that several silky strands had escaped to cling to her cheeks and temples like fine copper threads. She also seemed to be having trouble keeping her clothes on. Her shirt was partially open, with enough buttons undone to expose all of her satiny throat and enough of her full, firm breasts to make any healthy, red-blooded man squirm.

Frowning, Jack realized he was shifting his weight from foot to foot and forced himself to stand still. He transferred his gaze to the baby, who rewarded his scowl with a lopsided lift of her mouth.

"Oh, look!" Tess exclaimed. "She's smiling at you."

"It's gas," he said flatly.

She rolled her eyes and leaned close to the baby. "It is not, is it, pumpkin?" She scooped up a handful of water and dampened her daughter's dark curls. "She likes you."

"She's not old enough to know what she likes."

Lucky kid, he thought caustically, shifting his weight again as Tess scooped more water and her arm rubbed against his.

"Why do you do that?"

"Do what?"

Tess straightened and reached across him for the shampoo. "Always assume the worst."

He shrugged. "Beats the hell out of thinking like Pollyanna. At least you're prepared when things go to hell. Which they will."

Incredibly, she smiled. "Oh, I don't know. I always thought hoping for the best made good sense."

"I bet you also think the light at the end of the tunnel is a light," he said caustically, "and not the train."

"So?" She poured a scant amount of shampoo into her palm and carefully swished it through her daughter's ultra fine hair. "If it *is* the train, what good is knowing that going to do? You're just going to waste a lot of time worrying about what you can't change."

He shook his head, frustrated by her naive attitude. "Maybe you have to get run over to understand."

Her hand stilled, and she twisted around to look at him. "Maybe I have," she said evenly.

As simply as that, he found himself replaying the exchange he'd been trying to forget for a week.

I bet the kid's father is thrilled.

Save your sympathy. He's dead.

Damn, damn, damn. He stared blindly down at the sinkful of water, cursing a mental blue streak as all the questions he'd been avoiding about the man who'd been the baby's daddy crowded his throat.

Had the other man wanted his child? Had he even known about her? If he had, why the hell hadn't he married his baby's mother? How had he died? What happened to him?

The plastic cup Tess was using to rinse the baby's hair froze in midair. She swung her head around, her face mirroring a concoction of surprise and disbelief. "I'm sorry. What did you say?"

He took in her expression, then could have kicked himself as he realized he must have spoken that last out loud. "Nothing. It wasn't important. Forget it."

They stared at each other. He could see her uncertainty, and he realized with a sinking feeling that she was still trying to decide if he'd really said what she thought he had. To his relief, she didn't pursue it, however. "All right," she said finally, inclining her head. She resumed rinsing the baby's hair. "There. That should do it."

"Great." Five minutes more and he was out of here. Trying not to appear too eager, he slid one hand beneath the baby's back; took a hold of her upper arm so that she wouldn't squirm away and gently lifted her up, transferring her to a thick pad of towels on the counter.

Tess stepped close, caught up the edges of the topmost towel and wrapped it loosely around her child. Then she grabbed another and began the drying-off process, starting at the baby's head and working her way down. "Gray had what's called a hypocephalic glioma," she said quietly, her attention all for her daughter. "A form of brain tumor. Swift onset, lightning growth." She paused to lift the baby so that she could dry the back of her neck. "Last January he began to have headaches. Some problems with his vision. By the time he saw a doctor, it was too late. He was diagnosed in February, gone six weeks later." Satisfied that all the baby's wrinkles and folds were dry, she dusted the little girl's bottom with baby powder, reached for a clean diaper and began to fold.

Jack couldn't think what to say. "I'm sorry," was what he settled on finally, the words sounding inadequate as hell, particularly after his recent remarks about Pollyanna and trains. "It must've been tough."

She frowned at the diaper, shook it out and started over. "Yes. He was one of the real good guys. Like the pumpkin here." She sent her daughter a melting smile.

He heard a soft drumming and realized he was tapping his fingers against the counter. Damning his inability to stay still, he whisked the diaper out of her hands. "Here. Give me that." He made a few swift adjustments and slid it into place.

Tess carefully wielded the pins. "Thanks."

"You're welcome." To his disgust, he sounded anything but. He capped the shampoo, then let the water out of the sink as she began wrestling the baby into a clean sleeper.

"Jack?"

"Hmm." He wrung out the towel they'd used to pad the slippery porcelain and slapped it down next to the pile on the counter.

"About what happened earlier. I'm sorry if I did something to offend you."

His whole body tensed. He didn't want to think about that, much less discuss it. "Forget it. It didn't have anything to do with you." It was the truth, he thought fiercely. It hadn't had a damn thing to do with her and the uncanny way she had of getting beneath his defenses. It had been about him, and about hopes and dreams and old times best left forgotten. "I thought I'd left a space heater on out in the barn," he lied.

"Ah."

He could see that she didn't believe him. He told himself he didn't care about that, either.

The baby started to fuss, making the impatient mewing sounds that indicated hunger. He watched as Tess fastened the last snap on the sleeper, lifted the little girl up and cuddled her against her shoulder. Just for a second, he remembered what it had been like to be touched with such sweetness.

It was a struggle to keep his voice even. "Go ahead and go upstairs. She's hungry. I'll finish cleaning up."

"But—"

"Go. I want to catch the weather report, and I can't hear anything over all that caterwauling."

A faint flush rose in her face. She opened her mouth as if to protest, then shut it. "All right. Thanks for all the help. I guess I'll see you in the morning." She went across the room and up the stairs, pausing as she reached the corner landing. "Hey, Jack?"

"What?"

"Sweet dreams," she said softly. She disappeared from view.

Sweet dreams? Oh, God. His entire body jerked as the idea wrapped around him, as soft and enticing as her voice. He rubbed a hand over his eyes. He hadn't had a decent night's sleep since he met her.

He rolled his shoulders and tried not to think about how much a part of his life she'd become in only a week. Instead, he repeated the words that were beginning to sound like a litany: The sooner she was gone, the better.

With any luck at all, that shouldn't be much longer. According to the most recent forecast, the storm was expected to end sometime in the next seventy-two hours. Once it did, it might be another day or two before the roads were passable, but after that, he'd take Tess wherever she wanted to go and then his life would get back to normal.

All he had to do was hang on a little while longer.

Five

The sunrise began as nothing more than a shimmer of light.

Soon, however, fingers of pale yellow streaked the dawn twilight. The sky lightened, gray to lavender, pink into blue, azure to aquamarine, while the flame-red edge of the sun rose higher. A tide of gold washed slowly across the frozen landscape.

"Well, damn it all to hell, anyway," Jack muttered, staring balefully out the kitchen window. Except for the sparkling clouds of snow that danced before the gusting breeze, nothing moved across the frost-silvered terrain. Not a bird or a jackrabbit or a coyote could be seen.

Sure as shooting, it was going to be another lethally cold, treacherously windy day. A day when travel was impossible.

A day just like the previous nineteen.

Jack gave a little shudder as he recalled the pep talk

he'd given himself the night he helped Tess give the baby that very first bath.

Three more days he could have handled. Three more weeks was proving impossible.

No matter how often he told himself to dwell on the positive, to be grateful that at least the power and phones had come back on and that they had plenty of food, fuel, firewood and the other necessities, it didn't change one crucial fact: With each day that passed, he came closer and closer to losing the battle he was waging to keep himself aloof from Tess.

He heard a familiar step on the stairs. He didn't have to turn to know it was *her,* in search of a cup of coffee.

"Morning," she said softly, passing behind him.

As usual, she brought with her the now familiar fragrance of shampoo and soap on warm, moist skin and he knew she'd already showered. As usual, the smell went right to his head, filling it with visions of dim, steamy enclosures and long, lissome limbs and water-slick flesh—

No wonder he felt so edgy, so restless, so expectant. *Nothing like a self-inflicted dose of frustration to start off the day.*

He took a deep breath, listening as she took a cup from the drainer and lifted the glass pot from the coffeemaker. He heard her approach. His muscles strained in silent protest as she scooted close enough to read the thermometer attached to the siding on the other side of the glass. "Wow. Thirty below." She gave a theatrical shiver and turned to him with a sunny smile. "It's colder than it was yesterday."

"I noticed." She didn't have to sound so damn *pleased,* he thought sourly.

"How cold do you suppose it is with the windchill figured in?"

He considered a distant stand of leafless trees hunched beneath the breeze. The wind had been ceaseless the past pair of weeks, rarely falling below twenty miles per hour, and often gusting to two or three times that. "I don't know. Fifty, sixty below."

"You know, I don't remember it ever being this bad when I was a kid."

He grunted. "Maybe because it wasn't. Didn't you hear the guy on the news last night? This is the longest stretch of subzero weather Wyoming's seen since they started keeping records." It was also the first time in the six years he'd lived there that the snowplows had been too busy to get to his road. According to the county, unless he had a medical emergency, he was low-priority, since they were already stretched thin just trying to keep the main roadways open.

"Hmm," she said agreeably. She wrapped both hands around her coffee cup and took a long swallow, regarding him above the rim. Her eyes were big, dark, thoughtful. "So—" she lowered the cup and cocked an eyebrow "—is it the weather that's got you down? Or did you just roll off the wrong side of the couch this morning?"

He wasn't about to dignify that with an answer. Instead, he sent her his best black look. The one that always intimidated store clerks and gas jockeys and could be counted on to silence his mother when she started fussing at him.

Tess reached out and patted him on the shoulder. "Maybe some food would help. How about breakfast?"

Didn't she ever lose her damn composure? "No. Thanks."

She gave him an assessing look, then nodded. "All

right. Then how about this.'' For once, she sounded a little uncertain. ''I think I've decided on a name for the baby.''

''Yeah?'' He tried to sound uninterested and failed.

''Yeah.'' She took a deep breath. ''How about… Nicole? Nicki, for short.''

He considered a moment, then nodded, ashamed to admit, even to himself, that there was a part of him that was relieved she hadn't chosen Grace in honor of the late Gray. Not that he cared for himself, of course, or had a proprietary sort of interest; he just didn't think the baby looked like a Grace. He nodded. ''Yeah. I like it.''

Tess smiled. ''Great.''

Her eyes met his, and he felt that alarming sense of connection stir. He looked hastily away.

Tess took another sip of coffee. ''What are you up to today?''

''The usual.''

''Ah. See to the horses, work on the books?''

He nodded.

''Don't you ever get tired of the same old routine?'' she asked mildly.

''No.''

''Never?'' She strolled over to the coffee pot and freshened her cup.

He glanced at her. Something about her looked different. She seemed taller, slimmer…

''Because I was thinking—'' her voice deliberately casual, she turned to look at him over her shoulder ''—that maybe you'd like some help this morning.''

He jerked his gaze from her fanny to her face. ''With what?''

''The horses.''

He shook his head. ''Forget it.''

"But, Jack—"

"No way. You have to be here with the baby."

She made an impatient gesture with her hand. "I just fed her and put her down. You know darn well she'll sleep for at least another hour. Maybe two."

That much was true. Unlike her mother, the baby—Nicki-Nicole, he amended, trying it out—was the most amenable, most agreeable and least troublesome female Jack had every known. Although only three weeks and three days old, she'd already settled into a predictable schedule. "So?"

"So it's not as if she's going to crawl out of her cradle and wreck the place if I step outside for half an hour. Heck, she probably won't even roll over. She seemed really tired this morning. You'd think she'd been up half the night or something."

She looked straight at him. He could see the speculation in her eyes, but he ignored it. If some nights he couldn't sleep and chose to walk off his restlessness in the hallways, and if sometimes the baby stirred and was lonely and he was near... Well, there was no cause for Tess's concern. She ought to be grateful that she got an extra hour or two of undisturbed sleep.

"Please, Jack? I'd really like to see the horses."

"No."

Frustrated, she took in his expression and seemed to realize that nothing she said was going to change his mind. Even so, she let the look between them lengthen before she finally raised her chin and said, in that controlled way that always set his teeth on edge, "Fine. Tomorrow, then." She turned away and walked toward the fridge, turning her back on him and any further objections. "Now. You have any requests for dinner?"

You bet. Thirty-degree weather. You to go away and

*leave me in peace. Some relief for the constant itch be-
neath my fly.* He rolled his shoulders, feeling trapped in
his own skin. ''Whatever.''

She shrugged, but didn't turn. ''Suit yourself.''

''Yeah, right.''

Tess listened to the door close behind him.

How often in the past two weeks had she heard that
sound? Thirty or forty times? A hundred, if she added
in the solid snick of the den door swinging shut?

One time too many, she thought darkly. She wheeled
away from the refrigerator, slapped her cup down on the
counter before she threw it at something and paced
across the floor.

Darn it. Every time she thought she was making progress, connecting with Jack in some small way, she would
get just so far and then *wham!* He'd slam a door, either
real or mental, shutting her out, ensuring that she stayed
away.

If she wasn't so happy, she'd be miserable.

The absurdity of the thought made her miss a step.
But it was the realization that it was absolutely true that
stopped her in her tracks. Feeling slightly light-headed,
she stood smack in the middle of the kitchen and asked
herself why, but the truth was she already knew.

A large part of her contentment could be attributed to
the baby. She was crazy about Nicki. Like the best of
all miracles, her and Gray's daughter might have been
conceived during the harshest of sorrows, nurtured during a time of great uncertainty and born under circumstances that had been less than ideal, but that only
seemed to make the restored sense of joy she'd brought
to Tess's life all the more special. Tess felt as if the
baby's birth had completed a circle, linking her with her
past, providing a bridge to the future. Despite a long-

term responsibility that was awesome, having a child felt right.

So did coming back to Wyoming. She'd known she missed it, but she hadn't realized how very much until her plane touched down in Casper. It had been as if a weight had lifted off her shoulders. Gone was the restlessness that had plagued her teenage years. She'd left to get an education, to see the world, to find herself. Having done that, she'd come home because she wanted to. The vast plains, the huge sky, the solitude—even the extreme weather—made her feel complete, as if some part of her that she hadn't even known she was missing had been restored.

Not that she had any illusions. While she was happy at the moment to cook and keep house, to eat, read, sleep and spend hours marveling at the absolute perfection of her daughter, she doubted it would be enough to fulfill her much longer. Already she felt plagued with excess energy. She might revel in her motherhood, and be certain her future belonged in Wyoming, but soon she was going to need something more to keep her busy.

Something like cleaning stalls and hauling hay and getting to know the Cross Creek horses.

Damn Jack, anyway.

Well, what did you expect? This is the same guy who in the brief space of days after it stopped snowing and before it started blowing spent a day and a half with his fanny frozen to a tractor seat trying to clear a path to the road so he could get rid of you. Did you really think he'd welcome you into his private domain just because you asked?

Of course not. It was almost as unrealistic as her hope that she could fundamentally change his outlook on life with a few smiles and a little friendly conversation.

A reluctant grin twisted across her mouth. Talk about being arrogant! After the break with Mary, her only family, she'd spent nine years proving she could make it on her own and telling herself she didn't really need anyone. It had taken a tragedy and a blessing—Gray's loss and her pregnancy—to make her finally see how much she needed other people and to admit that they were what mattered, not money or success, not excess pride or always being right.

Why she should expect Jack to see things the same way simply because she willed it was a question she'd been asking herself for days. She'd pondered it almost as much as she had the problem of how to make him stop seeing her as a nuisance and start to see her as a woman.

Because she could no longer deny that she had feelings for him, even if most of the time he was difficult, aloof, evasive and unfriendly. He made her feel alive.

Tess sighed. A reasonable, sensible, prudent woman would give up. But the truth was, she'd never been any of those things. On the contrary, she'd always liked a challenge.

Still, she had to admit she was getting extremely tired of having doors shut in her face. It was clearly time for a change in strategy.

The question was, to what?

The following day brought no change in the weather.

Jack narrowed his eyes against the late-afternoon sunshine cursing the cold as he slid open the big barn door and stepped outside. The wind cut right through him, despite so much clothing—two pairs of socks and two sets of long underwear, flannel-lined jeans, a wool shirt, a down vest, an insulated duster, gloves, hat and a muffler—that he felt as overstuffed as a Thanksgiving turkey. Adding to his discomfort, the fine film of sweat he'd worked up doing evening chores was already freezing to his skin, while his fingers, toes, ears and nose had begun to ache.

He tried to ignore the discomfort, fixing his attention instead on the big bay mare named Cassiopeia at the other end of the reins in his hand. Making a soft clicking sound, he led her outside, slid the door shut, then set off for the arena. The mare danced along beside him, nearly pulling his arm from the socket as she jumped nervously at every shift of shadow and rattle of wind.

He pushed open the arena door and led her inside, shaking his head when she eyed the shadowy interior as if she'd never seen it before. "Settle down now, darlin'," he murmured, his breath billowing in the frozen air. His movements slow and deliberate, he reached up, gathered the reins, planted his foot in the stirrup and began to ease himself into the saddle. He continued to talk in that same soothing undertone. "Easy, now. It's okay, there's nothing to be afraid of—"

The mare wasn't buying it. The instant she registered his weight, she gave a giant shiver and flung herself sideways, doing her damnedest to scoot out from underneath him.

Jack quickly swung the rest of the way up. He'd barely touched denim to leather, however, when the mare abruptly dropped her head, planted her front feet and let loose with a crow hop that rattled his teeth.

"Aw, for heaven's sake." He shortened the reins and sat down hard to show her there was a price to be paid for her bad manners, then gave her a sharp rap with his heels and set her at a brisk walk around the rails. At first she continued to shy at every little shadow and sound, but eventually his gentle, soothing voice and quiet confidence began to pay off. The mare relaxed, giving him her trust. A faint smile touched his mouth. After a few more circuits, he nudged her into a slow, controlled trot.

Despite his easy posture, he could feel the strain in his muscles. Normally, he spent anywhere from three to six hours a day in the saddle, depending on the number of horses he had in residence. Now, however, with the extreme cold and the demands of doing all the chores single-handed, he was lucky if he could manage an hour. That meant the horses were getting about a tenth of their normal weekly exercise. Since they were also confined to the barn, their energy level was high and their nerves were on edge. Just like his.

So? You had an offer of help and you turned it down.

He gave a snort, his mouth flattening out, at the reminder. He and Tess had gone another round about that at lunch today. God, but the woman was stubborn! She refused to accept that he meant what he said and there wasn't a thing she could say that would change his mind.

She just didn't understand that more time with her was the *last* thing he needed. Not when he already knew more about her than he wanted to.

He knew she didn't like broccoli, that she had a thing for new wave Irish folk music, that she loved to read and could juggle numbers faster in her head than he could do on paper.

He knew she'd spent the past few years in San Francisco, where she and the baby's father had owned a successful import business together. He knew she'd traveled all over the world as the company's buyer and that she'd recently sold the business and didn't have to worry about money.

He knew she had a temper. He knew it wasn't in her

nature to pout, that she didn't expect to be entertained, that she didn't consider the ranch the middle of nowhere, the way Elise had.

He knew she sang in the shower, slept on her side and looked a heck of a lot better in his shirts than he did.

He knew Mary Danielson's abrupt decision to take a vacation had hurt her.

He knew the more he learned about her, the harder it was to keep a proper distance.

And he knew he spent too much time thinking about her. Like that foolishness yesterday, when he'd gotten it into his head that she looked somehow different. He'd been pondering it off and on ever since, had even caught himself staring at her like a randy teenager at the oddest moments, trying to figure out why he was so fascinated by the swell of her fanny and the curve of her hips—

He straightened in the saddle. God. That was *it*. How could he have been so blind? Why had it taken him this long to realize that for the first time since he'd met her, her shirttail hadn't been out? Instead, it had been tucked into her jeans, providing him with an unrestricted view of her very pretty backside.

Except that she didn't have any jeans. All she had were those stretchy things. Which meant... Well, hell. It meant that the damn jeans must be *his*.

Jack froze, transfixed at the thought.

Unfortunately, it was at that exact instant that one of the barn cats darted out of the shadows and dashed beneath Cassiopeia's feet. The skittish mare gave a violent start, seemed to leap straight up, then came crashing down onto a patch of frozen ground, only to have her front legs slide out from beneath her.

Jack never had a chance. One moment he was thinking about Tess and his purloined pants. In the next he was sailing over the mare's head and hitting the ground with a force that made him see stars. A second later, Cassiopeia fell on top of him.

For a while after that, he didn't see much of anything.

Tess settled deeper into the oversize chair by the kitchen fireplace. Trying not to smile, she gazed with exaggerated curiosity at her daughter, who was cradled in the crook of her arm. "Okay, kid. What's your secret? Why do the same dimpled thighs that look so bad on Mama look good on you? Come on, now—give."

The baby stared intently at her, big blue eyes wide in her little face.

"Not talking, huh?" It was amazing, Tess thought. After only three weeks and a few days, she couldn't imagine her life without Nicki in it. She felt enthralled, tender, protective and besotted, as saturated with love as a soggy sponge. "I guess you're just naturally diplomatic," she told the baby, leaning down to kiss the silk-soft little hand clutching her fingers. "Either that or you've been taking lessons in stonewalling from your buddy Jack."

The baby frowned. For a whimsical moment, Tess thought maybe it was an editorial response to her comment about a certain cowboy, and then, with the sort of psychic communication she still marveled at, she understood. She eased the child up and rubbed her back, smiling when Nicki gave a very unladylike belch. "My sentiments exactly."

At least one of them had a full tummy, she thought, her smile fading as she glanced at the clock. Dinner was ready, but she'd held off, waiting for Jack, who should have come in forty-five minutes ago.

She wondered uneasily if something had happened to

him. Then she told herself not to borrow trouble. It was
far more likely that he was simply taking his time, in no
rush to come in after the exchange they'd had earlier in
the day. The one in which she'd reiterated her desire to
help and he'd said he'd consider it when hell froze over.
To which she'd responded that it seemed pretty darned
cold to her all of a sudden, prompting him to get his
fanny in a sling and stomp off to the den, where he'd
stayed until time to do chores.

Tess sighed and shifted the baby into a more comfortable position. "Losing my temper wasn't exactly part
of my new strategy for winning him over," she confided
to her daughter. "But then, I don't have your advantage.
I'm not small and sweet and adorable. I can't make him
melt just by looking at him. As a matter of fact, I think
it's safe to say that mostly I annoy him—"

She broke off, saved from further confidences by the
dogs. Like a shaggy warning system, they suddenly
surged to their feet, trotted to the door and began to
whine in anticipation. A few seconds later, the door
swung open and Jack came in.

Tess took one look at him and felt as if a giant fist
had squeezed her heart. His hair was disheveled, his
coat, jeans and boots were dirt-stained and snow-caked,
his face was chalky, his mouth strained. He had his right
arm pressed protectively against his side, his gait was
unsteady, and he was shivering.

She scrambled to her feet and hastily laid the baby in
her makeshift bed. "My word! What happened to you?"
She hurried toward him.

His jaw tight, he swung the door shut with a careful
flick of his left wrist. "Nothing."

"Right." She snapped her fingers at the dogs, who
were dancing around him, and pointed at the fireplace,

using the seconds while they made their reluctant retreat to get herself under control. "You always come in looking like this." She made a broad gesture that enveloped him from neck to toes.

He looked down, surprise flickering across his face as he took in the state of his clothing. He sighed. "Okay. So I had a little problem." He headed unsteadily in the general direction of the sink, stopping before the cupboard where the medicine was kept.

Tess followed along in his wake, not certain what she felt most at that moment, concern or exasperation. "Like what? A horse fall on top of you?" He glanced sharply at her, and with a pang of dismay she realized that her facetious comment had been dead on target. "Good Lord," she murmured.

He ignored her. He opened the cabinet and took out the aspirin, moving with obvious difficulty. He stood there a minute, contemplated it, and then, with an exasperated sigh, turned and held it out to her, his expression stony. "Open that, would you?"

She took the bottle, twisted off the cap and poured a trio of tablets into his waiting palm, then grabbed a glass from the drainer and filled it with water. She took a deep breath and tried to match his detachment. "So…is the horse all right?"

"Never better."

"And what about you? Do you think anything is broken?"

He grimaced. "No. Just bruised." He tossed back the tablets and took the glass, spilling a little of the water when his hand shook.

He needed heat, she thought. Inside and out. "Can you make it over to the chair by the fireplace?"

He narrowed his eyes, the ultimate tough guy. "Yeah."

"Then why don't you go sit by the fire, and I'll bring you a cup of coffee?"

He started to shrug, then thought better of it. She watched as he made his way painfully across the room. Willful as ever, he passed the chair she'd mentioned and stopped instead in front of the fireplace, where he stood, head bent, soaking up the heat.

Tess dragged her gaze away from his broad back, unnerved by the contradictory emotions racing through her. Part of her felt fiercely protective and wanted nothing more than to walk over, smooth back his rumpled hair and somehow ease his pain. Part of her wanted to bury her head against his shoulder and sob with relief that he was all right. And part of her wanted to clobber him for daring to get hurt in the first place.

Shaking her head, she made a quick trip to the utility room. By the time she approached him with the coffee she'd promised, she had herself firmly under control. "Jack?"

He opened his eyes and took the cup she held out. He took a long swallow. She noted with relief that his hand was steady; the heat from the fire seemed to be doing its job.

He lowered the cup. "Thanks." He took another gulp and set it on the mantel.

"No problem." She reached up and began to unsnap his coat.

He gave an involuntary start, sucked in his breath at the pain from the imprudent action, but still had the strength to grab her by the wrist, stilling her movement. "What do you think you're doing?"

"Getting you out of these clothes so we can get a look at the damage."

He released her and took a step back. "Forget it."

She took a step forward. "Not a chance."

"I'm warning you, Tess—"

"What?" Her actions deliberate, she reached out and calmly undid another snap. "You're going to stop me?"

"That's right." ·

A faint shiver racked him. She raised her gaze to his and decided it was time to quit pretending. "Listen to me, Jack," she said, her voice trembling a little as she thought about what a close call he'd had. "As cold as it is, you could have died out there. If you're right and you've only got some bruises and a mild case of hypothermia, then that's great. But let's at least make sure."

"Fine. I can manage myself—"

"I'm sure you can. But after everything you've done for me, stopping after the accident, delivering Nicki…" She paused, never taking her eyes from his. "I'd like to help. Can't we declare a truce?"

He stared at her, his gaze searching her face before he abruptly looked away. "Aw, hell." He reached for the cup and tossed back half the contents as if it were straight whiskey instead of mere coffee. "All right. If it'll make you feel better…"

"It will." Before he could change his mind, she quickly undid the rest of the snaps on the khaki-colored duster, unzipped the quilted green vest underneath and unbuttoned his black wool shirt. Next, she undid his cuffs and tugged his shirttail out of his jeans, trying not to let herself think too much about the intimacy of what she was doing as she reached up and slid her hands between his shirt and his navy long-john top. "Left side first, okay?"

He nodded and set the mug back on the mantel, so that he could help as she pushed all three layers of clothing off first his left shoulder and then his right. "Leave them," he ordered, when she leaned forward to pick them up off the floor and brushed against him.

"All right." She straightened, trying not to stare when she saw how the knit top clung to the solid muscle in his arms and chest. She took a shallow breath. "This next part is going to be a little tricky."

"Just do what you have to," he said curtly.

"All right." She took a firm grasp on his left cuff and helped him free his arm from the close-fitting fabric, then carefully began to inch the shirt up his left side, one palm skating up his arm while the other worked the fabric up his chest. The first time he quivered when she brushed her fingertips against his rib cage, she thought she'd imagined it. But when it happened again, her fingers stilled and she glanced up in concern. "Am I hurting you?"

"No."

She didn't believe him. There was the harshness of his tone for one thing. For another, the nerve in his jaw was ticking like a metronome. She moved even more carefully. Biting her bottom lip in concentration, she slid her warm fingers over his cool skin with agonizing slowness.

"For God's sake! Would you hurry up and get it over with?"

The explosive sound of his voice startled her so badly she found herself clutching the velvety bulge of his biceps. She whipped up her head. "Yes! If you'll quit yelling at me!"

They stared at each other, practically nose to nose. For the space of one endless second, Tess found herself

wondering when the room had gotten so unbearably hot.
And why she suddenly couldn't remember how to
breathe. And why she couldn't seem to look away from
the brilliant green of Jack's eyes, except to gaze at his
mouth, which seemed unbearably, undeniably, excruci-
atingly beautiful...

And then she couldn't think at all. She could only
echo the low groan that exploded from deep in his throat
and thrill to the solid feel of him as his good arm en-
circled her and he tugged her close. To her shock, every
nerve ending in her body suddenly throbbed with desire.
It seemed the most natural thing in the world to part her
lips as his head dipped down. And to sigh with pleasure
when his mouth closed over hers.

His lips were cool and firm, his body was hard and
enticing, the kiss was hot and hungry. It was everything
she'd anticipated, in every way—except for the sweetness. That was devastating and unexpected, hinting at a
vulnerability she'd begun to think existed only in her
imagination. She was as unprepared for it as she was for
her response to it: a sweeping need that stole the last of
her breath and made her blood race.

Shamelessly she twined her arms around his neck and
pressed closer, fiercely glad for the first time in her life
for the height that made it possible for her to come up
on her toes and rock her pelvis against his.

He groaned. Louder than the first time. His body
strained against hers, and he opened his mouth, deep-
ening the kiss. Incredibly, it was hotter, sweeter, even
better...until the persistent rasp of a buzzer intruded.

Like a man awakening from a dream, Jack went still,
stiffened, then slowly raised his head, ignoring her vague
murmur of protest.

She pressed a kiss to the underside of his jaw, then to

the pulse in his neck, unable to think of anything appropriate to say. Awash as she was in a languorous haze, it took her a while to realize that the shoulder beneath her cheek was rigid with tension. She lifted her head. And felt the first stirring of uneasiness when she saw the cool, shuttered look on his face.

Instinctively she tried to head off whatever it was he was going to say. "Jack. Wait—"

"That," he said flatly, stepping away, "was a mistake." With a controlled savagery that froze her in place, he reached up and jerked the knit shirt over his head, down his right shoulder and arm and flung it to the floor.

"Oh!" She let out a soft gasp, but she couldn't have said what distressed her more: Her first horrified glimpse of the angry bruises already purpling his right shoulder and side. The mortifying discovery that her milk had let down and soaked the front of her shirt. Or his swift, unexpected rejection.

Surely she'd heard him wrong.... "What did you say?"

"You heard me. This never should have happened. I'm sorry."

He was *sorry?* She felt the blood leave her face.

The buzzer sounded again.

"What the hell is that, anyway?" Jack demanded, gazing irritably toward the utility room.

"The dryer." Under the circumstances, she couldn't decide what was more surreal, his question or her answer. "I put a shirt in to warm for you." With a further sense of shock, she realized that she'd done it no more than ten minutes ago.

It felt like hours.

"Thanks," Jack said. "But I don't need it."

"You don't seem to need anything," she murmured before she could stop herself.

She realized then that she had to get out of there. Out of the room, away from him. She had to leave before her unruly hormones combined with her wounded heart and she did something incredibly stupid.

Like burst into tears. Or smack Jack right in his beautiful, blockheaded face.

"I'd better get Nicki to bed." Blindly she stepped over to the table where the drawer-cum-baby bed sat. True to her easy-going nature, Nicki was already fast asleep. Without a word, Tess gathered the child into her arms, crossed the kitchen and went upstairs.

She was all the way to her room when her stomach growled and she realized she'd never eaten dinner.

It was simply one more thing for which Jack had to answer.

Six

Jack couldn't get his vest on.

Frustrated, he stood in the middle of the kitchen floor and tried to convince himself that this was just a minor setback. Okay. So he was running a little late this morning. And yes, the horses should have been fed an hour ago. But given how bad he felt—stiff, sore, exhausted and out of sorts—he was doing his best. Just as soon as he got the damn vest wrestled into place, he'd be out the door.

He gathered himself for another try. First he hunched his aching right shoulder to keep the quilted material from sliding off, the way it had twice before. Then he reached up, pulled the vest across his back, released the fabric and quickly attempted to push his good arm through the armhole.

To his relief, he finally seemed to have it. He slid his fingertips down, found the opening on his first try, and had just started to slide his hand through when a cool, feminine voice sounded behind him, catching him by surprise.

"Morning," Tess said quietly.

Startled, he twisted around. It proved to be a bad mistake. Pain exploded along his right side. His stomach rolled, and he swayed, struck by a wave of pain-induced vertigo. Perspiration popped up across his nose and prickled between his shoulder blades. Muttering a stream of invective, he cursed the weakness that left him shaking and jerked his hand free of the vest to reach across his chest and clutch his throbbing shoulder.

Seemingly oblivious of his predicament, Tess came the rest of the way down the stairs and strolled past him on her way to the coffeepot. A faint frown marred her face when she saw that it was empty, a situation she quickly set out to remedy. She put a filter in the basket, filled it with fresh grounds from the canister on the counter, picked up the glass carafe and carried it over to the sink. "I thought you'd be gone by now," she said after she filled the vessel with water, as if only then remembering he was there.

He narrowed his eyes. Despite her casual tone, there was an edge to her voice that he'd never heard before. "Well, I'm not."

"What happened? Oversleep?"

"Something like that." He wasn't about to admit that he'd actually spent a miserable night huddled in the chair by the fireplace, unwilling to lie down for fear he wouldn't be able to get back up again. It didn't concern her, any more than his secret suspicion that the only reason he was as dressed as he was because he'd been unable to get his boots off last night.

Bottom line, it was none of her business if he felt

lower than pond scum. Not when she seemed so fresh and energetic, with her skin all flushed from her shower and her hair as shiny as his mother's mahogany sideboard. Not when she was so sublimely unaware of him, while every traitorous inch of his body ached at the mere sight of her. And particularly not when he'd made a mistake the size of Texas by kissing her last night.

Even if she had seemed to enjoy it...

She walked past him again, and her soft, clean fragrance filled his head. Carefully he turned to keep her in view as she moseyed across the room, stepped lightly over his discarded long-john top and opened the screen on the fireplace. She stirred the coals and added a log to the fire. "Aren't you worried that the horses must be getting hungry?"

To hell with the vest. "I was just on my way out." He limped over and grabbed his coat, which earlier he'd tossed over one of the kitchen chairs.

"Ah."

There was something in that "Ah" that stopped him in his tracks. "What's that supposed to mean?"

To her credit, she didn't pretend not to understand. Still, she thought a moment before she answered. "I suppose it means you'd better leave me your mother's phone number."

"Why," he asked, trying not to lose his temper as she walked back toward the kitchen for coffee, forcing him to turn yet again, "would I want to do that?"

She took a mug from the cupboard. "Because when somebody dies, it's customary to notify their next of kin."

"Well, thanks for the concern, but the last time I checked, tardiness wasn't classified as a capital offense."

"No, but you won't last five minutes out in the cold dressed like that."

"Like what?"

She made a distinct sound of exasperation. "Oh, for heaven's sake, Jack. Get a clue. You not only don't have your long underwear on, but your shirt's not even buttoned."

He looked down, saw she was right and managed a one-shouldered shrug. "I just haven't gotten to it."

"Of course not. You were too busy celebrating your iron-man status doing handsprings."

"Yeah?" he said rashly. "Well, I wouldn't be in this condition if you'd keep your own damn clothes on."

"What on earth does that mean?"

Good God. Why couldn't he keep his mouth shut around her? "Nothing," he muttered, struggling to get his coat on. "Forget it."

"No. I want—"

"This isn't about what you want," he said, interrupting her. "Hell, it's not even about what *I* want. You grew up on a ranch. You must know that, like it or not, the stock has to be fed." Unable to do any better with his coat than he had with his vest, he gave up in disgust. He stuck his good arm in the sleeve and simply draped the other side over his sore shoulder. He took an unsteady step toward the door.

"Then let me do it."

"What?" He stopped and turned to stare at her, sure he must have misunderstood.

Tess didn't blame him. She could hardly believe she'd made the offer herself. Not after last night. After last night, he didn't deserve more than a quick shove out the door, unless it was a kick in the tush to go with it.

Except…he was hurting. Enough that it was a struggle

for him to put on his coat. And no matter how much she told herself he was a stubborn, insensitive, unfeeling oaf—and that *she* was nine kinds of fool—it bothered her to see him in pain. Even if he deserved it.

Besides, she could use the fresh air. She squared her shoulders. "I said I'll do it."

"Yeah, well…thanks for the offer, but…no. It won't work. You don't know where anything is, or who gets what, or who bites and who kicks—"

She resisted the urge to point out that if he had let her help out before, the way she'd wanted to, none of that would be a problem. Instead, she said reasonably, "You can tell me."

He looked skeptical. "I don't think so. There's too much to remember—"

"I had a baby, Jack, not a lobotomy. I can write it down."

"And there's an awful lot of heavy lifting," he went on, as if she hadn't spoken. "It's only been what—four weeks?—since you had Nicki…"

"It's closer to five. And I'm a fast healer."

"If something happened—"

"Nothing's going to happen. But if something did, you'd take care of it, just the way you've taken care of me and the baby and everything else these past few weeks." To her chagrin, her absolute conviction rang in her voice.

Judging from his sudden silence, Jack heard it, too. Separated from him by no more than a half-dozen feet, Tess could see the expression in his eyes change—from impatience to surprise to something that closely resembled dismay.

But surely that wasn't right. Why would he dislike the idea that she felt he could be depended on?

"You're not going to let this go, are you?" he said abruptly.

She studied his tired face and decided that now was not the time to pursue it. She shook her head no.

He sighed. "All right, then. If you're sure…"

"Yes. I'll get a pen and some paper." She did just that. Moments later, they sat down at the kitchen table together.

Warily at first, and then with increasing ease, they went over the barn's layout, identified each horse's stall, discussed the various animals' personalities and feed requirements, and the location of the hay, grain, vitamins and other supplements. Jack also explained how to check the heating unit on the tank that automatically supplied water to each stall.

Half an hour later, armed with several pages of instructions, Tess was finally ready to go. She glanced over at Jack. He was sitting back in his chair, his weight resting carefully on his left side, his long legs, in their dusty jeans, stretched out in front of him.

She wondered idly how he'd managed to pull on his boots when he couldn't manage something as simple as his coat—and felt her heart contract as the answer came to her. She suddenly understood why he had on the same clothes he'd worn yesterday. And why he had yet to shower, when the hot water would feel so good on his stiff muscles…

She came to a sudden decision. Quickly, before she lost her nerve, she stood, came around her chair and knelt at his feet.

He tensed. "What do you think you're doing?"

"Your boots are dirty," she said, careful to avoid his gaze. "And I washed this floor just yesterday." She knew him well enough by now to know he'd resist any suggestion that he couldn't take care of himself, and under the circumstances it was the best she could do.

She grabbed hold of a boot and tugged. It took a considerable amount of muscle, but eventually it slipped off. She set it aside, then repeated the procedure with the other one.

"Tess..."

She looked up. A mistake, she realized, as she found herself caught by the incredible green of his eyes. The specter of last night's kiss suddenly hovered between them. She could practically feel his mouth on hers, hot and drugging. And recall how cool and soft his hair had felt against her fingers. And remember the excitement that had twisted through her as she'd pressed against him and felt the warm weight of his sex thrusting back.

Her breath caught, growing hot and heavy in her throat as his eyes grew heavy-lidded. She came up on her knees. Let her eyes drift closed—

"You'd better get going," Jack said roughly.

Her eyes flew open. She was just in time to see him jerk back in the chair. "Of course." She surged to her feet, her face hot with mortification. What the heck was wrong with her? Why couldn't she seem to stop throwing herself at him? She was all the way across the room and had her hand on the doorknob when he finally spoke.

"Tess?"

She stopped, but didn't turn. "What?"

There was a long pause before he said quietly, "Just...take care of yourself out there."

Jack was asleep when Tess got back.

He was sprawled in a chair in her bedroom. Typical of Jack, he'd moved the chair so that he could keep an eye out for her, positioning it between the baby's cradle and the window that looked out on the barn.

A single glance told her he'd showered. His dark hair was fresh-washed-glossy, he had a pair of nicks in his chin from what she had no doubt had been a stubborn try at left-handed shaving, and he'd changed into a clean white shirt and an ancient pair of faded button-fly jeans.

Nicki, who was also asleep, was on his lap, her bottom propped on a pillow and the rest of her securely cradled in the crook of his left arm.

Tess couldn't take her eyes off the pair.

She stood as still as a statue a few feet away. She could feel the chilly wash of air from the unheated hall at her back. She knew she ought to turn around, retrace her steps and close the door.

She didn't. And though she told herself she was merely reluctant to do something that might disturb their slumber, on some level she suspected that the weakness in her knees might also have something to do with the decision. Besides, it wasn't often that she got to observe Jack without him observing her back. Why deny herself such a simple pleasure?

So she stayed where she was and indulged herself. She noted that his inky hair had grown so much since she first met him that it now touched the bottom of his collar. That he had a slight bruise on his right temple from yesterday's accident. And that even in sleep, the hold he had on Nicki was unwavering.

But then, he didn't look much more relaxed asleep than he did when he was awake. His strong features were still dark, dangerous and moody, and the line of his mouth was taut. The only soft thing in his face was the short, dense brush of inky eyelashes against the hard curve of his cheek.

It was an unsettling discovery. It had been her experience that most people looked gentler, kinder, or at least more benign in repose.

But not Jack. And the worst of it was, it didn't matter.

Maybe it was her recent exposure to so much fresh air after so long inside, but at some point in the past few hours she'd come to grips with some hard truths. One was that what she felt for Jack was more than mere gratitude. Another was that while she still wanted to be his friend, she also wanted to be something more. Something special.

Because she cared about him. So much so that maybe—just maybe—she…loved him.

A rueful smile tugged at her mouth. Okay. There. She'd said it. She wasn't certain yet, much less ready to declare herself. She was simply acknowledging the possibility. Even though she supposed that meant she had to concede that her melting response to his kiss had been prompted by something other than postpartum psychosis…darn it.

Her smile faded. She could joke, but the truth was that whatever she eventually decided, Jack wasn't going to make anything easy. While it was obvious he desired her physically—God bless the conspicuous nature of male anatomy—she was under no illusions that he'd welcome her feelings. But then, that seemed to be pretty much par for the course for Jack. He seemed determined to deny himself even the most innocent pleasures, from something as basic as owning a TV to spending time with friends and family to admitting to his own good, decent nature. Heck, even kissing seemed to be on his forbidden list, as he'd made quite clear last night.

She sighed. It was ironic that the same event that had

jolted her into facing her feelings had simply given him another excuse to avoid her.

Jack opened his eyes. "You're back."

"Yes." She stared at him in surprise. For a few seconds there, she would have sworn he actually looked happy to see her.

"I guess I dozed off for a second."

"I guess so."

He frowned and sat up straighter. Careful not to disturb the baby, he scrubbed a hand across his face, grimacing as the movement jarred his shoulder, but doing it anyway. "Everything go all right?"

Her heart melted a little as his hand dropped away and she saw the concern in his eyes. "Sure. It went fine. The horses were hungry, but they were all well-behaved except for the gray, and I fed him first, just the way you told me."

"What about the mare? Were you able to get a look at her?"

She walked over and sat on the edge of the bed. "She's a little stiff and has a slight bump on her near front knee, but otherwise she checked out okay. I'd say she came out of the encounter better than you did."

He grunted. "Anything else?"

She shook her head. "I don't think so. Everything was exactly where you said, the horses are beautiful, and the exercise felt good. Except for the cold, I enjoyed myself."

There was a moment's silence. Jack looked around the room. "This place looks different."

She hadn't done that much. She'd removed the frilly curtains and left the more functional shades in place. She'd replaced the fussy bedspread with an old wedding-ring quilt she'd found in the linen closet, taken down the canopy and yanked the checked slipcovers off the chairs, exposing the original blue corduroy. The room was now a little shabby, but infinitely more homey—which he knew perfectly well, given his sporadic late-night visits. "I asked you about it, remember?"

"I wasn't complaining. It looks better."

"I'm glad you feel that way." Encouraged, she gathered her courage and her thoughts. "Jack?"

"What?"

"About last night—"

The familiar guarded expression slammed into place on his face like a drawbridge coming down. All semblance of camaraderie vanished in an instant. "There's nothing to discuss."

"Actually, there is." She linked her fingers together in her lap, took a calming breath and told herself she could do this. That she had nothing to lose and everything to gain. "I've been thinking about what happened." That was certainly true. "I've decided you were right."

There was a moment's dead silence. "About what?"

She stared fixedly down at her hands. "About us getting involved...sexually. Obviously, it wouldn't work."

"Well...yeah. Obviously."

She glanced up and found he was staring at her with his eyes narrowed intently. She smiled, doing her darnedest to appear relieved. "Oh, good," she said blandly. "I was afraid you wouldn't understand."

There was another beat of silence. "Understand what?"

"The way I responded. The way I practically plastered myself to you. It's just..." She trailed off, searching for exactly the right words. "The truth is, it's been a long time since I've been kissed. And, what with that,

and all the hormone changes these past few months—
Well, I realize now it wasn't you. It was just…the moment. Just…one of those things.''

For the space of a heartbeat, you could have heard a
pin drop. ''Oh.''

''Not,'' she said hastily, not wanting him to think she
was trying to hurt his feelings, ''that it wasn't pleasant.
It was. It was really quite—'' she searched for exactly
the right word ''—nice.''

He stared at her with a look she couldn't decipher. He
nodded. ''Nice.''

She let out a gusty sigh. ''But of course you already
knew all this.''

''Oh, yeah.''

''I just don't want things to be awkward between us,
Jack.'' She stood up, closed the few feet between them
and held out her hand. ''Friends?''

His expression perfectly blank, he reached out and
gingerly grasped her proffered fingers. ''Sure.''

A jolt went through her at the contact; from the way
the nerve in his jaw quivered like a downed electrical
wire, she knew he felt it, too.

Not that he let on. ''I should get going,'' he muttered.

''Hold still a minute first.'' She let go of his hand, but
she didn't step away. Instead, she moved closer, leaning
over to examine the mark she'd noticed earlier on his
forehead.

''What the hell are you doing?'' he demanded, his
body going rigid.

She pretended not to notice that they were so close
she could feel his warm breath tickle the sensitive valley
between her breasts. ''This looks painful.'' Gently, she
brushed back a thick strand of his hair to get a better
look, then touched a finger as light as a feather to the

nickel-sized bruise. "You haven't been having head-aches, have you?"

"Not until now."

She looked down. He was staring up at her, his green eyes as dark and unfathomable as a forest pool. The seconds played out. Then, as if acting against his will, he slid his gaze from her eyes toward her mouth. A dull flush tinged his cheekbones, and his breathing increased.

It was Nicki who saved him. The baby, who'd been as silent as a clam ever since Tess first came in, abruptly emitted a squeaky wake-up call.

As if awakening from a trance, Jack wrenched his gaze from Tess's mouth with such speed he was lucky he didn't suffer whiplash. He surged to his feet. Scooting awkwardly sideways in a move that had to hurt his thigh and shoulder, he held out the child. "Here. She's awake. You'd better take her."

Short of letting Nicki drop to the floor, there was nothing Tess could do. She reached out. By the time she had the infant settled securely in her arms, Jack was gone.

She looked down at her daughter. "Great timing," she told her offspring.

Oblivious of adult concerns, Nicki's answer was to coo in excitement at the sight of her mother. Tess shook her head, but found it impossible to be out of sorts when confronted with the baby's bright little face. Besides, it was probably best that Jack had left. Another few seconds, and Nicki wouldn't have been the only female on his lap, a development that would no doubt have undermined Tess's entire "just friends" pitch.

She sat down in the chair Jack had vacated. A faint sigh parted her lips when she found it was still warm from his body. She thought about the look on his face when she'd told him his kiss had been...nice.

A smile tugged at her mouth. "You know, Nicki, I'm not positive, but somehow I don't think he liked that."

Tess could have sworn the baby chortled.

Jack, no doubt, would have sworn it was gas.

"Are you done?"

Jack tensed as Tess reached around him to retrieve his dinner plate. Her clean scent curled around him, almost as distracting as the soft weight of her breast, which she was unwittingly pressing against his arm. He shifted sideways, away from that provocative warmth, and looked up at her. "I told you I'd do the dishes."

"I know," she said serenely. "I just thought I'd clear some of these things away before I feed Nicki." Leaving him his coffee mug, she piled his silverware on the plate and whisked it away.

Jack watched moodily as she strolled toward the sink, stopping along the way to switch on the radio. When Trisha Yearwood's voice poured out in a soft but upbeat song, Tess promptly began to hum along.

She looked...good. Not that she hadn't looked good before, but now... Well, two days of fresh air and exercise certainly hadn't done her any harm. She looked healthy and vibrant and a hell of a lot more fit than anyone who'd had a baby so recently should, he thought gloomily.

Not that he cared, of course. After all, they were friends, with nothing more between them than a single "nice" kiss.

Jack scowled, hating to admit how much that particular four-letter word rankled. He found it almost as distasteful as his growing awareness that even though he still believed kissing Tess had been a terrible mistake, he wanted to do it again. And that he wanted to do certain…other things—not one of which could remotely be considered "nice."

He continued to stare at Tess. Blissfully unconcerned with his brooding, she set the plate on the counter, splashed some soap in the sink and turned on the water. Her tall, slim body swaying slightly to the music, she peered out into the dark beyond the window and gave a theatrical shiver. Then she turned off the water and headed back toward the table. She picked Nicki up out of her bed and carried her over to one of the chairs by the fireplace. She laid the baby down to check her diaper and glanced at Jack. "Did I tell you I've decided not to go back to San Francisco?"

"No."

"Well, I have."

Jack tried to tell himself her plans didn't interest him, but it didn't work. "What do you have in mind instead?"

She shrugged. "I won't decide for sure until I see how things go with Gram, but I've been thinking I wouldn't mind owning a dude ranch."

"You're kidding."

"No."

"I hear Montana is nice."

She laughed, soft and amused, as though he'd made a joke. The sound echoed through him, setting off a vague sense of yearning for…something. "Thanks for the suggestion," she said wryly, "but I think I'd prefer to be a little closer."

"Closer to *what*?"

"Home."

Words deserted him. While he'd known all along she'd eventually spend some time with Mary, he'd naturally assumed her stay would be temporary. It had never, ever occurred to him that she might decide to stick around and settle in the area permanently.

He tried to imagine what it would be like to know she and Nicki were close by. He had his answer as he was struck with an overwhelming sense of alarm and dismay. And though he tried to tell himself his reaction was triggered by the thought of her becoming part of a community that had viewed his dirty laundry and found him wanting, deep down he knew that wasn't it entirely. Deep down, it was more the idea of her being near but beyond his reach that really bothered him—and he didn't like the discovery. "Don't you think that's a pretty irresponsible thing to do to your daughter?"

Apparently satisfied that the baby didn't need to be changed, she lifted her up and sat down herself, crossing one long, slim leg over the other. Despite the receiving blanket she had draped over her shoulder, Jack had a clear view of the growing valley of pale gold skin between her breasts as she unbuttoned her shirt in anticipation of nursing the baby.

She stared at him in puzzlement. "What do you mean?"

He jerked his gaze from her breasts and climbed to his feet. "I mean," he said deliberately as he walked to the sink, "that the way of life here, the isolation and the lack of amenities, isn't for everyone. You must know that, since you hated it enough to leave the way you did." He pulled out the garbage can and began to scrape the plates.

"I never hated it," she protested. "But I was nineteen years old, and it was all I'd ever known. I wanted to go to college, try city life, see some of the world before I settled down. Only Gram wouldn't hear of it. With her, it was all or nothing, stay or go. There was no middle road. I'll never do that to Nicki.''

He could hear her sincerity. He could also hear the regret in her voice when she talked about Mary. He told himself to ignore it. All right. So there was more to her leaving and staying away than he'd realized. That still didn't mean she'd be happy here now. ''I still think you'd be making a mistake,'' he said stubbornly. ''Think about all the stuff you'd be giving up. Shopping malls. Movies, restaurants, dry cleaners. Fast food. Convenience stores. A nightlife. Six months and you'll be miserable.'' He picked up the washcloth and started sliding silverware and dishes into the warm water.

''You aren't.''

He shook his head. ''That's different.''

''Why?''

Exasperated, he turned around to pin her with his gaze. ''Because I don't need to be constantly entertained. To have endless diversions. To have other people around telling me who and what I am.''

''Neither do I.''

He snorted. ''You will. It's just a matter of time.''

''Ah.'' Her gaze sharpened on his face. ''Is that what happened with your wife?''

Jack shut his mouth with an audible snap. He stared at her, appalled to realize how much he'd just revealed— and by the discovery that, appalled or not, he was tempted to go on, to finally tell his side of the story and share every sordid, humiliating, hurtful detail.

Except…to what end? It was over and done. He'd vowed never again to open himself up or to need anyone. And if he did, the last person he'd want to confide all the ugly particulars to was Tess. He could just imagine what she'd think.

He hardened his expression. ''That's none of your business.'' To underscore his point, he deliberately turned his back on her and started in on the dishes.

''Jack?''

He heard a rustle of sound. To his disbelief, he realized she was approaching. Quickly he turned on the water and made a show of rinsing a plate. Maybe if he ignored her, she'd go away. He dumped the dish in the drainer and picked up another.

''Jack, I'm sorry.''

He stiffened as she walked up beside him and laid her hand on his shoulder. What the hell was wrong with her? Didn't she realize he was done with this subject?

Obviously not. ''I didn't mean to pry,'' she went on, just as if he weren't scowling for all he was worth. ''And although it's sweet of you to worry about me...''

She thought he was *worried* about her?

''...I'm not your ex-wife. You keep forgetting that I lived here for twice as long as I've lived anywhere else. My moving back isn't a whim. It's a decision that's been a long time coming.'' As if that settled that, she plucked a clean dish towel out of a drawer and took a plate out of the drainer.

Jack couldn't believe it. ''What do you think you're doing?''

She raised her eyebrows. ''I'm drying a dish. What does it look like?''

''What about Nicki? Don't you need to finish with her or something?''

''She doesn't seem to be hungry.''

Lucky baby, he thought grimly. Disgruntled, he turned to confront her, to make it clear once and for all that he didn't need her help—and knew immediately that he'd made a big mistake.

She was too close. She'd been close before, of course, but somehow he'd always managed to block the memory of their one and only nice and friendly kiss from his mind.

Not tonight. He looked down into her big, dark eyes and all he could do was remember. How perfectly she fit against him. How soft and sweet and hot her mouth was. How delicious her full, round breasts felt against his chest. How her tight little fanny was exactly the right size to fill his hands.

He took a deep breath.

There was only one thing to do. He had to get out of there. Now. Before he did something really stupid. "You sure you don't mind doing dishes?"

She smiled and shook her head.

"Good." He grabbed a handful of dirty silverware and thrust it at her. "Because there's some book work I really need to go do." He braced for her protest.

It didn't come. Instead, she gave him a long, shrewd, disconcerting look and, after what seemed like a very long handful of seconds, nodded. "Well, then, you'd better go on." She reached out and gently relieved him of his fistful of knives, forks and spoons. "I'll finish this."

Less than two minutes later, a little awed at how easy it had been, Jack found himself alone at his desk in the den, with the door shut and a ledger open, exactly the way he'd wanted.

So why the hell didn't he feel better about it?

Tess wasn't sure what woke her.

One moment she was dreaming; in the next she was wide awake, aware that something in the room was amiss.

Her first thought was of Nicki. She shifted her head
on the pillow and peered through the darkness at the
baby's cradle. Thankfully, it was drenched in a thin
wedge of moonlight that made it possible for Tess to see
that everything appeared fine, a conclusion that was re-
inforced when she heard her daughter make one of the
little smacking noises that often punctuated her sleep.
There was nothing distressed about the sound; on the
contrary, it was perfectly normal.

Yet Tess didn't shift or move. She continued to lie
there and listen, convinced she'd heard *something* out of
the ordinary.

Sure enough, less than half a minute later, a shadow
detached itself from the doorway and Jack padded silently into the room.

Tess forgot to breathe. Riveted, she watched as he
stopped by the cradle. He sent a surreptitious glance her
way, then leaned down. It took her a moment to understand what he was doing as he appeared to sweep his
hand from the bottom of the cradle up, and then she
realized he was pulling Nicki's covers up.

Once he had the baby tucked in to his satisfaction, he
straightened and padded back toward the door, as sound-
lessly as he'd come.

Tess waited until he was almost at the threshold. After
the way he'd maneuvered her into doing the dishes tonight, there was a perverse part of her that felt it was
only fair he should believe he was getting cleanly away
before he found out otherwise.

When his shadow reached the door, she spoke.
"Jack?" she said clearly, sitting up. "Did you need
something?"

He whipped around.

There was a loaded silence. She held her breath, curious as to how he was going to explain himself this time.

She didn't have to wait long to find out.

"No," he said gruffly. "I just came to tell you…you don't need to worry about feeding the horses tomorrow. I'll do it."

"Oh. That's all?"

"That's right."

"Well…sweet dreams, then."

"Yeah…right."

She smiled into the darkness, lay back down and listened as he disappeared down the hall.

When push came to shove, he really wasn't a very good liar.

Seven

Tess slept in the next morning.

Judging by the angle of the sunlight streaming in the windows, it had to be after ten, she realized as opened her eyes and pushed back the covers.

Yawning, she watched the dust motes dance in the rising currents of warmth, and tried to get up the energy to crawl out of bed and make a trip to the bathroom.

Eventually, she made it. Deciding she was on a roll when she returned to the bedroom and found Nicki still sleeping, she went ahead and showered.

The warm water helped clear her head. It did nothing, however, to improve her wardrobe, a sad fact she acknowledged as she tried to decide what to wear. Her choices were limited. She had three pairs of too-big panties, a bra that was too small, three pairs of maternity leggings, one tunic top and her long green sweater. Augmenting this delectable collection were Jack's things:

three flannel shirts, his old jeans, and a pair of long underwear. While she'd never considered herself a clotheshorse, she had to admit she was starting to long for something pretty—that fit—to wear for a change.

Still, there was no use dwelling on it, she decided as she pulled on the jeans and her own green sweater. Not when she had more important things to consider, such as Jack's visit to her room last night. Every time she thought about it, a curious combination of amusement and tenderness curled through her. He tried so hard to be tough and gruff and indifferent, and yet the caring side of his nature just kept surfacing, no matter how much he tried to suppress it.

As she headed downstairs, she tried to decide what kind of spin he was most likely to put on their latest encounter. Would he apologize? Enlarge on his explanation? Or pretend it hadn't happened?

It didn't take her long to find out. One quick glance from the top of the stairs told her the kitchen was empty, while a second, longer look revealed that there was a note propped against the empty coffeepot.

She walked slowly the rest of the way down and across the room. Jack's handwriting was big and bold, and his message was direct and to the point:

Did chores. It's warmer. Have gone to plow the driveway. Back later—Jack

Tess pursed her lips and walked thoughtfully over to the window to look out at the temperature gauge. It read a balmy fifteen above.

Well, of course. Bathing suit weather. Perfect for plowing roads. She only hoped he'd remembered to take his shades and some sunblock.

She shook her head and tried to convince herself it was no use getting angry. She'd known he was stubborn. She'd simply underestimated the extent of it. After all, while she was hardly a beauty queen, she wasn't so repulsive that men normally risked hypothermia just to avoid her.

But then, Jack wasn't like anyone else. He was stubborn and infuriating, yes. But beneath that thorny exterior there was an overdeveloped sense of responsibility, an old-fashioned kind of honor, and a truly generous heart. She knew he was worth an effort.

Even so, she hoped he froze his buns off.

The day seemed to drag on forever. She made lunch and ate it. She read. She did laundry. She nursed, changed and held the baby, who, as if sensing her tension, hardly napped. She read some more. She made popcorn on the stove, which she burned. She ate it anyway. She paced. She put a pot roast in for dinner.

She told herself she wasn't worried.

Not when the dogs showed up alone at two, cold and hungry and grateful for a place by the fire.

Not when the clock crept past three and the sun began to descend toward the far horizon.

And not when it was nearly four and Jack still hadn't shown up, not even to feed the horses.

By 4:10, when Nicki finally nodded off into an exhausted sleep, Tess made a decision. If nothing else, she could go out and feed the horses.

Anything was better than waiting. Or so told herself as she turned the heat down on the roast, ordered the dogs to keep watch over the baby, bundled up and headed out.

By the time she finished in the barn forty-five minutes later, she wasn't so sure. It might be warmer than it had been for weeks, but it was still chilly, there was still no sign of Jack, and she was thoroughly out of sorts. Before, she'd been worried, and a little annoyed. Now, she was worried, more than a little annoyed, and half-frozen. Where the devil was Jack? Had something happened to him?

She switched off the stable lights and walked outside. She was so deep in thought as she tried to decide whether she ought to go look for him that she'd taken several steps before the low rumble of sound issuing from across the yard started to penetrate. Finally, however, she looked up.

She saw the tail end of the tractor disappear into the shed. Relief swept through her. It increased, making her knees weak, when Jack appeared a minute later and slid the big metal door shut. He started toward the barn. Unaware of her presence, he made no effort to camouflage his exhaustion. It showed in the bowed set of his shoulders and in each slow, limping step.

Tess knew she ought to feel sympathetic, and she did—for all of ten seconds. But now that she knew he was all right, what she felt mostly was…anger. It surged through her, hot and potent.

She pushed away from the barn and began to walk stiffly in the direction of the house.

Jack came to a halt when he caught sight of her. "Tess. What are you doing out here?"

She stopped and glared at him. "I fed the horses."

"Yeah? Well, you shouldn't have. I would've taken care of it."

"It was getting late."

"Yeah." He frowned, regarding her with a slightly quizzical air, as if he'd finally sensed that something was wrong but couldn't imagine what it was. "I had a little problem."

"Like what?"

"No big deal. I put the tractor in the ditch and it took me a while to winch it out."

"Ah." He could have been killed. She shivered, the involuntary movement prompted by a mixture of relief that he was okay and ire at his self-imposed danger.

Jack apparently thought she was cold. "You'd better go on to the house."

"What about you?"

"I'll be in in a while. I want to check on the horses."

Well, of course. After all, she couldn't be trusted to toss a few flakes of hay into a manger. "Fine," she said tightly. Aware of his puzzled gaze, she started jerkily along the path to the house, her lips pursed and her eyes straight ahead.

Apparently he finally got it. Or so Tess surmised as she swept past and heard him make an exasperated sound, midway between a grunt and a snort. Her temper already on red alert, she swiveled around to tell him she wasn't amused—and was just in time to see him look pointedly up at heaven and give an exaggerated shrug as he started to stomp away.

Tess abruptly had had enough. Throwing caution to the winds, she gave in to temptation. She reached down, grabbed a handful of snow, molded it into a ball and took aim at his big broad back. She wound up and let it fly.

The throw went high. With a distinct *whomp,* it smacked him in the back of his head and sent his Stetson tumbling off.

He stopped where he was. He didn't move for a second, as if he couldn't quite believe what had happened.

Then he reached down, retrieved the hat and carefully knocked it against his thigh to get the snow off. Finally, he turned.

Tess was ready. She let loose with another. This one caught him square in the forehead, exploded on impact and showered him from the eyebrows down with snow.

He glowered and carefully wiped it away, clearly fighting to hold on to his temper. "Why the hell did you do that?"

She shrugged. "Because you deserved it."

"Because I *deserved* it?"

"That's right."

"For *what?*"

"Oh, get a clue, why don't you? You've been gone all day! I was worried, damn it!"

"Tess—"

"You're a royal pain in the backside, Sheridan, and I probably need to have my head examined, but I care about you—fool that I am! And not as your damn friend, either!" She swooped down, scooped up another handful of snow and drew back her arm.

He drew himself to his full height and sent her a warning glance. "Don't."

She gave an unladylike snort. "Oh, please. What are you going to do? Give me the silent treatment? Hide out in the barn? Run away on your nice little tractor?" She threw the snowball.

"Okay! That's it!" He ducked and lunged at her.

She gave a shriek and dived out his way, twisting around just in time to see him sail past her, clutching the space of empty air where she'd been. Off balance, he slipped and pitched forward, crashing facedown on the snow-covered ground.

He gave a muffled groan, tried to rise, then fell back without another sound. He didn't move.

Tess kept her distance and regarded him suspiciously. "Forget it, cowboy. I'm not falling for the old dead-duck routine," she informed him. "You might as well get up."

He didn't say a word. Or twitch so much as a single muscle.

She stared at him through narrowed eyes. "Come on, Jack. It's got to be cold down there. Get up."

Nothing. She sighed. She knew she was being suckered. Except...what if she wasn't? What if he'd cracked a rib the other day and he'd now managed to break it, piercing a lung? What if he'd knocked himself senseless on a buried rock?

What if you just admit that, sucker or not, you can't stand worrying about him another second?

She swallowed a sigh. Warily, she took a step closer, then another and another, until she was no more than a foot away from him. "Jack?" She gingerly nudged his hip with the toe of her boot. To her consternation, he groaned. For the first time, she really began to worry. "Hey...Jack. Are you all right?" She hunkered down. Swaying a little to maintain her balance, she reached out and touched her gloved fingers to his cheek.

Swift as a striking panther, his hand locked around her wrist. She gave a yelp of surprise, but it didn't do a thing to help her as he rolled onto his back. She tumbled across him, hollering incoherently with a combination of relief, surprise and outrage. "Let...me...go!"

He ignored her, his green eyes gleaming like a tiger's as he stared at her from no more than a few inches away. "You like snow?" He let loose of her wrist long enough to grab her by the front of her coat. Taking no notice of her struggles, he held her in place with one hand while he reached around and shoveled a handful of the white stuff down the back of her collar.

Tess gave a howl and tried to jerk away, only to find herself in an even worse situation when he rolled again, this time pinning her beneath him. "What's the matter? Can't take what you dish out?"

She refused to dignify that with an answer. Instead, she tried to push him off, but it was like trying to dislodge a boulder. So she walloped him on his good shoulder, for all the good it did her. Decked out in his heavy outer gear, he was better padded than a king-size mattress. "Oh, for heaven's sake," she murmured in disgust. "Get off me, you lunkhead. It's cold down here, and you're crushing me!"

He came up on his elbows, making it easier for her to breathe, but otherwise he didn't move. "You started it."

The juvenile answer made her eyes widen. As did the discovery that, despite the cold, there was a sizeable, singularly male part of him that was pressing boldly against her belly, generating enough heat to toast an army. "Jack?" she said uncertainly.

"Did you mean that stuff you said about not wanting to be my friend?"

His voice was raspy, and she suddenly saw the glitter in his eyes and the strain across his cheekbones in a whole new light. "Yes."

He squeezed his eyes shut for the barest moment. "You know this is still a mistake," he said hoarsely as he opened them.

"That's a matter of opinion."

"Tess—"

"Oh, for heaven's sake. Just shut up and kiss me, would you?"

With a hungry groan, he did just that, fusing his mouth to hers in a rush of heat.

Only this time, Tess was ready. She was ready for the sudden drop in her stomach, the needy ache that bloomed low in her belly, the haze of desire that fogged her brain. She tangled her hands in his dark, silky hair and dragged him closer. With a sensual talent she hadn't known she possessed, she parted her lips and slowly ran the tip of her tongue along the seam of his lips.

He groaned again, worked his gloved fingers under her head and met her tongue with his. Tess, who'd never been much of a devotee of French-kissing, felt almost faint with desire at the invasion of his smooth, slick warmth.

She couldn't get enough.

She shifted, wrapped her legs around his and pressed against him, aching to feel his strength and power and warmth without the bulky barrier of their clothes. And all the while, she feasted on his mouth, savored his flavor, shared his breath, trying to tell him without words how she felt.

Her heated response set Jack on fire, but it wasn't enough. He wanted to touch her. He wanted to strip her naked and cup her breasts in his hands. He wanted to yank down her jeans and thrust himself deep inside her.

And he wanted to see her face as he did it. Intent on doing just that, he rolled onto his back, too far gone in a haze of sexual need to care about snow or cold or any stiff muscles but one. He pushed her up and looked at her, his heart hammering as he took in her flushed cheeks, her swollen lips, the slumberous desire darkening her eyes.

Teetering on the edge of control, he yanked off his gloves and reached up to tangle one hand in her soft chestnut hair, while he slipped the other under her coat in search of a bare patch of skin.

He was frustrated on both accounts. While one hand struggled with what seemed like an endless amount of cotton knit and voluminous flannel, the other encountered an icy coating of snow.

Somewhere, deep down, a little voice of reason began to make a dreadful racket. *Hey, Jack. Get your brains out of your pants and pay attention. She has snow in her hair, and it's pretty damn cold out here.*

The realization pricked at him, and the little voice grew louder.

What do you think you're doing? You really want to have sex...here? Now? Like this? Even though it means freezing off some pretty essential body parts?

Yes. Hell, yes.

Well, hell, that's noble. And what about Tess? What if you hurt her? She just had a baby, remember? And speaking of babies, what about birth control? Yours is in the house, remember? Or don't you care? Are you so desperate that nothing else matters?

Yes.

No.

No? Jack groaned, but he knew damn well he was defeated, done in by an unfortunate conscience and a sense of responsibility that didn't seem to know they were outdated—despite a recent history where they'd made him a first-class chump.

And even so, he couldn't help it. Slowly, he removed his hand from Tess's coat, squeezed his eyes shut and uttered a curse that would have made his mother faint dead away if she heard it.

It made Tess stiffen. "Jack?"

Her voice whispered over him. "Tess...we've got to stop."

"What?" Her voice was thick and soft with need—and a tinge of indignation.

"We need to go inside."

"Okay." She leaned down and nipped at his lower lip. "In a little while."

He considered letting her persuade him. It wouldn't be hard. She wanted him. He wanted her. Did all the other stuff really matter?

Yes. Damn it.

He cursed again and turned his head away from temptation. "No. Now." He framed her cold face in his hands and gently pushed her away. "Listen to me. We're both going to have frostbite if we don't get inside."

She jerked away from him, reason slowly returning to her eyes. A shiver suddenly went through her, as if she were only then realizing how cold she was.

"Come on." He urged her to sit up.

"All right." She took a deep breath, then released it as she struggled to her feet, her movements suddenly clumsy from the cold.

He stood, as well, picked up his gloves and pulled them on. He started to brush the worst of the snow from his pants and coat, only to let it go when he glanced over and found Tess standing perfectly still, watching him.

There was a brief, awkward moment as they regarded each other. He took a deep breath and braced for a scene. After all... First he'd attacked her. Next he'd ravished her. And then he'd rejected her—for the second time in three days.

To his shock, an uncertain smile slowly curved her

mouth. She took a step toward him, and then hesitantly reached out and clasped his hand. "Come on," she said softly.

Jack stared at their gloved fingers twined together.

His stomach twisted as he realized that things had changed between them in the past twenty minutes. That, like it or not, there was no going back.

And that, worst of all, he no longer knew if that was good or bad.

With her usual impeccable timing, Nicki politely waited for the adults to get inside and peel off their snow-covered clothes before she woke up. Once actually awake, however, the baby began to fuss.

It was almost as if she knew the adults needed a buffer between them, Tess thought as she picked her daughter up. "Shh...sweetie," she murmured reassuringly. "Mama's here. It's okay." She jiggled the infant against her shoulder and watched as Jack added another log to the fire. Drawn by the promise of immediate heat, she walked over and turned her long-johns-and-flannel clad backside to the flames, sighing as their warmth washed over her.

Jack closed the screen and stood. "Cold?"

She glanced over at him. His face was in profile to her, the austere lines of cheek, chin and nose achingly beautiful in the flickering light. "Yes. I know it sounds strange, but I really didn't feel it...before. Not until we came inside."

He nodded.

There was an awkward silence. He looked tired, she realized—and strung so tight he'd snap at the slightest touch. "Why don't you go take a shower?" she suggested.

His expression was impossible to read. "You sure you don't want to go first?"

"Yes." She regarded him over the top of the baby's head, smiling faintly when the infant gave an unconvincing whimper. "Nicki seems to be hungry, and for once she doesn't seem inclined to wait. You go ahead."

"All right."

Tess watched him walk away. If truth be told, she was ready for some time alone. She needed to think, to try to sort through the events of the past few hours. She'd never known she could feel the way she had outside. She'd been so swept away by desire, so wild with the need to have Jack inside her, that nothing else had mattered.

It was a stunning admission for someone who'd always prided herself on the strength of her will. Yet it was also a testament to her instinctive belief in Jack's character. She trusted him. And today, as usual, her faith had been well-founded. Despite all his tough talk—and his obvious, very impressive need—he'd put her safety and well-being first.

Although she hadn't a doubt he'd deny it vigorously.

She started to sigh, only to wince instead as Nicki's attempt to suck on her neck reminded her that she, too, had certain responsibilities. Her face softened as she glanced down at the baby, who was doing her best to look pathetic. "I'm sorry, little one. Here you've been so good, and Mama just ignores you. Come on." She sat down in the chair by the fireplace, adjusted her clothes and guided the baby into place. "Let's fill up that poor empty tummy."

Nicki's response was to grip a fistful of flannel in her little fist and latch on like a pint-size vacuum cleaner.

Tess shook her head. No wonder she felt slightly...

unhinged. Between Nicole and Jack, her emotions seemed to be constantly maxed out. Yet she wouldn't change one thing that had happened—not in the past hour or week or month—for all the world's riches. She felt more challenged, more fulfilled, more *alive* than she'd ever imagined she could.

She reached down and gently smoothed a flyaway lock of Nicki's hair. Tenderness curled through her as the baby abruptly quit suckling and sent her a quizzical look. Tess could no more stop the indulgent smile that curved across her face than she could stop the jolt that went through her as she glanced over and saw Jack standing in the doorway, watching her.

She took in his damp hair, his shadowed jaw, the green glint of his hooded eyes, and her pulse skipped a beat. Barefoot, dressed in jeans that were zipped but not snapped and a faded denim shirt, he looked big and forceful and enigmatic. And yet, there was something in his eyes, in the set of his mouth...

Longing, she realized, her heart turning over.

She wondered if he knew it. Or if he'd acknowledge it if he did. Somehow she doubted it.

But that didn't mean *she* couldn't. She widened her smile, leaving no doubt about how glad she was to see him. "Hi," she said softly.

Maybe it was her imagination, but some of his wariness seemed to evaporate. He motioned with his chin in the direction of the oven. "Something smells good."

"Pot roast. We can eat after I shower—if that's all right?"

"Sure." He came a few paces closer and gestured at the baby. "Is she about done?"

"Yes." Feeling a tad self-conscious, which under the

circumstances was really ridiculous, she pulled her shirt into place and stood. "Would you mind taking her?"

He didn't move. "You sure?"

"Of course." She handed him the baby, watching as he gingerly tucked the infant against his shoulder. "I'll be back in a little while."

"Right." Jack nodded, careful to keep his expression dispassionate, afraid she'd see how much her easy manner—and that soft smile—meant to him. Already feeling off kilter, he watched her start toward the stairs, and was totally unprepared when she abruptly stopped and retraced her steps. "What's the matter?" he said gruffly, assuming she'd had a change of heart and had decided not to leave him with the baby. "You forget something?"

"Uh-huh. This." To his stupefaction, she went up on tiptoe and kissed him, joining her mouth to his in an ardent union that was all the more devastating for the fact that she didn't touch him anywhere else. Her lips were slick, warm, soft and delicious. By the time she was finished with him, he was as hard as a fence post. Without saying a word, she turned and walked away.

He stared after her, his eyes riveted by the sway of her hips, his mind reeling from the promise he could still taste on his lips. Instinctively he cuddled the baby closer and patted her on the back in the universal gesture of comfort, although he wasn't sure whose he was after—hers or his own. He did know he'd had about all he could take. Every time he started to think he understood how Tess's mind worked, she did something that left him feeling as off balance as a drunkard during an earthquake.

He was thinking about that when Nicki let loose with

an enormous burp. Surprised, he leaned back so that he could see her. "Hey, what was that?"

The baby gazed steadily back, her dainty little brows raised in an expression startling like her mother's.

Jack shook his head. "Well, hell. Who knows what either of you are going to do next?"

The baby's answer was to burp again.

Jack frowned. "Listen, kid. You think you've got it rough?" He tugged at the front of his jeans. "Thanks to your mama, I can barely walk."

Still, he couldn't just stand around, he thought, filled with a sudden surge of restless energy. He might as well set the table. After a short detour to switch on the radio, he walked gingerly over to the table. Taking a firm grip on Nicki, he reached for the place mats stacked in the center, only to falter when he heard what the radio announcer was saying.

"….a long-awaited warming trend. Overnight winds will be out of the north at ten to twenty, but are expected to subside by morning. Tomorrow's daytime highs should be in the mid-twenties at Gillette, with temperatures five to ten degrees lower at Sheridan and Rapid City. The projected five-day forecast is for highs to climb into the thirties, with overnight lows at or above zero. County officials say they expect the last local roads to be cleared and open for travel by Thursday. These include Stilson, MacDwyer and Black Gulch, as well as Johnson County Number 9 and 13. In other news…"

Jack couldn't believe it. Finally, the weather was going to improve. In another day or two, his road and all the others would be cleared and open for travel. It was the news he'd been hoping and praying for all these weeks.

So why wasn't he relieved?

Relieved, hell. Why wasn't he breaking out the Scotch to celebrate? This meant he could get rid of his unwanted guests and get back to his real life. He wouldn't have to put up with anybody asking inappropriate questions or stealing his clothes or invading his space. He'd be alone. The way he liked it. With no ties, no commitments, no pain or disappointments to bring him down.

Yet, for some reason, the prospect of being alone again didn't seem nearly as appealing as it should have. As it *had* as recently as this morning, when he was so anxious to send Tess on her way that he'd been willing to spend the whole damn day plowing the driveway to achieve it.

Why this sudden reluctance? God knew, it wasn't as if he'd miss her…much. Sure, he liked homemade meals. And he supposed it was nice to have someone around again with whom he could discuss business. And she wasn't hard to look at…

But none of that was enough, either separately or together, to cause this sudden churning in his gut. Not when his entire focus for weeks had been on effecting her imminent departure.

Unless… He considered the heavy ache in his groin. Well, hell, of course. That must be it. The answer wasn't that he didn't want Tess to leave. He did. He just didn't want her to go until *after* he'd had her in his bed.

And why not? After everything he'd gone through the past few weeks, didn't he deserve some satisfaction? Damn right he did. For once in his life, he was going to take what he wanted, and to hell with the consequences.

Nicki made a soft little sound. Jack started to glance down, then found himself looking away, reluctant to meet her gaze. With a surge of impatience, he realized his damn conscience was acting up again.

Only this time it was way out of line.

Because Tess wanted him as much he wanted her. Oh, he'd bet the ranch she probably thought of it in some sort of off-the-wall romantic way, with him cast as the black hero into whose life she was going to bring some sweetness and light. But even so, given their last two kisses—definitely not nice, thank God—she wanted him.

Who was he to disagree?

"Jack?" Tess's low voice yanked him out his reverie. He spun around to find her partway down the stairs.

She looked...beautiful. He wasn't quite sure what it was—the haphazard way she had her hair swept up or the extra button on her shirt that she'd left undone or the way her mouth softened when she looked at him.

After more than a month of avoiding the truth—looking the other way, turning his back, leaving the room if she was in it—he couldn't deny she took his breath away.

Tess cocked her head. "Is something the matter?"

"No. I was just listening to the weather report."

"Oh." She came the rest of the way down and crossed the room, not stopping until she was so close her scent filled his head. She leaned forward to examine the baby, then raised her head, her eyes filled with indulgent tenderness as her gaze met his. "She's asleep."

"What?" He glanced down in surprise. Sure enough, Nicki's eyes were closed and her mouth was open in a slack little O.

"Poor little tyke." As light as a feather, Tess touched a finger to a silky strand of the baby's hair. "She was up most of the day, and I guess it's finally caught up with her. Why don't you give her to me and I'll take her up to bed." She laid her hand against his shoulder.

He felt her touch as if it were a brand. Need twisted through him, sharp and strong. "I'll do it."

"Are you sure? I mean, it's no problem for me...."

Her voice trailed off as he looked straight at her, making no effort to mask the desire riding him.

A faint flush crept into her cheeks. "Jack?"

He wanted to touch her...all over. And he wanted to hear her say his name in that same breathless tone...over and over. He cleared his throat. "Earlier. That kiss. Did you mean what I think you did?"

She didn't pretend not to understand. She searched his face, and whatever she saw there seemed to bolster her courage. "Yes."

"You realize...I'm not making any promises? I was married once, and I don't intend to do it again. I don't want you to think—"

She reached out and touched her hand to his cheek. "Jack. It's okay."

"Good." He tried to sound calm. It was hard to pull off, with his heart suddenly slamming against his ribs like a pile driver. "I won't be long." He started for the stairs.

"Jack?" Her voice whispered over him, siren-soft.

He froze. "What?"

"Hurry back."

Eight

Tess sat on the couch, her legs curled beneath her, and stared into the fire. Low and steady, the flames licked at the log, curling around it with fingers of yellow, tangerine and gold.

She heard the muted thud of Jack's bare feet on the stairs, but she didn't turn. Instead, she continued to watch the fire, waiting, savoring the way her pulse picked up as his step came closer and closer.

"Tired?"

His low, raspy voice brought her chin up. She shook her head in response to his question and absorbed details: the taut line of his mouth, the strand of dark hair falling over his forehead, the way he stood on the balls of his feet as if he were ready for...anything. "No. I got to sleep in this morning. What about you? You must be beat after being out in the cold all day."

He nodded, his gaze as intent on her as hers was on

him. "A little. But there'll be time to sleep…later." He held out his hand. "Come here," he said softly.

Anticipation hammered through her, making her light-headed. She took a deep breath, waited for the moment to pass and came to her feet.

He took a step forward and framed her face in his hands. His green eyes dark with desire, he bent his head and fit his mouth to hers. The kiss was achingly gentle to start, his lips rubbing against hers in an unhurried caress that quickly had her aching for more. As if he sensed her need, his hands slid into her hair. Anchoring her in place, he angled his head, and she opened her mouth for the thrust of his tongue.

A hollow warmth swirled through her stomach. It made her knees feel watery, so she twined her arms around his neck and leaned against him, needing to feel his solid strength against her breasts and hips. She rocked her hips and he groaned, nipped at her lower lip, then ran his mouth along her jaw to the sensitive spot where it met her neck.

He nuzzled her there, out of breath. "Tess?"

"Hmm?" She pressed a kiss to his hair, enjoying the silky coolness against her face.

"I want you. But I want this to be good for you, too. Are you sure, so soon after the baby…?"

"I'm fine, Jack. Really."

"The books all say six weeks…"

"People heal at different rates. Trust me. I really am okay."

He raised his head. "All right."

She took in the raw need that made the strong lines of his face appear stark. Tenderness curled through her, and she reached up to brush a lock of hair off his forehead. "I brought the quilt from the den. I thought we could lay it here by the fire."

He nodded. He pushed the chairs to one side while she spread the heavy, flannel-backed blanket, soft side up, over the thick green rug. Unselfconscious as only a man could be, he reached into his back pocket and tossed a pair of round foil packets onto the quilt. Then he undid the buttons on his shirt, shrugged it off and tossed it over the back of the couch. Moments later, his jeans came off, along with his briefs.

Tess stared at him in awe, taking in the strong curve of his jaw, the long lean line of thigh and torso, the bunched power of his shoulders, chest and arms. His skin looked like bronze in the flickering light from the fireplace, the warm color a stark contrast to the dark hair that curled at his armpits and bisected the washboard hardness of his belly, ending in a cloud at the top of his thighs. There, just like everywhere else, he was utterly male—every taut, thick inch of him.

"Your turn," he said softly.

Her head jerked up. She could feel a wash of heat rise in her cheeks as she undid one button, then another, with unsteady fingers. She hesitated.

His expression went very still. "What? Change your mind already?"

"No." She took a deep breath. "If you have to know, I was thinking about my less-than-flat after-the-baby tummy."

Instantly, his expression changed. He stepped close. Before she realized his intent, he slipped the rivet free of her jeans, pulled her shirttail free and slid his fingers underneath the flannel. One hand slipped around her side to fill the hollow of her back, while the other slid under her waistband and settled below her navel, cradling the gentle rise of her belly. "You're perfect," he said softly, staring into her face. "Understand?"

She sucked in a breath as his fingertips brushed against her woman's mound. "Yes."

"Good." He brought his hands up and around and slid them over her breasts, and it was his turn to catch his breath. "What happened to your bra?"

"I left it off after my shower."

He cupped her soft, firm weight against his palms. His hands felt hot and hard. He lowered his head, rasped his tongue across one jutting peak, then took her nipple into his mouth and sucked, fabric and all.

Tess felt as if she were going to explode. "Jack. Oh. *Oh!*" She arched her back, the warmth in her belly exploding in a pleasure so intense it bordered on pain. She stroked her hands over his back, feeling the smooth, satiny stretch of skin over muscle. There was something terribly erotic about being fully dressed while he was naked, and it was never more true than when the warm, velvety weight of his sex nudged against her belly. Wild from the need he was creating as he suckled and stroked her, she reached down and measured the thick length of him with her hand.

His head came up in a hurry. "Don't." He closed his hand around hers and moved it away. "I'm already more than ready."

"That makes two of us," she said with a shaky breath.

"Then let's get you out of those clothes." Suiting action to words, he undid the last few buttons on her shirt and stripped it off. He stood back, his face growing taut as he looked at her full, rose-tipped breasts. He reached out and touched the end of his index finger to one stiff, swollen tip.

She shivered.

So did he. "Take off your jeans." His voice was hoarse.

The rasp of her zipper was loud in the sudden silence. Trying not to be too self-conscious, Tess hooked her fingers in the denim and worked it over her hips and down her thighs to her knees, then let it drop to the floor. She stepped out of the encircling fabric and straightened, her heart pounding with a apprehension, excitement, and shyness.

Jack groaned. "No panties, either?" His gaze traced the long slim length of her legs. He seemed to be having trouble breathing.

She shook her head and he swore, soft and sibilantly. "Thank God I didn't know that before...."

He reached out, pulled her close, and they sank to the quilt, facing each other. His skin felt hot and his fingers seemed to burn right through her as he rolled onto his back and pulled her astride his thighs. He hooked his hand around her neck and guided her mouth to his. Their tongues tangled, and Tess whimpered at the heat building between her thighs, where the rigid length of his sex rubbed against her. She made a sound low in her throat and rocked against him as he began to touch her... everywhere.

Her hands slid into his hair. She felt wild, hot, out of control.

So did he. Or so it seemed as his hands stroked over her bottom and he pulled her closer at the same time he tipped her onto her back.

He rose above her. "Are you ready?" His voice licked against her like a rasp of velvet.

"Yes."

There was a momentary pause, a tearing of foil, and then he was poised above her. He reached down to guide himself, and she felt the first incredible pressure as his shoulders rose and his hips fell, and then he was slowly, slowly sliding inside her.

He felt huge. She caught her breath and angled her hips as he pressed forward. "Oh."

Jack froze. "Am I hurting you?"

"No. Oh, no." She'd been prepared for discomfort. Instead, she felt a hot jab of pure pleasure that made her shiver. She stroked her hands down his sides and clutched at his back. "More."

He shuddered, unable to hold back any longer. He began to thrust, carefully at first, and then, at Tess's urging, faster and faster.

Breathing hard, he leaned down and fused his mouth to hers.

The pleasure started for her first. It was a hot, building pressure that grew more and more concentrated with each stroke of his body in hers. She arched, straining for more. "Oh, Jack, yes, more—"

"Tess, damn it, don't move like that—"

She felt his back hollow out, and then the pulsing warmth as his climax ripped through him and he practically lifted her off the floor. He seemed to swell inside her, and suddenly all the sensation in the world seemed to be concentrated in one sensitive, swollen spot. She pressed against him and he rotated his hips, and her world exploded in a shock wave of pleasure.

"Yes. Oh, Jack. Don't stop Don't...stop..." She wrapped her arms around him and held on.

Together, they rode out the storm.

It was after ten when they finally ate dinner. By then, the pot roast had been reduced to a dry cinder, so they ate sandwiches on plates in front of the fire.

They talked a little, comparing their experiences growing up on a ranch, sharing tales of their respective travels, Tess's as the buyer for Maxwell and Danielson Imports, Jack's on the rodeo circuit. When their stomachs were finally full, however, they set their plates aside and simply sat, shoulders touching, and watched the fire.

Their easy, companionable silence made Jack feel more than a little bewildered. He couldn't help but compare it to his marriage. Even during the first year, when he and Elise were still getting along occasionally, they'd never been able to just be together. Elise had craved talk, action and constant attention, and it hadn't taken long for him to resent it. They'd had sex, but that had pretty much been it. Once it was over, they'd gone their separate ways.

He looked over at Tess. She looked perfectly at ease with her long legs stretched out before her. She was naked except for his denim shirt. "What happened to your flannel?" he asked her.

"It's here somewhere," she said easily. "But I like this one better."

"Why?"

She leaned sideways and nuzzled his ear. "Because this one smells like you."

The simplicity of the answer caught at him. Without knowing what he intended, he turned to her. To his shock, he heard himself say, "Did you love him?"

Tess looked at him in surprise. "Who?"

"Nicki's father." He didn't know why it was so important all of a sudden—it simply was.

She met his gaze steadily. "Yes. He was my very best friend. I miss him every day."

"I see." Well, he'd asked. He had nobody but himself

to blame for the sudden tightness in his gut. The tightness that he told himself wasn't jealousy.

Tess must have heard something in his voice, however. "It wasn't how it is with you and me," she said quietly. "There was no spark between Gray and I. We were friends," she said again.

"There must've been at least an ember," he said gruffly. "You have a daughter."

She linked her fingers with his. "We were together only once. He'd just been diagnosed with the tumor, and we were both so devastated... Things got out of hand. But I don't regret it. Not for a moment. My only regret is that he died before I found out I was pregnant."

Jack saw the tenderness blaze through her face as she spoke of the other man. For some reason, he had to look away.

"What about you?"

It took him a moment to change gears. When he realized what she was asking, he tensed. "What about me?"

"Did you love your wife? At least at first?"

He shrugged. "I suppose. It's not a subject I spend much time thinking about." He sent her a look meant to convey that the subject was closed.

She got the message and looked away. There was a long silence, one that wasn't as tranquil as those that had preceded it. Finally, she said, "So. What did the weatherman say earlier?"

Gratefully, he latched on to the change in subject, feeling a little rueful when he realized he'd forgotten all about that piece of news. "He said that it's finally going to warm up and the wind's going to stop."

"Does that mean they'll come and plow the road?"

He nodded. "We should be able to get out Friday at the latest."

She was silent. "Do you want me to go?" she asked finally. "There's no reason I can't stay in a motel until Gram gets back. You certainly don't have to put me up because of…this."

His stomach flip-flopped. "Is that what you want?"

She shook her head. "No."

"Then don't. The baby's settled here. Why upset her schedule now, when you'd just have to do it again when Mary gets back?"

For once, the emotion in Tess's dark eyes was impossible to read. "All right," she said slowly. "For the baby's sake…I'll stay." She stood abruptly and picked up their plates. "I'd still like to make a trip to town, though. Nicki should be seen by a doctor, and there are some other things I need to see about."

"*You* need to be seen by a doctor." He considered. "Things should be clear enough by the end of the week that we can make Gillette if we start early enough."

"Oh, no," Tess said matter-of-factly. "Gweneth will do just fine."

He stared at her, fighting to control his expression. The last place he wanted to take Tess was the town where Elise had spent the end of her pregnancy. The gossipmongers would have a field day. "Gillette's four times the size. And it's got more doctors."

"It's too far. Besides, I want to see Dr. Isaacs. He's still practicing, isn't he?"

"Yeah, but—"

"Good." Tess carried the plates to the counter. "That settles it, then."

Jack opened his mouth to disagree, then shut it. There was nothing to be gained by arguing. If they went anywhere, it was going to be Gillette. For her sake, that was all there was to it.

Tess strolled back toward the quilt. Jack's groin tightened at the sight of her long, bare legs. The knowledge that she was naked under his shirt didn't help matters.

She reached down and offered him her hand. "Come on. Let's go upstairs. It's been a long day."

He climbed to his feet. Sex was one thing. Sleeping together was something different, which he realized the second he thought about what it would be like to fall asleep and wake with her in his arms, to feel her softness against him all night long. He shook his head. "I don't think that's a good idea."

"Please?" If she'd begged or complained or tried to entice him, he might have stood firm. Instead, she simply stood there, looking at him. "I don't want to sleep without you," she said quietly.

She was close enough for him to note the change in her scent. Four hours ago, she'd smelled of herself and soap and baby powder. Now, she smelled like him—and the sweet, musky odor of sex. The scent went to his head like an exotic aphrodisiac.

Well, hell…why not? He wasn't foolish enough to think in terms of forever, but for now, for the space of the next few days, what could it hurt? "Okay."

Deep down, he knew it was a mistake.

He went anyway.

Nine

"So?" Jack opened the pickup's passenger door, his green eyes scrutinizing Tess as they stood in the miniature parking lot outside Dr. Isaacs's office. "What did he say?" He reached out to her and took the baby, lifting her in her new infant carrier with an effortless strength Tess envied.

She watched his expression soften as he glanced down at Nicki, whose little hands had started to wave in excitement the instant she heard his voice. Ducking his head, he leaned into the truck.

"He said you're three years overdue for your annual physical." She leaned forward to watch as he snapped the carrier into the base and began securing straps. "And that you ought to stop being such a stranger."

"Tess."

"He also said that Nicki is perfectly healthy and seems to be thriving. That he'd get the ball rolling on getting her a birth certificate. That I need to bring her back in two weeks for her first set of shots. And that you did such a good job delivering her, he's going to start giving out your name as an emergency midwife.''

"Terrific," Jack muttered. He took a step back and straightened, turning to confront her. "And what about you? Are you okay?"

She met his probing look with a slight smile. "I told you. I'm a fast healer."

"Good."

She felt a distinct thrill as his eyes got the heavy-lidded look she'd seen quite a bit of the past three days. "Yes." Her smile got a little wider. "It certainly is."

He moved to one side and motioned her into the truck. She stepped forward and he gave her a boost onto the high seat, bending over to press a hot kiss to her mouth before he shut the door.

He was halfway around the hood of the truck before she caught her breath. She watched the weak sunshine glint off his dark hair and wondered if she'd ever understand him. She was starting to doubt it.

She knew darn well he hadn't wanted to come to Gweneth. He'd resisted the trip every step of the way, coming up with all sorts of elaborate reasons why Gillette was the superior choice, while refusing to explain his opposition to the smaller town. In the end, it had been that refusal that lost him the argument, since he couldn't dispute the fact that Gweneth was a good hour closer to the ranch and he wouldn't provide a reason why Tess shouldn't see Dr. Isaacs, who was an excellent doctor and had the added advantage of being someone she knew.

So here they were, although so far "they" meant her and Nicki, while Jack went his separate way. She'd told him she wanted to buy a car seat, and he'd dropped her in front of the general store and gone to gas the truck. When it was time to see the doctor, he'd walked her as far as the clinic door and said he had an appointment to see a man about a horse.

If not for that kiss, she might have thought he didn't want to be seen with her. Barring that, she was starting to think he didn't want to be seen, period.

It was a notion that gained credence as he climbed into the cab and gave her a sideways glance she couldn't interpret. "Doc say anything else?"

She shrugged. "Sure. We talked about his son Mike, who's a veterinarian in Cody. And about the mare you trained for his wife. We discussed Gram, and the ranch, and who's still around and who's not."

"Hmm." He fastened his seat belt, started the truck and pulled out of the parking lot. "I suppose he was surprised when he found out you were with me."

Tess glanced at him. His voice was too casual. "Maybe a little. At first. Then he seemed pleased. He said you'd had a bad time and deserved a little happiness."

He gave an elaborate shrug, but seemed to relax a fraction. "Nice of him."

"Maybe you'd like to elaborate?"

He shook his head. "Don't think so."

She swallowed a burst of frustration, but let the subject drop. She didn't want to have to pry information out of Jack; she wanted him to trust her enough to volunteer it.

She looked out at the town. They'd come only as far as the general store on the town outskirt's this morning, then backtracked to Dr. Isaacs's office, which was among the scattering of houses that made up the residential area.

"So?" Jack slowed the pickup to a stop at Gweneth's one and only traffic light. "Does it look the way you remember?"

She glanced around and nodded, taking in the string of storefronts. The feed store was still the largest and most prosperous-looking establishment, not too surprising given that ranchers made up the bulk of the population for a hundred miles. The rest of the town consisted of a general store, a bank and a service station, a barbershop-beauty parlor, three taverns, two churches and two cafés, all located along the street that bisected the highway. "I guess so—except for the video store. That's new."

He shook his head. "They went out of business two years ago."

She smiled. "So where to next?"

"Home."

She turned to look at him. "Excuse me?"

He stared straight ahead, acting as if what he was proposing were the most normal thing in the world. "We got the car seat, you've been to the doctor's. What else is there to do?"

"Feed me, for one."

"We've still got all those sandwiches you made in case we got stuck. I thought we'd stop and eat at the rest area at Madeline Butte."

"Think again. I've been eating my own cooking for the past month. I want to go to Mabel's. Doc said she's still in business, and I dreamed about her chocolate cream pie the whole time I was pregnant." Tess didn't add that she wouldn't mind having a chance to show off Nicki, but there was that, too.

"We have to get started back," he said stubbornly.

She narrowed her eyes. "It's just past noon. It won't take that long to eat. Please?"

"No."

She sighed. "All right. But it's on your head."

He was silent a moment before he said reluctantly, "What is?"

"Doc says I'm slightly anemic." Desperate times called for desperate measures, and it was only a tiny lie.

"I thought you said you were fine."

"I am. I'm just supposed to eat on a regular basis. It's been a long time since breakfast, and we're forty minutes from Madeline Butte."

"So have a sandwich now."

"Eating in the car makes me nauseous." She had to bite her lip as the nerve in his jaw suddenly started to throb.

He took a deep breath, then released it. "Mabel's it is."

The light changed. He fed the truck gas and proceeded up the street. When they reached the café, which was fronted by half a dozen other pickups, he angled the truck into a parking slot.

Several people looked up as they entered, and a few of the men nodded to Jack as they made their way to one of the booths on the wall. A murmur of sound seemed to follow them, but it fell off as soon as they were seated. Tess told herself she'd imagined it.

And she might even have believed it, if not for Jack's obvious tension. He was so stiff, it was a miracle he could unbend enough to sit down.

Their waitress bustled up. She was a short, buxom woman in her fifties whose name tag read *Betty*. Tess had never seen her before, but it was obvious the woman knew Jack from her very first hello.

"Why, Mr. Sheridan," she said cheerfully. "I haven't seen you in a coon's age." Her eyes brimming with curiosity, she inspected Tess and the baby. "Now, who are these nice ladies?"

Tess waited for him to make introductions.

Instead, he stared at the menu and said, "Just friends," in a tone cold enough to freeze steam. "We'd like to order. Two coffees to start, one decaf. Then I'll have the chicken-fried steak, and the lady will have...?"

"The cholesterol special, please," she said, rattling off the menu's name for the cheeseburger platter as she stared at him, shocked by his rudeness.

Only Betty seemed unfazed. She nodded, started to say something, then dashed off with a quick apology as a bell sounded in the kitchen and the cook yelled, "Order up!"

"Jack—"

He gave her a hard look. "Let it go, would you, Tess?"

Short of making a scene, she didn't know what else to do under the circumstances. She nodded.

The meal passed in almost total silence. By the time Betty returned to clear away their plates, Tess was actually glad to see her.

"You two want anything more?" the waitress asked.

"Yes," Tess said, in the same breath that Jack said, "No."

The waitress laughed. "So which is it, folks?"

"I'd like a piece of chocolate cream pie," Tess said firmly, shooting Jack a look that dared him to disagree. "And I wondered...is Mabel back in her office, by chance?"

Across the table, Jack's fingers threatened to snap the handle off his coffee cup.

"Nope. Today's her day off."

"Oh." She swallowed her disappointment, although she was relieved to see Jack's grip relax.

"That's sure a cute baby." The waitress took another long look at Nicki, then looked speculatively from Jack to Tess and back again. "You *sure* you two are just friends? 'Cause I gotta tell you, that little darling looks just like you, Mr. Sheridan."

Jack stared coolly back, his face impossible to read. "You're mistaken," he said stiffly.

"If you say so. I'll get your pie and be back in a jiffy."

Aware of Jack's strained expression, Tess ate her pie in a hurry. The second she was done, he tossed two tens on the table to cover the bill, picked up the baby in her carrier and stood. "Let's go."

Mystified and more than a little irritated by his behavior, she went willingly along to the truck, waiting until they were inside before she confronted him. "Okay. You want to tell me what that was all about?"

He shrugged and started the truck. "I don't like restaurants. Too many people."

"Is that it, really? Or are you just acting like this to pay me back for not agreeing to go to Gillette?"

"Hell, no."

"Then you won't mind if we make a quick trip to Marden's."

"Damn it, Tess—"

"Listen," she said reasonably. "I've got to have new underwear. Mine were in pretty sorry shape to begin with, and now that you've ripped that pair last night and—"

"All right," he said hastily. He backed out, drove down to the end of the street and did a U-turn, then came back up and parked on the other side of the street, in front of the town's clothing store. He set the emergency brake and turned off the engine. "Go on. I'll stay here with the baby. There's no reason to drag her along."

She looked at him, wishing with all her heart she had a clue what was going on.

"I shouldn't be much more than half an hour."

He gave her a long look, then nodded. "All right."

She started to reach for the door handle.

"Tess?" She turned to look at him, her eyes questioning.

He leaned over, slid his hand under her hair at the nape of her neck and tugged her toward him, holding her still for his mouth. Her breath caught. She could feel his heat, his hunger, his need. And, for a fanciful moment, a hint of desperation, which she quickly forgot beneath the suggestive thrust of his tongue. When he finally lifted his head, she felt as weak as a kitten. His green eyes gleamed with banked desire. "Don't take too long."

She cleared her throat. "I won't."

Her knees still weak, she climbed out of the cab.

Marden's Clothing Emporium hadn't changed at all in ten years, Tess thought with a sense of nostalgia. There was still the same curious hodgepodge of items, which ranged from a rack of chiffon prom dresses to an entire wall devoted to jeans in every imaginable size to a corner filled with accessories that ranged from rawhide roping gloves to satin hair bows.

Conscious of her limited time, she quickly grabbed a shopping cart. After a quick survey of the men's section, she picked out a few things for Nicki, unable to resist some little pink sleepers and drawstring nighties, a fuzzy hat, a well-insulated bunting and some fluffy booties. Then she grabbed two pair of jeans for herself, a pair of stretchy T-shirts and a dark purple sweater, some socks and a half-dozen pair of panties. Two new bras, by far the most time-consuming part of her shopping, since she had to try them on to find the right size, rounded out her selections—until she caught sight of a short, filmy black chemise. She grabbed that, too.

By the time she arrived at the cash register, she felt as though she'd run a marathon. In a way, she supposed she had; according to the clock above the cash register, only thirty-nine minutes had passed since she left Jack. She started piling things on the counter.

The clerk, a woman about Tess's age, rang up the first few items. "Hi," she said with a friendly smile. "Did you find everything you need?"

"Yes, thanks." Things had certainly changed, Tess thought philosophically. Just like the waitress, the clerk was a stranger. Once upon a time, she'd pretty much known everyone in Gweneth. Now, she didn't seem to know anyone.

"Are you new in town?"

"Not really. I grew up about seventy miles south of here."

The woman's fingers flew over the cash register keys as she worked her way through the pile of clothing. "It looks like you're here for more than a visit."

"Maybe. I'm Tess Danielson. My grandmother owns the Double D."

"Oh, I know Miss Mary. I'm Carole Marden."

Tess did a little mental juggling. "You must

be...Jeff's wife? We went to high school together," she explained.

"How nice." She beamed. "We've been married eight years. His parents are retired, so now we run the store," she added unnecessarily.

The bell above the door rang, and they both turned to look as a pair of teenage girls burst in, talking and giggling excitedly. "Hey, Mrs. Marden," they chimed, sending two distracted waves in the older women's direction before they scurried over to stare covertly out the main display window. "I'm telling you, Elsa, that's him," the taller of the two, a plain, prim-looking redhead said in a carrying whisper. "I saw him last spring at the charity rodeo in Elmo. He rode in the cutting event. Whose baby do you suppose that is?"

"I don't know, but I bet it's not his," said her companion, a compact blonde. "My mama says it broke his heart when his wife up and left him, and them with a brand-new baby. That he's just pining away."

Tess followed the path of their gaze. Her chest constricted when she saw that the only person in sight was Jack. He was sitting in the truck, holding Nicki in the curve of his arm.

The redheaded girl shrugged. "Well, my mama says it's a disgrace the way he let that two-timing Jezebel have custody. She says there's not a judge in all of Wyoming who would have let her have that precious baby boy. Not after she left her husband for his very own brother."

"Well, I don't know about that," the blonde said uncertainly. "I feel sort of sorry for him. It must be hard having everyone in town know your wife cheated on you—"

The other girl gave an unattractive snort. "Mama says

it's his own fault. That he must not have any backbone. That a real man would've kept what was his.''

Tess stood, rooted to the spot, stunned by what she was hearing. It was suddenly very clear why Jack had been so reluctant to come into Gweneth. Her hands clenched into fists as she fought a very real desire to inform the redhead that her mama wouldn't know a real man if she found him naked in her bed.

Yet she knew that wouldn't help matters. Nor would it do anything to change the fact that it was Jack's *brother* who'd been—was?—the other man. She thought about how guarded and wary and alone Jack seemed at times. Now she knew why; the extent of the betrayal was staggering. *Oh, God. Oh, Jack. I'm sorry.*

She must have made some sound of distress, because Carole Marden suddenly spoke up sharply. "Girls! That's enough. I'm paying you to stock shelves, not gossip.''

The two teens jerked around, as if only then realizing they could be overheard. "Yes, Mrs. Marden,'' they chorused. They turned slowly away from the window and headed for the back of the store.

Tess barely noticed. She was too busy trying to put what she'd just heard into some sort of perspective.

"I'm sorry you had to hear that.'' Carole began folding Tess's purchases and sliding them into bags. "But since you grew up around here, you must know how people love to gossip.'' She glanced in Jack's direction and clucked her tongue, a frown marring her pleasant features. "That poor, unfortunate man. It's just so sad…''

It took a moment for the woman's words to penetrate. Tess's head came up. "What did you say?''

"Oh, that it's just so sad how that poor man's life was ruined—"

Tess's eyes narrowed. It was bad enough that "Mama" seemed to blame Jack for his own misfortune, without having this stranger—no matter how well-intentioned—pity him. "Excuse me. But there's nothing sad or unfortunate about Jack Sheridan. And his life is certainly not ruined. Trust me." She dredged up a meaningful smile. "I'm in a position to know, since I live with him."

"Oh." The other woman's eyes widened. "Oh, but— I mean—" In the process of placing the last pair of Nicki's new booties in the bag, she suddenly appeared to make the connection between Tess's purchases and the pair out in the truck. "Oh, dear. I'm sorry. I didn't mean…"

There was a strained silence that Tess made no effort to ease. She took out her billfold. "How much do I owe you?"

The other woman turned her gaze to the register display with an air of relief. "It comes to $386.42."

There was a certain grim satisfaction to being able to pay with cash. Tess handed over the money and collected her change. "Thanks. Tell Jeff I said hello."

"I—I will."

Her thoughts churning, Tess barely heard her as she hefted the bags and set off for the truck.

Tess was too quiet.

Jack glanced at her out of the corner of his eye. He'd known something was wrong the instant he saw her come out of Marden's. Everything from the set of her chin to the length of her stride had telegraphed her agitation. As had the way she jerked open the door, stuffed her trio of bags behind the seat and climbed stiffly onto the seat.

He'd braced for an explosion. But all she'd said was "I'd like to go home. *Now.*"

Except as related to the baby, she'd barely said a word since—and that had been close to an hour ago.

He put on the turn indicator and slowed the truck for the turn onto Johnson Number 9. Behind him, the weak winter sun was beginning to descend over the Bighorn Mountains, which stretched across the western horizon like a jagged curtain. In front and to each side, the terrain unrolled in an uneven sea of wind-scoured white.

Even with four-wheel drive, their trip on the county road this morning had been slow going, with four-foot drifts and patches of ice making for treacherous driving. Now, with dusk no more than an hour off and the temperature starting to drop, anything that had warmed today would be starting to refreeze.

It promised to be a hellish drive, demanding total concentration. And all he could do was think about Tess and wonder…if she knew.

Yeah, right. Do you really believe she's staring out the window with that remote expression on her face because she's so enamored of the view?

His stomach twisted. All right. So what if she did know? What the hell did he care? It wasn't as if he needed her or something. He'd been doing just fine before she came into his life.

The only reason he was upset was because this probably meant no more sex. Which was pretty damn stupid. As far as he knew, there was no such thing as an uncomplicated sexual relationship. And even if there was, he and Tess were the last two people on earth to make it work. Neither of them had your garden-variety white-picket-fence sort of past. Both had their share of baggage.

Especially him.

So why don't you just admit it, Sheridan? Why don't you own up, at least to yourself, how you hate the thought of her knowing you weren't man enough to satisfy your wife? And that your own brother betrayed you? Or that you let your son go without a fight?

Well, that was pretty stupid, too. Hadn't he known that if she stuck around long enough she'd hear something? That it was just a matter of time? That there'd been a real risk in agreeing to go to Gweneth?

He sighed and tried to convince himself that this was probably best for them both, in the long run. It made sense to cut things off now, before there was any real involvement. She could go her way, and he'd go his, and—

"Jack?"

He was so absorbed, it took him a second to realize she'd spoken. He came to attention, surprised to find he'd been driving on automatic pilot and that they were already past the draw where Tess's car had been until he winched it out yesterday. "What?"

"Is the man your ex-wife's married to now...is he your brother?"

Even though he thought he was prepared, the direct question felt like a punch to the belly. His hands tightened on the steering wheel as he fought to get a grip on his emotions. "Who told you that?"

"No one. I overheard some people talking, saying the two of them had an affair, and I wondered. Is it true?"

He stared straight ahead. "Yes."

She released a long, pent-up breath. "Why didn't you tell me?"

"Why should I? It's not the sort of thing you brag about."

"But, Jack—"

"I don't want to talk about it."

"Really?" She stared at him in undisguised amazement. "Well, maybe I do."

"That's too damn bad, because you're out of luck. The discussion is closed."

She tried a different tack. "Do you have any idea the sort of things people are saying?"

He shrugged. "Sure. I just don't give a damn."

"Then why did you spend most of today sitting in this truck, doing your best to avoid the entire population of Gweneth?"

He was silent.

"Why, Jack?"

"It doesn't matter."

Out of the corner of his eye, he could see the pink in her cheeks getting a little deeper. "I guess that's good. Because that means you won't care that I told Carole Marden that we're living together, will you?"

"What?" He jerked around to look at her, and nearly put the truck in the ditch. "Why the hell would you do that?"

"What was I supposed to do? She called you 'that poor, unfortunate man.' She said your life was ruined. It made me mad."

"Maybe you should have listened to her."

"Why should I do that?" she shot back. "It seems to me that there's already one person too many feeling sorry for you."

That cut it. She might not be done, but *he* was finished. He sent the truck shooting across the Cross Creek

444 THE BABY BLIZZARD

cattle guard. Up ahead, he could see the solid rise of the barn. All he had to do was hold on.

He hit the brakes and sent the truck fishtailing to a stop in front of the house. He slammed the transmission into park, switched off the ignition, shoved open the door and clambered out.

"Where do you think you're going?" Tess demanded.

"I've got chores."

"But—"

Disturbed by all the commotion, Nicki began to whimper.

"You'd better see to your daughter." He shut the door and walked away.

Tess told herself she didn't care that Jack had retreated to the barn. After all, a barn was the appropriate place for a man who was as blind as a bat, as stubborn as a mule, as pigheaded as a...pig. He could stay out there until the Fourth of July, for all that it mattered to her.

She repeated the sentiment regularly over the next three hours, muttering it as she put away her purchases, restating it as she fixed and ate a solitary dinner, reminding herself of it again as she bathed and fed the baby and put her to bed in a new pink sleeper.

She told herself the same thing as she stood in the dark and stared out the bedroom window at the barn.

The problem was, part of her didn't believe it.

It was the same part that kept remembering the hint of desperation in that kiss outside Marden's. And the way Jack's knuckles had turned white on the steering wheel when she asked that very first question about his brother and his ex-wife. And the stubborn way he'd refused to discuss anything.

If she didn't know better, she'd think he felt ashamed. But why?

Oh, for heaven's sake, Tess. Think about it. How would you feel if it had happened to you?

She turned it over in her mind. She'd be hurt, of course. And she'd feel angry and betrayed and determined to never again make the same mistake.

And, she supposed, if the hurt went deep enough—as it would if you were cuckolded by your own sibling—she might start to wonder what was wrong with her, what she'd done to deserve such a fate. Particularly if her neighbors made it clear they were wondering the same thing.

It might very well be enough to make her shut down. To cut herself off from everyone and swear she didn't care…about anything.

And yet…what about the child? Try as she might, she couldn't square what she knew of Jack with a man who would voluntarily turn his back on his own child, no matter how battered he felt. Not when he was so tender with Nicki. And not when he'd been there for her, even when they were strangers…

She sighed, the last of her anger fading.

She no longer wondered if she loved him, she realized. She knew. But her loving him wasn't going to do either of them any good if he wouldn't talk to her.

And as quickly as that, she knew what she had to do. She turned her back on the window and strode across the room to check on Nicki. Assured that the baby was fast asleep, she wasted no time, going swiftly along the hall and taking the stairs two at a time before she lost her nerve. She slipped on her boots and pulled on her coat in the mudroom, then plunged out into the night.

A full moon and a smudge of stars hung in the sky.

While not nearly as frigid as it had been, it was still cold. She turned up her collar and stuffed her hands in her pockets, her feet crunching against the top layer of frozen snow.

She paused in front of the barn door to gather her courage.

Then she pulled it open and stepped inside.

Midway down the corridor, Jack jerked around to stare at her. He gave her a long, impenetrable look, then turned back and resumed rubbing the curry comb over Obsidian, who was loosely tied to an iron ring in the wall.

Tess took a deep breath and walked closer, moving to the gelding's head. The horse stretched out his nose to smell her. Recognizing her scent, he nudged her until she began to scratch his neck.

"I thought you'd be packed and gone by now," Jack said.

She looked over at him. Despite the chill, his coat was off, his shirt was unbuttoned, his sleeves were turned up. A light sheen of perspiration filmed his face and chest, while the muscles in his arms and back bunched as he worked the brush along the horses barrel. He didn't look at her.

Clearly, he wasn't going to make this easy.

"Are you throwing me out?" she asked.

He shrugged. "After today, why would you want to stay?"

She let the silence spin out before she answered, telling herself, as she had so many times before, that she had nothing to lose and everything to gain. Even so, her heart was pounding. "Because I love you."

The words momentarily froze him in midmotion.

"You don't mean that." Although his voice was steady, the downward stroke of the currycomb jerked sideways.

Tess took it as an encouraging sign. "Yes, I do." She took a step toward him.

"No. You don't." He retreated around the back of the horse, came up the other side and jerked the lead line loose. He turned the gelding in such a way that Tess had to jump back to avoid being hit in the face by the horse's haunches.

She watched through narrowed eyes as he led the gray away into the far stall.

She waited.

He reappeared a few minutes later. His face impassive, he came down the corridor toward her.

When he was too close to easily avoid her, Tess stepped into his path. "Jack, listen. Please. I realize what you went through must have been awful. And I'm sorrier than I can say that two people you so obviously cared about betrayed you. But is it really worth ruining your life over?"

"You don't understand."

"Then explain it to me. Explain to me why you're so determined to be alone. Why you refuse to get on with your life. Why you've turned your back on your own child. Because I don't get it! Did you really love your ex-wife so much you can't let go?"

He recoiled. "Hell, no!"

"Then *what?*"

His face worked. "Isn't it enough for you that I wasn't man enough to satisfy my wife? Or smart enough to know I was being deceived in my own house?"

"*No.*"

"Then try this on for size. *My son* isn't mine, and

never was!'' He stared at her, his expression hard with challenge. "Does that explain it?''

"Do you know that for sure?'' Even as she asked, she knew the answer. Just as so many other things she hadn't understood now were clear.

"Oh, yeah. I've got the test results to prove it.''

She squeezed her eyes shut. "I'm so sorry—''

"Save it. I don't want your pity.''

Her eyes snapped open. "That isn't what I feel—''

He leaned forward so that they were standing toe-to-toe. "What I want is to be left the hell alone!''

"Well, that's too bad—because that's the one thing I can't do!''

"Why the hell not?''

He was so close she could see the dense green of his irises expand as his pupils contracted. It was like trying to stare down a tiger. There was a hint of danger in the air, a sense that one rash move might push him over the edge.

She looked steadily at him. "I told you. Because I love you.''

Stubbornly he shook his head. "You don't mean that. You can't. Haven't you been listening—''

"Yes. You're the one who doesn't understand. It's over and done with. You didn't have a choice about what happened then, but you do have one about what happens now, about whether you put it behind you and get on with your life…or not.''

"Damn it, Tess—''

She touched her fingertips to the seam of his lips. "You can swear all you want, but it's not going to change anything. So for now, why don't you just kiss me and make us both happy?''

With an explosive oath, he did just that. One second

Tess was staring into his green eyes, and in the next she was in his arms, the cool wood of the tack room wall against her back, the solid strength of his hard length against her front, the drugging force of his mouth on hers.

A tangle of emotions rolled through her—relief, joy, tenderness. Fast on their heels came complete and total arousal as his lips slanted across hers again and again. She pressed against him, her pulse racing as heat spread through her core. It stole the strength from her arms and legs and consumed the air trapped in her lungs.

His tongue found hers. She felt faint, feverish, flushed.

She whimpered, wanting more. He complied, nudging her legs apart with his thighs until he was as close as he could be without being inside her.

An ache started low in her belly and concentrated downward. With a sob of need, she tangled her hands in his hair and nipped his bottom lip, trying to convey her growing urgency.

Jack groaned. He knew he should stop—but he didn't want to. Everything about her, her taste, her touch, the soft little sounds she was making deep in her throat, excited him. So did the way she was suddenly touching him, sliding her hands from his hair, down his neck, to the top of his shoulders. She trailed her fingers down his arms, then dragged his shirt out of his pants, echoing his sudden moan of satisfaction as she rubbed her palms over his hard belly. He wondered how much more he could stand as she explored the deep valley of his spine and the sleek flesh of his sides. He got his answer when she found his nipples. When she rubbed the pads of her fingers across them, he felt as if she'd touched him with a live wire. His entire body jerked with an overload of sensation.

He dragged his mouth away. Breathing hard, he rested his lips against her temple. "Tess…I can't— I want— You have to stop, or I'm going to take you right here…"

"For heaven's sake—*yes*."

It was too much. She was the most unpredictable, exasperating, enticing woman he'd ever known—and he'd never wanted anyone so much. With a low, rumbling sound of need, he reached out, unsnapped her jeans and shoved them down, then did the same to his own.

He started to reach for her, but she held him off.

"Wait." Gripping his forearm for balance, she hastily toed off one boot and reached down to extricate her foot from her pant leg.

The sight of her long, smooth flanks and bare bottom destroyed the last scrap of his restraint. Unable to wait a second longer, he wrapped his arm around her waist as she straightened. He pulled her close.

She came to him without hesitation. Linking her arms around his neck, she lifted her face to his and rocked up on her toes in a provocative move that made his heart slam against his ribs.

He flexed his knees and thrust himself inside her, holding her gaze with his own. He saw her eyes widen, saw the pulse leap in her silky throat, saw the way her thick, russet-tipped lashes swept down. He heard her whisper of gratification, a long, breathless, "Oh."

"Look at me," he demanded, gritting his teeth for control as her wet, slick warmth closed around him.

She opened her eyes. Color rose in her cheeks as he established a steady rhythm. She rolled her hips, trying to make him hurry. He retaliated by manacling her wrists in his hands and raising them to the wall above her head.

The labored sound of their breathing filled the big barn.

Her lips parted, and one long leg climbed the back of his thigh, to hook around his waist to take him deeper. He felt her tense, saw the glazed look come into her eyes as her concentration turned inward, saw the moment when her head fell back. He reached down and slicked his thumb across the top of her wet, swollen folds, searching for the center of her desire.

She quivered. "Jack. Oh, don't, it's too much—"

He found it and pressed. For one long moment her body went rigid, and then her smooth, inner muscles clamped down. She shuddered and cried out, holding on to him as if he were her only link with the world.

Her pleasure triggered his own. Gripping her hips in his hands, he held her against the concentrated slamming of his hips. He felt the pressure build, so intense it was almost painful, and then the gushing rush of release as he poured himself into her, his entire body jerking with a sensation almost too exquisite to bear.

When he could think again, he realized Tess was still rocking him against her, gently stroking her hands down his spine.

He raised his head and looked at her.

Her mouth was wet from his kisses, her cheeks were flushed, her eyes were soft with satiation. Her expression soft and dreamy, she smiled at him. "Hi."

To his shock, he felt a tickle in his loins. "Tess. We shouldn't have—"

"Shh..." She stroked a hand through his damp hair, then leaned forward to press a kiss to his lips. "It was wonderful. Don't ruin it with regrets."

Jack tried to tell himself that she was right. But deep down, he was remembering all the things she'd said. And the vow he'd made never again to care too much.

And deep down, a part of him knew he was in trouble.

Ten

The soft murmur of Tess's voice woke Jack.

It took him a few moments to realize she wasn't in the bed with him. He rolled onto his side and found her standing at Nicki's cradle. Because it was dark in the big master bedroom, with only the faintest edge of gray framing the window shades, she was nothing more than a shadow against the night.

He propped himself up on one elbow. "Everything all right?"

"Uh-huh." Her voice was hushed. "I just finished feeding the little glutton here, and she's drifting off to sleep…aren't you, sweetie?" she said soothingly to the baby.

Jack laid his head back down on the pillow. There was something soothing about lying in the dark, listening to her talk to the baby. And about feeling included instead of excluded, for a change. A surprising sense of peace washed over him. For the first time, it didn't feel the least bit strange to find himself back in the same room and the same bed he'd once shared with Elise.

But then, nothing was the same as it had been. Not the room. Not the woman with whom he was sharing it.

And not him. He lay there, tested the unfamiliar emotion threading through him, and realized after a moment that it felt like…happiness. He still wasn't in the market for a long-term commitment, but for now…well, for now, this would do fine.

The mattress shifted as Tess climbed back into the bed. He reached out, pulled her close and stroked a hand down her back. He frowned at the goose bumps on her skin. "Cold?"

"A little. But you're not. You feel nice and warm." She nestled against him, and for a long space of time they simply lay there, both lost to their own private thoughts.

She stroked one slim, long-fingered hand across his chest. "Jack?"

"Hmm?"

"Tell me about them."

"Who?" he said, although he already knew.

"About…Elise and—?"

"Jared," he said finally, saying his brother's name out loud for the first time in more than three years. He waited for the familiar bitterness to surface. It didn't. To his surprise, all he felt was a curious sort of indifference.

Even more surprising was the discovery that he was finally ready to talk about what had happened—as long as it was to Tess.

He tried to decide where to begin. "Ever since we were little kids, Jared and I were best friends. I was two years older, the big brother, the serious one, while

Jared…well, Jared could make folks smile just by walking into a room. We rodeoed together. We double-dated. We dreamed about having a ranch.

"So we saved our money, and when we could afford it, we bought this place. At first, things were great. I worked my butt off. Jared charmed everybody in sight. Life was good.

"And then I met Elise at a cattle auction in Las Vegas. She was something. She sang in the chorus at one of the shows, and she was brash, sophisticated, wild. I'd never known anyone like her. I put off coming home for a week. We were married eight days after we met.

"Things started to go sour within a year. According to her, the ranch was too isolated, I worked too much, I didn't talk to her enough. I was always tired. I didn't take her to town. I wasn't *fun*. We fought—a lot—but I wasn't willing to give up. Instead, I asked Jared to help me out. To run interference. To keep her entertained."

He took a deep breath. "You would've thought I'd have caught on when she turned up pregnant, since by then our sex life had pretty much gone to hell. And I think I did know, deep down. I just didn't want to believe it. Not because of Elise, but because of Jared. So I acted as though nothing was wrong. I pretended not to notice the way he avoided me whenever he could, and wouldn't look me in the eye when he couldn't. I convinced myself it was normal for Elise to ask me to move out of our room and to want to go to Gweneth for her last trimester.

"When Matthew was born, I was the only one who was happy. I had my son. If I just held on, everything else would work out. And it did—for a few months. And then Jared and Elise came to me. They were sorry, they said, they'd never meant to hurt me, but they'd fallen in love and they were leaving."

Tess's arm tightened around him, and he found himself groping for her hand. "They needed money, of course. And under the circumstances, they were willing to be reasonable—I didn't have to give Elise a penny, they'd settle for Jared's half share in the ranch," he said, unable to keep a trace of remembered bitterness out of his voice. "I said fine, anything, just as long as Matthew stayed with me…and that's when they told me the rest. I didn't believe them. God, I was angry. So we did the tests." Jack sighed, remembering. "The day after I got the results, I sold the entire herd to get them their money. And I told myself *never again.*"

Yet for some reason, he realized slowly, the wound didn't seem as raw now as it had been. As a matter of fact, it felt as if it had happened long ago, to somebody else.…

Tess squeezed his hand. "I'm so sorry."

Her words jerked him back to the present. He heard the sincerity in her voice and found himself thinking that in some ways, they'd shared more in the past five weeks than some couples shared in a lifetime.

The thought was disturbing. As was the sudden memory of what she'd said to him out in the barn about it being time to make a choice. It occurred to him that now that he'd opened himself up a little, it would be natural for her to pick up the theme.

Only she didn't. Instead, as if she understood his sudden wariness, she shifted in his arms and came up on top of him. Robbed of his sight by the darkness, he was acutely aware of the way she felt against him—the firm mounds of her breasts pressed against his chest, the lithe strength of her thighs cradling his hips, the satiny slide of her sheath as she settled it against his sex.

He began to feel another sort of tension. "What do you think you're doing?"

"I'll give you a hint," she said softly. Slow and unhurried, she leaned down and began to kiss him. She paid homage to his temples, his eyes, his cheeks, his chin, before she settled her mouth over his with a sweetness that made him tremble. He raised his hands to touch her, but she caught them in her own and pressed them into the mattress on either side of his head. Then she began to explore him, sketching a line of kisses down his throat and along each shoulder. She lingered at the notch of his collarbone, at his nipples, at each shallow depression between his ribs.

She found his navel. She lingered there, too, and at the hollows that adjoined each hip, brushing her mouth over him, tickling him with the very tip of her tongue. She blazed a path to his thighs, rubbing her peach-soft cheeks against the long, hard muscles that were now rigid with his struggle for restraint.

And finally, when he was certain that he couldn't stand another second, she turned her attention to the rampant proof of his desire, rising full and thick to meet her. She kissed him there, too, with agonizing thoroughness, refusing to hurry, despite his heartfelt urging. Her mouth was wet, hot, hungry. She didn't relent until he'd gripped the mattress so hard he yanked the bottom sheet off the bed.

Only then did she move up his body, hold him steady, and fill herself with him. Bracing her hands on his chest, she began to ride him, slow and easy at first, then harder and faster.

Her technique didn't matter. Jack was lost from the

first downward slide of her body over his. He wanted to make it last, wanted to guarantee her pleasure, but his control was gone. Breathing like a bellows, he surged upward, crying out as his climax struck him, so powerful that it made him feel as if he were being turned inside out. He was only vaguely aware of Tess calling his name as her completion was triggered by his.

Twined together, they held each other in the darkness. Jack felt Tess's heartbeat against his chest. A deep sense of possessiveness rolled over him.

At least for a while, she was his.

"Tess. Come here."

Tess frowned at the urgency in Jack's voice. Hastily adding the sleeper she was folding to the stack of clean laundry atop the kitchen table, she hurried over to the sink where he was bathing the baby.

"What's the matter?" She glanced curiously from him to Nicki, who was merrily splashing her arms and legs, secure in Jack's steady hands. Everything looked all right to her.

"Watch." Ignoring the water that soaked the front of his shirt, he leaned over. "Hey, little sweetheart," he crooned. "How're you doing?"

The baby went still, her expression growing sober as she focused all of her attention on him. She stared intently. And then her eyes lit up like the sun coming out, a brilliant smile curved her mouth, and she beamed at him.

It was impossible not to smile in response. And Tess did, although she wasn't sure exactly what the big deal was. After all, Nicki had been smiling for weeks.

She turned to ask Jack—and suddenly her heart stood still. To her astonishment, he, too, was smiling, his firm, chiseled lips curving in a way that took years off his face. She stared at him in amazement.

"What?" he demanded, the smile faltering as he saw her expression.

"Nothing. I just... That's the first time I've seen you smile."

"Oh." Now he looked mildly embarrassed. "Well, forget about that. You're supposed to be watching Nicki. She *smiled* at me," he added unnecessarily.

She regarded him for all of half a second before she reached up to give him a sympathetic pat on the shoulder. "I don't think so. Probably just gas."

He opened his mouth to object, then caught himself as she raised her eyebrows at him. Understanding dawned, and his expression turned sardonic. "Very funny."

Tenderness rippled through her. The last thing she wanted to do was embarrass him further, however, so she simply leaned forward, wiped a bead of water off the point of his chin and said lightly, "*I* thought so." As if nothing special had occurred, she walked calmly back over to the table and resumed folding clothes.

Inside, however, her heart was soaring. It had been a week since they made the trip to Gweneth, and with every day that passed, his guard seemed to come down a little more. Oh, he was still prickly and private and, despite what had just happened, not prone to wearing his heart on his sleeve. Yet some sort of internal barrier definitely had been breached. He was more open, more at ease, more willing to share his feelings.

She wanted to believe he was starting to let go of the past. That he was finally starting to look toward the future. Because she knew that they'd reached a crossroads of sorts. As much as she might wish otherwise, she couldn't will Jack to want a life with Nicki and her. It was a decision he had to make on his own, of his own free will. She'd made all the other moves in their relationship; now, it was up to him.

For that reason, over the past few days she'd come to a painful decision. When the time came for her to go, she would. No matter how hard it was, no matter how much it hurt, she would abide by his decision.

In the meantime, there would be no long faces for her. She meant to take each day as it came and savor every moment they had together. Losing Gray had taught her that life was too short to waste a second worrying about what you couldn't control.

Her gaze swung back to Jack like a compass seeking true north. She watched as he lifted the baby out of the water and laid her on a towel, talking in a low, confidential tone as he dried her off. With a deft touch that was astonishing, given the size of his hands, he diapered and dressed the little girl, then picked up a tiny yellow brush and styled her hair.

When he was done, he propped her up for Tess to see. "What do you think?"

She dragged her gaze away from him to glance at her daughter, and gasped. *"Jack!"* The baby's hair stood straight up in an outrageous rooster tail that made her look like a wide-eyed Woody Woodpecker.

"No?" Although his expression was solemn, there was a hint of a twinkle in his brilliant green eyes.

"No," she said with a laugh.

Chuckling, she rescued her daughter from him and took her upstairs to nurse before her nap.

When she came back down forty-five minutes later, Jack was still in the kitchen, talking on the phone in the kitchen. He turned at the sound of her footsteps. His expression was carefully blank.

"It's for you," he said quietly. "It's Mary."

Jack stared out the kitchen window, listening to the quiet murmur of Tess's voice as she talked to her grandmother. He wondered what was taking so long. His own conversation with the old lady had been blunt and to the point. She'd thanked him for his hospitality, while making it clear it was no longer needed. She wanted Tess and the baby at the Double D with her.

So? That was always the plan. How come you suddenly wish otherwise? Why do you suddenly want to rip the phone off the wall?

He rolled his shoulders, shying away from the answer. He told himself that his sudden sense of aggravation was simply resentment at having somebody else calling the shots. It had nothing at all do with Tess leaving.

So what if she did leave? They'd been thrown together by circumstance, they'd had their normal defenses stripped away by the extraordinary experience of birth, they'd made a mutual decision to explore their undeniable sexual chemistry.

It wasn't as if she were his wife or anything.

That's right. You care for her a lot more than you ever did Elise.

The realization froze him in place. He tried to deny it, but it refused to go away.

So ask her to stay.

Right. And then what? She might think ranch life was all right at the moment, but who knew how long that would last? She'd left once before. She could do it again.

Besides, she could do better than him. What did he have to offer except an empty house and a questionable future? And what about Nicki? She'd already lost one father. Under the circumstances, how could he ask Tess to stay, when he wouldn't—he couldn't—make any promises?

He took a deep breath as the decision was made.

The best thing he could do for everyone concerned was let her go. He looked over at her as she finally hung up the phone. "Well?"

Tess took in the grim look on Jack's face. Her heart felt unsteady, not because of her conversation with her grandmother—as challenging as it had been—but because of the decision that was surely coming.

She tried to keep her voice light. "Ten years doesn't seem to have mellowed her any. She says that my coming here without her consent proves I'm as 'precipitous as ever.' As does my 'blatant disregard for convention' in staying with you." At his questioning look, she shrugged. "Apparently she stopped in Gweneth on her way home and got an earful, thanks to my big mouth. She's willing to overlook all that, however, since I've had the good sense to provide her with a great-granddaughter. I've been commanded to pack my things and get myself to the Double D without delay." She tried to read his face and drew a blank. "All and all, I think it went pretty well." *Come on, Jack. Say something. Ask me to stay. Suggest I only go for a visit. Meet me halfway.*

"How soon do you want to leave?" he said woodenly.

The question was like a punch to the heart. She swallowed—hard—and told herself she was not going to make a scene that would only embarrass them both. Hadn't she told herself, promised herself, that she'd abide by his wishes? That whatever happened, it had to be what he wanted?

Yes. She'd gone into this with her eyes open. Jack had been honest with her from the start, had warned her not to expect anything. She ought to be glad this was happening now...while she still had a semblance of pride left and could take her leave with dignity.

It also didn't hurt that she felt more than a little numb, as if this were happening to somebody else.

She plastered a smile on her face. "The sooner the better, I think. If I start packing now, I'll be ready by the time Nicki wakes up."

He nodded, still wearing that same unreadable look. "I'll go put the infant seat in your car."

To her shock, he turned and walked out of the kitchen without another word. Tess stared after him, feeling as if she were suddenly caught in a bad dream. Everything seemed to be happening too fast. Only an hour ago they'd been joking and laughing, and now... *Now, it's over. Get a grip on yourself.*

It didn't take her long to gather her things; despite the shopping she'd done in Gweneth, neither she nor the baby had much. Of the items Jack had lent her, she kept, from necessity, a dozen diapers and the pale blue blanket with the rocking horse embroidered on the corner—and a single flannel shirt.

"Ready?"

She looked up. Jack stood in the doorway, as if he couldn't wait to get rid of her. He looked big and tall and as formidable as he had the first time she'd ever seen him. She could see nothing in his face. Not a hint of regret. Not a speck of affection.

She nodded and picked up the baby, watching as he

came slowly into the bedroom and picked up her overnight bag and the suitcase he'd lent her.

Nicki was still fast asleep, but Tess cuddled her close anyway, needing the comforting contact, and stopped to take a final look around. She remembered that first night, how frightened she'd been, and how Jack had been there for her. She thought about how drastically her life had changed in the past weeks.

She took a deep breath and straightened her spine. Then she turned and walked out the door.

Eleven

Eleven

Jack wasn't sure when he finally knew he'd made a mistake.

But he knew where he was when he got the first inkling. He was in the barn, where he'd gone to clean stalls after Tess left.

Added to his regular feeding and grooming tasks, the additional chore took him nearly four hours. Four hours in which to make countless trips past the spot where he and Tess had made love only days before. It was plenty of time to remember every detail of the passion they'd shared. To reflect on exactly what it was he'd given up. And to hear her clear, uncompromising voice in his head.

You didn't have a choice about what happened then. But you do have one now.

He tried to ignore it. But hour by hour, he started to wonder. Could it really be true? *Was* it his choice? But if it was, how could he be trusted to make the right decision about the future, when his choices in the past had been so disastrous?

Hell. He hadn't even had the brains to kiss Tess goodbye when she left, he thought tiredly as he switched off the barn's interior lights.

He stepped outside. To his surprise, night had fallen, taking the temperature with it. He shivered as the cold washed down his spin and clung to his sweat-damp body.

A smart man would have hurried toward the house.

But not him. He stayed where he was. If the barn was full of memories, the house would only be worse. Especially now, when it looked so dark and empty.

So? You've got nobody to blame but yourself. You knew better than to get involved. But you did it anyway, even though you knew better, and now you're paying the price.

There was always a price.

Only this time, it seemed inordinately high. And try as he might to convince himself that the reason for that was because he knew what to expect, knew down to the minute how long the days could stretch when there was no one to share them with, he didn't believe it. Not for a minute.

Because he didn't want just anyone, he admitted as he started along the path to the house, his feet dragging with every step. He wanted Tess.

The admission—as obvious as it was—knocked another hole in the shield he'd thrown up around his heart.

He let himself into the mudroom. Unmindful of the snow on his boots, he walked into the kitchen and switched on a light. He looked around at the cold, empty room. The folded laundry still sat on the table. The towels he'd used to dry Nicki after her bath still littered the counter. There was no fire in the fireplace, no food in the oven, no voice of welcome.

He tried to convince himself one last time that Tess's departure had been inevitable.

But suddenly, it just wouldn't wash. He could no longer deny that his stubborn refusal to ask her to stay was all tied up in that startling moment when he'd realized he cared for her more than Elise...or Jared...or even little Matthew.

He let out his breath and stood stock-still. *Come on. Admit it. Plain and simple, you panicked. You drove her away to save yourself from rejection. The same thing you've done to everyone the past three years.*

Only losing Tess was worse.

Because somehow, in just a matter of weeks, she'd made him care about life again. Because all of a sudden he *wanted*—her, Nicki, a future—more than he needed to hold on to the past.

Because...he loved her.

The realization rolled over him, knocking away the last of his defenses.

The only question was, what was he going to do about it *now,* when he'd already sent her away?

Tess looked out the Cadillac's windshield. Narrowing her eyes at the dazzling display of sunlight on snow, she decided—not for the first time—that she was probably crazy.

Why else would she be out at the crack of dawn, driving down a deserted county road in the middle of nowhere? After all, things had gone well at the Double D. After a little jockeying for position and some blunt talk, she and her grandmother had made their peace.

It had helped that they both agreed that Nicki was probably the most perfect baby ever made.

Yet Tess's heart had been heavy.

And, oddly enough, it had been Mary who put things in perspective. Sitting in the big leather chair in her study, her great-grandchild secure on her lap, the old lady had looked over at Tess during a pause in their after-dinner conversation last night and said, "So? How long are you going to mope?"

"Excuse me?" As she'd noticed on the phone, time hadn't done a thing to soften her grandmother's blunt manner.

"Why'd you let that Sheridan fellow run you off, anyway? I thought I raised you better than that, Tessa. I thought I taught you to go after what you want."

Tess had narrowed her eyes at the old lady and told herself that Mary didn't know what she was talking about. And yet the idea had stuck. Is that what I'm doing? she'd wondered. Letting Jack run me off, because it's easier than fighting for what I want?

She'd denied it at the time, but sometime in the middle of the night she'd realized her grandmother was right—drat her. And that she was going to have to do something to remedy the situation.

So here she was, going back for one last try. Somehow, she was going to make Jack see that they were meant for each other. That he needed her and she needed him. And that life was too short to waste on regrets.

She was so lost in thought, she didn't see the steer until it was almost too late. Feet planted in the middle of the road, the beast looked as big as a bus.

Tess hit the brakes. Too hard. The Cadillac began to slide. As if it were moving in slow motion, the car glided slowly to the right, skidded gently along the verge for a hundred feet, then burst through the snow bank, bumped down the slope that edged the road and rolled to a stop.

She clutched the steering wheel. Well, heck, she thought with a strong sense of déjà vu. Now what was she supposed to do?

She pondered her options—all one of them. There was nothing for it; she'd have to walk. With a disgusted sigh, she took a good look around. To her relief, the steer had finally hightailed it away, and could just be seen disappearing over the far hill. Shaking her head, she climbed out of the car, stuck her purse under the seat and locked the car up. Then she tramped up the slope onto the road. She brushed the loose snow off her boots and jeans. At least this time she was better dressed and in better shape for a hike, she reflected.

She had gone perhaps half a mile and was just starting to hit her stride when she heard the sound of a vehicle approaching. Shading her eyes with one gloved hand, she gave it a good look.

She stiffened. She recognized that pickup. It was Jack's.

She knew the instant he spotted her. The truck slowed, then sped up, then slowed again as it rolled to a stop in front of her.

Jack climbed out. A nervous flutter went through her stomach. On some level she realized he was dressed more formally then she'd ever seen him, in a good white shirt and a brocaded vest, black cords and a leather jacket. Yet mostly what she saw was the strain around his mouth, the way he had his hands closed loosely into fists, the way he hurried toward her as if he'd missed her as much as she'd missed him—

"Tess?" The sunglasses he was wearing didn't do a

thing to camouflage his ferocious scowl. "What the hell are you doing out here?"

She stopped in her tracks. Yep, she was definitely crazy. Here she'd been making him into a needy romantic hero, while the truth was, he was as impossible as ever—and totally annoying. What on earth had she been thinking? That she'd waltz up to him, speak a few hard truths, tell him what a fool he was, and that he'd drop at her feet and make a passionate declaration of love?

Right. There was a better chance Nicki would get up from her nap and recite the soliloquy from *Hamlet*.

She lifted her chin. "I needed some fresh air and exercise," she lied.

He planted his hands on his narrow hips. "So you decided to go for a walk out in the middle of nowhere?"

"If you have to know, there was a steer in the road a mile or so back. I tried to avoid it and had a little accident."

There was a dead silence. His jaw worked with what she assumed was annoyance. "You going for a record or something?" he said finally. "Most encounters with a snowbank by an expectant or nursing mother in a single season?"

"Very funny. Are you going to give me a ride or not?"

"What do you think?" With the air of a man operating under a great restraint, he walked around to the pickup, opened up the passenger door and stood there, waiting. He was careful not to touch her as she climbed up, Tess noticed with a sinking heart.

"Fasten your seat belt," he ordered as he climbed in on his side.

She ignored him. What did she care about seat belts when her heart was breaking...again?

He waited.

Sighing, she complied. "Could we go now?"

He put the truck in gear. There was a silence that probably lasted a minute but felt more like an eternity. Finally, she couldn't stand it. She looked over at him, praying her heart wasn't in her eyes. "So...are you on your way to town?"

"No."

"Then how come you're out here, dressed like that, at this hour?"

He continued to stare straight ahead without saying anything for so long that she thought he hadn't heard her. And then, as he tightened his hands on the steering wheel, she realized he had.

She braced for him to tell her to mind her own business.

"If you have to know, I was coming to see you."

"Oh." It was all she could manage, since her heart seemed to be jammed in her throat.

"I've been thinking. About your dude ranch idea. And I thought...well, my place would work pretty well...if you're really serious. We work pretty well together, and I thought... I mean..." He cleared his throat. "The thing is, it would be good for everybody. You'd be close to your grandmother, and Nicki needs a father. Not that you couldn't do a good job raising her on your own, but I did help bring her into the world. In a way, that makes me responsible for her." When she still didn't say anything, his voice took on a desperate note. "I don't know if you've realized it yet, but that night in the barn, and then later...well, we didn't use any birth control. I know it may be too soon, and that you're nursing and all, but..." He trailed off. After a second, he glanced over at her. "Are you going to help me out here?"

She shook her head. "No."

His jaw bunched and he shifted his gaze forward again. "Well, what I'm trying to get you to see is that you ought to marry me, damn it."

"Jack?"

"What?

"Stop the truck."

Still looking straight ahead, he did, as she asked. She unfastened her seat belt and scooted across the seat. When he turned to face her, she reached up and slid his sunglasses off. Her breath caught as she saw the jumble of emotions in his eyes. Hope, fear, uncertainty...*trust*.

"Say it," she said softly.

He looked at her, and it was as if she could see straight into his soul. "I love you, Tess. I love you more than I've ever loved anybody in my life, and I want you to be my wife."

She blinked against a sudden rush of tears. "Oh, Jack. I love you, too."

"Is that a yes?"

"Yes."

"Thank God." The words were a prayer and a celebration. He pulled her into his arms. For a long space of time, he just held her, as if afraid to let her go. And then his mouth found hers and he kissed her, long and sweet, with nothing held back.

Tess realized it was his promise for their future.

Happiness filled her. She smiled as his mouth lifted from hers. He smiled back, and she suddenly knew that whatever happened, they'd get through it.

He rested his forehead against hers. "So how did it go with Mary?"

"Fine." She leaned against him. "She's every bit as impossible as she ever was."

"Then how about we go rescue our daughter? I miss her. And I'm ready to go home."

Together, they did just that.

* * * * *

SPOTLIGHT

"Debra Webb's fast-paced thriller will make you shiver in passion and fear...."—*Romantic Times*

Dying To Play

Debra Webb

When FBI agent Trace Callahan arrives in Atlanta to investigate a baffling series of multiple homicides, deputy chief of detectives Elaine Jentzen isn't prepared for the immediate attraction between them. And as they hunt to find the killer known as the Gamekeeper, it seems that Trace is singled out as his next victim...unless Elaine can stop the Gamekeeper before it's too late.

Available January 2005.

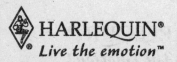

HARLEQUIN®
Live the emotion™

Exclusive Bonus Features:
Author Interview
Sneak Preview...
and more!

PHDTP

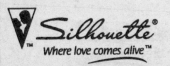

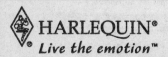

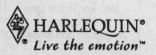
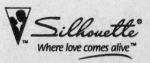